THE
COUTURIER
OF
MILAN

THE COUTURIER OF MILAN

THE TRIAD YEARS
AN AVA LEE NOVEL

IAN HAMILTON

SPIDERLINE

Published in Canada in 2017 and the USA in 2017
by House of Anansi Press Inc.
www.houseofanansi.com

House of Anansi Press is committed to protecting our natural environment.
As part of our efforts, the interior of this book is printed on paper that
contains 100% post-consumer recycled fibres, is acid-free, and is processed
chlorine-free.

21 20 19 18 17   1 2 3 4 5

Library of Congress Control Number: 2016950831

Book design: Alysia Shewchuk

**Canada Council
for the Arts**

**Conseil des Arts
du Canada**

ONTARIO ARTS COUNCIL
CONSEIL DES ARTS DE L'ONTARIO
an Ontario government agency
un organisme du gouvernement de l'Ontario

*We acknowledge for their financial support of our publishing program
the Canada Council for the Arts, the Ontario Arts Council, and the
Government of Canada through the Canada Book Fund.*

Printed and bound in Canada

RECYCLED
Paper made from
recycled material
FSC® C103567

Again, for Lorraine —
and hopefully again and again and again.

AVA LEE THOUGHT SHE KNEW LONDON. SHE'D BEEN there as a tourist and on business countless times. After nine months of owning part of a designer clothing line, she also thought she was beginning to understand the fashion industry. But three days into London Fashion Week, she felt far removed from any sense of her usual reality. When she voiced this feeling to May Ling Wong, her friend and business partner, May's reaction was surprise.

"What are you talking about?" May said. "You've been the only calm one this week. Everyone else is running around like headless chickens, me included."

"What you think is calmness is actually me not knowing how to react to so much chaos. Between preparations for the show, all of the public relations activity, and the hosting of lunches and dinners for existing and potential customers, I've had more contact with people in my three days here than I've had over the last three months."

"It does seem a bit mad, I admit, but according to our show director and the public relations people, it's very typical for

Fashion Week here, or any of the big four fashion weeks, for that matter."

"What a crazy business," Ava said. "New York, London, Milan, and Paris in four consecutive weeks, and twice every year. I don't know how people survive it."

"We're thankful we got into even one of them. It isn't easy for new designers to be accepted into the official part of the week."

"Clark did graduate from Central Saint Martin's," Ava said, referring to the famous London design school.

"He did have contacts, thank goodness, but we still had to lobby."

"I've been thinking that I should have arrived just the day before, as I did for the launch in Shanghai. Everything moved so fast there that I didn't have time to feel out of place."

"And what would we have done with Pang Fai? You're the only reason she's here."

Pang Fai was the most talented and famous actress in Chinese cinema and had a massive following in Asia. Her films were now also commonly screened in the West, and her fame there was on a rapid upswing. Her popularity had grown accordingly, and in the past few months she'd made many of the "World's Most Beautiful Women" and "Sexiest Women" lists. Her decision to promote the PÖ line was a coup.

"She's being paid well enough."

"We both know that she's never promoted any products before, let alone a fashion designer. She only agreed to do it because of you, and she only came to London because of you. I don't know what happened between you and her in Shanghai, but you certainly made an impact."

Ava shrugged and then shivered. It was late February, and a cold, damp winter still had its grip on London. She and May Ling were standing outside the Corinthia Hotel waiting for their partner, Ava's sister-in-law Amanda Yee, to join them for the taxi ride to the Shard, the tallest building in the European Union. In just over an hour they were scheduled to introduce their PÖ fashion line there, to the European market and the Western world.

Despite having already been featured on the cover of Hong Kong *Vogue* and having had a remarkable initial selling season in Asia, PÖ wasn't a known name in Europe or North America. Their hope was that the launch at the Shard would correct that, and Pang Fai was an important part of their strategy.

While it wasn't uncommon for actresses to affiliate themselves with specific fashion designers and to attend shows to give support, Pang was going several steps further. Although no one outside the PÖ inner circle knew it, she was going to model in the show. And that was even more remarkable because Pang zealously guarded her privacy and was rarely seen in public outside of film promotion activities.

Ava had originally come up with the idea for having Pang Fai promote the PÖ brand and had secured the actress's agreement. But the decision had been made to withhold any public mention of her involvement until London Fashion Week. Instead, a stealth campaign was set in motion by the PÖ partners and their British and Chinese PR companies. Hints were dropped on social media and in the local press about the possibility of Pang's presence and participation in London. The fashion and style magazines were quietly contacted and told to expect a major surprise at the PÖ launch.

When they asked if the rumours about Pang were true, no one from PÖ would either confirm or deny the possibility, fuelling even greater interest and making the brand's debut one of the most anticipated events of Fashion Week.

Ava believed in luck, but she knew that one of the key elements in good fortune is timing, and it seemed to her that things had fallen into place for the PÖ business in an almost preordained way. She had managed to secure Pang Fai's agreement just before the actress's profile began to rise in the West. Asia was now the fastest-growing market for luxury-brand companies, and there was an increasing Asian presence on runways and in the magazines. A few Chinese designers had made some impact in the West, but there was still anticipation that a star was going to emerge. Those factors, the PÖ launch, and the promise of Pang Fai's presence had galvanized public attention, and Ava couldn't help but feel that the stars were aligned to make PÖ an international hit.

"She's going to cause a sensation," May said. "I just hope it doesn't distract from the clothes."

We'll find out soon enough, Ava thought as she checked her watch. Amanda was running a little late, and Ava hoped there wasn't a last-minute crisis.

Amanda, May Ling, and Ava owned an investment company called Three Sisters. Amanda, still in her late twenties, handled the day-to-day operations from their office in Hong Kong. May Ling, who was in her mid-forties but looked at least ten years younger, lived in the city of Wuhan in central China and acted as senior advisor and strategist. She and Ava had put in most of the money and were majority sharehold-ers. Ava's role in the business wasn't as clearly defined but was no less important. Since the company's inception, her involvement had cut across finance, marketing, planning, and the building of relationships.

Three Sisters had put money into a furniture-manufacturing company in Borneo, a warehouse and distribution firm that operated out of Shanghai and Beijing, a Hong Kong trading business, and a start-up company that was making revolutionary—or so they hoped—carbon-fibre containers for ocean and air freight shipments, and they had decided to gamble on the talents of Clark Po by putting more than $10 million into his Shanghai-based fashion line.

Despite the Asian locations of all the businesses, Ava still lived in Toronto. The distance and time difference between the partners didn't present any real difficulties. None of them worked regular eight-hour days, and they were able to communicate well enough by phone, text, email, and video call. It helped that, in addition to being partners, the women were extremely close and shared an extraordinary level of trust.

"I'm sorry for being late," a voice said.

Ava turned to see Amanda rushing towards them.

"Was there a problem?" she asked.

"No, just the opposite," Amanda said breathlessly. "Chi-Tze called to tell me that the event site is already buzzing. They're expecting a full house, and the PR people are predicting that Pang Fai's appearance will generate outstanding press coverage."

"Did Chi-Tze mention how Fai is doing?"

"She's as cool as can be. The other girls, especially the Chinese ones, aren't quite so composed. The fact that they're going to be sharing the runway with her might have something to do with it."

"Do we know what she's going to be wearing?" Ava asked.

"I don't have a clue, and neither does Chi-Tze or Gillian. Clark and the show director have been huddling together for days, and Fai was with them yesterday. None of them are talking about what she's going to wear or when she'll make her entrance."

"We should be going," May interrupted.

They stepped into a taxi and began the trip that would take them across London Bridge to Southwark, on the south side of the Thames River. Ava gazed out the window. The last time she'd been to London she had been working for the debt-collection company she ran with her old partner, Uncle. They had worked together for more than ten years, chasing scam artists and thieves around the world. Uncle had passed away more than a year ago, but he was still part of her life, often appearing in her dreams and memories. She had started the transition into Three Sisters partially at his insistence, just before his death.

"I don't know if I'm more nervous or excited," Amanda said as they neared the bridge.

"How is Clark?" Ava asked

"He's a mess."

"Good. He was the same in Shanghai, and look how well that turned out."

"Is Elsa here?" May asked, referring to Elsa Ngan, a friend of Amanda's and an editor at Hong Kong *Vogue*. Elsa had been one of PÖ's first fans.

"Yes, she said there was no way she was going to miss our introduction to the West," Amanda said. "And by the way, she told me that Carrie Song flew in from Hong Kong yesterday."

"You say that like it's unusual. Doesn't Carrie attend these fashion weeks every year?"

"Evidently not. Normally it's the head buyers from Lane Crawford and Joyce Boutiques who come to the shows."

"Thank god for her support," May said. "Getting probably the best retailer of women's clothes in Hong Kong and Asia to carry our line was such a coup."

"Carrying the clothes and selling them are two different things," Amanda said. "I have no doubt Carrie is here only because we've been selling very well."

"That and the fact that she still feels she owes Ava a debt of gratitude," May said.

"Are you still having doubts about the setting for the show?" Ava asked, slightly uncomfortable about discussing her relationship with Song. She preferred to believe that it was the quality of Clark's clothes, not her *guanxi*, that had been the determining factor in Carrie's decision to take on the line.

"No. I was thinking about it last night and I believe the director we hired to create the show is being honest when he says it's the coolest venue he's ever worked in."

"Clark loves it," Amanda said.

The show was to be staged on a vacant floor more than halfway up the eighty-seven-storey Shard. With its floor-to-ceiling windows as a dramatic backdrop, the venue had been converted into a theatre with a stage and a U-shaped runway extending more than thirty metres. Three rows of seats were placed on each side of the runway for the press, photographers, bloggers, retailers, and purchasing groups. The front-row seats were reserved for the major buyers and people of huge influence in the fashion world.

"It is dramatic," Ava said. "And those silk warlord banners we used in Shanghai are going to look fantastic in that light."

"We debated about using them again," Amanda said. "But they worked so well in Shanghai, and we have almost an entirely different audience here, so the director decided to do it."

"And did you finally decide what to do about music?" May asked.

"We're going with Cantopop — loud and upbeat," Amanda said.

They reached the Thames, crossed the bridge, and in a few minutes found themselves on London Bridge Street looking up at the glass-encased Shard.

"This is crazy," Ava said, as they got out of the taxi and stepped into a crowd of people. "They can't all be here for the launch."

"No, this is a busy building most days," Amanda said. "Follow me."

It took them ten minutes to work their way through the lobby and into an elevator. The doors opened onto a throng of photographers taking shots of people posing on the red carpet against a backdrop emblazoned with the PÖ logo. Ava didn't recognize any of them, but Amanda whispered, "The woman with the red hair is a senior editor at *Elle*."

Another crowd was gathered near the door to the venue. Ava had never seen so many well-dressed people together in one place. Inside, at least a third of the seats were already taken, mainly those in the second and third rows. Ava, Amanda, and May had been offered front-row seats, but May had been quick to say no.

"We don't need our egos stroked," she said. "I'd rather have someone sit there who can help make our company a success."

"Do you want to go backstage and wish everyone good luck?" Amanda asked as they stepped inside.

"No," Ava said. "We didn't in Shanghai. I don't want us to jinx them."

"Then I guess that's a no from me as well," May said with a laugh.

They took their seats and looked anxiously around. The runway ran from the far end of the room towards the main entrance. The U-shaped design had the added advantage of enabling a maximum number of front-row seats. Five minutes before the show was scheduled to start, there was hardly an empty seat. Ava looked at the seats front-row centre and saw they were full. She breathed a sigh of relief. The director had made it clear that if some of the major buyers and media people were running late, the show wouldn't start until they got there.

"I saw Carrie and Elsa arrive," May said. "Besides them, I don't know a soul."

"We're not on home turf anymore," Ava said.

The lights dimmed and Jacky Cheung's voice filled the room. Ava felt a slight breeze, and the banners they had brought from Shanghai began to flutter.

Ava sat down between May and Amanda, and when the first model appeared, she reached for their hands. For the next twenty minutes, she didn't let go.

After seeing the show in Shanghai, Ava was familiar with the rhythm of the models appearing seconds apart. She knew they were going to show about forty outfits, or "exits" as the director called them, but she quickly lost count. The show was tightly paced, and because of that Ava noticed that instead of one outfit being singularly prominent, it was the general impression that stayed with her. And in this case she was taken by how beautifully cut everything was, how vibrant the linens — Clark Po's favourite medium — and how well he straddled East and West. His designs hinted at a Western sensibility but still had distinctly Eastern touches, such as cheongsam and bell collars and voluminous cuffs.

Unlike the Shanghai show — where the workers from the PÖ sample factory were in attendance and cheered loudly — the reaction in London was muted, although Ava thought she could hear muttering that seemed to indicate approval. But success in the fashion world was all so subjective, she knew, and skewed to reputation and expectation, and PÖ still lacked the former. One thing that did bode well, she thought, was the number of people taking photos or filming with their smartphones. It seemed as though every other person had a phone aimed at the runway.

Ava lost track of how many models walked by, but she knew the end of the show was approaching and there was still no sign of Pang Fai. "I'm beginning to worry about Fai," she whispered to May. "Maybe she's changed her mind about doing this."

The constant flow of models stopped quite suddenly, and Ava watched the last three women walk past them and disappear backstage. There was a buzz in the air. Ava could detect disappointment in it, and felt a rush of anxiety. Was it possible Pang Fai wouldn't appear?

Then all the models began streaming onto the runway, followed by Clark, who was wearing white linen slacks with a red silk scarf tied around his waist and a loose-fitting white linen shirt with colourful glass buttons. He took five or six steps forward, stopped, turned, and extended his right arm back towards the runway entrance.

Ava felt time stand still. Seconds seemed to stretch into minutes. Then an extraordinarily tall woman stepped onto the runway. She wore a delicately spun black linen coat shot through with thin strands of red and gold. All three colours shimmered under the lights. The coat was tightly fitted and came to just below the knee. The clean, minimalist cut was juxtaposed with a scalloped hem and bell sleeves. The model's face was obscured by a multi-layered hood trimmed in red.

"Is that Fai?" May said.

The model took three steps forward and then stopped. She rolled her shoulders back and held out a hand towards Clark. He walked to her, took her hand, and led her slowly down the centre of the runway.

Ava could hear herself breathing and realized that the entire room had fallen silent.

Clark faced the woman and whispered something to her. When she nodded, he began to undo the onyx coat buttons. When he had finished, he moved back and took two steps to the side.

Her hands reached up and pulled the coat off. It floated to the ground. May gasped, and Ava felt her own breathing stop for a second.

Pang Fai raised her head. She wore no makeup and her hair was cut in a simple pageboy. She had on a white linen T-shirt that barely reached her thighs, exposing nearly all of the famous Pang legs. The word "PÖ" was written on it in red, and along the bottom were the date and the word "London."

The models lined the runway, surrounding Clark and Fai. May, Amanda, and Ava hardly noticed the steadily rising applause. Their attention was fixed on Pang Fai.

"Whoever thought of having her so plain under that coat is a genius," Amanda said.

"So plain?" May said. "I've never seen anyone so beautiful."

Clark picked up the coat and placed it over Pang Fai's shoulders. She smiled affectionately and leaned down and kissed him on the lips. He turned and bowed, waved to the crowd, and took Fai's hand and led her backstage.

Ava felt her body sag and realized she had been caught up in the drama of it all. The applause abated and the crowd began to disperse. Most people were already making their way towards the exit, while a few headed backstage. The director had warned them about rapid audience departures. There were shows going on all over London and schedules were tight.

Ava was turning to talk to May when out of the corner of her eye she saw Carrie Song hurrying towards them.

"What did you think?" Ava said.

"I wouldn't have missed this for anything," Carrie said, shaking her head. "The clothes were wonderful, and Pang Fai...My god, only a real superstar could have pulled that off."

"She was amazing."

"There's something I want to tell you. Do you see that stocky man in the grey suit and light blue tie?" Carrie said, motioning towards the exit.

"The one surrounded by three or four other men in grey and black suits?"

"Yes."

"Who is he?"

"Dominic Ventola, the chairman of VLG, the world's second largest luxury-brand company."

"I know the name, and I know of VLG. Why would he come to our show?"

"Like everyone else, he may have wanted to see if Pang Fai would make an appearance. But I can tell you that once the show started, he had his assistants — those other men in suits — taking photographs of every outfit."

"Why would they be so interested?"

"Not to steal Clark's designs, if that's what you're thinking. They don't operate like that," Carrie said. "But, among other things, Dominic likes to invest in talented young designers."

"We don't need any investors."

"I'm not suggesting you do or that that's what he wants," Carrie said. "I probably shouldn't have said anything at all."

"No, I'm glad you did, and I'm sure Clark will be pleased to hear that a man like Ventola saw fit to attend his show and thought enough of his designs to record them."

"He should be."

"And I need to tell you how pleased I am that you came today," Ava said.

"I feel as if I have a stake in all of this, and all of you."

"A big enough stake that I can entice you to join us for a celebratory lunch?"

"Will Pang Fai be there?"

"Of course, as well as May, Amanda, Clark, and our entire Shanghai team."

"I didn't mean to sound quite so star-struck," Carrie said with a laugh.

"Fai does that to people."

Carrie looked at her watch. "I have two more shows scheduled over the next two hours. One is in Soho and the other is in the Docklands. I can't miss them."

"I understand, but by the time they're done, in all likelihood we'll just be getting started. It won't be a problem if you're late."

"I'll try to make it."

"Great. We've reserved the private dining area at Hakkasan Restaurant in Hanway Place. It's near Tottenham Court Road, about a twenty-minute cab ride from here."

"It sounds like it's Chinese," Carrie said.

"It is Chinese — actually, Cantonese. We're a predictable bunch."

"That's the very last thing anyone would ever call you."

2

IT WAS MADNESS BACKSTAGE.

When Ava, May, and Amanda entered the dressing and staging area, they stepped into a sea of noise. Most of the models had other shows to get to and were quickly changing into their own clothes. Clark was standing in a corner, surrounded by well-wishers. Gillian and Chi-Tze were deep in discussion with several people Ava didn't recognize.

"Where is Pang Fai?" Ava asked.

"Over there," Amanda said.

Fai was seated, and some of the Chinese models stood around her. The monstrously large bodyguard her agent had hired was hovering by her side.

"I'll go talk to her," Ava said.

"I'm going to see who Clark is with," Amanda said.

"And I recognize one of the people talking to Chi-Tze," May said. "I'll join them."

Fai beamed when she saw Ava approaching, and rose to her feet. She was still wearing the T-shirt but had removed the high-heeled shoes. The models grouped around her parted.

"You were magnificent," Ava said, giving Fai a hug.

"So the girls keep telling me."

"It's true."

"I didn't think I would be so nervous."

"It didn't show," Ava said, surprised at Fai's insecurity. "Who came up with the idea?"

"I did," Fai said. "They wanted me to just do a runway walk, but I said to Clark, 'What is the point in hiring an actress if you don't let her act?'"

"I'm glad they listened to you."

"I didn't give them much choice," Fai said, laughing. "I am hard to resist when I'm in full drama-queen mode."

"Ava..." a voice said. She turned to see Amanda.

"Elsa brought some colleagues to meet Clark," Amanda said. "Do we have room for them at lunch?"

"How many are they?"

"Two, plus Elsa."

The Ling Ling Lounge at Hakkasan was designed to accommodate about twenty people. They were already at twenty-three, and Elsa and her friends would make it twenty-six. "Sure," Ava said, figuring that she would insist — as she had seen her mother do countless times — that the restaurant find a way to fit everyone in.

It took close to an hour for the backstage activity to calm. The PR people had lined up a series of interviews and photo ops for Clark and Pang Fai. Clark spoke fluent English but Fai needed an interpreter — a role that Amanda and Chi-Tze took turns filling.

They left the Shard in taxis. Ava, Amanda, May, and Elsa rode together in one; behind them were Pang Fai, her body-guard, Clark, and the show director; and trailing, Chi-Tze,

Gillian, Elsa's friends, some of the director's staff, and the models they'd flown in from Shanghai.

"You are going to be pleased with the coverage you'll get," Elsa said as they were crossing London Bridge. "I heard nothing but compliments from the press I talked to."

"Thank you for saying that, and thanks for all the support you've given us," Ava said.

"Now all we have to do is convert that support into orders," May said.

"We have lots of follow-up to do," Amanda said. "Chi-Tze and Gillian were approached by at least five buyers who want to talk to us about carrying the line."

"Does Clark know?" Ava asked.

"He does, and I was amazed at how composed he was about it. He was so high-strung before the show, but now he's like a different person."

"He is a bit of an actor, isn't he," May said. "I was thinking that when he came down the runway with Pang Fai. What you've said just reinforces that idea. He played the eccentric, emotional designer before the show and then morphed into the cool and collected professional after it."

"Maybe that's because he knew the show was a success," Ava said.

"Still, I think May is right," Elsa said. "When we did that photo shoot with him in Shanghai, he was like a chameleon, fitting whatever role our photographer wanted him to play. He's a bit like Dominic Ventola in that regard."

"Did you know Ventola was at the show?" Ava asked, surprised.

"Yes, I saw him, and Amanda tells me that Carrie Song spotted him as well."

"Have you ever met him?"

"No, but I know people who have."

"What do they say he's like?"

"Apparently it depends on the day. I've been told he's charming, incredibly intelligent, and generous," Elsa said. "And I've also heard people swear they've never met anyone coarser, greedier, or more ruthless. It's like a switch goes on or off and his personality does a complete about-face."

"Why was he there?" May asked.

"That's anyone's guess," Elsa said.

It took them more than half an hour to negotiate the mid-day London traffic to get to Hakkasan. Ava had called the restaurant from the cab to tell them more seats were required and then requested extra servings of every dish she had pre-ordered. As the group slowly gathered, Ava functioned as hostess. She put Elsa Ngan on one side of Pang Fai and left the other seat open for Carrie Song. Clark sat directly across from Fai, flanked by Gillian and Chi-Tze, with May Ling and Amanda on either side of them. Ava sat in Song's seat, leaving the one next to her empty. The director, a few key members of his staff, Elsa's friends, and the models filled the rest of the chairs. When everyone was more or less settled, Ava asked the servers to bring the dim sum platters she'd ordered and to start serving the Louis Roederer champagne.

When everyone had a glass, Ava stood and raised hers. "On behalf of May, Amanda, and myself, I want to say how proud we are of our talented and wonderful Clark. He continues to go from strength to strength, and his collection is spectacular. We don't know how much business we'll generate from the show today, and frankly we don't care. We're just so proud to have helped bring his creations to the world's attention."

"Ava, don't be so quick to say you don't care how much business we do," Gillian said, and everyone laughed.

They toasted and then settled in to eat. The first course was scallop *siu mai*, *har gow*, and celery prawn dumplings. Then the main dishes were served: Peking duck with Qiando caviar, silver cod with champagne, wagyu beef with white asparagus, Singapore noodles with prawns and squid, and stir-fried bok choy and morning glory. The food was uniformly excellent, but the models, Clark, and the director and his staff just picked at the dishes.

"I'm going to have way too much food left if these people don't start eating," Ava said to Fai. "What's the matter with them?"

"They're used to starving themselves. Once you get into that habit it's hard to break."

"They're flying to Shanghai tomorrow. They should have a hearty meal here before they go."

Fai nodded then said to the table, "Who would have thought we could find Chinese food this good in England?" she said. "Why don't we show the chefs some respect by eating a bit more."

"That goes for you too, Clark," Ava said. "You could eat six meals a day for two months and still not be fat."

"Well, what they won't eat, I will," May said. "And here is Carrie to help."

Carrie gave Ava a hug and then worked her way around the table before sitting next to Fai.

"How were the other shows?" Ava asked.

"Good, but not quite as good as PÖ," she said. "All I heard was talk about Clark and, of course, Pang Fai."

Fai smiled.

"You were fantastic," Carrie said.

"Because of a brilliant designer and a great director."

"Don't be so modest."

Fai shrugged and then smiled again. "Okay, maybe I did have something to do with it."

Carrie reached for a slice of beef, and then the others really began to eat and enjoy themselves. Ten minutes later, Ava was pleased to see that some of the platters were almost empty. She ordered three more bottles of champagne.

Carrie had just finished her second glass when she checked her phone. She turned to Ava. "Good god, look at this."

"What?" Ava said.

"It's a text from Raffi Pandolfo, asking me if I know who he should talk to about the PÖ brand."

"Who is Raffi Pandolfo?"

"You really don't know?'

Ava shook her head.

"Dominic Ventola's right-hand man," Carrie said.

"And long-time partner," Elsa added.

"Yes, but strictly in the business sense," Carrie said. "He's a minority shareholder and partner in VLG. He has a well-earned reputation for being astute, especially when it comes to managing the group's finances."

"Does everyone know that Ventola was at the launch today?" Ava asked.

"Yes, we all heard," Chi-Tze said.

"But I didn't see Pandolfo there," Carrie said.

"What does this mean?" Gillian asked.

"According to Carrie, we should assume that Ventola likes Clark's work."

"Do you think he wants to get involved with us?" Gillian said.

"I don't know," Ava said.

"VLG is a spectacular company," Gillian said.

"We do understand their significance," May said.

"Tell Mr. Pandolfo he can contact me," Ava said to Carrie. "I'm curious to hear what he has to say."

3

"I CAN'T SAY I'M VERY HAPPY ABOUT GILLIAN'S REACTION to that text from Raffi Pandolfo," May said. She, Ava, and Amanda were in a taxi on the way back to their hotel.

"I'm sure she was just flattered by the attention," Amanda said. "She and Clark have been trying for so long to get his work known. It must be overwhelming to have had Dominic Ventola at the show and then Pandolfo trying to contact us."

"What do you think they intend?" May asked.

"Carrie made a point of saying that Ventola likes to invest in young, talented designers," Ava said.

"We don't need his money," May said.

"No, but he brings many other things to the table," Amanda said.

"Influence with high-end retailers?" May suggested.

"And that only scratches the surface," Amanda said. "It's true he's got many friends and allies in retail and in fashion media around the world, but he and Raffi also know how to take someone like Clark, and a brand like ΓÖ, and spin it off into perfumes, leathers, watches, and other merchandise."

"I know it's a cliché, but we need to walk before we run," Ava said.

They reached the Corinthia and were walking through the lobby when Ava's phone vibrated. She looked at the screen and saw it was a private number. She hesitated and then answered. "Ava Lee."

"This is Xu."

"It's the middle of the night in Shanghai."

"I woke around one and started thinking about the show and couldn't get back to sleep. How did it go?"

"Fantastic."

"How did Pang Fai do?"

"It was like watching a dream. She was sensational."

"Your partners must be happy."

"Yourself included," Ava said, referring to his silent investment in Three Sisters.

"It's nice to hear you sound so happy."

"Happy is the right word."

"So now what?"

"We don't know yet. We'll have to see how much media coverage we get and what kind of orders come in."

"Keep me updated."

"I will," Ava said.

"Who was that?" May asked when Ava ended the call.

"Xu."

"Oh."

Ava glanced at her friend. Recently May had been acting oddly whenever she was with Xu or when his name was mentioned. Ava wondered if there was something going on between them, or whether she was reading too much into May's reaction. "He sends his congratulations to everyone," she said.

"There must be times when he finds it tiresome having to stay in the background," May said.

"I'm sure that's true, but he doesn't plan on that being a permanent situation."

In addition to being a silent investor in Three Sisters, Xu ran the triad organization in Shanghai and was chairman of the triad societies in Asia. Like Ava, he had been mentored by Uncle, and that bond had initially drawn them together. Now they were forging their own strong relationship. Xu often referred to Ava as *mei mei*, little sister, and she thought of him as *gege*, big brother.

"I'll let you both know if I hear from Pandolfo," Ava said as they got in the elevator.

"And if you don't?" Amanda asked.

"Then I'll see you at seven for drinks and dinner," Ava said. "We're meeting here in the lobby before heading over to the Dorchester Hotel. Fai wants steak, and the Grill at the Dorchester is supposed to be terrific."

Ava's room was on the third floor and she was the first to exit the elevator. She opened the door and walked into a room that had almost taken her breath away the first time she saw it. Originally known as the Metropole Hotel, the Corinthia had been constructed in 1885. The unique triangular brick building had been used for other purposes throughout the years, including as a government office. It wasn't until 2007 that the Corinthia group, owned by the Pisani family of Malta, took control of the property and turned it into a five-star luxury hotel. What surprised Ava was how originally and richly decorated every room was. Hers was furnished in an ultra-modern style and the wooden floor was laid out in a herringbone pattern in shades of taupe, tan, and brown. May's room was styled with a purple and red palette and Amanda was in a blue room. Regardless of colour and decor, the overriding impression was of tremendous quality.

She slipped off her shoes and went into the bathroom. She washed her face and hands and then undid the ivory chignon pin that held her hair in place. She had left Toronto four days before and was still feeling some minor effects of jet lag. She contemplated taking a nap but knew from experience that it might throw off her body clock even more. Instead, when she returned to the room, she sat at the desk and turned on her computer.

There was a long list of emails from friends, most of them asking how the launch had gone. Ava answered them all, detailing the tremendous reception the show had received. When she was finished, she turned to emails from her girl-friend, Maria Gonzalez, and her mother, Jennie Lee, both of whom also asked about the show, and then ventured into other areas that were more problematic.

Five months before, Jennie had won almost $100,000 playing baccarat during a week-long gambling binge at some local casinos. In the excitement of the moment she'd offered to take Ava's sister, Marian, and her two daughters to Disneyworld in Florida, and Ava and Maria to Italy. The Florida trip had taken place in early December. The Italian tour was scheduled for early May, but two issues had arisen since Ava had accepted the invitation. First, she was con-vinced that her mother had burned through most, if not all, of her winnings. They hadn't discussed it directly, but she knew her mother had taken a week-long trip to Las Vegas in January and was going to the local casinos on a regular basis.

When Ava asked her how she had done, Jennie sidestepped the question. And when Ava tried to discuss the trip to Italy, her mother did so without enthusiasm. That could mean only one thing: Jennie had lost money, and probably a lot of it. If that was true, Ava didn't imagine she could still afford to pay for the three of them to go to Italy.

Jennie was the second wife of Marcus Lee, a Hong Kong businessman. The relationship had soured quickly and Jennie was sent to Vancouver with the two young girls. A few years later Jennie moved to Richmond Hill, a northern Toronto suburb and the place Ava thought of as home. Marcus looked after Jennie and his daughters financially. He visited Canada for two weeks every year and talked to Jennie every day by phone. As strange as the arrangement might seem to outsiders, neither Jennie nor her daughters found it odd. As far as Jennie was concerned, Marcus was her husband. To the girls he was their father, and the children from his first marriage, and later from a third to a woman now living in Australia, were their siblings.

Ava wasn't privy to the details of the financial arrangement between her mother and father, but she understood that he looked after the house and car expenses and provided Jennie with a monthly allowance. That allowance, Ava knew from experience, was spent every month and often before the month had ended. When Ava and Marian were still living at home, they knew that Jennie had burned through her monthly budget when there was increased rice in their diet. Now it was when Ava called her mother and asked what her plans were for the next few days and was told she didn't have any. When Jennie had money, she rarely spent an evening at home.

What am I going to do? Ava thought. Finding an excuse to cancel the trip would be awkward. Offering to pay for it herself would offend her mother's pride. Ava had been mulling over postponing the trip, which would allow Jennie to save face and give Ava more time to deal with her second problem — her relationship with Maria.

Maria and Ava had been together for almost two years. It was the longest relationship Ava had ever been in. Aside from a one-night stand she'd had on a business trip to the Faroe Islands, she had been faithful and had no interest in pursuing other women. She had no doubt that she loved Maria, who was warm, caring, beautiful, and a wonderful lover. The problem was that Maria wasn't satisfied with the status quo. Months earlier, her appointment as assistant trade commissioner for Colombia in Toronto had been extended for an additional two years. The instant it was confirmed, she began to press Ava about moving in together. She was less insistent about marriage but dropped plenty of hints that it was what she wanted in the long run. Ava wasn't ready for either of those steps and wasn't sure she ever would be. Strangely, the idea of marriage was less stressful for her than the thought of living with someone.

Ava had been living by herself since she left home for university at the age of seventeen. During her years working with Uncle, she was often alone on the road for weeks on end. Even when she was young, she'd never minded solitude, and as she got older she grew more and more comfortable with being on her own. The longest time she'd been under the same roof with anyone was the two weeks she'd spent in Thailand with Maria near the start of their relationship. Although it had gone well, she was still happy to come home, close the door of her Yorkville apartment, and sit quietly by herself at the kitchen table looking out onto the street. Since then, she and Maria had taken several shorter holidays and spent most weekends together, usually at Ava's. As much as Ava enjoyed those times, she was almost relieved when Maria went back to her bungalow for the week. It was so much easier to breathe that Ava swore the oxygen level in the apartment had doubled.

The email that Maria had just sent addressed the subject of cohabitation again. She was leasing on a month-to-month basis and her landlord wanted her to make a long-term commitment. What should I do? she had written. Ava slowly shook her head. She couldn't think of an answer that would make both of them happy.

Hello my love, it has been a wonderful day. The launch went very well. Pang Fai was fantastic, and there's all kinds of interest in Clark's work. I'm going to be staying in Europe for a few days longer than planned, but the schedule is still fluid. I'll let you know the moment it's finalized, she wrote. As for your house, I think you should extend the lease. I'm always so comfortable there, and we're so lucky to be able to go back and forth, enjoying our two different neighbourhoods the way we do. Love, Ava.

She reread the note and thought about waiting until the morning before sending it. But she disliked procrastination, and putting this off wasn't going to make things any easier. She hit SEND. Almost immediately her phone rang, and for an irrational few seconds she imagined it was Maria.

"Hello," she said.

"Is this Miss Ava Lee?" a man's voice said.

"Yes, it is."

"I am Raffaello Pandolfo. I'm with the Ventola Luxury Group. I believe that Carrie Song told you to expect a call from me?"

"She did. We saw that Mr. Ventola and some of his associates were at our launch today. Were you one of them?"

"No, unfortunately, I had other obligations, but Dom came away very impressed with what he saw."

"Thank you. Clark Po will be thrilled to hear that."

"Miss Lee, when I spoke to Carrie, she explained a bit about how your company is structured." Pandolfo spoke softly, his tone rising and falling as if he were sharing a secret. "She couldn't be precise, of course, but I was given the general impression that you and a Ms. Wong are financing the Po siblings."

Ava hesitated, not sure how to respond. "I'm not sure why our structure is of interest to you, Mr. Pandolfo," she said.

"*Mi scusi* if it was impolite on my part to enquire," he said.

"*Momentai*," Ava said.

"What does that mean?"

"It's Cantonese, and it means 'no problem.'"

"I'll try to remember that. It sounds like a useful word," he said. "Now, do you have any notion why I'm calling?"

"I'm not much of a mind reader, Mr. Pandolfo."

"Call me Raffi, please."

"And I'm Ava."

"Well, Ava, our company, VLG, has an interest in discussing the PÖ line with you."

"And what exactly is your interest?"

"Well, Asia — and China in particular — is becoming an increasingly important market for us, both in terms of sales and as a source of raw materials and some finished goods.

We'd like to expand our footprint there, and having an affiliation with a brand like PÖ would be a start in that direction."

"'Having an affiliation,' as you put it, is a very broad
concept."

"I'm partial to the phrase. It implies caution, and we're
not a company that acts in a precipitous manner," he said.
"What we would like to do is sit down together with you and
your partners and exchange information. You'll have a better
understanding of who we are, how we operate, and perhaps
what we can do for you. We'll have a better sense of your
business and what your plans are for the future. Who knows,
there might be some common ground for us to build on."

"We don't need investors," Ava said.

"I haven't suggested that you do."

"And as for the rest of it, I'm not sure —"

"Ava, what harm is there in a simple conversation? No one
is asking you to make a commitment or do anything except
have a chat with us. We don't bite," he said with a laugh. "And
if all that comes from it is that Clark Po gets the opportunity
to meet Dominic, then at least we'll have been entertained
by their exchange of views."

Ava admired the way he had woven Clark's name into the
conversation and connected it with Ventola's. "We already
have dinner planned for this evening," she said.

"Do you plan to be in Milan next week, for the next show
on the Fashion Week merry-go-round?"

"No, we're all going home. Most of us leave London tomorrow and the day after for various parts of the world."

"Instead of doing that, come to Milan," he urged. "We'll
talk there."

"I don't know if that's even possible."

"How many people would you want to include in a meeting — assuming you agree to one?"

"I have two partners, May Ling Wong and Amanda Yee. PÖ is run by Clark, his sister Gillian Po, and a woman named Chi-Tze Song."

"Are they all in London?"

"They are."

"Discuss it with them, yes? Tell them that Dom has issued a personal invitation for them to join him in Milan."

"I'm sure they'll be flattered, but even if they want to go, there's still the matter of getting there and finding accommodation. We were told that during the run-up to Milan Fashion Week, hotel rooms in the city are booked months in advance."

"You shouldn't have any problem finding flights, but you are correct that accommodation could be challenging. Rooms are booked years, not just months, in advance. I'll tell you what, if you can't find a suitable hotel we have a guest villa in Menaggio, on Lake Como, that I'm sure can be made available. It is big enough for all of you."

"That is generous, but —"

"Ava, don't say no to me, please. I take rejection very hard," Pandolfo said. "Besides, you're all here in London, only a few hours from Milan. The timing is perfect for us to sit together."

She hesitated.

"Can I assume that your silence means you are at least thinking about talking to your colleagues about our invitation?" he said.

Ava smiled. "You are very, very persuasive."

"So, you will talk to them?" he pressed.

"I will."

"*Molte grazie.*"

"But I'm not making any promises that they'll agree to go."

"I understand, but you will get back to me sometime today with their response?"

"I should be able to do that."

"You can reach me at the number I'm calling you from."

"You shouldn't expect to hear from me until after our dinner tonight."

"You can call at any time."

"Okay, then we'll talk later," Ava said.

"And hopefully we'll see some or all of you tomorrow or the day after in Milan. *Ciao*," Pandolfo said.

Ava put down the phone and sat back in the chair with her hands clasped behind her head. *What just happened?* she thought. She couldn't remember the last time a man — any man — had convinced her to do something she didn't want to. And this man had done it in such a smooth way that she couldn't bring herself to be annoyed.

She called May Ling.

"*Wei*," May said.

"I've just had the most remarkable conversation with Raffaello Pandolfo."

"What did he want?" May asked.

"He wants us all to get together in Milan tomorrow or the day after for a chat."

"About what?"

"He wasn't specific, but generally about their interest in PÖ."

"How did you respond?"

"Eventually I agreed that I would talk it over with our team."

"Really?"

"May, how do you think Clark would respond if he found out he had a personal invitation to meet with Dominic Ventola in Milan and we didn't tell him about it?"

"He wouldn't be happy, and frankly, it would make us look insecure."

"And if we just put off Pandolfo, he would eventually find a way to approach Clark directly."

"That would almost certainly happen."

"I agree, so we need to take the high road and be completely proactive," Ava said.

"I also can't deny that being approached by the Ventola Group is quite a compliment and kind of exciting."

"Exactly, and who knows what could result? They're a tremendous company and could provide us with types of support that we haven't even considered."

"I just can't help being wary about their intentions," May said.

"That's just your natural Wuhan nature."

"You're right," May said, laughing.

"After dinner tonight we'll pull the entire team together and talk it through."

"I find it hard to imagine that Clark and Gillian won't find the idea of meeting with Ventola irresistible."

"And if they do, we'll agree to go to Milan. Even if nothing concrete comes from the trip, we'll get a glimpse inside one of the world's greatest luxury-brand companies and the chance to meet a legend."

(4)

THEY RODE IN TWO TAXIS TO THE DORCHESTER HOTEL
on Park Lane, less than two miles west of the Corinthia.

Ava, May, Pang Fai, and her bodyguard were in one cab,
and Gillian, Clark, Chi-Tze, and the show director were in
the other. Amanda was meeting a friend for dinner elsewhere. The group was far more subdued than they'd been
earlier in the day. The combination of jet lag, too much food
and wine, and adrenalin burnout made for a quiet dinner
and an early night. As they left the Dorchester, Ava pulled
aside Chi-Tze and both of the Pos.

"We need to chat when we get back to the hotel," she said.
"We're going to have a short meeting in May's suite." She had
phoned Amanda earlier and left the same message.

Clark started to protest, but he quieted immediately when
Ava said, "It's about Dominic Ventola and VLG."

Ava called Amanda from the taxi to tell her they were
on their way back to the hotel. "I'm in the lobby already,"
Amanda said.

They gathered in May's sitting room. As they arranged
themselves on couches and chairs, Ava couldn't help but

notice the natural groupings. Gillian and Clark were slouched side by side on a couch, her hand placed casually on his knee. They weren't just siblings; they had worked together in their father's garment business for more than ten years before he died and their uncle sold the business out from under them. At thirty-two, Gillian was two years older than her brother, and in addition to having the stronger head for business, she thought of herself as a protective shield between Clark and the rest of the world.

Amanda and Chi-Tze also sat together. Amanda was Hong Kong–born and raised; Chi-Tze had grown up in Kota Kinabalu, in Borneo's Sabah province. Now in their late twenties, they had met at Brandeis University, where they were both taking a master's degree in business administration. Amanda had brought Chi-Tze into Three Sisters with the specific task of managing PÖ together with Gillian. So far she had been very successful. Both the young women were barely five feet tall, fine-boned, and delicate. In Ava's mind they were becoming as inseparable as the Pos.

May took a seat at the small dining table, slightly apart from the others. Ava joined her there. Still in her mid-thirties, Ava was closer in age to the others than to May, but her time working with Uncle had given her experience that went far beyond her years, and she and May had had a special bond from the beginning, intellectually and emotionally.

"First of all, thanks for interrupting your evening plans. I know it's been a long day, but I didn't think this should wait," Ava said.

"You mentioned Dominic Ventola," Clark said.

"Yes. His business partner, Raffaello Pandolfo, called me earlier today," Ava said. "He wants us to go to Milan tomorrow or the day after to meet with him and other members of VLG, including Dominic."

"Meet about what?" Gillian asked, sitting upright.

"They were impressed with Clark's designs and want to discuss his work and our company," Ava said.

"Are we having financial issues?" Gillian asked abruptly.

The question caught Ava off guard. "I don't understand what you mean."

"Is Three Sisters having any difficulty financing us?"

"No."

"And in the next year or so, if we keep growing and expanding, do you foresee any financial issues?"

"We can finance any amount of growth you, Clark, and Chi-Tze can generate," Ava said.

Clark cut in. "What did you actually say to him?"

"I said I had to talk to you — to all of you."

"Apart from the fact that I'd love to visit Italy and the idea of meeting Dom Ventola is exciting, I don't know why we'd bother going to Milan," Amanda said. "We've been pretty successful at opening doors, and we need to keep our growth manageable."

"They sell their goods everywhere. There isn't a door they couldn't open for us," Gillian said. "And they can take the PÖ brand and extend it into perfumes, watches, bags."

"Except the PÖ brand — at this point in time — doesn't have that kind of international cachet yet. We're still building recognition," Amanda said.

"If we got the right kind of support from VLG we wouldn't have to wait too long to become a truly international brand," Gillian said. "With their reputation, marketing dollars, and skills, and all their connections with fashion editors, bloggers, and stylists, we could get there much faster than we could on our own."

"That may well be true, but before we get too far along talking about what the Ventola Group can do or not do for us, don't you think we should consider what the price might be for any help they might want to give us?" May said.

"In recent years they've expanded their company by acquiring other brands. They own ten or more," Gillian said. "They prefer to buy an up-and-coming brand at a reasonable cost and tie the designer into a long-term contract. But they've also bought some well-established fashion lines too."

"I have zero interest in selling our interest in PÖ, and I think I speak for both of my partners in Three Sisters," May said.

Ava nodded.

"I was only explaining how Ventola likes to operate," Gillian said quickly. "I wasn't making any suggestions."

"And I don't want to give up any control over how I work," Clark said. "It took long enough to get the independence I wanted, and I'm not about to give it up after six months."

"Okay, so where does this leave us?" Ava said.

The room fell quiet. Then Clark leaned in towards Ava and said, "What do you think we should do?"

"Well, we don't know what they want and we're all making assumptions," she said. "I've never been afraid of having a discussion with someone, so I'm prepared to talk to them. But I think this decision is really yours to make. They only want to meet with us because of you."

"I would actually have a chance to meet personally with Dominic Ventola?"

"I was told that, but we can confirm it," Ava said.

"He's been my idol for years."

"If we do decide to go," Amanda said, "what will we do about flights and hotels? Milan Fashion Week starts in a few days. It will be hard to get there and the hotels will be jam-packed."

"I'm told that flights shouldn't be a problem, and Raffi Pandolfo offered us the use of a villa on Lake Como if we want it."

"A villa," Chi-Tze said. She looked at Gillian. "What do you think?"

"It seems to me that we have nothing to lose by talking to them," Gillian said. "And if there's nothing to be gained on the business side, we'll at least get a bit of a holiday."

"And I'll get the chance to meet Dominic Ventola," Clark said.

"Does anyone disagree with Gillian?" Ava said.

"Who would go?" Chi-Tze asked.

"I think it should be everyone who's here," Ava said.

"Then I'm for it," Chi-Tze said.

Ava looked at Clark and Gillian. They both nodded.

"I'll have to call Wuhan and move some meetings," May said. "I'll do it as soon as we're finished."

"I'm in," Amanda said.

"How does tomorrow look for everyone? Pang Fai leaves early tomorrow afternoon and I should see her off," Ava said.

"And we have some meetings scheduled with buyers," Amanda said. "They'll be done by three."

"Okay, then we should leave sometime late in the afternoon or early the next morning," Ava said. "Amanda, why don't you look after the flight arrangements. I'll call Raffi Pandolfo and let him know we're coming but that our schedule isn't finalized."

"I'll text the flight details to everyone," Amanda said.

"Perfect. Anything else?"

No one spoke. Then the younger women and Clark stood up and started to walk towards the door. Gillian, Amanda, and Chi-Tze were talking, and even from where she was sitting, Ava sensed their excitement. Clark turned when he reached the door and looked back at Ava and May, who were still at the table.

"Thank you for everything you've done for me — for us," he said. "This week has been the most amazing of my life and now the adventure continues."

When the door closed and they were left alone, May said to Ava, "I know that telling the group about the invitation to Italy was the right thing to do, but I still wish we weren't going."

"What do you mean?"

"Did you see Clark's face?"

"He's thrilled about meeting Dominic Ventola. It's to be expected."

"I know, but I don't like what he said when he left just now."

"What did you hear that I didn't?"

"'Thank you for everything you've done for me?' He sounded like a man getting ready to ditch his girlfriend or quit his job."

"You're paranoid," Ava said, laughing.

"Twenty years of doing business in China will do that to you," May said.

"We're going to Italy."

"I've heard that the Italians and Chinese have a lot in common."

5

IT WAS ALMOST ELEVEN O'CLOCK IN THE EVENING WHEN the British Airways Airbus began its descent into Milan–Malpensa Airport. They had left the hotel at five to get to Heathrow in time for the eight-o'clock departure. It had been a long day. May spent most of hers on the phone with her husband, Changxing, tending to various business issues. Chi-Tze, Gillian, and Amanda ran from meeting to meeting, following up on the interest that had been generated by the show. Ava had slept in, went for a run, and then lunched with Pang Fai before seeing her safely into an airport limousine with two of the models. They were all headed for Beijing.

Ava thought the lunch had been a bit odd. For the three days leading up to the show, Fai had been a bundle of nervous energy, constantly chattering and barely able to sit still for more than a couple of minutes. At lunch she was so subdued that Ava found it difficult to get more than a few words out of her. Ava knew very little about actors but wondered if this was a natural post-performance comedown. When she asked Fai, the actress just shook her head and looked even gloomier. Ava wondered if she'd offended her somehow, but when they said goodbye at the hotel entrance Fai wrapped her arms around Ava and gave her a long, intimate hug.

"I'm going to miss you and the others," Fai whispered.

"And we'll miss you. But we'll see you soon enough. There's lots more for us to do together in the next few months," Ava said.

"Ava, I like everyone on the team, but I don't want to do anything unless you're involved."

"Why do you say that?"

"I think you understand me, and I feel so safe around you," Fai said.

"What?" Ava replied, but Fai had quietly settled into the back seat and the chauffeur closed the door.

As the plane continued its slow descent, Ava replayed that conversation with Fai and the one she'd had the night before with Raffi Pandolfo. He had responded enthusiastically to the news that they were coming to Milan.

"I'm sorry we arrive so late," Ava said.

"We're just thrilled that you decided to come," he said. "I'll arrange to have you met at the airport. I can't come myself, but you'll be well looked after."

"And we'll need to stay at the villa. I hope that's okay."

"I've already reserved it for you. Our drivers will take you directly there. Coming to Milan was the right thing to do."

Ava closed the Moleskine notebook that sat on her lap and put it in her bag. When she worked with Uncle, she had kept a separate notebook full of names, numbers, and facts for each job they'd done. She used a fountain pen because the process of writing in longhand helping crystallize her thoughts. She wasn't on a job now, but it was a habit she couldn't break. *Dominic Ventola* was now written across the top of the first page of the new notebook. She had made notes about her impressions of Raffi Pandolfo, the information about VLG and Dominic Ventola that Carrie Song and Elsa Ngan had passed on, and the data she'd unearthed online.

VLG was a huge enterprise. Its sales ran close to $15 billion a year, and its annual profits exceeded a billion. Dominic Ventola controlled the business, even though he owned less than ten percent of its publicly traded shares. When VLG first went public, it had issued two types of shares. The first ten million were common shares, entitling the shareholders to dividends and an ownership position in proportion to the number they owned. The second type was voting shares, and only one hundred had been issued. Ventola owned eighty of them and Pandolfo the balance. Those voting shares gave the two men the power to make every major decision concerning the company, regardless of how many common shares they held. As the company grew and needed additional capital, it had issued more common shares, which diluted their ownership stake but not their authority to run the business. Ava knew that a dual share structure wasn't uncommon, but it took someone with foresight to put it in place. She wondered if that had been Pandolfo or Ventola. Or both.

Ventola had started his career as a designer of men's clothing, specializing in suits. It wasn't until Pandolfo joined the firm that ties, shoes, and shirts were added to the lineup. The business was then known simply as Ventola. Their initial partnership lasted ten years, until a disagreement over the direction of the business prompted Pandolfo to leave. The company had floundered without him, and after a year's absence Ventola asked him to return and agreed to the strategy that Pandolfo wanted to pursue. That was the start of a twenty-year period of growth and the birth of VLG.

Pandolfo's vision was to build a global company that could offer the broadest possible spectrum of high-end consumer goods to as many buying sectors as possible. VLG did this by buying other brands, integrating them into the business, and then extending their lines. Ventola identified the brands he thought they should buy and grow, while Pandolfo orchestrated the acquisitions. It was, Ava thought, a partnership that obviously worked, and it showed no signs of slowing down.

The plane landed and they exited the baggage area at just past midnight to see a man wearing a white linen suit and white shirt holding aloft a sign that read "PÖ."

"We're the PÖ group," she said.

"Welcome. My name is Riccardo. Signore Ventola and Signore Pandolfo have sent me and my colleague Giacomo to greet you," he said. "The cars are just outside. Follow me, please."

They were led to two silver Maserati Quattroporte sedans. Out of the corner of her eye Ava saw Clark nudge Gillian and whisper something to her. He was obviously impressed.

"How long is the drive?" Ava asked Riccardo.

"About one hundred kilometres, almost straight north from here," he said. "At this time of night it should take us a bit more than an hour."

"I'll ride with you and Amanda," Ava said to May.

Ava slid into the front seat and May and Amanda got into the back. Ava took a hard look at the interior of the Maserati. She wasn't a car aficionado, but the Quattroporte was one of the most luxurious cars she'd ever been in.

"Do you know what our schedule is?" Ava asked Riccardo as the car pulled out of the terminal.

"One moment," he said, reaching for his cellphone. He entered a number and then a few seconds later began to speak rapidly in Italian. He paused to listen, smiled, and then turned his head towards Ava. "Signore Pandolfo wants to speak to you," he said, passing her the phone.

"Welcome to Milan. I hope the flight was okay."

"It wasn't bad."

"Riccardo will take you to the villa. You'll be met there by Francesca, the housekeeper. She's prepared a late-night snack for you."

"You shouldn't have gone to such trouble."

"It isn't any trouble, and besides, I'm sure you're all hungry after the flight," Pandolfo said. "You asked about the plans for tomorrow."

"Yes."

"Given your late arrival, we thought we'd let you get a full night's sleep," he said. "I've tentatively arranged for the cars to pick you up at nine-thirty. That should get you to our offices here in Milan at around eleven. Is that satisfactory?"

"It sounds just fine."

"Excellent. Enjoy Francesca's hospitality and we'll see you tomorrow," he said.

Ava handed the phone to Riccardo and then turned to May and Amanda. "We're on tomorrow morning at eleven in Milan."

"Good, that gives us some time to talk as a group before we leave the villa," May said in Chinese.

"Did Chi-Tze and the Pos talk much about this trip today?" Ava asked Amanda.

"Not really. We were preoccupied with our meetings."

"I'm glad the concentration was where it should have been," May said.

"Although when it was mentioned, both Gillian and Chi-Tze seemed excited about the business possibilities it might present. Clark is enamoured with the idea of meeting Dominic Ventola," Amanda said.

The Maserati quietly accelerated. Ava glanced at the speedometer. They were going one hundred and fifty kilometres an hour. The surge in power had been effortless and the ride was incredibly smooth.

"I like this car," she said.

"We have six of them," Riccardo said. "They're Signore Ventola's favourite."

"How nice for Mr. Ventola."

"He likes quality in everything."

Ava looked outside. They seemed to be on the outskirts of the city, but it was too dark to be sure. She'd never been to Milan or Lake Como, though business had taken her to Rome once for two days and to Naples for another. Those memories triggered thoughts about her mother. Jennie wanted them to visit Rome, Florence, and Venice. As she was again pondering how to delay the trip, Maria came to her mind. Maria's response to Ava's email about extending her lease had been abrupt: I'll talk to my landlord in the next day or two. Maria. Ava knew she was very unhappy and definitely hurt. Her hope was that those feelings would have started to fade by the time she got home.

"The villa is in Mennagio," Riccardo said, tearing Ava's thoughts away from Toronto. "It's on the west side of the lake. Signore Ventola bought it fifteen years ago and lived there for about a year, but the travel to Milan was too cumbersome on a daily basis. So now he just uses it on weekends or makes it available to special guests, like you."

"Does Signore Pandolfo ever stay there?" Ava asked.

"No, never," he said, pursing his lips and with a quick shake of his head.

They rode in silence. Ava looked back at May and Amanda. Their eyes were closed and their heads were resting against the back of the seat. She did the same and was just about to fall sleep when Riccardo pointed to a sign and said, "There is the route to Bellagio. Whenever we have American visitors they're always excited to see that the place really exists. Signore Ventola tells them that while it was complimentary of Steve Wynn to model his hotel after our town, it pales by comparison."

"I'm sure it does," Ava said. "You could also tell the Americans that St. Mark's Square at the Venetian Hotel, the Eiffel Tower at the Paris, and the pyramid at the Luxor bear no relation to the real things either."

"Do they think they do?"

"Well, two-thirds of Americans don't have passports. Vegas is one of their windows on the world."

"Are you serious?"

"About the passports, yes. For the rest, I'm just joking."

"Will we go near Bellagio?" May asked.

"No, it sits at the tip of a peninsula in the middle of the lake. Mennagio is almost halfway up the western coastline," Ricardo said.

Even in the dark, Ava noticed major changes in the elevation. As they drew near Mennagio, she could see more and more lights glinting on the mountainsides. Via Milano SS340 became Via Statale and they entered the outer town.

Riccardo took four or five right-hand turns that led them through streets lined with houses and shops, and then one more gentle right brought them to the lake. They drove along Viale Benedetto Castelli. Ava looked at the lake shimmering under the light cast by a line of street lamps along a promenade. The other side of the road was lined with small hotels, shops, restaurants, and houses with large windows looking out onto the water. Riccardo braked several hundred metres along, reached under the visor, and pressed what looked like a garage-door opener. A ten-metre-wide ornately carved steel gate swung slowly open.

"We're home," Riccardo said.

He drove into the brown-and-black-tiled courtyard and stopped just past the house entrance. Giacomo stopped several metres behind. The villa was floodlit. The mixture of weathered red brick and pale pink stucco glimmered in the night. Ava climbed out of the car and took in the structure. She counted ten windows across the top floor and six across the ground floor, with two immense ones flanking the door.

As Riccardo popped open the trunk, the front door opened.

"*Benvenuti*," a tall middle-aged woman said.

"Hello, I'm Ava Lee," Ava said, walking towards her.

"I'm Francesca."

"And this is May Ling Wong and Amanda Yee," Ava said, indicating each in turn. "And behind us are —"

"I know who everyone is," Francesca said. "Raffi sent me your names and photos."

"That was clever of him."

Francesca smiled. "Do all your bags have name tags?"

"I think so."

"Excellent. Then I'll have the men take them directly to your rooms," she said, and spoke rapidly in Italian to Riccardo and Giacomo. She turned back to Ava. "Now please come inside. We've prepared a late-night snack for you. And if anyone wishes to use a washroom, there are two downstairs."

Ava walked through the doors and onto a white marble floor. The foyer was oval, with doors to the left and right and in the centre. The ceiling was at least twelve-feet high and the walls were covered in art.

"The dining room is on the right," Francesca said. "I'll join you in a moment."

Ava stepped inside and paused. There was a wooden table in the centre of the room surrounded by twelve chairs. The table was laid out with cured meats, cheeses, olives, peppers, breads, a platter of marinated squid and octopus, smoked mussels, and oysters on the half shell. Two bottles of red wine and two bottles of white were resting in ice buckets.

"Look at that food," May said from behind. "There's enough for twenty."

"Never mind the food, look at what's on the walls," Amanda said. "Those are Picassos."

"And that's a Warhol," Gillian said.

"Are they real?" Chi-Tze asked.

Amanda looked at her, amused. "Of course they are."

"Don't be so sure," May said. "I first met Ava because Changxing and I hired her and Uncle to track down thieves who sold us fake paintings, all of which came from supposedly reputable dealers."

"The art world may be filled with crooks, but given Dominic Ventola's reputation for being thorough, it's difficult to believe that these paintings are anything but genuine," Amanda said.

"Are you discussing our art collection?"

Ava turned and saw Francesca standing in the doorway. "Yes. It's wonderful," she said.

"Dominic started buying many, many years ago, before some of these artists had earned their reputations and before others skyrocketed in value. The past few years have seen a tremendous rise in prices. He focuses now on new and emerging artists."

"As he does with designers," Ava said.

"He has a keen eye for talent, and he knows how to appreciate and nurture it."

"You've been with him a long time?"

"More than twenty years. I'm his longest-serving employee," Francesca said.

"Here at the villa?"

"Hardly." She laughed. "But I don't want to talk about me. There's all this marvellous food here that mustn't go to waste. Why don't we eat."

Francesca wasn't the only household staff member. Over the next hour a man and a woman came to fill wineglasses and take away empty plates. When they had finished eating, the woman was joined by another and together with Francesca they led them upstairs to their assigned rooms.

"How many people can the villa accommodate?" Ava asked as they climbed the stairs.

"We've had as many as twelve guests," Francesca said.

Chi-Tze and Amanda were the first to reach the second floor. They took five steps before stopping.

"Wow," Chi-Tze said.

Francesca took Ava by the arm and guided her around the others. They faced down a long corridor with paintings on the walls and a line of nude male sculptures in bronze and marble.

"Do you need wakeup reminders?" Francesca asked.

"We have to leave at nine-thirty, so would you mind knocking on our doors at eight?"

"We'll do that."

Ava said goodnight to the others and went into her room. It was large enough to have its own bathroom, a king-size bed, a small desk and chair, and a chaise lounge. She took some clothes from her bag and headed to the bathroom. She emerged in a T-shirt and underwear and climbed immediately into bed, the white duvet covering her like a cloud.

She had barely closed her eyes when her phone rang. "Yes," she said.

"It's May."

"I just got into bed. The room is fantastic."

"Mine too, but I can't help wondering what we're doing here."

"You called to tell me that?"

"No. I've started worrying again."

"About what?"

"They're going to try to seduce Clark."

"We can't worry until we know for sure what they want."

"Maybe, but this is different."

"Different how?"

"It's a different kind of wealth, a different kind of culture, a different kind of sophistication than anything I've ever seen."

"May, we're not about to lose Clark."

"How can you be so sure?"

6

AVA WOKE AT SEVEN, MADE A BATHROOM RUN, THEN nestled under the duvet for another fifteen minutes. When she couldn't get back to sleep, she pulled herself from the bed and went to the window. The sun was just beginning to rise, its light faint behind a huge bank of grey clouds that hovered over the horizon. Rain streaked the window. She saw it spatter on the street and on the lamp-lit promenade, where not a single pedestrian was in sight. She shivered. It was probably five or six degrees outside, but damp, dank winters got into her bones.

She returned to the bathroom, brushed her teeth, stripped, and turned on the shower full force. She stepped inside and let the hot water pound her for ten minutes before picking up the bar of soap. When she got out, the room was filled with steam. She wrapped a thick towel around her head and another around her body before going back into the bedroom. Her bag sat by the side of the chaise lounge. She emptied it, placing her clothes in several piles.

She eyed two black dresses that Clark had made specifically for her. They were sleeker and sexier than anything she'd have bought for herself. Her tastes ran mainly to button-down shirts, slacks, and pencil skirts. During her years working with Uncle, she had thought of those clothes as her uniform. She was an accountant, after all, and they signalled that she was a professional who should be taken seriously. Now, given her involvement with the fashion world, she had a less clear idea about what image she should be presenting. She reached for her phone.

"Sorry to call a bit early," she said.

"I've been up for a while," May said. "We have a few issues in Wuhan that still need my attention."

"It's miserable outside."

"I know."

"What are you going to wear today?"

"I brought my pale blue Chanel suit, the one with the coral trim."

"I love that suit. You were wearing it the first time I saw you."

"I remember," May said. "How about you?"

"I was thinking about a dress, but I decided just to go with one of my white Brooks Brothers shirts. It's a plain button-down but it has French cuffs, so I can wear my jade cufflinks," Ava said. "But I can't make up my mind between slacks and a skirt."

"Go with the skirt and wear your crocodile stilettos as well. You have great legs; it's a shame not to show them," May said. "One more thing: make sure you put your hair up with that ivory chignon pin."

Ava smiled. She had bought the pin in Kowloon after finishing her first job and agreeing to become partners with Uncle. It was hundreds of years old and she could hardly afford it at the time. She believed it brought her luck, and she always wore it when she thought she needed it. So far it had never let her down. "I'll be downstairs in about fifteen minutes," Ava said.

"See you there."

Ava walked over to the mirror that hung above the desk. She dried and brushed her hair and pulled it back, securing it with the ivory pin. She put on some black mascara and a light application of red lipstick. Next she put on the shirt, the black pencil skirt, and the stilettos. She stared at herself in the mirror. *Not bad*, she thought. She slid on her Cartier Tank Française watch and left the room.

"Good morning," Francesca said from the top of the stairs. "We've laid out breakfast in the dining room. If anyone wants something warm like eggs or crêpes, the chef will be pleased to make it."

"Thank you," Ava said.

As Ava started along the corridor, May emerged from her room, wearing her Chanel suit, large diamond and platinum earrings, and an incredibly old and expensive white jade necklace and bracelet set.

"If you don't mind me saying it, both of you ladies look absolutely stunning," Francesca said.

"Well, we have these boys to compete against," May said, pointing to the sculptures.

Francesca laughed and moved past them down the hall.

Ava and May walked into the dining room to find that the massive spread from the evening before had been replaced by an equally large breakfast. There was a bowl of yogurt; other bowls of strawberries, raspberries, and blueberries; plates of smoked salmon and smoked trout; baskets filled with rolls and sliced bread; a plate layered with prosciutto; and a row of cheeses. Two coffee urns and another marked HOT WATER with a selection of teabags next to it were set up on a side table.

"This is never-ending," May said. "I'm still full from last night."

"Coffee is all I can handle," Ava said.

"We should eat a little something, if only to be polite."

"I might be able to manage a slice or two of smoked salmon," Ava said.

"Another feast," Amanda said from behind them.

"They're certainly being hospitable," Gillian said.

"Well, let's enjoy it and then we can chat. Where's Clark?" Ava said.

"He wants to sleep in. He doesn't have to be here — I know what he wants," Gillian said.

"And what's that?" Ava said.

"To meet Dominic Ventola."

Ava cast a glance at May.

They settled around the table with cups of coffee or tea and a sampling of food.

"I was wondering, should we take our luggage with us when we leave this morning?" Chi-Tze asked.

"Yes, I think we should," Ava said. "If there's a reason for us to stay longer, we can always bring it back."

"The only reason to stay is if, as we expect, VLG wants to buy into PÖ," Amanda said.

"We discussed that in London. Has our position changed?" Gillian said.

"No, we're all still on the same page," Ava said. "But they may make us an offer that we want to consider. And if they do and we like what we hear, it will take more than one day to sort things out."

"As enticing a prospect as that sounds, are we all still agreed that the only offer that interests us is one that won't change our basic structure and control, won't threaten Clark's independence, and will make a real contribution to our growth?" Gillian said.

"We are absolutely in agreement about that," Ava said

"Offer or no offer, I think we need to agree on how we're going to conduct ourselves during the meeting," May said.

"What do you suggest?" Amanda asked.

"First, we should be doing more listening than talking," May said. "And next, we should let Ava handle any business questions they have and Clark should respond to everything on the creative side."

"That makes sense to me," Gillian said.

Ava looked at Amanda and Chi-Tze. They both nodded.

"Then, if we're set, why don't we spend the rest of the next hour or so talking about something more relevant," Ava said.

"Like what?"

"How do we fully capitalize on the success of the London show? How do we use Pang Fai to maximize our advantage over the next six months?"

"That's all Gillian and I have been talking about," Chi-Tze said.

"Then let's hear your thoughts," Ava said.

They were still strategizing by the time Clark emerged from his room. He said good morning, reached for a plate, and sat by himself. He wore black jeans and a plain long-sleeved black cotton shirt that was buttoned to the neck.

"You're dressed so simply," Ava said.

"With a man like Dominic Ventola, I don't have to draw attention to myself," he said. "He's seen my work. My personal image doesn't matter."

"Clark knows how this game is played," Gillian said.

7

RICCARDO AND GIACOMO ARRIVED AT THE VILLA JUST before nine-thirty to pick up the team. They hadn't driven more than ten minutes when they ran into heavy traffic.

"It's the weather," Riccardo said. "You would think people around here would be used to rain and fog in the winter, but every time it gets like this, traffic crawls."

"We're not in a rush," Ava said.

As they continued the long, slow trek to Milan, Riccardo tried to point out the sights, but visibility was atrocious. Every fifteen minutes he got on the phone. She imagined he was updating the office with progress reports.

The weather began to lift and traffic flow improved when they reached the outskirts of Milan.

"Where is the office?" she asked.

"On Via Borgospesso. Do you know it?"

"I've never been to Milan."

"But you've heard of the street maybe? Or the streets surrounding it, like Via Santa Spirito, Via Sant'Andrea, Via Monte Napoleone?"

"No, I'm sorry I haven't."

"They're famous for their designer shops and offices," he said. "From our offices you can kick a football in any direction and hit Salvatore Ferragamo, Dolce and Gabbana, Paul Smith, Valentino, Stella McCartney, Versace, or Armani."

"Impressive."

"It's Milan."

They left the highway and merged onto a six-lane boulevard, which soon became four lanes and then narrowed into two. Ava saw a sign for Via Santa Spirito and knew they had to be close to VLG. A moment later, Riccardo turned onto Via Borgospesso. It was a short, narrow one-way street lined with buildings that were two or three storeys high. They drove for thirty metres, then Riccardo slowed and parked the car on the sidewalk. The other Maserati was directly behind them.

"That is Signore Ventola's first store," Riccardo said, pointing to the left. Ava saw a shop window with two mannequins in men's suits. There was no sign on the window or above the door.

Riccardo climbed out of the car and opened the doors. After they had all assembled on the crowded sidewalk, he said, "Follow me."

As they walked past the shop window, Ava saw a small brass plaque on the wall with VENTOLA on it. They walked ten metres, to another door with a brass plaque that read VLG. Riccardo pressed the intercom button. There was a rapid response in Italian, an equally rapid reply, and the door clicked open.

"Signore Pandolfo will call me when you're ready to leave," Riccardo said. "Enjoy your visit."

Ava stepped inside a large circular foyer that was eerily reminiscent of the villa. She stood there awkwardly, looking at the multiple doors and trying to figure out which one to enter. A door in the middle opened and a man she recognized from photos appeared. He had a large black moustache and thinning hair that curled around his ears.

"Mr. Pandolfo?" she said.

"Ava Lee and the rest of the Po family, welcome," he said. "We've been waiting."

"The weather and the traffic delayed us."

"So Riccardo said. How was your stay at the villa?"

"It couldn't have been better."

"Wonderful. I'm just sorry that you didn't get to see Lake Como and the surrounding countryside at their finest."

"Maybe another time."

"Perhaps later today, or tomorrow."

"We brought our luggage with us," Ava said. "We don't anticipate staying another night. And besides, we don't want to abuse your hospitality."

He smiled and gently bowed his head. "Then let's not waste the time we have. Follow me, if you will. We'll make all the appropriate introductions when we're in the boardroom." He led them into a corridor lined with closed doors.

Ava's heels clicked on the marble floor as her eyes flicked right and left. She took in the artwork that hung on the walls. "Was this a house?" she asked.

"Yes. We converted it years ago into an office. We have another, more modern and much larger office about two kilometres from here, but Dominic loves this place too much to leave. Our senior executive team works here."

At the far end of the corridor Ava noticed a door slightly ajar. As she drew near she saw a woman seated at a boardroom table working on a computer.

Pandolfo opened the door and stood to one side. When the PÖ team had filed past, he stepped in behind them.

"Let me introduce Gabriella Rossellini and Roland Fuda," he said, motioning with his arm. "Gabriella is our vice-president of marketing and Roland is our chief financial officer. They'll be joining us."

"Pleased to meet you both," Ava said. "Now let me introduce our team. May Ling Wong and Amanda Yee are my partners in the Three Sisters investment company. Chi-Tze Song is part of the management team, with Gillian Po, in Shanghai. And I guess I don't have to tell you that this is Clark."

Gabriella and Roland stood and walked towards them. After a round of handshakes, they returned to their seats at the head of the table.

"You can sit on either side," Pandolfo said.

As the PÖ group settled in, Clark asked, "Is Mr. Ventola going to be joining us?"

"Eventually," Pandolfo said. "He had a meeting he couldn't cancel, but he should be here in an hour or so."

"Would anyone like coffee, tea, water?" Roland asked. When no one answered affirmatively, he said, "Then I think we can get started."

"We thought it would provide a useful frame of reference for you if we took a few minutes to detail how VLG is structured and how it operates," Pandolfo said.

Gabriella dimmed the lights and started a PowerPoint presentation that detailed in depth the history of VLG. She traced the company's growth by market, by region, by product category, and by acquisition over the past thirty years. There was so much information it was almost numbing. Ava glanced at Clark more than once to see how he was coping. To her surprise, he seemed intensely interested.

After more than half an hour, Gabriella paused. "Does anyone have questions before I turn over the floor to Roland?" she asked.

Ava had been making notes in her Moleskine during the presentation. She did have a number of questions, but she suspected Roland was going to answer some of them and decided not to pre-empt him. "I think we can continue," she said. The others nodded.

Roland's presentation was dominated by charts as he out-lined VLG's corporate structure. Ava paid particular attention to where the acquisitions fitted in and how many layers of management were between the acquired brands and the two VLG offices in Milan, especially the group that worked on Via Borgospesso. It was, to her mind, a surprisingly lean company. How the structure manifested itself in terms of control wasn't explained and wasn't obvious, but Ava did note that there were designated global corporate offices for finance, sales, marketing, planning, creative development, purchasing, and manufacturing. She had no idea how large these subsidiary organizations were, and the charts gave no indication.

With hardly a pause, Roland said, "Now, as to our financials…" and unleashed another flurry of charts that showed thirty years of uninterrupted sales and profit growth. Ava had seen most of the numbers in the VLG annual reports online, but as she checked her notes she saw that Fuda's profit margins and net profits were higher than those that had been made public.

"Now, like Gabriella, I'll be pleased to answer any questions you may have," Roland said.

"Why are the profit margins and the net profits different from the numbers I saw in your annual reports?" Ava asked.

Roland turned to Pandolfo and Pandolfo leaned in towards Ava. "We have exceeded our profit estimates every year for the past twelve, but as a public company we are continually being scrutinized and judged against the estimates that various industry analysts post. We decided to build a 'contingency fund.' That is a deliberately vague term for a large amount of cash we keep on hand to use for acquisitions and to pump up our profit numbers if the need should arise. So far, thank God, the fund has been used only to make acquisitions."

"That seems to be a rather complicated way of doing things."

"My understanding is that you are an accountant."

"I am."

"Well, you're correct that from an accounting standpoint we could make things simpler, but we're in the marketing business, and we've taken that marketing mentality and extended it to the marketing of our financials. Unlike most companies, we understate rather than overstate our real position. It gives us flexibility, and we're in a business that requires that."

"I was curious, not being critical," Ava said.

"Critical about what?" a voice said from the doorway.

Everyone at the table turned.

"Dominic, your timing is impeccable," Pandolfo said.

8

DURING THE COURSE OF HER LIFE AND CAREER, AVA had met only a few people whose sheer physical presence could dominate a room. There had been Captain Robbins, an enormous man who was the head of security services in Guyana. Her father, Marcus, looked like someone important; she had seen him quietly command attention by simply walking into a room. Xu had an aura, a bearing, that was similar to Marcus's, but he also gave off the impression that he was a man not to be refused anything. To that short list she now added Dominic Ventola.

He walked into the boardroom with a slight smile on his face and a wave of his hand. "Sorry to be late," he said. "I hope I didn't miss anything important."

"Roland and Gabriella have just finished their presentations," Pandolfo said.

"And I'm sure they did their usual admirable job."

Ventola was short, not much more than five foot six, but his physique was sturdy and muscular. He was clean-shaven, his skin a pale pink that highlighted the depth and richness of his dark blue eyes. He had a wide-set jaw and brow that were offset by a slender nose and thin lips. He wore a light blue shirt and crisp grey slacks with a crease as sharp as a razor's edge. The shirt was tightly tucked in and the middle of his belt buckle was perfectly aligned with the shirt button above it. His nails were manicured. *This might be the cleanest, neatest man I've ever seen*, Ava thought.

Roland and Gabriella had stood when he entered the room. They moved, almost subconsciously, back from the table to give him space. Ava noticed that the four youngest members of the PÖ group had stood as well, their eyes locked on him. He walked directly up to Clark.

"How are you, Clark?" he said, his hand reaching out.

"I'm well, thank you."

"And so you should be," Ventola said, one hand shaking Clark's, the other gripping his forearm. "You are an extremely talented young man with some great years ahead of you. Our hope is that you'll permit us to take that ride with you."

"Dom, we haven't gotten to that part yet," Pandolfo said.

"Then my timing really is impeccable." Ventola grinned and walked to the head of the table. Roland pulled a chair back for him.

"I need some water," Ventola said. The room went quiet while Roland filled a glass with sparkling water and brought it to him. He took a small sip, just wetting his lips.

"I have been a fan of yours for so long," Clark said.

"You're not going to make me feel old, are you?" Ventola said. "It's bad enough that I find myself surrounded by so many young and beautiful people."

"We're all admirers," Gillian said.

Ventola nodded as if he was acknowledging the obvious.

"I'd rather talk about PÖ," he said. "Your show in London was brilliant — wonderful designs married to spectacular theatre. How did you convince Pang Fai to do it?"

"I asked her to help and she agreed," Ava said. "The actual runway performance was her idea."

"She was paid well?"

"Of course."

"Do you have her under contract?"

"No, we have a verbal agreement."

"Really?" Ventola said, cocking his head slightly. "Will she work for you again?"

"Of course."

"How do you know that? Her star is on the rise and so will be the demand and the cost."

"PÖ is the only design house she will work for."

"You seem so sure."

"We have an understanding."

Ventola sat back in his chair and folded his arms across his chest.

"Ava," Pandolfo said, "I'm wondering if you could explain your partnership structure to us. You are obviously aware that we have an interest in the PÖ company. We'd like some idea of who owns what."

"For the purpose of this discussion you can assume that we're equal partners."

"Our understanding is that Three Sisters owns forty-nine percent of PÖ," he persisted. "Is that true?"

"I don't know where you got that number," Ava said.

"So it isn't true?"

Ava shrugged. A moment passed. She felt the discomfort in the room rising.

"Ms. Lee, over the years we have invested in many young designers and most often have been successful," Ventola said. "We have money, of course, but more importantly we have design, manufacturing, marketing, and merchandising support mechanisms. We understand the business and know how to nurture and grow young talent. We believe that Clark would benefit from an affiliation with us."

"Your success has been remarkable. We don't doubt that you could help PÖ grow, and we're prepared to discuss how that might happen," Ava said. "But you'll need to explain what you mean by 'affiliation'."

"We'd buy into PÖ," Pandolfo said.

"To what level?"

"It's our company policy not to take minority positions when we invest," Pandolfo said. "If we're going to commit to a designer and put the full force of our organization behind him, then we want a majority, a controlling interest."

"Fifty-one percent?" Ava asked.

"At a minimum, but it is normally more. We do pay fair market value, and often a bit extra," Pandolfo said.

"I don't doubt that. But while I expect we could assign a value to the company as it currently exists, I think it would be far more difficult to assess its potential value. These are early days for PÖ. Who knows what we're capable of accomplishing?"

"Our financial and marketing people have considerable expertise in making that kind of projection — we have done it often enough. If we agree there is a potential for a deal, then I'll ask them to run numbers for PÖ. You obviously don't have to make a commitment until you see what we're prepared to pay," he said. "And you won't find many people who regret partnering with us. They may own a smaller share of their business than they once did, but that share is worth far more than the value of their business would have been if they'd tried to go it alone."

"I'm sure all that is true, but we're not ready to concede control of our company. Are you firm on your policy of wanting a majority interest?"

"We are."

"And we're not willing to be in a minority position, so we appear to be at an impasse."

"Do all of you feel this way?" Pandolfo asked, his attention blatantly focused on Clark.

Ava saw Clark glance at Gillian. She pursed her lips, and for a second Ava thought she was wavering.

"Ava speaks for Three Sisters, and we are in complete agreement," May said.

"That is also the view that Clark and I share," Gillian finally said.

Pandolfo turned towards Ventola with a resigned look on his face.

"Let me switch topics for just a moment," Ventola said. "Clark, I'm interested in how you construct your clothes. I know you're using high-thread-count linens, but I've never before seen linen flow so beautifully. What are you doing to achieve that effect?"

Clark hesitated and then smiled self-consciously. "It's amazing that you ask about the draping, because when I start to create a piece, that's exactly what I'm thinking of. And I find that when I can see it in my mind's eye, every-thing else — the cuts and angles and seams — takes on a life of its own."

"I told Raffi that I saw a hint of genius in your work," Ventola said, and then turned to Ava and May Ling. "You can't teach what Clark has. There are designers who learn the tools of the trade and then go about constructing clothes by rote, like bricklayers. Then there are the few who see things that no one else can. I was a bricklayer — a good one, but a bricklayer all the same. What separated me from the rest of them was that I knew what I was and accepted it. It was that acceptance, I think, that allowed me to see the greatness in others. And there is greatness in Clark."

"We think that as well, and that's why we decided to support Clark and are committed to keep on doing that," Ava said.

"Even though you're not as well equipped as we are to ensure success?"

"That's an unfair remark, Mr. Ventola," Ava said.

"Perhaps it was, and if so I apologize," he said. He turned to Clark. "When I saw your linen creations, I couldn't help but think about sea silk. Have you ever seen sea silk?"

"No," Clark said.

"You know of it?"

"Only in a general way."

"It's the rarest, finest, and most valuable silk in the world," Ventola said. "It's made from byssus, the long silk filaments that pen shells use to attach themselves to the ocean floor. Pen shells have been disappearing, and the silk with it. A few years ago I visited a woman in Sardinia who may be the last person alive to weave sea silk the way it was done to make robes for the kings of Mesopotamia. I spent an entire day with her and came away determined to save as much sea silk as I could. I have a studio in the basement of this house with perhaps the largest amount in any one place in the world. When I saw the way you made linen flow, I thought, *What could he do with sea silk?* Would you like to see it?"

"That would be incredible."

"Then let's take a break," Ventola said. "Gabriella, why don't you take Clark and his sister down to the studio? Tell Jacob that I said Clark is to have unfettered access to the sea silk."

"Yes, sir," she said and stood.

Clark and Gillian looked questioningly at Ava.

"Go ahead," Ava said.

As they left, Ava saw Pandolfo glance at Ventola. "Could I have a glass of water now?" she asked.

"Anyone else?" Roland said.

"Sure, I'll have some," May said.

While Roland was pouring the water, Ventola leaned towards Pandolfo and whispered. Pandolfo whispered in return.

"So, my understanding is that the four of you are partners in or connected with Three Sisters," Ventola said.

"We are," Ava said.

"Then why don't you ladies do me and Clark Po a favour and get the fuck out of his life."

9

THE BOARDROOM WAS SILENT. THE FACES OF THE THREE men across from her were blank. May hadn't reacted to Ventola's outburst; Ava knew she'd seen and heard worse while doing business in Wuhan. Amanda and Chi-Tze were startled, and Chi-Tze seemed especially flustered.

"I think I've stated our position quite clearly," Ava said calmly.

"I believe in being blunt," Ventola said.

"Obviously."

"There's nothing you can really do for him."

"We haven't done so badly thus far."

"You're playing around the edges. You don't have the muscle to get him into the centre of the action, and you don't have the experience or contacts to maximize his brand."

"All of that may be true —"

"So stop being so hard-headed and selfish. Let him go."

"As I was saying, all of that may be true but we have a plan and we made a commitment. We also have some hard-working, smart young women in Gillian, Chi-Tze, and Amanda. They may not have the specific contacts and talents that you have in your organization, but as a team they'll learn what they need to know soon enough."

"You're being naive."

"I disagree. We know what our shortcomings are and we know they can be dealt with."

Ventola shook his head in frustration. "You should know that we're approaching you first as a courtesy, out of respect for the fact that you did finance PÖ to bring it this far. We could have gone directly to the Pos to cut a deal. Raffi tells me they have fifty-one percent of the business to your forty-nine."

"That's the second time those numbers have come up. How do you know what the split is?"

"People talk," Pandolfo said.

"Did the same people tell you that the Pos can't sell a single share without our specific approval?"

"Is that true?"

"And did they tell you that if Clark leaves the company he's bound by a five-year non-compete agreement?"

Ventola glared at Pandolfo.

"And did they tell you that the PÖ brand name is owned by Three Sisters?"

"You thought of everything, didn't you," Ventola said.

"May Ling is one of the most successful businesswomen in China. Amanda and Chi-Tze each have an MBA from a leading American university and have run multimillion-dollar family businesses. And we weren't reluctant to pay for very good legal advice. So we did think of a lot of things."

"How much money are we talking about?" Pandolfo asked, reasserting himself.

"I beg your pardon?" Ava said.

"How much did you invest? Two million, three million?"

"The actual number is ten million."

"That's impressive. You went all in. Most of the young designers we encounter are underfunded."

"The only way we know how to operate is to go all in. We put our money where our beliefs are, and we believe in Clark."

"So how much will it take to get you to walk away?" Pandolfo said. "How much will it cost to acquire all the rights you've assembled and your shares?"

"I'm not sure that's open for discussion."

"You're businesspeople. You made an investment, you expect a return. What is it?"

"We've never talked about it."

"No endgame?"

"No."

"Well, you've got one staring you in the face. Don't you think you owe it to yourselves to talk it over? Come back to us with a number."

"And don't concern yourselves about what will happen to Clark," Ventola said. "Designers like him are our lifeblood, our most prized assets. We know how to look after them. We'll make him rich and we'll keep him happy."

"Dom truly believes that Clark is special," Pandolfo said.

Ventola nodded. "We've been waiting for years for a talent to break out of Asia. There have been a few other designers with some potential, but none of them had what I call 'the gift'. Your boy has it, and with his personality, we can create a highly marketable package."

Ava looked at May, Amanda, and Chi-Tze. May raised her eyebrows. Amanda seemed pensive. Chi-Tze still looked flustered.

"I hope you'll understand that we didn't anticipate you'd

make an offer so quickly. When I first spoke with Raffi, he used words like *cautious*, and this hardly qualifies," Ava said. "And Mr. Ventola, while your assessment of Clark's talent and potential is highly complimentary, and one we share, I'm wondering how you can be so sure after seeing just that one show in London."

"We've been watching you for months," Ventola said.

"Pardon?"

"The show director you hired in Shanghai has worked for me in the past. He sent me a video from your launch there and told me he thought the boy was special. We've tracked your sales at Lane Crawford and elsewhere in Asia. I had my people talk to some of his teachers from Central St. Martin's, and they raved about him. So I went to the London show to see for myself. I'm naturally a skeptic and I was prepared to be disappointed. Instead, everything we'd been told was confirmed. I was won over," he said.

"Asia is also an increasingly important market for us in terms of sales and manufacturing. But we have no real footprint there, no presence. We think that Clark and PÖ could become the face of VLG in that part of the world," Pandolfo added. "So you see, Ava, we have given this considerable thought and we're not being precipitous. Now, would you like to come back to us with a number?"

"We need to talk," Ava said. "Could you leave us alone for a few minutes?"

"Sure, we can," Ventola said. "And don't worry, the room isn't bugged."

10

"I CAN'T BELIEVE THE IMPACT CLARK'S WORK HAS HAD on them," Amanda said as soon as the door closed behind the VLG group.

"You mean had on Ventola," May said.

"Who else matters?"

"No one, and I wasn't being glib. His opinion reaffirms every decision we've made, and it tells me the reactions we got in Shanghai and London are genuine responses to Clark's work. We've invested in a remarkable talent."

"And that leaves us with the decision about what to do with it," Ava said.

"You were firm enough with Ventola," Amanda said.

"That doesn't mean he didn't make some very good points," Ava said. "Do any of you doubt that VLG could grow the PÖ brand faster than we can?"

"No, and with their public relations machine they'd make Clark a star in no time," Chi-Tze said.

"We have our own PR people," May said.

"Yes, but their influence is mainly in Asia. We had to use freelancers in London, and we have no one in North

America or the rest of Europe," said Chi-Tze.

"I thought you were happy working with the Pos," May said.

"I am and I'd love to keep at it, but there's a business decision to make and we can't ignore certain realities."

"The fact that VLG can give the Pos more support than we can?"

"That may or may not be true," Chi-Tze said, "but what I mean from the business side is that we have an opportunity to double or triple the Three Sisters initial investment by selling even a part of the business and the rights to VLG. And whatever part we keep could appreciate and produce revenue for Three Sisters for years."

"Is that what you're recommending?"

"No. Like I said, I love the path we're on. I don't want to change it. I just thought I should make the business argument."

"What do you think, Amanda?" Ava said.

"Given Ventola's enthusiasm, I think Chi-Tze is correct that we might be able to more than triple our investment and hang on to a piece of the action," she said. "But I don't want to sell. It's too early. I want to find out what we're capable of doing on our own. I think we've all made an emotional as well as a financial commitment, and I'm not ready to let go."

"May?"

May drew a deep breath. "I love being involved in this business as well. There's nothing more satisfying than building something from the ground up. I also take some irrational pride in the fact that we're helping to introduce a rare Chinese talent to the rest of the world," she said. "But I have a problem."

"And that is?"

"I think we need to let Clark and Gillian make this decision," she said. "We need to tell them that Ventola wants to take us out and replace us as their partners, with the same rights we have. We have to be honest about telling Clark it wouldn't have a negative financial impact on us, but we have to be clear and firm that we don't want to sell unless it is their wish. They need to know that we're still totally committed."

"What would you do if you were them?" Ava asked.

May hesitated. "I don't know."

"Do we really have to ask them to make a decision now?" Amanda said. "Is this the right time or place to put them on the spot?"

"I don't want them to learn about the VLG offer from anyone else," May said. "And the longer we delay, the more likely that becomes a possibility."

"I agree with Amanda that the timing is atrocious, but I also agree with May that we can't drag our feet," Ava said. "If Clark and Gillian are going to remain our partners, I want it to be for the right reasons, not just because we've tied them up contractually."

"What if he and Gillian want to see those sales and marketing projections that Raffi Pandolfo was talking about, before they make a decision?" Amanda said.

"That could take weeks, and I can't imagine that any of us want to be dangling in suspense for that long. Besides, we all know, including Gillian and Clark, that VLG can make those numbers read any way they want, and you can be certain they will look wonderful," Ava said. She turned to Chi Tze. "Could you please go and find Clark and Gillian? We might as well be direct and try to resolve this right now."

When Chi-Tze had left the room, Ava rose from her chair and poured a glass of water.

"We shouldn't have come to Italy," May said. "All my instincts were telling me it was the wrong thing to do."

"They would have made their interest in buying PÖ known whether we were in Italy or not," Ava said.

"Chi-Tze and I have talked many times about something like this happening," Amanda said. "But we never thought it would be this soon. We thought maybe it would take a few years, until after Clark was more firmly established."

"Yet here we are," Ava said.

"What do we ask for if they decide they want to be with VLG?" Amanda said.

"Let's not prejudge their reaction. Uncle taught me to take one step at a time. Getting too far ahead of ourselves is almost inviting bad luck."

They sat quietly for a few minutes.

"I think —" Amanda began to say when the door opened. Chi-Tze led Clark and Gillian into the room.

"What's going on?" Gillian asked. "Chi-Tze is suddenly so tight-lipped and mysterious that I'm afraid of what I'm going to hear."

"It's nothing that dramatic," Ava said. "Dominic Ventola wants to buy the Three Sisters shares in PÖ."

"Some of them?"

"We haven't discussed a specific number, but it's safe to assume they'll want most of them," Ava said. "And of course they will want all the rights. If we agree, then I imagine they'll also want to buy enough of your shares to own more than fifty-one percent of the company."

"Jesus Christ," Clark said, taking the chair next to Ava.

"How did you respond to him?" Gillian said.

"We haven't. We wanted to talk to you and Clark first."

"Why?"

"We believe it's a decision that you should make."

"You want us to decide if you should sell your shares?" Gillian said.

"To be absolutely clear, the last thing we want to do is sell our shares, and there isn't a monetary value VLG could put on them that would persuade us otherwise."

"Then what's this about?"

"This is about PÖ and Clark's career," Ava said. "We can't ignore the fact that joining VLG could give PÖ and Clark a huge boost. You would instantly have more money, more customers, and more marketing and PR muscle. We don't want to deny you that opportunity if it's what you want."

"We know what VLG can give us, and it is tempting," Gillian said.

"But we also know what they can't give us," Clark said.

"Do you want to review the pros and cons?" May asked.

"No, we know what they are," Clark said with a brisk shake of his head. "Gillian and I talked about them last night, and again when we were in the studio just now."

"So what do you think?" Ava asked.

"We've been in this business for our entire adult lives, and for nearly all that time we've worked for other people. Some were nice and some not so nice, but when all was said and done, they were the bosses and I was expected to do what I was told," Clark said. "I understand that Three Sisters has some level of control over PÖ, but I've never felt it. I'm free to do whatever I want to do. You've kept your word. You've let me be me."

"That's a wonderful compliment," Ava said. "And not that I'm arguing VLG's position, but what makes you think it would be any different working with them?"

"When Mr. Fuda showed us the corporate organization chart as part of his presentation, I searched it for the names of some of the design firms I know they've bought," Clark said. "I found them halfway down or lower, buried in boxes below other boxes. I don't want to be in a small box on the VLG organization chart. I know people who are in those boxes, and some of them are miserable. "

"I can understand that," Ava said.

"I also know that when disagreements arise between the designer whose name is on the label and VLG, it's the corporation that always wins. The designer leaves but VLG still owns his name, and they bring in a hired gun to replace him," he said. "I don't want to risk losing my name, and I don't want PÖ creations being designed by someone who may be French or German."

"I think what my brother is saying is that we're happy where we are," Gillian said.

11

RAFFI PANDOLFO RETURNED TO THE BOARDROOM WITH Gabriella Rossellini and Roland Fuda. He looked confident and smiled at everyone as he sat down.

"Mr. Ventola?" Ava queried.

"He has a meeting out of the office. Don't worry, we're authorized to act on his behalf, and he's available by phone if we really need him," Pandolfo said. He looked at Clark. "What did you think of the sea silk?"

"It's wondrous."

"I won't tell you what it costs because I don't think you'd believe me," Pandolfo said. "But that's the way it is with Dom. When he wants something, cost becomes irrelevant."

"He's a remarkable man," Clark said.

"As, hopefully, you're going to find out first-hand."

"I'm afraid that's not going to happen," Ava said.

Pandolfo's eyes narrowed and Ava thought she detected a touch of malice in them. "Is that a no or a backdoor start to negotiations?"

"That's a no."

"You have no interest in what we might have to offer?"

"No, we don't."

"So no, just like that? No negotiations at all? I had expected we'd be haggling for a while."

"There's nothing to haggle about."

"Even though you didn't seem to have any interest, we were prepared to offer you a handsome premium over your investment."

"We invested in PÖ for a multitude of reasons, only one of which was money, and the others have prevailed," Ava said.

Pandolfo looked at Clark and glanced at Gillian. "I understand that Ms. Lee and her group have you bound by a rather onerous contract, and I'm sure she's reminded you of that," he said. "But if you're prepared to leave them and join VLG, we're prepared to finance and manage the legal battle to void it."

"Ava hasn't mentioned the contract once since the day we signed it," Clark said. "We're staying where we are because we like where we are. I have my independence and I'm surrounded by people who understand me."

"They can't do for you the things that we can."

"No, but they give me the unconditional support I need to grow. I'll succeed or fail based on my own merits and not because I'm part of the VLG empire."

"Our empire, as you call it, is not a monolith. It consists of a large number of talented designers like yourself, all of whom we've invested in for a reason that sometimes goes beyond the talent."

"Why Clark, aside from the talent you think he has?" Gillian asked

"As I told the other ladies a few minutes ago, we've been searching for an Asian identity. I probably shouldn't be so frank, but that is my nature," Pandolfo said. "We believe that Clark and PÖ could become the face of VLG in Asia."

"I think my brother already feels that he is the face of PÖ."

Pandolfo shrugged. "What do you have to say?" he asked Ava. "We can't entice you?"

"Mr. Pandolfo, I want to thank you and Mr. Ventola for the interest you've shown in us," Ava said. "I wish there were some way we could have reached an understanding, but there obviously isn't. I can only hope that there are no hard feelings."

"Dominic really wanted this deal to go through, for all the reasons we explained to you earlier," he said.

"We are aware of that, and again thanks for the interest."

"And he's not going to be pleased that you're turning us down."

"I'm sure you can explain our position."

"I won't even try. He'll have no interest in listening."

"I'm sorry about that."

"It may not be the only thing you regret."

"What is that supposed to mean?" Ava said.

Pandolfo shook his head. "I've already said too much."

12

THE MASERATIS WERE STILL PARKED OUTSIDE THE OFFICE.

"Where can we take you?" Riccardo asked, less effusive than he'd been in the morning. Ava guessed he'd been told that they were no longer welcome guests.

"The airport, please," she said and then turned to her colleagues. "I'll have Amanda check on flights for all of us. Do any of you mind going through Hong Kong?"

"Just get us out of here," May said.

"My feelings exactly," Ava said.

Ava, May, and Amanda rode together in one car. They were silent as Amanda worked her phone searching for flights. They were almost at the airport when she said, "There's an Alitalia flight at 7:20 p.m. to Rome that connects to Abu Dhabi and from there to Hong Kong."

"What is the seat availability in business class?" May said.

"It appears to be wide open."

"Put everyone in there if you can. They've earned it."

"Okay, and Ava, there's a KLM flight at 7:30 p.m. to Amsterdam that connects to Toronto."

"Perfect," Ava said.

"I don't have everyone's passport information, so we can't buy the tickets until we get to the airport."

"We have lots of time," Ava said. She turned to Riccardo. "Could you let us off at the Alitalia departures door, please."

The Maseratis stopped directly in front of Alitalia and the drivers unloaded the bags. Ava took two fifty-euro notes from her purse and gave them to Riccardo. Chi-Tze gave the same amount to Giacomo.

It took almost two hours to purchase the tickets, check their bags, clear Customs, and work their way through security. By the time they had reached the business lounge, Ava was ready for a drink.

They found a table in a bar that had a full selection of liquor. Chi-Tze, Clark, and Gillian ordered Heinekens, Ava and Amanda a large glass each of Pinot Grigio, and May her usual gin martini with two green olives.

"Cheers, my dears," May said when they were served.

"Well, this trip wasn't exactly what we expected," Ava said. "But it's only a day out of our schedules, so we can get back to our normal routine tomorrow."

"Yesterday in London was really productive," Chi-Tze said. "Now we need to follow up and do some closing."

"How many new accounts do you think we picked up?" May asked.

"Five or six large ones," Chi-Tze said.

"Maybe even more than that," Gillian added. "There are some still sitting on the fence, but I think a phone call from Clark and a little wooing will get them onside."

"Do you enjoy doing that?" Ava asked Clark.

"I didn't have to do it when I was designing private labels, and I was reluctant when Gillian and Chi-Tze asked me to do it after the Shanghai launch, but they persuaded me."

"You mean we browbeat and strong-armed you," Gillian said.

"That too." He laughed. "But I found that I kind of enjoyed it, maybe because it was more about talking about the clothes than actually selling them."

"But he can sell," Chi-Tze said. "He closes every conversation with the same question: 'When can we expect the first order?'"

"Speaking of wooing, I was surprised there wasn't more of that from the VLG group," Ava said.

"Me too," Amanda said. "I thought they were rather abrupt, verging on being rude. It was as if they thought we would be so pleased to get their offer that we'd accept instantly."

"Dominic Ventola telling us to get the fuck out of Clark's life *was* rude, not verging on rude," Ava said.

"He really said that?" Gillian asked.

"He did, and we were all remarkably restrained," Ava said.

"More like in shock," Amanda said.

"He's a man who's obviously accustomed to getting his way and reacts badly when it doesn't happen," Ava said. She heard her phone ring and took it from her bag. "That's uncanny."

"What is?" May said.

"Dominic Ventola appears to be calling me."

"Answer it."

"I'm not sure I want to."

"Ava!"

She pressed the answer button. "This is Ava Lee."

"This is Dominic Ventola. Where are you?"

"At the airport."

"Raffi told me about your decision earlier, but I was in a meeting and couldn't contact you," he said. "That's probably just as well. It gave me a chance to calm down."

"I'm sorry you felt it necessary to calm down."

"I don't take bad news very well. I've been that way my entire life, and I don't apologize for it, because it has helped more often than not," he said. "Now tell me, what can I do to improve the offer that Raffi made to you earlier?"

"Our position hasn't changed. We're prepared to sell a minority stake in the company and nothing more."

"We don't buy minority stakes."

"We understand that, but we are unanimous in our position. We will not give up control of PÖ," Ava said. "Mr. Ventola, we are very appreciative of the interest you've shown in Clark and the brand. I hope you understand that our decision is in no way a negative reaction to you or to your company. We simply want to follow our own path."

"The boy has an enormous amount of talent."

"We know."

"It's too bad that it's going to be wasted."

"I don't see why that should be the case."

"You've been given the chance of a lifetime and you're pissing it away. Worse, you stay in my house, you come to my office, and then you piss on me."

"That's a completely unfair and inaccurate characterization," Ava said.

"You're smooth, I'll give you that," he said.

Every eye at the table was on her, and the group seemed to be holding its collective breath. Ava hit the speaker button and placed the phone in front of her. "I'm not sure where this is heading, Mr. Ventola," she said. "It's obvious that you're upset about our decision, but I have to say I don't want to listen to much more of this."

"You are a bunch of dumb bitches, and you deserve to be called worse for what you're doing to that boy's career."

Ava saw May's face contort in anger. The others looked stunned.

"Mr. Ventola, please, you've said enough."

"Is that a warning?"

"No, it's a request that we end this conversation in a more professional manner."

"Well, let me say something that you might find completely unprofessional," he said. "I have to decide what I'm going to do about your little company. I could ignore you, I guess, or cause you some problems in the marketplace. Or I could even go all out and try to destroy you. It wouldn't be that difficult, you know, to make the PÖ brand disappear."

"Mr. Ventola —"

He spoke right over her. "A few phone calls to the right people, some favours cashed in, some favours requested, and a couple of nudges can do a lot of damage."

"Mr. Ventola, we're a tiny dot in your universe. Why should our existence matter to you?"

"Raffi and I think of anyone who isn't associated with VLG as the competition. The easiest way to get rid of competition is to go after it before it has any strength."

"We're hardly a threat."

"Not yet."

"And not in the foreseeable future. Maybe not ever," Ava said. "Mr. Ventola, when we spoke in your office, you said that Clark's talent had won you over. Please stay won over and become his mentor. Let Clark do his thing and let us manage our company."

"It doesn't work that way with me."

"That's unfortunate."

"I have to go," he said abruptly. "You'll know soon enough what I decide to do about PÖ."

"Mr. Ventola —"

The phone went dead. The group was silent, everyone looking at Ava with eyes full of questions and concern.

"Wasn't he charming," Ava said as lightly as she could.

"I didn't quite believe Elsa Ngan when she told us he has something of a dual personality. I know we had a glimpse of his coarseness when we were at the office, but I never expected that kind of reaction," Amanda said.

"He's crazy," Gillian said.

"Or it was only a performance, a tactic," May said.

"To achieve what?" Gillian asked.

"To scare us enough that we'll go back into negotiations."

"That isn't going to happen," Clark said. "If I didn't want to work with them a few hours ago, I feel ten times stronger about it now."

"In a strange and almost perverse way that was quite the compliment he delivered," Ava said. "If he recognizes the quality of Clark's work to that extent, then others will as well. What I think we should do is forget about Dominic Ventola and VLG and get on with building our business, our way."

"Can we afford to ignore him?" Chi-Tze asked.

"What do you mean?" Ava said.

"I know he was angry and might not have meant everything he said, but if he decides to try to damage our business, don't you think he's capable of doing it?"

"Are you suggesting we do something?"

"No, I'm just concerned."

"Then take that energy you're using to worry and transfer it into closing the deals we have on the table," Ava said. "That's the best way to respond to his threats."

13

AS THE PLANE BEGAN ITS DESCENT INTO TORONTO'S Pearson International Airport, Ava looked down on the familiar landscape and saw that it was blanketed with snow. She groaned. The airport was in the northwest corner of the city and her condo was near its centre, near Avenue Road and Bloor Street. It was three p.m. and the start of rush hour. A one-hour limo ride would turn into two or more in this weather. Still, of all the things that were weighing on her, the prospect of a torturous commute barely registered.

Despite the message she'd conveyed to Chi-Tze and the positive attitude she'd displayed with the others, she had been alarmed by Dominic Ventola's threat. It had been her experience while working with Uncle that threats from people who were scared or in a position of weakness rarely amounted to anything. They were face-saving gestures, a last-gasp attempt at hanging on to a shred of dignity. It was different with people who had power. They didn't need to bluff. They could say what they meant without any fear of repercussion, and they had the ability to execute their threats.

She had no doubts that Ventola would indeed try to damage them. What she had struggled with during the flight was how to respond if he did attack. She couldn't think of much beyond continuing to promote Clark, and she wasn't the least bit sure that would work if someone as credible and powerful as Ventola wanted to damage PÖ's reputation.

The ride from Pearson was worse than she had imagined. The snowfall continued wet and heavy, and the combination of numerous fender-benders and tricky road conditions meant the limo stopped, started, and crawled when it moved at all. She turned on her phone and found a text from Maria. We need to talk when you get back. I can't continue like this, it read. Ava felt her stomach tighten. She contemplated answering the message, but she had a sense which way the conversation would go and she wasn't ready for it.

It was past seven p.m. when she finally reached her building. She quickly unpacked, took a shower, checked the fridge, and found an unopened bottle of Pinot Grigio. She poured a glass and went to sit at the kitchen table, where she could look out the window. It was her favourite spot, a place to think while she viewed the outside world. It was still snowing, the flakes glimmering under the light of the street lamps.

She looked at her phone again. There was nothing from May, Amanda, or the PÖ group. They were all probably still in transit. None of the other messages she had received needed her immediate attention. She thought for a second about calling Maria and then let the idea go. She was too exhausted for an emotional discussion. Instead she sent a text saying Will be in Toronto tomorrow. Are you available for dinner? Then she turned off her phone, topped up her glass, and went back to watching the snow swirl.

She went to bed just before ten, certain that she would have trouble falling asleep. That was the last thought she had before waking up at a quarter to nine, the sun streaming through her bedroom window. She looked outside. The streets had been ploughed and salted and were now coated in slush. The sidewalks hadn't been cleared yet and pedestrians were trudging through a foot of snow. She liked to go for a morning run when she was at home, but conditions looked too messy for that. Maybe she could fit in a workout with Grandmaster Tang, her bak mei instructor. His house was only a ten-minute walk away in good weather.

She went into the kitchen, made a cup of instant coffee, and sat down at the table. She turned on her computer and saw a flood of overnight emails from Shanghai, Hong Kong, and Wuhan. Everyone was back at work and following up on London. So far there hadn't been any negative reactions from potential customers.

This has been a very encouraging day, Amanda wrote in the last email. I think that Dominic Ventola may have decided to ignore us.

Or he's not in a rush, Ava thought. She started to respond to Amanda with advice that they should be closing deals as fast as possible, but then she deleted the message. They didn't need to be told the obvious.

She made another coffee and looked at her phone. She expected to see a text from Maria, but there wasn't one. Ava knew she would probably be at her office at the Colombian Trade Commission by now. She thought about calling and then decided to give Maria more time to respond to the dinner invitation. Besides, Ava's message had said she was arriving today. Maybe Maria saw no need to answer so quickly.

Ava phoned her mother in Richmond Hill. When Jennie Lee's cell went directly to voicemail, Ava called the house number. It rang five times and then prompted a message. "It's me. I'm back. Call me when you're up," Ava said. Her night-owl mother was probably still in bed.

She went into the bedroom and put on a black sports bra and black T-shirt, a thick wool sweater, and black leggings. Ten minutes later she left the apartment dressed in an Adidas track suit and walked along Cumberland Street to Avenue Road. She turned right and headed north to Lowther Avenue. It had stopped snowing, but the temperature was well below zero and a brisk wind bit into her face. She pulled her tuque down over her ears and zipped her jacket up to her chin. The sidewalk was slippery and she had to concentrate on every footstep. The effort was made more difficult by the fact that the wind was making her eyes water. She almost felt like turning around and going home. When she reached Lowther, the wind shifted direction and the temperature became more bearable.

Grandmaster Tang's home doubled as his dojo. There wasn't any sign on or near the house to indicate that this was the pre-eminent martial arts facility in the city. Those who were skilled in any of those arts knew of the Grandmaster and where to find him. Ava had been his student since she was a teenager. She'd been sent to him by an instructor in Richmond Hill who recognized she had special talents that he couldn't develop any further. Grandmaster Tang had tested her, agreed with the instructor's assessment of her potential, and decided to teach her bak mei. It was one of the oldest of all the martial arts. Chinese in origin, it was always taught one-on-one, traditionally passed on from father to son, but in Ava's case from mentor to student. The Grandmaster had only two students he deemed talented and disciplined enough to learn bak mei: Ava and her friend Derek Liang.

The main objective of this fighting style was to do as much damage to your opponent as you could, by attacking nerve-endings, eyes, ears, and other sensitive body parts. The classic strike was the phoenix-eye fist — the middle knuckle of the first finger driven into the target with all the concentrated force that the body could generate. It was devastating when properly executed, and Ava had used it more often than she could remember. Derek was as capable, and until he married Ava's best friend, Mimi, she had taken him on some collection jobs as backup.

Now that she wasn't in the collections business anymore, Ava wasn't sure she would need to use bak mei on such a regular basis. But she liked the physical workouts. Her body never felt more alive than when training, and it always cleared her head. This morning she felt that her head needed it more than her body.

She climbed the front steps to the Grandmaster's house, hoping he was in. She didn't know if he even had a phone. When she first started training with him, he would tell her when to come for the next session. In later years she would simply show up at his door and more often than not he was there. Most of his regular students came in the evening, so his days were usually free. She knocked at the door and waited, preparing to bow to the small grey-haired man in his black T-shirt and black jeans. A moment later she knocked again, then stood on tiptoe to peer through the high window next to the door. The house looked deserted.

"Shit," Ava said. She turned and retraced her steps back to the condo.

She was hungry by the time she got back and found some shrimp dumplings in the freezer. She put them in a pot of water and brought it to a boil, then replaced the water with chicken broth and brought it to a boil again. She ladled the dumplings into a bowl, added chili sauce, and sat at the kitchen table to eat. But first she checked her phone and email account for messages and found nothing new. Maria's lack of response was beginning to irk her.

She ate slowly, then washed the bowl and pot before returning to the table, where she picked up the phone and without thinking called Maria.

Maria answered on the second ring with a hesitant "Hello?"

"Hi, I'm back," Ava said. "Did you get my text about dinner?"

"I did."

"Can you make it?"

"You sound as though nothing has happened."

"What has happened?"

"You got my message about not being able to continue like this?"

"I did."

"Is that why you're suggesting we meet for dinner?"

"Among other reasons."

"Ava, unless we resolve this, there are no other reasons I care about."

"By 'resolve,' do you mean am I prepared to change my position?"

"Yes, I guess that's what I mean."

"No, I'm not," Ava said as gently as she could. "I've thought about it, I've agonized about it, and I know I can't live with anyone else. I love you, but I like the way things are now."

"I thought the longer we were a couple, the more our relationship would develop. I don't think it's unreasonable to expect that."

"No, it's not unreasonable. I just can't give you much more."

"All I'm talking about is living together. I'd like to be married, but that can wait. I'd also like to have children sometime down the road, but that can wait too."

"I'm not ready for any of that."

"So you keep telling me."

"Would you rather I be dishonest?"

"No."

"I really have thought about it," Ava said. "But I always end up in the same place."

"Then there's no point in having dinner," Maria said.

"What do you want to do?"

"I think we need to take a break, or maybe I should say I need to take a break," she said calmly. "I have to decide if what you're prepared to give to this relationship is enough for me to stay in it."

"Yes, I think you do have to make that decision," Ava said.

"It won't be easy."

"Maria...I hope you decide to stay."

"Do you really feel that way?"

"I love you. You know that."

"And I love you, but I've got this overpowering need to be part of a family, part of something bigger than myself."

"So where does this leave us?" Ava asked.

"I need to make the decision, and I have to make it knowing that I'm not going to get more from you. I don't know how long that will take. Will you wait until I do?"

"By 'wait,' do you mean that I won't abandon our relationship?"

"Yes."

"That's an easy thing for me to agree to."

"Thanks."

"And in the meantime, do you want me to contact you at all?"

"No, I think it's best for me to sort this out quietly by myself."

"Okay. I'll be here when you're ready to talk."

"Thanks," Maria said softly, then ended the call.

Ava stared at the phone for a few seconds. She had half expected the conversation to go like that, but it hadn't made it any easier. Still, it was a relief to have everything out in the open. And no matter what happened, she wasn't going to do anything that ran contrary to her nature and, ultimately, cause more distress and pain than she and Maria were experiencing now.

Her phone rang. She blinked in surprise. "Hello," she said.

"Ava, it's Amanda."

Ava checked her watch. It was almost midnight in Hong Kong. "What's happened?"

"Elsa Ngan just phoned. There's an online publication called *Fashion Times*. She just saw an advance copy of tomorrow's edition. Dominic Ventola is the lead story."

"What does it say?"

"It's what he says. He trashes Clark."

"Trashes?"

"He was asked for his opinion about the highs and lows of London Fashion Week. Or, Elsa thinks, he called the reporter and offered opinions he knew they'd want to print," Amanda said. "However it came to be, the main focus of the article is on the lows — predominantly on the work of Clark Po. Ventola found the collecton 'unimaginative, pedestrian, and totally lacking in originality.' He said it was by far his biggest disappointment in London. He wondered how someone like Pang Fai could associate herself with the brand. He went on to say that the world is still waiting for a design star from China, and despite all the hype surrounding Clark, he isn't even close to being one."

"Shit. So much for ignoring us as one of his options."

"Elsa was appalled. She called the editor and argued that she'd seen Clark's show and the reaction to the collection in London. She said Ventola was being biased and unfair. She was told that they reported news and that Ventola's opinions were news."

"When he strikes, he strikes hard."

"He does. *Fashion Times* is read by just about everyone in the trade, including the buyers we're currently pursuing. On top of that, Elsa says we should expect other publications to pick up the article."

"Have you told May yet?"

"No. I wanted to talk to you first."

"And there's no way we can get the story killed?"

"Absolutely not."

"Then I'll call May right away," Ava said. "You phone Chi-Tze and give her a heads-up. Let her communicate the details to Clark and Gillian."

"He'll be shattered."

"I don't blame him if he is."

"This is a disaster," Amanda said.

"It certainly has that potential," Ava said. "So we need to do damage control right away. If we move fast enough, maybe we can blunt its impact."

"What do you suggest?"

"Can we get hold of all our existing customers?"

"I don't see why not, since most of them are here in Asia. A few went to London, like Carrie Song, and some may even go on to Milan, but we have contact numbers."

"Then you, Chi-Tze, Gillian, or Clark — whoever gets along best with the particular account — should call all of them as soon as they're open for business tomorrow. If they're going to hear something ugly, it's better that it come directly from us, with our spin on it."

"What is our spin?"

"The truth. VLG tried to buy PÖ. We turned them down. Now they're being vindictive."

"If that becomes public, Ventola will deny it. It will be our word against his."

"When isn't it someone's word against someone else's? We have to believe that the people who know us will grant us some level of credibility," Ava said. "And while you're at it, get Chi-Tze or Gillian — not Clark — to send a letter to *Fashion Times* stating the very same thing. They tried to buy us and we declined. This is their payback."

"Gillian is officially the CEO."

"Then she should sign the letter."

Amanda drew a deep breath. "I thought it was too good to be true today. Nearly every prospective European and North American customer we contacted gave us a positive response."

"Well, you're going to have to call them all back."

"Some of the Americans flew home after London, and it's the middle of the business day there. We should be able to reach them and the Europeans before the end of the day."

"Let's reach out right now. Most of the industry is already in Milan for Fashion Week, and the fact that they're on VLG's home turf already gives Ventola an advantage. We don't want him talking to them before we do."

"There will be a great many awkward conversations."

"For all concerned, I would imagine."

"Yeah, well, let me start the ball rolling by calling Chi-Tze. No one in Shanghai, or me for that matter, is going to get much sleep tonight."

"I'll talk to May. Some of our Asian customers are friends of hers. She might be able to help."

"How about Carrie Song?"

"Do you know where she is?"

"She flew back to Hong Kong after London."

"I'll call her myself first thing in the morning."

"What's the best way to keep you updated?"

"Phone me. I'm not going anywhere and this has my full attention."

Ava closed her eyes after she ended the call. She couldn't remember the last time a day had gone bad so progressively. Crummy weather. Grandmaster Tang. Maria. And now this.

Her phone rang and she almost jumped from the chair. She glanced at the number. It was her mother. She hesitated before answering, afraid that more bad news was about to be delivered.

"Hi, Mummy."

"I'm so happy you're back. It sounds like London was terrific."

"It's too soon to say."

"I was going to invite you to dim sum. There's a place I've discovered in Richmond Hill that's the best I've eaten in years."

"Mummy, you do know it snowed all night and I'm not comfortable driving in ice and slush? Besides, traffic will be a nightmare."

"It isn't so bad up here."

"Tomorrow."

"But not too early. I have a mah-jong game and it will go on late."

Ava smiled. At least one person in her life could be depended on to be predictable.

14

AVA CALLED MAY LING'S CELL, BUT IT WASN'T ON. SHE left a message and called her office phone. That led to another message. She then sent her a text and, for good measure, an email. They all said essentially the same thing: "We have a big problem. His name, to no one's surprise, is Dominic Ventola. Call me whenever you can."

She went online and found *Fashion Times* but couldn't find the Ventola story. She guessed it hadn't been posted yet and then immediately began to worry if it had been premature to tell Amanda to phone customers. No, she thought, the direction she'd given Amanda was correct, and it was the same that Uncle had always given her: If there was bad news for a client, it had to come from them. Coming from anyone else always made it seem worse than it was and in the process made them look untrustworthy. "We may not always be able to succeed," he said, "but we can always be honest, and that will be remembered."

How would their current and potential customers react to the story and their explanation for Ventola's comments, she wondered. She didn't like to think that their existing

Asian customer base would desert them based on an article in an English-language publication, especially given their sales success. But she actually wasn't sure how they would react, given the strong influence that European brands had in Asia. The companies they were wooing in Europe and North America were another story. PÖ had no track record in either of those markets. Why would those companies support them when Dominic Ventola deemed the collection a failure? How many buyers would be brave enough to tell their bosses that the great Ventola's assessment of PÖ was wrong?

Her phone rang and she saw Amanda's number. "Did you reach Chi-Tze?"

"I did, and then she conferenced in the Pos," Amanda said.

"How did it go?"

"Badly. Even though they knew it was a possibility, they obviously didn't believe Ventola would go through with his threat."

"How bad was it?"

"Gillian was really upset, and so was Chi-Tze. For the first five minutes Clark pretended that it didn't bother him that much, but then he fell apart. I think he was crying."

"I'm surprised he was able to even pretend," Ava said. "He's worked all these years to get to this point, and now his work is publicly lambasted by the same man who two days ago called him a genius. It has to be devastating."

"Gillian and Chi-Tze are being incredibly supportive."

"Are they all, including Clark, prepared to call customers?"

"Of course, and I'm sure it's happening already. Clark did pull himself together before we ended our conversation, and he said he will do whatever is necessary."

"It's the best thing to do."

"That's what Clark said."

"Now we sit and wait."

"Not for that long. I imagine we'll have some idea in the next hour or so about how things are going."

"Keep me posted."

"I will," Amanda said. "Have you spoken to May?"

"No. I couldn't reach her."

"Chi-Tze thinks that May's *gaunxi* is so strong that her friends will never go against her."

"You think you know what people will do, but then money gets in the way and all predictions are off," Ava said. "Call me when you have any updates."

She knew that waiting to hear back from Amanda was going to be torture. *What can I do to kill time?* she thought. The twelve-hour time difference between Toronto and Asia was seldom an issue, but now it was. She couldn't reach May, wasn't going to call Carrie Song so late, and had nothing to contribute to what Chi-Tze and the others were doing. She looked out the window. A mixture of sleet and snow was falling again, discouraging any idea of going outside.

She went to the living room and turned on the television. She scanned the English cable channels for something to watch, but nothing captured her interest. She checked the Chinese channels. There was a soap opera on one, a news show on the next, and — to her delight — one of Pang Fai's early films on the third. The film, called *Family*, followed the life of a young woman who was trying to support her parents, her younger sister, and two aged aunts during the Cultural Revolution. The film ended on a sombre note with the young woman's death. Made by the wrong hands, it could have been a maudlin tear-jerker. But the director, Lau Lau, was brilliant and Pang Fai was magnetic, so emotionally raw and bare that it didn't feel like a performance.

Lau Lau had been in his thirties when he made the film. Pang Fai was in her early twenties. He had discovered her during a casting call for a supporting role in an earlier film. They had moved in together and then married, but the marriage didn't last long. Fai had left him just as the government began to withdraw financial support for his films and his career started a slow fade. It was common now for the Hong Kong tabloids to characterize her as an opportunist, marrying Lau to advance her career and then dumping him when he was no longer of use. Ava wondered if that was true. Maybe she'd have a chance to ask one day.

Regardless of what happened to him in later years, Lau Lau had made a number of films that were to Ava's mind some of the best ever to come out of China. *Family* was at the top of that list. Even though she knew the storyline in detail, Ava watched it again with fresh eyes and quickly became absorbed in Pang Fai's performance. She physically inhabited the role, her body language subtle but powerful and her eyes large and luminous. There was a scene late in the film when her character confronted a government official and begged him for food for her family. The look on her face as she made the request and then when he denied it moved seamlessly from hope to humiliation to despair. Ava wept every time she watched it. Now she wept again.

When the film ended, she went to the bathroom to dry her eyes and splash some cold water on her face. When she came back, her phone was ringing.

"It's Amanda."

Ava looked at her watch. It was almost one-thirty. "What's the news?"

"Well, some of the calls were very complicated, particularly with the prospective customers. Frankly, some of them weren't pleased to hear from us."

"Had they seen the article?"

"I don't know if any of them had seen it, but they'd all heard about it," Amanda said. "The reporter at *Fashion Times* wasn't the only person who heard from Dominic Ventola or his company today. Senior marketing people at VLG have been at work trying to poison our business with every major retailer in Europe and North America. They started contacting them around noon, Milan time, which was after we'd closed shop for the day in Shanghai, feeling very good about ourselves."

"My god, they're eager. Many of those companies will be in Milan in the next day or two. You would think they'd have waited to talk to them then."

"It sounds like their plan was to coordinate the calls with the release of the *Times* article. Then the news would dominate the talk in Milan."

"And it was employees, not Dominic or Raffi, who made the calls?"

"I guess Dominic thought it was beneath him or Raffi, at least so far."

"What did they say?"

"They pretended the article was the reason they were making contact. The message was 'We don't know if you're considering carrying that new PÖ line, but if you are, you might want to read what Mr. Ventola has to say about it in *Fashion Times*.'"

"I can't believe those companies would buy into what he has to say. Surely they're capable of making their own judgements about Clark's work."

"Yes, but some of the mainstream retailers are quite conservative. They want a sure thing. They don't want to gamble on a relative unknown, especially when Dominic Ventola, as you said earlier, publicly decimates his work."

"Did they tell you that?"

"Not directly, but they made it clear they weren't going to be buying from us anytime soon. We were told to come back in three to six months. They said they'd reconsider the line then, based on how well PÖ was doing in the market," Amanda said. "They just want us to go away."

"How many companies are we talking about?"

"We were negotiating with ten different companies. That conservative group represented six of them."

"What about the other four?"

"This is where the conversations between our team and the buyers became a little bizarre," Amanda said. "Even those who still maintained that they liked Clark's work and wanted to carry it wouldn't make any kind of immediate commitment. When we pushed them, two said they didn't want to have issues with VLG."

"Issues? What does that mean?"

"Evidently when one of the buyers told the VLG representative that she still intended to carry PÖ, the rep said it would be unfortunate if she found herself having to decide between carrying PÖ or the entire VLG line, because it was unlikely she could carry both."

"Good god."

"Chi-Tze was stunned when she heard it."

"So how many new accounts do you think we have a chance to land?"

"As of right now, none that amount to anything," Amanda said.

"Are you worried about the existing ones?"

"Why wouldn't I be? So are Chi-Tze and Gillian. We'd like to think we've built some solid relationships and developed a loyal following, but how are those customers going to react if VLG drops a big hammer on them?"

"As in either sell VLG or PÖ but not both?"

"Exactly. I can't even begin to count how many designer brands VLG controls, and that includes shoes, clothes, perfume, bags, and even liquor. They have to represent a big percentage of those retailers' sales. We're a sliver, a decimal point."

"Do you really believe that VLG is willing to throw away business to get at us?" Ava said, and then quickly answered her own question. "Of course they're not. They know damn well that the retailers have only one option."

"Drop PÖ."

"Yes. But we are making the assumption that VLG will take the same approach with our Asian customer base as they did with the European and North American companies. I don't think that's necessarily certain. They may be less willing to try to strong-arm an Asian company to drop an Asian supplier."

"Ava, I know it's nice to think that VLG might be culturally sensitive, but they know this is all about money, and that's how our customers will think as well. We can't expect them to stay with us because of our home base. But we'll know soon enough. We start making phone calls to Asia at eight."

"I'm going to call Carrie Song then as well."

"That will be an interesting test case."

"I guess so."

"Have you talked to May yet?"

"I haven't been able to reach her."

"Well, the way I look at it, if you can't convince Carrie to keep us in her stores, and if May can't get her friends to hang in there with us, we're not going to have much of a business left," Amanda said. "We need a break of some kind. Maybe the story won't run."

"Just a second," Ava said, checking her computer. "The story is online now."

"So much for a break."

15

AVA CONTEMPLATED THE HOURS SHE HAD TO KILL before she could call Carrie Song or expect to reach May, and she knew she'd never last that long in the condo. She bundled up again and headed outdoors. She walked to Lowther Avenue and knocked on Grandmaster Tang's door, but there was still no answer. She walked back to Avenue Road and began heading south, but then she came to an abrupt halt, turned, and walked north.

The snow had turned to sleet and the wind had picked up, driving more fiercely into her face. She pulled down her tuque as far as it would go, burrowed her chin into her scarf, and concentrated on taking one step at a time.

She walked for close to an hour in a straight line towards Upper Canada College, the all-boys private school for Canada's elite. She knew from her running route that it was just over three kilometres from her condo to the school, a distance she usually ran in twelve to fifteen minutes, depending on traffic lights. If the sidewalks had been dry, it would have taken her thirty minutes to make the walk, but this was a slog.

As she reached the college, the pale winter sun began to ebb behind a bank of clouds. The greyness suited her mood. She stopped and turned south. She walked methodically, one foot in front of the other, trying not to slip.

"You bastards, you fucking bastards," she said under her breath more than once.

It was completely dark by the time she got near Yorkville. She wasn't sure of the time, but she'd walked long enough to focus her mind, work off some anger, and build up an appetite. There was an Italian restaurant near her condo that she liked, but anything Italian was anathema to her right now. It came down to a choice between Chinese and Japanese. She opted for Dynasty, a Chinese restaurant on Yorkville Avenue.

It took her several minutes to warm up enough to take off her hat and scarf. She sipped tea while she read the menu and then ordered hot and sour soup for two, steamed bok choy, and a glass of Chardonnay. While she waited for the wine, she took her phone from her pocket and checked incoming calls. May had phoned an hour ago. Ava hadn't heard a ring or felt any vibration. "Shit," she said as she hit May's number.

"May, sorry. My phone was in my pocket and I was outside walking and didn't hear it."

"I got your messages," May said.

"It isn't a good situation," Ava said.

"I know. A few minutes ago I got a call from one of my business acquaintances who put the PÖ line into her stores in Hubei. It isn't a big operation, only four stores, but she does well enough. She told me that the local VLG rep called to say they had been told to pull all their lines out of her stores unless she dropped PÖ. I couldn't reach you, so I phoned Amanda. She told me what's going on."

"I was hoping they'd tread more carefully on our home turf," Ava said. "I'm surprised at how direct a threat that is."

"It could be a case of the VLG rep getting a general directive and then taking it to the extreme. The closer you get to the ground, the more ferocious the competition."

"I hope it's an isolated incident."

"I don't think it is. I've talked to some other people and they've received the same message, although not quite as blunt."

"How are they reacting?"

"They don't want to cut and run from PÖ, but from a practical viewpoint they don't want to lose VLG. I have a friend in Wuhan who owns a high-end designer-label boutique but is also the agent for VLG's liquor business in the province. I can't blame him if he chooses to drop us. Others are hanging in there, probably because they're more afraid of me than VLG."

"It also doesn't seem like we're going to be picking up any new North American or European accounts."

"So Amanda said. Have you talked to Carrie Song yet?"

"No. I'll call her when I get back to my condo."

"Well, her reaction will tell us just how large this problem is. If she bails after everything she owes you, then I don't know what we can do."

"She doesn't own Lane Crawford; she works for it. I can't expect her to put her job and her future at risk for me."

"I know. I've been wracking my brains for the past hour trying to figure out if there's anything we can do to stop them. Changxing suggested we hire some topnotch lawyers and go after them. But for what? Ventola offering an opinion? And even if we did find some reason, how long would it take to get some resolution?"

"I've spent two hours walking around in the snow and slush thinking about the same thing."

"And what did you come up with?"

"I kept coming back to something Uncle used to say to me."

"What's that?"

"He said that everyone has a weakness, but sometimes we're so blinded by how strong someone appears that we don't take the time to look for it."

"Have you found one for VLG?"

"Not yet. I'm still thinking about it," Ava said.

"We don't have a lot of time."

"I know, but we still have more phone calls to make. Maybe something will come to me before we're finished. In the meantime, I need to contact Carrie Song."

May sighed. "The girls in Shanghai will be making more phone calls in a little while as well, and I'll be doing the same. We can compare notes when we're finished and see where we're at."

"Do you have much doubt where we'll be?"

"No. Those pricks seem to have done a number on us."

16

AVA SAT AT THE KITCHEN TABLE WITH THE NOTEBOOK she'd started on the flight to Milan open in front of her. She crossed out *Ventola* and wrote *VLG*. The situation had become bigger than one man. She turned on her computer and began to verify, add to, and cross-reference the information she'd initially uncovered about the conglomerate.

Fifteen billion dollars in sales. Six major international brands. Flagship stores in more than fifty countries. Product lines that encompassed the very best in leather goods and fashion, jewellery, watches, shoes, perfume, and liquor, including premium whisky and cognac labels and one of the world's top champagne producers. *What a great job Ventola and Pandolfo have done building this company*, she thought. *And what a massive footprint they've made.*

She entered the web site for Plouffe, VLG's major French fashion and accessories business, and was starting to identify its component parts when the alarm on her phone sounded. It was time to call Carrie Song. *Please be there*, she thought.

"Lane Crawford, Carrie Song's office," a receptionist said.

"This is Ava Lee. I'm calling from Toronto to speak to Ms. Song."

"Good morning, Ms. Lee," the woman said. "Just one moment, I'll see if she's available."

Ava closed the notebook and turned towards the window. The sleet had morphed into rain. The forecast called for general warming. She hoped they had passed the freezing rain stage.

"Ms. Lee, she's on her way from the boardroom and will be right with you," the receptionist said.

"Ava," Carrie said breathlessly, "I already know why you're calling and I'm so sorry about it all."

"I wanted to give you a heads-up. I guess I'm a bit late for that," she said.

"Raffi Pandolfo phoned me at home an hour ago."

"Raffi himself. You must be important to them. They've been using underlings to do their dirty work elsewhere."

"I've known Raffi a long time. We're a key account and it was me who referred him to you," she said. "I feel terrible for Clark. I mean, I know that you, May, and Amanda have a lot of money tied up in the business, but on a personal level I feel most keenly for him. What a horrible thing for them to do. What happened?"

"We met with them in Milan. They wanted to buy PÖ, to buy Clark. To get control they needed the Three Sisters' shares. We have no interest in selling, but we left it to Clark to make the decision about who he wants to be his partners moving forward. He chose us. Ventola was angry and made threats. Quite truthfully, we didn't take them seriously enough."

"Even if you had, what could you have done?"

"Talked some more, but apart from that not much else."

"So here we are," Carrie said.

"Yes, and here am I calling you to ask — probably unfairly — what you're going to do. VLG has been phoning potential and current customers and telling them to drop us. I imagine they've made the same request of you."

Carrie didn't answer immediately, and in her hesitation Ava felt a lead-up to a complicated rationalization of her decision to drop PÖ from her stores.

"Nothing," Carrie said. "I'm going to do nothing."

"What?"

"I wish you didn't sound so surprised."

"I'm sorry. It's been a day and night of nothing but rejection."

"I'd read the article in *Fashion Times* before Raffi called me. I figured something had happened between you, and this was payback," Carrie said. "I didn't actually expect to hear from them, but I'd already been thinking about possible repercussions from the story, so I was kind of prepared."

"What exactly did Raffi say?"

"Oh, he wandered around the subject a bit. He claimed that when Dominic and his design team got back to Milan, they reviewed the PÖ show in London and concluded they'd been blinded by Pang Fai's appearance. He said that when they got into a detailed examination of Clark's clothes, they found them lacking."

"Lacking? That's it?"

"No, he also went on to say that in the next few weeks we'll be contacted by some of their marketing and mer-chandising people to review our in-store plans for their brands over the next few quarters. He said it was only fair that I should know their people have been instructed to make sure that their products aren't sold alongside or anywhere near PÖ."

"That was subtle."

"Not subtle enough. I told Raffi that I will decide what is sold where. I told him I have PÖ inventory and outstanding PÖ orders and that I intend to honour every commitment," Carrie said. "He hemmed and hawed and then said he understood, and hadn't expected me to do anything else."

"Thank you."

"It's too soon to say that," Carrie said. "I told him we'd honour our commitments, and we will. We'll support you one hundred percent in that regard. But, Ava, you can't put me in the middle of an ongoing battle between you and Dominic Ventola, or between PÖ and VLG. I'll back you over the short term, but you need to find a way to resolve this. If you let it drag out, you have no way of winning."

"Thank you again for the support, and for being honest. I do know the situation can't carry on. I was debating about going to Shanghai tomorrow, and I've just made up my mind. I can't solve anything from Canada."

"The faster you move, the better it will be for everyone concerned."

"Obviously," Ava said.

"Could you keep me advised? I don't want to hear any more news from Raffi. So, good or bad, please call me."

"I will."

Ava thought about calling Shanghai but instead went online. She booked a business-class seat on an Air Canada flight leaving Toronto at one p.m. the next day. It was a direct flight and would get her into Shanghai at three in the afternoon the day after.

She phoned her mother's cell and, as usual, got voicemail. "I can't make dim sum tomorrow. I'm leaving for Shanghai on some business that just came up. I'll stay in touch," she said.

She started to hit Maria's number and then froze when she remembered she wasn't supposed to call. It felt strange not following the usual routine, but she needed to respect Maria's wishes. She stood and walked to the bedroom. She hadn't completely unpacked from the London trip, and in a matter of minutes she had everything she needed for Shanghai in the bag. She returned to the kitchen, sat at the table, and re-entered the world of VLG online. For the next hour she read and made notes, but for everything she found out there were about ten questions that she couldn't answer. The good thing was that the questions were becoming similar, almost repetitive — mainly variations of who, what, where, when, and how. As she contemplated the list of questions, she smiled. She knew she had the means to answer them all, sooner or later.

Her phone rang, and she saw it was May.

"Hi. How is it going on your end?" Ava asked.

"So-so. We're not losing everyone, but those who are sticking by us aren't doing it with much enthusiasm."

"Have you talked to Amanda?"

"Yes, and she's getting the same feedback from Chi-Tze and Gillian."

"Raffi Pandolfo called Carrie."

"Oh," May said, apprehensively.

"Not to worry, or at least not to worry just yet. Carrie told him she's honouring all their commitments to us, but she's asked us to get this behind us as fast as possible."

"Or?"

"There was no 'or,' and there didn't have to be. She's never going to choose us over VLG unless she doesn't care about keeping her job."

"What constitutes putting this behind us?"

"We didn't define it, but I imagine she'd be happy enough if our relationship with VLG was neutral."

"Me too."

"I'm flying to Shanghai tomorrow," Ava said. "I'd like it if you could join me."

"Have you told the others?"

"Not yet. I just emailed Xu to tell him I'm coming. We may need his help."

"So you have a plan? You've identified a weakness?"

"I'm getting there, but I'm still working on it. What I do have is a firm idea of an end result."

"Do I have to ask what it is?"

"I want to see Dominic Ventola on his knees, begging for Clark's forgiveness."

"Couldn't you come up with something more dramatic?" May said.

Ava laughed. "I have a lot to do before I get to Shanghai. And when I get there, I'm going to need everyone's time and support."

"My husband isn't going to be happy about me running off again."

"I know, but I need you too."

May paused. "Do you really think you can get Ventola to back off?"

"Why not?" Ava said. "He's just another man who thinks women were put on this earth to do what they're told or get run over. There isn't a man alive who can tell me what to do. And I'm certainly not about to be run over."

17

AMANDA'S FLIGHT FROM HONG KONG HAD ARRIVED at Shanghai Pudong International Airport an hour before Ava's, and she was waiting at the arrivals door when Ava exited. They hugged and then walked to the limo stand. Ava had her Shanghai Tang Double Happiness bag in one hand and her Louis Vuitton case in the other. Amanda rolled an enormous suitcase behind her that Ava knew contained more clothes than she could wear in a week. Amanda never travelled light.

"How's Michael?" Ava asked as they settled into the limo.

"He's great. He and Simon are on a roll. He sends his love," she said. "So does Marcus. We had dinner with him and Elizabeth last night."

Elizabeth Lee was her father's first wife, and the pre-eminent female in the Lee clan.

"I haven't seen my father in a while," Ava said.

"He's aging well. He doesn't look fifty, let alone sixty-plus."

"Any new wives on the horizon?"

"Ava!"

"Sorry."

Amanda shrugged. "You're entitled to say that, I guess. I don't get it myself, this need to keep trading up for younger women. I know there's a tradition, but I've already told Michael that if he ever suggests doing the same, he'd better sleep with one eye open."

"You've become bloodthirsty all of a sudden."

"Not really. I've always felt that way, but now I'm just prepared to admit it."

Ava laughed. "Okay, now we should talk about why I wanted you and May to meet me here in Shanghai. I've decided that the only way PÖ can survive is for us to go after Ventola and Pandolfo and VLG. Being passive isn't an option."

"I knew that was why you wanted me to come here," Amanda said. "I told Michael, 'They've tried to bully the wrong person. Ava won't put up with their shit.'"

"So you're onside with whatever I want to do?"

"You know I am, and you know May will be as well."

"How about Gillian, Clark, and Chi-Tze?"

"What do you mean?"

"Do you think they'll be willing to do whatever is necessary to help?"

"After what you did for her in Borneo, Chi-Tze would do just about anything for you. But I don't know about Clark and Gillian. It may depend on what you have in mind. They haven't been exposed to the Ava who worked with Uncle."

"I'm not envisioning anything as dramatic as Borneo, and this isn't taking on thugs for a collection job. Our egos, Clark's reputation, and our bank accounts are maybe at risk here, but not our physical well-being."

"So what will you want from them?"

"I don't exactly know yet. I just need to know they're going to be completely behind us."

"If it means saving PÖ, I imagine they'll be willing to do anything."

"That's the answer I want."

"I called Chi-Tze when I landed," Amanda said. "She said you asked her to schedule a meeting at the Peninsula Hotel at five."

"I did. I also asked May to book a small conference room next to the business centre. We thought about meeting at the factory, but I decided it might be less distracting in the hotel."

PÖ leased a small sample factory in Pudong, where Clark created his designs and his team of seamstresses put them together. If the samples generated orders, those were jobbed out to a large garment factory sixty kilometres away that was owned by one of Xu's companies.

"I think that's a good idea. Chi-Tze says it's gloomy at the factory right now. No one has said anything to the workers, but they can sense from Gillian and Clark's mood that things aren't right," Amanda said. She reached over to touch Ava's arm. "What's your plan?"

"You'll have to wait," Ava said. "I want to tell everyone at once."

Amanda gently squeezed her arm but didn't pursue the question.

"Look at the construction going on around here," Ava said, looking out the window. "I keep waiting for it to slow down, but it doesn't."

"Gillian told me that more than five million people live in Pudong now. When Pudong became a special economic zone in the early nineties, I think there were only a couple of hundred thousand inhabitants."

"At least we can see the buildings today. The first time I was in Nanjing, the air was so thick and yellow you could barely see through it."

Pudong was a district of Shanghai located on the east bank of the Haungpu River. When people on the west bank looked across the river, they faced the looming façades of the two tallest buildings in China — the 101-storey Shanghai World Financial Centre and the 128-storey Shanghai Tower — and two of the next six largest, including the Oriental Pearl Tower. As imposing as they were, Ava thought they paled in comparison to the majesty of the Bund, the walkway lined with banks, trading houses, and consulates that fronted the west bank. Built in the late 1800s and early 1900s in what was then the Shanghai International Settlement, the Bund had fifty-two buildings that had somehow survived civil war, Japanese occupation, the early days of communism, and the more recent mania for razing and redeveloping entire cities.

Quaintly numbered "No. 1, The Bund" to "No. 52, The Bund," the buildings showcased a mixture of beaux arts, art deco, Gothic, and Renaissance revival architecture. The original tenants had all left or been displaced, and many of the buildings had been modernized and transformed. Their hotel, the Peninsula, was on the Bund. It was an art deco masterpiece built on property that had been part of the Consulate General of the United Kingdom.

Traffic in Shanghai was unpredictable, and gridlock wasn't uncommon along and near the Bund. As they crossed Waibaidu Bridge, Ava expected the worst when they reached the other side, but traffic was moving smoothly and they were at the Peninsula in good time.

May had made their reservations and as usual had put them in suites. Amanda had a river suite, and Ava one that overlooked the former gardens of the British Consulate and a stretch of Suzhou Creek, which flowed into the Huangpu River. Ava had stayed in the same room on three previous visits, and she almost felt at home. She quickly unpacked, showered, slipped on a pair of a black linen slacks and a plain white cotton shirt, and headed out the door, carrying the bag that contained her notebook, pen, and phone.

The others were already there when she got to the conference room. They stood when she walked in and there was a general round of hugs and kisses. When they sat down, Ava felt the tension in the room.

"How was the flight?" May asked Ava.

"It was okay. I was so anxious to get here it seemed longer than it was."

"Our thanks to you, May, and Amanda for coming," Gillian said.

Ava looked at her and Clark. Both of them appeared distracted.

"How are you holding up?" Ava asked.

"I haven't slept in two nights," said Clark.

"I'm the same," Gillian added.

"Have you talked to any more customers over the past twenty hours?"

"That's all we've been doing," Gillian said.

"And what kind of reaction are you getting?"

"The smaller and more regional the customer, the more loyal they are."

"I guess that was to be expected," Ava said.

"What are we going to do?" Clark said, his voice hoarse. "It can't continue like this."

"It isn't going to. Is it fair to say that they've made good on their threats and they can't cause much more immediate damage?"

"The damage so far is bad enough," Clark said.

"I'm not downplaying the severity of this," Ava said. "I'm just pointing out that they've done just about everything to us they can. They've effectively shut us out of every major account in Europe and North America, and they've scared some of our biggest Asian customers away. What's left? Kicking us out of some small accounts here and there? I don't think they'll bother. I imagine they're feeling very satisfied with themselves."

"I don't understand your point," Clark said.

"We don't have that much left to lose. If we did, our response to their actions might be tempered by the fact that we'd want to hang on to whatever we still had. I don't feel any restraint in that regard. In fact, I don't feel any restraint at all," Ava said. "I want to go after them full bore. I want to hurt them the way they hurt us — financially and in reputation. I want to hurt them so badly that they'll beg us to stop. And when they do, they're going to have to apologize to Clark and call all those major accounts and set things right."

Ava hadn't raised her voice as she spoke. She was calm and measured, her eyes focused in turn on everyone sitting at the table. May nodded when she finished and then glanced at Amanda, who was smiling at Chi-Tze. Gillian looked confused. Clark's eyes were closed and his head was bent.

"How is any of that even remotely possible?" Gillian said.

"They're a fifteen-billion-dollar-a-year conglomerate. What could we possibly do to cause them harm?"

"Gillian, if Ava says we can hurt them, then you'd better believe she has a plan for doing exactly that," Amanda said.

Ava opened her notebook and turned to Gillian and Clark. "You have to stop thinking about VLG as a fifteen-billion-dollar-a-year corporation. It isn't one large monolith. It's constructed from a great many parts. There are at least six brands that we can multiply by four or five major product categories and then another two or three sub-categories, and then multiply each of them by market segments. When you work through those numbers, you're left with a whole bunch of small entities that you can attack individually. Our first job is to identify them."

"Attack them how?" Gillian said.

"One step at a time," Ava said. "Let's start by identifying who we're really dealing with, where they are, and how they operate. If we can do that, then I promise you we'll find the means to attack them."

"What do you mean by 'identify'?" Chi-Tze asked.

"We need to do research on VLG," Ava said, ripping sheets of paper from the back of her notebook. "Here are lists that I've made. They identify every major brand that VLG owns, and as many sub-brands and products as I could find. I'm sure you'll find more. The more details you can unearth, the easier it will be to go after them."

"What kind of details do we look for?" Gillian asked.

"The first priority is to find out what they're selling and to whom and where. That includes everything, from clothing to liquor to perfume."

"That's a lot," Gillian said.

"There are the three of you and Clark. If you divide up the work by brand or market or product or whatever you think makes sense, it shouldn't be that hard to get some data pulled together in a few days," Ava said as she passed the lists to them. "I apologize that these notes are handwritten, but they will give you a bit of a head start.

"Even more important, we need to know what products they're getting made in Asia, especially in China, and that includes Hong Kong. Who are they selling to in these markets? Who are they buying from? During our conversations with Pandolfo and Ventola, they mentioned that Asia is becoming an increasingly important supplier of goods to them. They weren't specific, but the implication was that it isn't only raw material. Some products are made here or, more likely, product components might be made here. In either case, it is absolutely essential that we know who their suppliers are, for both raw materials and finished goods."

"What about the logistical side?" Amanda asked. "It would be really useful to know how their distribution chain operates."

"That's the next thing on my list," Ava said with a smile. "That's going to be a job for May and our friend Suki Chan. We haven't discussed it with Suki yet, but I don't imagine she'll be reluctant to help. What do you think, May?"

"I'll be happy to do it, and so will Suki. Between us there isn't much we don't know about distribution in this country, and there aren't many contacts we don't have."

"You'll need to feed what you're discovering to the girls and Clark."

"And vice versa."

"One of you should be the research coordinator for your

group. Someone needs to divide the work among you and pass the results along to me and May in a fairly organized way."

"I think that should be Gillian," Amanda said.

"I'm okay with that," Gillian said.

"May will be the point of contact for the logistical team," Ava said.

"That's fine," May said.

"And in case anyone is wondering what I'll be doing," Ava said, "I'll put together everything you're gathering and create a plan of execution."

"I know you said we shouldn't leap ahead," Gillian said, "but even if we know what they're buying and selling and transporting, what can we do about it?"

"We have friends who can cause things to happen," Ava said. "They're here in Shanghai and in Hong Kong, Guangzhou, and other places all over Asia. I'm going to meet with one tonight and we'll start the process of getting organized to act. There isn't much more I want to say about that right now."

"Gillian," May said, "Amanda and I have worked with Ava in the past on situations that were almost as difficult as this. When she says that things will happen, you can believe her."

"I want to get started," Clark said abruptly.

"I've made a dinner reservation for us all at the Mercato restaurant," May said.

"I want to get started now," he said.

"Does everyone else feel the same way?" May asked. They nodded. "Then I'll cancel the reservation."

"I do love your attitude," Ava said. Then she looked at her phone. It was buzzing, and a number that was vaguely familiar appeared on the screen. "Ava Lee," she said.

"This is Raffi Pandolfo."

"I'm very surprised to hear from you."

"I'm calling to tell you that I regret everything that's happened over the past forty-eight hours. It was unfortunate that you made it unavoidable."

"Your regrets don't help us very much."

"I know, but it's my way of reaching out and perhaps keeping the door even slightly ajar," he said. "Dom can be mercurial, and when he loses his temper he takes no half-measures. He always goes for the jugular. That isn't my style. I don't always approve of the way he behaves, but I can never prevent it."

"But neither he nor you will be making an effort to repair the damage that has been done, will you."

"No, that won't happen."

"How is your French, Mr. Pandolfo?"

"It's passable."

"My mentor, a man I called Uncle, used a phrase in Chinese that I discovered he'd borrowed from a French aphorism. It goes: *Cet animal est si féroce. Quand on l'attaque, il se défend.*"

"That animal is vicious. When you attack it, it defends itself?"

"Exactly. We've been attacked, and now you're going to find out just how viciously we defend ourselves."

18

MAY AND AVA SAT AT A TABLE NEAR THE FIREPLACE IN the Compass Bar, which was on the Peninsula's ground floor. May sipped her second martini while Ava worked on her second glass of Pinot Grigio. Amanda had left with the rest of the team half an hour before to go to the sample factory. They were full of enthusiasm. Ava's conversation with Raffi Pandolfo had added to their sense that all was not lost.

"How do you think it went?" Ava asked.

"You gave them hope."

"If we all dig deep and come up with enough useful information, we'll have more than hope."

"Do you really believe we can make an impact on VLG's operations?"

"I do."

"I assume we're going to try to disrupt everything they're doing in this market in terms of imports, export, and distribution."

"We are."

"It isn't going to be easy."

"I know. I'm going to ask Xu for some favours and get favours from anyone else who I think can help."

"Does Xu know you're in Shanghai?"

"Yes, I sent him my flight schedule before I left. I texted a half-hour ago, telling him we need to get together tonight. He's in a meeting and said he'd call me as soon as he's free."

"Does he have any idea why you want to see him?"

"Not a clue."

"You seem confident he'll do what you want."

"I think all I have to do is ask," she said. "You know the favours I've done for him."

"What a couple you two are."

"We're not a couple," Ava said. "We're friends. Like me and you. My relationship with him is something close to what I had with Uncle. There's a deep attachment, a lot of trust, and not many boundaries when it comes to give-and-take."

"My problem is that I think of Xu in another way," May said, looking carefully at Ava for her reaction.

"May, please."

"Nothing's happened."

"I hope not."

"We need to talk about this at some point."

"Maybe we do, but not now. I can't handle it."

"I can wait," May said.

"Thank you."

May looked at her watch. "I should call Suki. We're going to need her help, and I have to get her briefed and started."

"Do you think she can find out what we want to know?"

"I'd be surprised if she can't."

"And how about her contacts with the customs department?"

"They're solid, but it still won't be as easy as you think."

"I'm not taking anything for granted, but with a bit of money placed in the right hands, some favours exchanged, and *guanxi*, we should be able to get some information."

"*Guanxi* will probably work best."

"Still, tell Suki that obviously we'll reimburse her for whatever she has to pay out."

"She'll expect that," May said, and then stood up. "Okay, I'd better go. One more drink and I won't be fit to talk to anyone, let alone someone as sharp as Suki."

"Breakfast?"

"Sure. How about nine o'clock in the Lobby Lounge?"

"That's perfect. Good luck with Suki," Ava said, getting up. The two women hugged.

"Say hello to Xu for me," May said.

Ava smiled but didn't respond. As she watched May leave the bar she thought, *There's not a chance I'll do that. What I have to do is keep the two of you apart.* She felt a twinge of guilt and then pushed it aside. Nothing messed up friendships more quickly and more permanently than sex. If Xu and May ever connected and it didn't work, Ava knew she'd be caught somewhere in the middle, trying to juggle her relationship with each of them. That was the last thing she wanted. As selfish as it was, she liked the way things were and didn't want them to change.

She sat down again and contemplated another drink, but she knew that more wine would only hasten jet lag and the need to sleep. She picked up her phone and called Xu. If he couldn't see her in the next few hours, it might have to wait a day.

"Hi. Welcome back," he said after one ring, the sound of traffic in the background.

"Hey, I'm at the Peninsula. Do you have any idea when we can meet?"

"I was going to call you when I got a bit closer to Shanghai. I'm on my way back from our new factory, about half an hour away. Do you want me to pick you up or do you want to meet me at the house?"

Ava smiled at his assumption that they would meet at his house in the French Concession. It had become her second home in Shanghai. "Pick me up, please."

"Have you had dinner?"

"No. We were supposed to eat at Mercato but decided not to."

"Me neither. I'll tell Auntie Grace to prepare some noodles."

"And *dou miao* if she can."

"She always can, and it'll make her happy to know you asked for it."

"See you in half an hour. I'll wait near the entrance."

Ava settled the bar tab and went up to her room. She turned on her computer, did a quick check of her emails, and then sent one to her mother saying she'd arrived safely. There was nothing from Maria.

She went to the bathroom, freshened up, and went downstairs to meet Xu.

Suen, a mountain of a man who was Xu's Red Pole — his enforcer — leapt out of the front passenger seat to open the back door of the silver Mercedes S-Class sedan. Xu stepped out and grinned at Ava.

"*Mei mei,*" he said.

Ava had been uncomfortable when Xu started calling her *mei mei*. Now it was as natural as his using her given name.

Xu was a lean six feet with a full head of slicked-back hair and a handsome, chiselled face. The last time she'd seen him, he'd been under tremendous stress and his manner and movements were stiff and forced. Now he seemed completely relaxed. The grin was one indication. Another was that the thin black tie he always wore with a black suit and white shirt was loose, and the top button of his crisp white shirt was undone. For Xu that was being casual.

He held out his hands. When she grasped them, he bent over to kiss her on the forehead. "I don't know why you're here, but I'm very happy to see you."

"It's business trouble that brings me," she said.

"I thought it would be business. I'm sorry it's trouble," he said. "We can talk in the car."

"I'd rather wait until we're at the house."

"That's fine too." He stood to one side so she could slide into the back seat.

As the car pulled away from the hotel, he said, "When I told Auntie Grace you're going to have dinner at the house, she asked why you aren't staying with us."

"May and Amanda are at the hotel. We need to stay in contact and it's easier that way."

"Of course it is."

Auntie Grace had been Xu's nanny and was now his housekeeper. She was the most constant presence in his life, and there wasn't much she didn't know or had heard or seen. She and Ava had become friends and confidantes.

"I hope Auntie isn't upset about that."

"I don't think it's possible for you to offend her. You lead a life that might have been hers if she'd had the opportunity. She lives vicariously through you."

"And I think she's amazing."

"You both are, and that makes me a lucky man."

"What is the lucky man doing opening a new factory?" Ava asked. "Have things calmed down with the provincial authorities?"

"There's a new governor and a new provincial secretary. They approached me with a request to provide employment in a town about forty kilometres from here. I'm doing what I can to help."

"Are you paying them off?"

"Not yet. After the Tsai family debacle, everyone is sensitive to the fact that Beijing has many eyes fixed on Jiangsu. It's too soon for the new players to start accumulating wealth. That will probably change in a year or two, but right now I'm getting a free ride."

"What's happened to the Tsais?" Ava said, referring to the family that had run Jiangsu province politically for many years, until a corruption scandal brought them down.

"The governor and his cousin are serving ten-year jail terms. The governor's sister lost her gold-trading business. About ten billion in other assets was seized."

"I'm guessing they're still not poverty-stricken."

"They were left with enough to get by on," Xu said, and smiled.

"So what's this new factory making?"

"Something I wish I had discovered years ago," he said. "We're now in the perfume business."

"Counterfeit?"

"Of course."

"Which brand?"

"Several."

"How complicated is the process?"

"It isn't. The perfumes are all made primarily from distilled water and alcohol. The only difference among them is the aromatics that create the scent. We hired a young couple from France who are science grads with five years' experience working in the labs of two of the biggest European perfume manufacturers. There aren't many scents they can't match."

"What are the profit margins like?"

Xu glanced at her. "You normally have no interest in our knockoff businesses. What's so different about perfume?"

"Humour me."

He shrugged. "The margins are terrific. It costs about sixty U.S. cents an ounce to make a perfume that sells for sixty to eighty dollars. The most expensive and difficult job is getting the bottles made. After a lot of trial and error we finally found a glassmaker in Pudong who has a knack for it. He's expensive — we pay between three and five dollars for a three-and-a-half-ounce bottle — but I would defy anyone to tell the difference between his copies and the originals."

"How big is the market?"

"We expect we'll do about a hundred million dollars in sales over the next twelve months, mainly in Europe and Asia. That doesn't even begin to make a dent in a market that's worth more than thirty billion dollars worldwide."

"Who are your customers?"

"You'd be surprised at how big the demand is. One of the largest duty-free companies in Europe just became a customer."

"They know your perfumes are counterfeit?"

"We took them on a tour of the factory."

"Won't the real brands catch on?"

"That isn't my problem. I have to assume the company will find a way to integrate our products into their system and program their sales data to disguise how much of it they're selling."

The Mercedes reached the French Concession, a neighbourhood that abutted central Shanghai. In 1849 the area had been ceded to the French in an international settlement. They had constructed a replica of a French town with broad, tree-lined avenues, shops, and houses. Xu lived in a small brick house in the middle of a narrow lane lined on both sides with stone walls. Xu owned other houses on the lane, and fruit carts positioned at either end were manned twenty-four hours a day by his men. It was in many ways his private enclave.

As they drove towards the house, Ava couldn't help but notice that developers had started to worm their way into the Concession. There seemed to be fewer trees and more highrises under construction than she remembered. She mentioned it to Xu and he shrugged.

"The construction has actually slowed a bit in the neighbourhood. It will never be as pretty as it was five or ten years ago, but I think we've been able to stop the development."

They reached the lane and turned left. The driver stopped the car at the fruit cart and Suen had a quick chat with the man there. The car then drove slowly down the lane, its side mirrors threatening to scrape the stone walls. The wooden gate opened just as they arrived. Two men on security detail nodded as the Mercedes eased past.

Ava saw Auntie Grace standing at the door to the house. She was tiny, grey-haired, and dressed in a plain black Mandarin jacket and pants.

At five foot three, Ava rarely towered over anyone, but she had to bend down to kiss the older woman on both cheeks.

"You look tired," Auntie Grace said.

"I just arrived today and I didn't have a chance to nap or eat."

"The noodles and snow pea tips are ready, and I even have a bed if you want one."

"You're too kind."

"You shouldn't feel obliged to say that. I feel like you're part of my family now, and some things should be expected," Auntie Grace said with a smile. "Mind you, the other side of the coin is that I have the right to criticize if I think it's warranted."

Ava looked at her and saw there was a little tension behind the smile. Auntie Grace's comment was loaded with questions that she could either ignore or answer. She chose to answer. "I'm happy to be part of the family, and of course I could use any advice and wisdom you want to impart."

Auntie Grace reached for Ava's hand and squeezed. "I keep telling Xu that he should persuade you to move to Shanghai."

"One thing at a time," Xu said. "Right now we need to eat."

They went to the kitchen and sat on wooden folding chairs at a small round portable table. Two empty plates, chopsticks, a bowl of chilis, and a pepper shaker were set out on the table. As soon as they sat, Auntie Grace filled two bowls from her woks. The first contained noodles with beef, spring onions, and what smelled like XO sauce. The second held snow pea tips fried in garlic and oil. The mouth-watering aromas were overpowering. Ava found that her chopsticks almost had a mind of their own as they dug into the dishes.

"What do you want to drink?" Auntie Grace asked.

"Tea, please," Ava said.

"My whisky," Xu said.

They ate quietly for about ten minutes. The only word spoken was "Thanks" when their drinks were poured.

When they had finished, they pushed their plates into the centre of the table. Xu half-filled his glass with whisky and said, "I'm going outside for a smoke. Do you want to join me?"

"Sure," Ava said, accustomed to his after-dinner routine. She turned towards Auntie Grace, who hadn't left the stove. "That was a wonderful meal."

"I just wish he wouldn't end it by smoking."

"I told you, Auntie, I'll stop in the new year," Xu said.

"You've been saying that for five years."

"I didn't say which new year."

She flicked a tea towel in his direction. "Take your whisky and go for your smoke before I get really angry."

They sat by the fish pond. It was dark. The full moon was barely visible through what was either a bank of clouds or a smoggy haze. Ava guessed it was smog. "So, your business is going well?" she said.

"Yes, but evidently yours isn't. What's the problem?"

"PÖ."

"Really? I thought London was another success."

"Maybe too much of one."

"How is that possible?"

"After the show we flew to Milan to meet with a luxury fashion conglomerate. We naively thought they might be interested in some kind of joint venture. Instead, the only offer they made was to buy Three Sisters completely out of

PÖ. We said no. They didn't like our answer and now they seem determined to destroy us."

"How?"

"By poisoning our reputation within the trade and by telling existing and potential customers that their brands and the PÖ brand can't co-exist in stores."

"Forcing the customers to choose one or the other?"

"Precisely, and it isn't exactly a fair fight. As it stands, we won't be able to add any new business in the foreseeable future and we're having problems hanging on to what we do have."

"Who would want to do that?"

"VLG."

"Dominic Ventola?"

"Yes."

"Personally?"

"Unfortunately, very personally."

"Shit," Xu said. "I'm wearing one of his suits."

19

XU LISTENED ATTENTIVELY AS AVA DESCRIBED IN DETAIL how the London show, the trip to Milan, and the meetings with Raffi Pandolfo and Dominic Ventola had gone. When she was finished, he lit another cigarette and said, "When you mentioned trouble with business, I had no idea it was something of this magnitude. But what I don't understand is why a company that size would go to all that trouble over a startup like PÖ."

"I don't really know. Ventola says he's simply eliminating possible future competition, but I think that's bullshit. His partner, Raffi Pandolfo, said that he doesn't handle people saying no to him very well. Or maybe we offended him in some other way and he's coming after us just because he can."

"Well, whether it's personal or not, the end result is the same, and he's thrown the full weight of the company against you."

"That's true enough."

"What are you going to do?" he asked. He put his cigarette butt in a tomato can filled with water that was beside his chair and which Auntie Grace refused to empty. "You could try to bypass the system by opening your own stores."

"It's far too soon for that. We could maybe justify a flagship store in Shanghai, but we don't have the reputation or an extensive enough line to go anywhere else. Besides, going the bricks-and-mortar route would cost a fortune."

"You could try to wait him out. People have short memories. Six months from now you could revisit the potential and existing customers you've lost."

"We will also have lost all the momentum we built in Shanghai and London. I don't want people to forget us. I want to be front of mind. Right now we are, even if it's because Ventola has decided to make us an issue. I think we're better off staying on everyone's radar rather than retreating into silence."

"You very obviously have something in mind that I can't guess."

"I do, but what I don't know is if it's workable," Ava said. "I told our team that I think it is, but some of that was just bravado. I don't want them getting discouraged, so I'm trying to keep their spirits up."

"But there is some kind of plan and an objective that underscores the bravado?"

"The objective is to force Ventola to publicly apologize to Clark and for VLG to withdraw its opposition to our entry into the European and North American marketplaces," Ava said. She glanced at Xu to gauge his reaction to what even she knew sounded far-fetched.

"That's certainly ambitious." His face was impassive. "How do you propose to get to that point?"

"Well," Ava said, drawing a deep breath, "we need to hurt their business. We need to cause them so much aggravation and cost them so much money that playing nice with us will be a small price to pay for a return to civility."

"Ava, I don't doubt your intentions and your determination, but how can you possibly have that kind of impact on a company as large as VLG?"

"For starters, we pretend that they're small."

"What?"

"It's like I told the team. VLG is huge only if you think of it as one giant corporation. In reality it's made up of fifty or sixty separate companies, each with its own brands, markets, and distribution systems. If we can identify and isolate those businesses, our project immediately becomes less imposing."

"Except, even as stand-alone businesses, those brands have great reputations and strongholds in the market."

"And according to Raffi Pandolfo, Asia might now be their most important market."

"There you are."

"Exactly, here we are. He also told me that Asia, and China in particular, has become an increasingly important source of supplies for them."

"Supplies of what?"

"I don't know yet but I'm going to find out, as well as where their products are made. That's what Amanda and the others are working on right now. And while they're doing that, May Ling is figuring out what goods they're exporting into the Asian market and how they're shipped, warehoused, and distributed."

Xu smiled and slowly shook his head. "You intend to screw up their lines of supply and their importing, don't you."

"Yes," Ava said. "What do you think?"

"It's a clever concept, and it might really hurt some of the companies they own."

"I need more than just some companies. And I'm going to need help, especially your help, to make it happen."

"I would think that May Ling and the woman who runs your Shanghai logistics company would be useful."

"Suki Chan's influence is centred in Shanghai and May's in Hubei province. I think we'll need to go further afield."

"You know I'll do what I can."

"Hong Kong and Guangzhou are major entry and exit points for these kinds of goods."

"Lop has very strong contacts in Hong Kong, and no one is more powerful in Guangzhou than Lam."

Ava knew Lop Ying and Ban Lam well. Lop had been an officer in the Special Services Unit of the PLA before joining Xu's gang as Red Pole. After a dispute with Sammy Wing, the head of the triads in the Wanchai district of Hong Kong, Xu had assumed control of that gang and placed Lop in charge. Lam was the Mountain Master — the gang leader — in Guangzhou, and owed his ascendancy to that position in part to contributions from Ava and Xu.

"Can I still count on them?" she asked.

"Of course. Lop will do whatever I ask, and Lam owes you and me some big favours. I think Lam may be particularly pleased to have a chance to help you."

"How about the rest of China?"

"I can make calls."

"Would you be prepared to make some to outside the country?"

"We have good contacts and working relationships in Singapore, Taiwan, Malaysia, Vietnam, and Indonesia. We're not as strongly connected elsewhere, and I don't want to request any favours from the Yakuza — they have a tendency to backfire on us."

"I guess we don't need Japan to make an impact."

Xu's smile turned into a broad grin. "Uncle told me more than once that you have an incredibly nimble mind. He said that what makes it particularly special is that you combine an accountant's focus on order and detail with the ability to see the bigger picture in an imaginative way. He called it 'structured flair.' I've seen it twice now, with the triad election and the Tsai family crisis, but I don't think even those schemes were as audacious as what you think you can pull off this time."

"'Think' is the operative word. In fact, it might be more accurate to say 'hope.' There's a lot of data to collect, and until we have it I have no idea what will be possible," Ava said quietly, surprised again by how openly Uncle had discussed his opinions of her with Xu. It reinforced how close they'd been. What did it say about her relationship with Uncle that he'd never once mentioned Xu?

"How long will it take to get the first pieces of information?"

"Unless I'm badly mistaken, May and Amanda are working on it already. I expect to get an initial blast tomorrow."

"Then how quickly will you act?"

"As fast as possible."

"Depending on what you want me to do and where you want it done, I might not be able to move at the pace you want."

"I'm not going to be unreasonable."

"Thanks, booo." He smiled.

"I thought I was called *xiao lao ban* around here."

"Who told you that?"

"One of your men — Wen, I think. It was at your house after we resolved the Tsai family problem. He called for the car and said *xiao lao ban*, the 'little boss,' was leaving. I asked Auntie Grace who called me that and she said everyone did, including you when I wasn't around."

"Do you mind?"

"Auntie Grace said I should take it as a compliment."

"And so you should."

"I will, especially if it helps me get the action I want."

20

DESPITE BEING FATIGUED, AVA WOKE AT TWO IN THE morning and after a bathroom run had to force herself to go back to sleep. She woke up again at five. Her body was in a time zone somewhere between Toronto and London and wasn't about to be persuaded otherwise.

She made a coffee and carried it to the window. She looked out onto the gardens below, where the grass and leaves were glistening under the lights. What she could see of the Bund was quiet. She figured that if she dressed quickly she'd be able to get in a run. She finished the coffee and hurried to the bathroom to wash her face and brush her hair. She put on a sports bra, T-shirt, tights, her Adidas jacket and pants, and a Toronto Blue Jays cap and headed downstairs.

"How is the air quality right now?" she asked the concierge. Morning was always the worst time for pollution.

"It should be okay. It rained about two hours ago and there's a brisk west wind. Those usually help improve it."

She stepped out of the hotel and crossed the street to reach the promenade, which ran for fifteen hundred metres along the length of the Bund. The concierge had been correct about the wind. It was a brisk westerly that blew directly against Ava as she turned right and began to run. She went past the China Everbright Bank, the Agricultural Bank of China, the Bank of China, the Peace Hotel, and the Shanghai Customs House, and then she reached No. 1, The Bund — the former home of the China Pacific Insurance Company. It had taken her more than seven minutes to negotiate the distance, but with the wind at her back she retraced her steps in six. She ran without any interference from pedestrians; she could count on one hand the number of times that had been the case on the Bund. She made a mental note of the time but knew the weather had to be a contributing factor. Whatever the cause, it was a treat to be able to go back and forth without breaking stride or having to dodge around people walking.

As she ran she thought about VLG and her plans. When she had woken at two it was the first thing on her mind, and she had still been considering strategies when she fell back to sleep. She had a firm idea about what she wanted to do, but she couldn't do anything without hard information, and that meant waiting for Gillian and May Ling. She decided to call both of them after eight o'clock.

"How was the air?" the concierge asked when she walked past him in the lobby.

"Good enough."

"There was a time when I didn't have to ask that question."

"I guess you can't stop progress."

"In China, progress is going to kill the lot of us," he said. "May I ask where you're from?"

"I live in Canada."

"The cleanest air in the world."

"If it isn't, it's close," Ava said. She took off her cap and walked to the elevator.

She made another coffee and sat at the desk to check emails. Maria continued her silence, but Ava's friend Mimi, her sister, Marian, and Jennie Lee had all sent messages. She answered them all and then looked at her phone. May had called rather late to say that Suki was excited by their request for her help and had already plunged into the project. She had also texted Tremendous progress already. There was no news from Gillian or Amanda. Ava headed for the bathroom to shower, encouraged about how the day would unfold.

She called May's room at ten after eight. "I hope it isn't too early," she said when she heard her friend's groggy voice.

"I didn't get to bed until after three. Suki kept me and some of her staff working until two on our project."

"I saw your text."

"It was fantastic what they could find out in such a short time."

"Do you want to share your information over breakfast?"

"Sure, but I'll need at least half an hour to put myself together."

"I'll give you an hour and meet you in the Lobby."

"I've got pages of printouts."

"Bring them with you," Ava said.

"That Suki is such a character," May said. "I met her at a bar near the office, but I barely had a chance to explain our problem and what information we needed before she had me and a couple of her staff back at the office making phone calls and working the computers. You would think it's her business that's being threatened."

"Maybe she views PÖ as an extension of us, and we're an extension of her, and that connects us all."

"There's no doubt about that."

Ava thought of Suki and smiled. She was a short, round woman in her mid-fifties who normally dressed in grey Mao jackets and slacks and never wore a trace of makeup. But beneath the plain exterior was a dynamo. She and her husband had owned the Shanghai-based warehousing and distribution company for many years, but he had always resisted expanding the business. When he died, Three Sisters had invested in it, unleashing Suki. In two years she had already almost doubled the company's size, and her appetite for growth was still not sated.

"What a wonderful partner she is," Ava said.

"Speaking of which, have you heard from Gillian yet?"

"No. I'm just about to call her."

"While you do that, I'll get myself organized," May said.

Rather than phoning Gillian, Ava tried Amanda's room first. When there was no reply, she called her cell.

"Good morning, Ava," Amanda said.

"I'm just checking in. Where are you?"

"I'm in a taxi heading over to Pudong."

"How did it go last night?"

"Haven't you heard from Gillian?"

"Not yet."

"She's probably waiting until she's sure you're up and organized."

"So you found something worth reporting?"

"We made good progress, but we need to make a lot of follow-up phone calls today to confirm things."

"Was Raffi Pandolfo exaggerating?"

"What do you mean?"

"Are they really buying a lot of raw material and partially finished goods from Chinese companies?"

"It certainly looks that way. In fact, it appears that over the past six months they've also started buying finished goods."

"What are we talking about specifically?"

"Ava, you should wait for Gillian to tell you," Amanda said. "I don't want to steal her thunder."

"I can't help being impatient," Ava said. "I just spoke to May, and she and Suki seem to have amassed a ton of logistical information. If your team has had the same kind of success, then we could be ready to move far sooner than I imagined possible."

"That's great news about May, and I know how you love speed, but I still want you to wait for Gillian."

She's right, Ava thought. "Of course, and I won't let on that you and I talked."

"That would be best," Amanda said. "She's quite pleased that you asked her to coordinate on our end. Now you need to let her do that."

Ava ended the call and put the phone back on the desk. There were times when some of the nuances of teamwork escaped her. She had spent so many years working basically alone, involving others, including Uncle, only when and as she needed them. She had forgotten that there were lines of communication that needed to be respected.

She made one more coffee and went to sit by the window and look out on the garden. Her sliver of the Bund was now teeming with traffic and pedestrians. Her mind gravitated to VLG. *If things continue to move at this pace*, she thought, *I'll have to speak to Xu again today*. She had some idea of how far his influence extended, but now she was going to find out how strong it actually was. She also wanted to find out more about his new perfume-manufacturing business. She hadn't asked which brands he was counterfeiting and realized it would be useful to know that, as well as how quickly the factory could duplicate other scents. Her room phone rang and she left the window to answer it.

"Ava Lee," she said.

"It's Gillian."

"How are you?"

"We're well. We worked last night until one, and then started up again an hour ago. But no one's complaining."

"What have you found?"

"The VLG brands are being sold everywhere to just about everyone. Their market penetration is even more impressive than we thought."

"Is there any one brand or customer that looks dominant? Is there anything we can target?"

"Not really."

"Damn," Ava said, wondering why Amanda had been so upbeat.

"But from the supply side, it's a different story," Gillian said.

"How so?"

"VLG is buying container-load after container-load of silk in China, and nearly all of it from Chongqing," Gillian said. "That's not surprising, since China produces seventy-five percent of the world's silk and controls ninety percent of the silk export business."

"Where's the silk going?"

"Mainly France, Italy, and Germany."

"Do we know which factories are making it and export-ing it?"

"Not yet. That's what we're working on. The numbers we have are composites, so we need time to break them down."

"Still, that's encouraging."

"We think what we've found on the leather side is even more so," Gillian said. "We never knew that China is a player in this market, but we certainly appear to be."

"The quality is good enough for VLG brands?"

"Evidently. From what we've discovered, several of their brands are making women's footwear in Huidong and at least two of them are making luggage and handbags in Huadu. Both of those districts are in Guangdong province."

"Near Guangzhou?"

"Yes. And the other major leather centre seems to be Shenzhen. We're not certain if they're making specific prod-ucts, but high-end leather from there is a growing export and VLG is one of the customers."

"Do you know which factories they're using?"

"Not yet, but give us until the end of the day."

"This is fantastic information. Well done."

"We've all made a ton of phone calls, and it's amazing how much information is available online if you know what you're looking for and have even a basic idea of where to start. The Chinese government publishes detailed export data, but only in Chinese. Companies like VLG would have a fit if they knew what kind of information is available."

"You've done a great job. Please pass along my thanks to the rest of the team."

"I haven't forwarded anything to May yet. I thought I'd wait until we confirmed the list of factories and exporters doing business with VLG."

"Don't wait past late afternoon," Ava said. "Whatever you have, send it along by then."

"Okay, and I'll let you know when we do."

Ava checked the time and saw it was ten to nine. She took her notebook from her bag and wrote on a new page:

Chongqing: Silk — Xu?
Huadu and Huidong: Leather bags and shoes — Lam?
Shenzhen: Leather — Lop and Sonny?

21

MAY WAS ALREADY IN THE RESTAURANT WHEN AVA arrived. She had a table near the rear windows, which afforded a marvellous view of the two massive floor-to-ceiling jade-green murals by Helen Poon. The murals had been commissioned from the Hong Kong artist and were a perfect complement to the hotel's art deco style. What Ava loved about them was the way they shimmered and changed colour with the shifting light.

As was becoming customary in the morning, May wore sunglasses. She complained that her eyes were puffy when she woke up, and the glasses had become a fixture. In Ava's mind they were completely unnecessary. May had beautiful eyes, and Ava hadn't seen a single line or puffiness on any morning, except for after a night of heavy drinking.

"Hey," Ava said when she reached the table.

"Hey, yourself," May said, looking up from the menu. "I've just ordered a pot of coffee. I'm not sure if I want to eat. Suki and I shared a midnight snack."

"Coffee will be fine with me. I had a late dinner at Xu's."

May started to say something and then stopped. She

closed the menu and reached for the brown leather briefcase that rested against her chair. "Here's what we found," she said, depositing a thick pile of printouts on the table.

Ava leafed through the first few pages. "Could you summarize for me?"

"We focused entirely on what VLG and its subsidiaries are sending to China. Suki and her people contacted friends who work at the major shipping lines and air freight operations. They persuaded them to send us their import records for VLG and the VLG companies on your list. Some of the most exclusive designer clothing comes in by air, and so do jewelry and watches. Other clothes are shipped by sea. The leather goods are transported by air and sea. The liquor and perfume all seem to arrive in ocean containers."

"Is this information up to date?"

"As of yesterday evening."

"What does it detail?"

"A list of the air shipments arriving over the next forty-eight hours at various entry points; the ocean containers that VLG companies on your list have in transit to China; and containers in Chinese ports that are waiting to be cleared by Customs."

"How comprehensive is the data?"

"Well, it isn't complete. Suki doesn't have friends at every company, but she seems to think it represents a fairly high percentage of VLG's import activity."

"This is wonderful."

"We thought it might make you happy."

Ava shook her head. "Between this and what Gillian and the Pudong team have found, we're miles ahead of where we were last night."

"What did Gillian find?"

"VLG is buying raw material, mainly leather and silk, it appears, and even finished goods in China."

"Do you want Suki to start looking at those exports?"

"Not yet. She needs to focus on imports," Ava said. "Do we have ETAs and ports of entry for the inbound goods?"

"They're listed under every container and air shipment."

"That's all we need."

"What do you have in mind?" May asked as their coffee arrived.

Ava waited until the server had finished pouring and left the table. "Containers will need to get lost or misplaced. Can Suki's friends at the shipping companies help make this happen?"

"I imagine it's possible — all it takes is an incorrect computer entry. But we can't ask them to go crazy. They have jobs they need to protect."

"Can air shipments disappear?"

"I don't see why not. It happens all the time anyway."

"How about at Customs?"

"What do you mean?"

"Can she arrange for Customs to delay clearing air and sea shipments?"

"Maybe in Shanghai, but I doubt she has that level of contacts anywhere else."

"Okay, we'll have to work something out when it comes to that," Ava said. "But for starters, why don't we get Suki's contacts at the shipping companies to temporarily lose one inbound container each, and for each of the air freighters to screw up a shipment or two."

"Do you care what's in the shipments?"

"By sea, I don't think it matters. By air, it would be nice if it were watches and jewelry. Whatever it is, I want to know the bill of lading numbers for the air freight and the container numbers for the ocean shipments."

"Why?"

"So I can tell Raffi Pandolfo."

May lowered her sunglasses and looked at Ava over the rims. "I'm not sure I heard you correctly."

"What's the point of hurting them if they don't know it's us?"

"Do you really think we should tip them off that quickly?" May said. "Why put them on alert? Why not wait until we've got some other things in motion and they're wondering what the hell is going on? Then we can drop an even bigger mess on them."

Ava hesitated and then tapped the printouts in front of her. "On second thought, I think you're right," she said. "It could be more effective to have them confused, and it would certainly make it easier for us to attack other parts of their business if they're not overly suspicious. We can do a lot of damage before they figure out what's going on. But at some point they need to know we're the ones causing them pain, and that we have the capacity to keep doing exactly that."

"They might figure that out for themselves."

"All the better if they do, but we can't count on it."

"Would you mind telling me what else you have in mind, after Suki gets her contacts to misplace some containers and air freight?"

"I don't know specifically. We need to hear from Gillian first, and I'll need to talk to Xu again."

"Are you going to try to cut off their Chinese supply lines?"

"Yes, but I can't do anything unless I know which factories are making goods for them, and for that I have to wait for Gillian. Once I do, we then have to see what pressure Xu can exert."

"How about asking Suki to tie up some of their outbound shipments?"

"Let's not ask too much of Suki's contacts for now. It can always be a backup option if Gillian and Xu can't give us what we need."

"Ava, how far are you prepared to go with this?"

"I don't know. I haven't set any limits. Does that bother you?"

May sat back in her chair, pushing her sunglasses back into place. "When I was with Suki last night, she asked me about Dominic Ventola. I told her about him telling us to get the fuck out of Clark's life. Then I told her about his phone call to you at the airport. Later, when I was alone in my room, I thought about the story in that fashion paper and the phone calls his people made to my friends."

"What are you trying to say, May?"

"If you had set limits, I'd really like you to forget them. We're at war. And I don't care if there's collateral damage."

"I don't care either. But I'm not sure what that says about you and me."

22

AVA CALLED XU AFTER MAY LEFT FOR SUKI'S OFFICE.

"How is your day?" she asked.

"Do you need me?"

"I think I will."

"Then my day is open. I have a couple of meetings, but none of them are urgent and they can be postponed or cut short. I'll keep my phone on. Call me when you're ready to meet or talk."

"There's something you can do for me in the interim," Ava said. "Could you look at the list of perfumes you're making right now and see if any are VLG brands? If there aren't any, can you let me know how long it would take to get started on at least one?"

"I can do that."

"And Xu, whose territory is Guangdong province? I'm assuming it's Lam's."

"It is."

"Does that include Huidong and Huadu?"

"It does."

"How about Shenzhen?"

"It's run by a different gang, but they have an association with Uncle's old organization in Fanling. Lop stays in touch with both of them."

"In touch?"

"Let's just say they're happy to have him as an advisor."

"So if we need help in Shenzhen..."

"It shouldn't be a problem."

"Last: Chongqing?"

"It's run by some locals I don't know very well. If you needed something done there I'd send Suen and some of his men."

"The locals wouldn't mind?"

"This is Suen we're talking about."

"Of course."

"When will all of this become clearer?" he asked.

"Maybe by late today."

"You're not wasting any time."

"We can't afford to."

"Then I won't mention anything until I hear from you."

"I think that's best."

Ava ended the call and looked at her watch. It was only quarter past ten and an entire day stretched out in front of her. She looked at the paperwork May had left and decided to take it back to her room.

Three hours later, she had filled four pages in her notebook and had acquired a grudging admiration for how cleverly Ventola and Pandolfo had built their company. During the presentation in Milan she had seen how functions such as administration, sales, and marketing were centralized, but as she examined the shipments brand by brand, another pattern emerged — VLG had also centralized most of its production.

The company had seven perfumes under different labels, for example, but all of them were manufactured in or near Grasse, a town northwest of Nice, France. Ava was sure that if she could see the bills of lading accompanying the perfume shipments, they would confirm that several of them came from the same factory. The shipments of four watch brands had all originated in and around Geneva. Designer clothing was being made in Italy, France, and Germany, and the Italian products all came from Florence, Milan, and Como.

Ava noted that the leather goods were also Italian in origin and that manufacturing was centred in Naples and Florence. She wondered how much Chinese leather was now finding its way into that production process, and if any was, whether it was declared as such. And how about the shoes being made in Huidong — where were they shipped to and what did their labels say? Surely not "Made in China."

It was early afternoon when she closed the notebook. She hadn't eaten all day and now felt hunger pangs. She thought about ordering room service and then decided that going downstairs to Yi Long Court, the hotel's Chinese restaurant, made more sense. She pushed back from the desk, put her phone and notebook in her bag, and got up to leave the room. She was halfway to the door when her phone rang. It was May.

"Hey. Are you with Suki?"

"Yes. We're still working on those containers and air shipments."

"Any progress?"

"Some envelopes filled with cash are being delivered here and there, but some of Suki's contacts aren't in their offices yet. This is all person-to-person dealing. We have to wait for them."

"I understand."

"But I can tell you that a container of Scottish whisky has been put in the wrong slot in the Port of Shanghai, and that a shipment of watches won't be able to be found at Pudong Airport until her contact decides it's time for it to reappear."

"That's a start."

"You don't sound particularly pleased."

"I've spent the past few hours going over the import records. A few lost containers and air shipments will probably just be an annoyance. We're going to have to jack it up to get their attention," Ava said. "Did Suki speak to anyone at Customs?"

"She had coffee with a friend who's a customs supervisor at the port."

"And?"

"He can delay any number of shipments, but he really pressed her about why she wanted it done."

"What did she tell him?"

"The truth. She said that VLG is screwing over a young Shanghai-based designer and a small Chinese company that she has shares in, and she's looking for a way to get back at them," May said. "She's known this friend for a very long time. In fact, he's her husband's second cousin."

"How did he react?"

"He was very sympathetic. And he told her that if she really wants to give VLG some grief there's a far better of way of doing it."

"And that is?"

"He didn't tell her. He said it would involve several of his colleagues and that it would cost eighteen thousand renminbi to get them to go along. But he promised her she'd like what she got for the money."

"I thought he was family."

"Maybe eighteen thousand is the family discount."

"It's only three thousand U.S.," Ava said. "What do we have to lose? Tell her to tell him she'll pay."

"I already did. She'll be visiting him at his house tonight."

"How are you going to spend the rest of your afternoon?" Ava asked.

"I'm going to stay here. Along with sticking it to VLG, Suki and I are going over the last-quarter results for her actual business and talking through her plans for next year."

"I'm waiting to hear from Gillian. The moment I do, I'll be in touch with Xu."

"Keep me posted."

Yi Long Court was still quite busy when Ava approached the host, but a moment later she had a window table and a view of the congested Bund and the laboriously moving Huangpu River. She ordered hot and sour soup with abalone, sliced pork knuckle with shredded jellyfish, and Fukien-style fried rice. The dishes came in rapid order and Ava dug in as if she hadn't eaten in days. The rice was heavy — fried egg, scallops, spring onions, and shrimp mixed in with a brown sauce — and she normally couldn't get through a serving, but this time she had no problem. She was even considering ordering some custard tarts for dessert when her phone rang.

"Ava Lee."

"It's Gillian. I thought you'd like an update."

"You sound pleased."

"Well, we've got the names of three companies in Chongqing that are shipping silk to VLG, and we know who is making shoes for them in Huidong and where they're buying leather in Shenzhen."

"What about the luggage and bags from Huadu?"

"We're still working on it."

"Email me everything you have so far."

"Right away. And Ava, how are May and Suki doing?" Gillian said.

"They're about to inflict a little pain on Mr. Ventola, and over the next two or three days we're going to increase it. The information you've unearthed is going to make a major contribution."

"In what way?" Gillian's abruptness surprised Ava.

"I would prefer to tell you as things materialize," she said. "But essentially our intention is to eliminate or disrupt as much of their Chinese supply base as we can."

"Do you really think we can do that?"

Ava hesitated. She wasn't sure how much Gillian knew about her previous life, and this wasn't the time to start explaining it. "Yes, I think we can."

"And how soon will we start to see some results?" Gillian asked. "I'm sorry if I sound pushy, but Clark is anxious and I'm worried about him. He was fine when we left the hotel last night, but he's been inundated with phone calls from friends, from people who went to Central St. Martin's with him, and from some of our old private-label customers. They've all seen or heard what Ventola said and are appalled by it. The problem is that all their concern and anger is getting him wound up."

"And you can't calm him?"

"I'm trying, but every time he talks to one of them he gets upset all over again. Several suggested he call the newspaper, and one even said he should fly to Milan and confront Ventola."

"He wouldn't do that, would he?"

"Of course not. The point is that he's getting increasingly agitated and I'm worried about him losing control."

"He needs to give our plan a chance to work. He needs to be patient," Ava said. "Is he nearby?"

"He's in the boardroom with Chi-Tze and Amanda."

"Are you talking to me on your cell?"

"Yes."

"Put it in speaker mode and carry it to the boardroom. I'll speak to everyone when you get there."

Ava heard a door close and then Gillian's footsteps striking the tile floor of the sample factory. A moment later she heard other voices in the background, and then Gillian said, "Ava's on the line. She wants to talk to us."

"Can you hear me?" Ava said.

"Yes," replied a chorus of voices.

"I want to thank you for everything you've done over the past twenty-four hours. The information you've provided is invaluable. May and Suki have been equally successful," Ava said. "Over the next twenty-four hours, the information you've collectively uncovered will be put to good use. It is too soon to go into any details about what we're going to do. I can only promise you that we'll make an impact and get VLG's full attention. My hope is that within a few days they'll be motivated to start negotiating a resolution to this dispute."

There was a long pause before Chi-Tze said, "Is there anything more we can do to help?"

"Yes. Find as many Chinese sources of supply for VLG as you can, and when you can't find any more, look at Vietnam, Indonesia, and Malaysia and see what you can find there. Our reach can extend that far and even farther."

"We're on it," Chi-Tze said.

"Good. So let's all stay calm and keep gathering information. I'm more confident now than I was yesterday that we'll succeed," Ava said. "Gillian, email me the names of the factories as soon as you can."

"Right away."

"Clark, I know this has to be harder on you than for the rest of us. How are you doing?"

"I'm good."

"I don't expect you to be 'good' and I won't be disappointed if you aren't. What I do want is for you to be determined to see this through with us to the end," Ava said. "We are all completely devoted to you, and no one more so than your sister. So please, just hang in there and believe that we'll win. I promise you we will."

23

XU DIDN'T ANSWER HIS PHONE, SO AVA LEFT A VOICE message and then sent a text saying, I'm eager to meet. When are you available? She signalled for the server to bring her bill. Before he returned with it, her phone rang.

"Where are you?" Xu said.

"At the hotel."

"I'll pick you up at the entrance in about twenty minutes, if that works."

"Perfect," she said.

She checked her emails and saw a message from Gillian. It was the list of factories and exporters they'd found in Chongqing, Shenzhen, and Huidong. Ava took her notebook from the bag and copied the names into it. Then she tore a page from the back and made a separate list for Xu. Having the names gave her a feeling of some momentum, but they'd mean nothing if she couldn't make use of them.

She went out the hotel's main door and stood to its right, where she was shielded from the elements. The sky had turned almost black. The pedestrians on the promenade were leaning into the wind, which seemed to have intensified since the morning. The temperature was probably eight or nine degrees, but the damp air and biting wind made it feel colder. She was certain it was going to rain, and when it did, anyone on the promenade without a large umbrella was going to get soaked. She shivered and bundled herself more tightly into the small alcove, where the wind couldn't get at her and an overhanging roof would keep her dry.

She saw Xu's Mercedes turn into the hotel driveway but waited until it was almost directly in front of her before stepping into view. Suen started to climb out of the front passenger seat but Ava shouted at him to stay where he was. A gust of wind caught her as she reached for the back door handle, a sheet of rain following in its wake and almost blinding her. She opened the door and leapt in.

"I'd forgotten how miserable winter can be here," she said, wiping water from her eyes.

"It isn't much different from Hong Kong," Xu said.

"That doesn't make either of them pleasant."

"Do you prefer snow and ice?" Xu asked, bemused.

"A Canadian winter can be dry. It doesn't get into your bones the way this weather does."

"I'll have to experience it some time."

Ava sat back in the seat. "Thanks for coming so quickly."

"I was at a meeting nearby," Xu said. "I assumed from your message that you have some information for me."

"We've found out where VLG is buying silk and some leather goods."

"Is it from a number of companies?"

"Yes, three in Chongqing for silk and one in Huidong for shoes. And two companies in Shenzhen are supplying them with various types of leather."

"We'll go over them when we get to the house."

There was loud crack of thunder, followed by a lightning flash over the river. As the car pulled onto Zhongshan Road the rain began to pound, beating on the car as if it were a drum. Ava felt sympathy for the poor souls caught on the promenade.

"I had the manager of our perfume factory send me the names of all the brands we're making, and I asked him to talk to our European perfumers about VLG's products," Xu said.

"European perfumers?"

"The two people we hired. They refer to themselves as perfumers, though the manager calls them 'les nez,' the noses."

"Have you seen what he sent?"

"Not yet. We can look at the information together."

The car twisted its way through the French Concession. Despite the number of times she'd gone to Xu's house, she could never remember the route. They never seemed to go the same way twice, and she wondered if that was deliberate.

After fifteen minutes of stop-and-go driving with the windshield wipers slapping at full speed, she saw through the rain-streaked window a familiar neon sign advertising a bakery, and then another identifying a restaurant called Les Deux Garçons. She knew they were close, and a moment later the car turned into the lane that led to Xu's house. The fruit cart was where it always stood, its contents getting pelted by the rain while the vendor stood under a Wilson golf umbrella. As they crawled past, Suen waved at him through a closed window.

The wooden gate swung open and the car squeezed through. The driver inched as close to the front door of the house as possible. The door opened and Auntie Grace stood just inside. Wen, the head of Xu's security detail, appeared at the back door of the car with an umbrella.

Ava climbed out of the car. Wen sheltered her with the umbrella and led her to the door. Then he turned and went back for Xu.

"I hate rain," Auntie Grace said.

"Especially when it's so cold and gloomy and windy," Ava said.

"Well, it's warm and bright inside."

"Where do you want to sit?" Ava asked Xu as he entered the foyer.

"I have to go to my office to print the names of the perfume brands. Why don't you wait for me in the kitchen."

"Will you eat?" Auntie Grace asked.

"No, thank you," said Ava. "I just finished lunch."

"Some tea would be perfect," Xu said.

Ava followed Auntie Grace into the kitchen and sat at the table. She took out her notebook and placed it in front of her. She looked at the information Gillian had sent. Beside the names of the silk companies in Chongqing that were supplying VLG she wrote: *How many others sell silk to VLG?*

Auntie Grace put a pot of tea and two cups on the table. "You look worried," she said.

"We have a few business problems, but nothing we shouldn't be able to handle," Ava said.

"We're already making one of the VLG perfumes," Xu said, coming through the doorway with a piece of paper in his hand.

"That's great."

"Here's the list," he said, sliding the paper over to her.

"Some very famous names here. You didn't start out small," she said.

"The perfumers say the better known the brand, the easier it is to copy, because they were analyzing them in their old job and already know the composition," Xu said. "Does VLG own a company called Pomminville?"

"Yes."

"Then Rêves Blancs is their perfume. It's selling very well for us."

"How long would it take for the noses to create copies of two more?"

"Which ones?"

"Diva and Suddenly."

"I'll ask, but as I told you, it's the bottle that usually takes longer to perfect."

"When can you call the factory manager and start the process?"

"Right now if you want," he said.

Ava noticed that Xu had a small smile on his lips. "Sorry, I know that sounded pushy," she said. "It can wait until you have the time."

"I'll do it later today. Now, what do you have for me?"

She passed him the page she'd ripped from her notebook. "Here are the names and addresses of the companies that are making and/or shipping goods from China to VLG operations. At the top are the ones in Chongqing that make or export silk for VLG. We need your help getting those silk companies to stop."

"For how long?"

"A week, two weeks, a month. I really don't know, but for as long as it takes to make an impact."

"No more manufacturing for VLG?"

"No, and I don't want them to ship anything they've already made, and if it's possible I'd like them to freeze any shipments that are already en route."

"That will cost those companies an awful lot of money."

"I know...Maybe they can divert production time and goods to their other customers."

"And if they can't?"

"Then we'll find a way to offset their short-term losses or cash-flow problems. All that matters is that VLG's silk supply gets cut off."

"Assuming that's possible, what's to stop VLG finding alternative supply sources? From what I understand, there are dozens of suppliers in the Chongqing region."

"We should warn off as many as we can from selling to VLG. Even if we don't get to all of them, it will take time for the Italians to find new suppliers."

"That may work over the short term."

"Yes, we can't reasonably expect to shut down their supply completely for any substantial length of time."

"You mean 'unreasonably'?" Xu said, clearly amused.

"My goal is to get VLG's attention," Ava said, ignoring his gibe. "Interfering with their silk supply, even for a short time, is only part of the strategy. We're also going to disrupt some of their imports. And then there is the leather and leather-goods business in and around Guangzhou and Shenzhen that has to be halted. I know these measures won't be indefinite, but if we can affect VLG's activity in all those areas, it will cause them enough pain that they'll be forced to take us seriously."

"For this to have an impact, they'll have to know who's orchestrating the disruptions."

"I know."

"How will you do that?"

"I haven't figured it out yet. First we need to make things happen."

"You mentioned imports."

"That's already started. By the end of the day they're going to be missing containers and air shipments at the two Shanghai airports and the Port of Shanghai."

"Lop could arrange the same delays in Hong Kong if you want. Remember, we have terrific working relationships with Customs and the freight companies there."

"Then please ask him to do it," Ava said. "The more valuable the loads, the better. I'll need some idea of the contents, the container numbers, and the bill of lading details."

"Consider it done," Xu said. "Now, as for Chongqing, I'll personally call my local contacts there and tell them what I want to happen. If they think they'll need help — which I expect they will — I'll send Suen with a group of his men."

"What about the factory in Huidong that's making shoes?"

"Lam is the man to make that come to a halt. Do you want me to call him or will you do it yourself?"

"I would prefer if you talked to him. He may owe me a few favours, but I don't have any official standing with him. He might be inclined to do more and move faster if the request comes from you."

"I don't think that's necessarily true, but I'll make the call anyway."

"When you do, could you also mention the factories in Huadu that are making luggage and handbags? We don't have any detailed information about them yet, but I imagine we'll get it later today."

"Okay, I'll let him know."

"That leaves the leather exporters in Shenzhen."

"Lop can deal with them."

"Xu, would you have any objections if Sonny played a role? He has a lot of contacts in Shenzhen, and of course he was part of the Fanling gang for many years."

"I think Lop would be happy to have him along. He has a lot of respect for Sonny. The two of them socialize quite a bit in Hong Kong."

"Would Lop be okay if Sonny had equal responsibility?"

"I don't see why not. I'll tell him to treat Sonny as a partner."

"Let me talk to Sonny first and make sure he's okay with this," Ava said. "He's rather territorial when it comes to anything involving me. If he found out about the job from anyone else he'd be offended."

"I understand. Lop and Suen are the same where I'm concerned. Let me know when you've had your conversation."

Ava nodded. "So where does this leave us?"

"I believe I have a lot of phone calls to make, while you go off to dream up new ways to make Dominic Ventola's life as miserable as possible."

24

XU AND SUEN WERE SITTING BY THE FISHPOND MAKING plans when Ava left the house to go back to the Peninsula. Despite Xu's support, she had no sense of how successful they might be. It was one thing to think that Xu could bring the full weight of his organization down on the businesses in Chongqing, but another to expect those businesses to follow through. She had the same reservations about Lam and Huidong, but absolutely none about what Lop and Sonny could accomplish in Shenzhen. Who would have the nerve to say no to them?

Despite being only a wiry five foot nine, Lop Ying was one of the most terrifying men she'd ever met. It was his manner that people found alarming. His eyes didn't focus on any one thing for long and his body was constantly moving. He seemed permanently on edge, always poised to strike. But in Ava's mind, Lop paled in comparison to Sonny. Maybe that was because she knew him better and had seen him in action more often. But even if she hadn't, there was no denying Sonny's physical threat at six foot four and 260 pounds. Despite his size, Sonny had the agility of an acrobat, was a skilled martial artist, and had a cold, dispassionate, and — when aroused — vicious temperament. Sonny had been Uncle's bodyguard and driver. When Uncle died, Ava inherited his loyalty and his willingness to do absolutely anything to defend his boss, a trait he shared with Lop.

Ava didn't need Sonny in Toronto, which was just as well, because he would never have adjusted. Their understanding was that he would drive for her brother and Amanda when Ava wasn't in Hong Kong or if she didn't need him elsewhere in Asia. But when she was there, she got one hundred percent of his dedication and attention.

She waited until she got back to her room at the hotel before calling him. He answered immediately with a loud, "Hey, boss!"

"Are you in Hong Kong?"

"I'm in Tai Wai New Village. I drove your brother and Simon To to the grand opening of another of their noodle restaurants."

"Are you free to talk?"

"Sure. I'm standing outside by the car."

"I have a job for you," she said.

"Where?"

"Shenzhen."

"Are you going to be there?"

"No, I'm in Shanghai and I think I'll be here for at least a few more days, if not longer," Ava said. "This is a job that's really important to me and my business, and I need you to handle it in my absence."

"Whatever you want."

"It isn't something you can do alone, though, and Xu is going to ask Lop to help. Do you have any objections to working with him as a partner?"

"None. We get along fine."

"Good. And I was told that your and Uncle's old gang in Fanling has some strong contacts in Shenzhen. Do you stay in touch with that crew?"

"Yeah."

"It might be smart to talk to them about what you're going to do. If there are any local gangs involved with the people I want you to meet, then at least you can give them a heads-up. And who knows, they might actually be able to help."

"What is it you want me to do? If it's important enough to involve Lop and bring the Fanling gang into the loop, then I'm obviously not delivering gifts for you."

"Sonny, an Italian company called VLG is trying to put us out of business. We need to retaliate. They're buying leather from three companies in Shenzhen. That has to stop, and stop now. I don't want them doing any more production for VLG. Whatever they have on hand that's earmarked for VLG can't be shipped. If they have products in transit, I want to see if we can pull them back."

"Okay," he said without hesitation.

"If we can work out an accommodation with the Italians, this won't be a permanent situation. It might last a week or two and then the companies can go back to business as usual. But they don't go back until we tell them they can."

"Do you want us to shut them down entirely or just stop that one part?"

"Just their VLG production and shipments. And hopefully they have other business to pick up the slack."

"I get it."

"Now, I don't mind paying them a bit of money to

co-operate. And I'll certainly look after any costs associated with having goods shipped back or put into storage."

"What if we arrange it so you don't have to pay?"

"I understand what you're saying and we may end up there, but why don't you start by making a goodwill offer."

"Lop isn't so keen on goodwill. He thinks it wastes time."

"Convince him to make it anyway."

"I'll try."

"And I have no doubt you'll succeed," Ava said. "Now I'm going to call Xu and tell him you're onside when it comes to working with Lop, and then I'll send you the names and addresses of the companies."

"I'll wait to hear from you before I contact him, and after I get those names I'll contact some of the guys in Fanling and see if they know any of the companies."

"What are the chances?"

"If they don't know them, it's more than likely they know someone in Shenzhen who does. The triads have made serious inroads in that city in recent years."

"Sonny, I'd like to make this happen quickly."

"Yes, boss."

"That doesn't mean taking chances or being so aggressive that outside authorities get involved."

"Lop can be smooth when he needs to be, and after watching Uncle operate for so many years, I'm not so bad myself."

Smooth was the last word that came to mind when Ava thought about Lop or Sonny, but she said, "I'm sure you both can be."

"But the bottom line is that you want these shipments stopped, right?"

"That's the bottom line."

"We'll get it done."

"I'm sure you will," Ava said. "Now, what's the best way for me to send you the information?"

"Phone me, and if for some reason you can't get me, then send a text."

"Until then," Ava said.

She turned on her computer to check emails and saw nothing of any importance. She picked up her phone and sent a text to Xu that said, Sonny is onside. He'll be happy to work with Lop. Please set it up on your end. I'm sending the contact information to Sonny, so you can do the same with Lop if you want.

Sonny's phone went directly to voicemail. Ava texted him the factory information and added, You should call Lop tonight and organize your Shenzhen visit.

It was almost five o'clock when she had finished. She yawned as her adrenalin ebbed and jet lag rushed in to fill the space. She imagined she'd be having dinner with May and whoever else wanted to join them, but normally May ate quite late and Ava knew it would be a struggle to stay alert for that long. *A nap would help*, she thought, and then discarded the idea. She'd tough it out, she decided, and that meant staying active. She went to the window and looked outside. The rain had stopped and the wind seemed to have settled. She figured there was about forty-five minutes of daylight left. Ten minutes later she had left the hotel in her tracksuit and cap and was walking along the promenade.

She worked her way around the slower pedestrians. The wind had abated, but not to the extent she'd imagined while standing by the window in her room. It still blew in bitterly cold gusts that made her eyes water and her nose run.

As annoying and uncomfortable as that was, it did provide enough of a distraction that she hardly noticed when the sun set and the street lamps came on.

Back in the hotel, she stepped into the shower for the second time that day. When she emerged, she felt refreshed. She put on a clean shirt and slacks and sat down in a green leather chair by the window. She looked at her mobile phone and saw she'd missed calls from Gillian and May. They'd left messages simply saying to phone them back. Ava tried May first.

"I called an hour ago," May said.

"Sorry, I went out for a walk."

"Suki wanted to be here when I told you how we've done, but she just left to have dinner with her husband's cousin, the customs officer."

"I remember who he is. Let's hope she has some luck with him."

"Well, after hearing her sweet talk and/or browbeat freight and shipping agents for most of the day, I don't think luck or even the money we spend has anything to do with it," May said. "She's an unstoppable force of nature."

"So you did well?"

"There are now four inbound containers filled with VLG products misplaced in the Port of Shanghai. And when I say 'misplaced,' I mean they aren't going to be found until we decide they are."

"Is it that easy to lose them?"

"I knew the port was busy, but the actual numbers are beyond anything I imagined. As it turns out, the equivalent of more than thirty-five million twenty-foot containers go in and out of the port every year. That's three million a month. One hundred thousand on any given day."

"Then I guess it is."

"She's also arranged for three air shipments to go astray. The warehouses are smaller and the goods are harder to hide, so they've put them into trucks and parked offsite."

"That sounds a bit like theft."

"Only if they're not returned, and that's the plan... eventually."

"Do you have the container numbers and the air waybill numbers?"

"Are we having dinner?"

"I'd like to."

"Then I'll bring them with me."

"Will Suki join us?"

"I don't know how long she'll be with the cousin. She said she'd phone when she was done."

"Have you asked the girls and Clark?" Ava said.

"I haven't spoken to them."

"I'll call Gillian and invite them."

"I'm holding a table at Mercato. Again. It's at No. 3, The Bund. I can meet you at the hotel and we can walk over there together."

"What time?"

"Eight, so let's say we hook up at seven forty-five in the hotel lobby."

"Perfect."

"Wait, don't go yet," May said. "You haven't told me what kind of day you had."

"Things are in motion. I met with Xu and, as I thought, he's happy to help, but it's going to be a day or two before we know the outcome."

"You're optimistic?"

"He plans to send Suen and some men to Chongqing if that's necessary."

"Oh."

"We also think that Lam — the guy who runs the triads in Guangzhou — will help us in Huidong and Huadu."

"I see."

"And in all likelihood, Sonny and Lop will be paying a personal visit to the leather manufacturers in Shenzhen."

"Who in their right mind would say no to any request from those two?"

"That's exactly what I thought when I asked them to do it," Ava said. "And, in answer to your question about me being optimistic, let's just say that I'm cautiously so."

25

AVA PHONED GILLIAN PO AND FOUND HER SOUNDING
much happier than the last time they'd spoken. Gillian's
team had not only found the names of the two factories in
Huadu that were making luggage and handbags for VLG,
they had actually spoken to senior marketing people at those
companies and had a list of the specific brands they were
manufacturing in part or in whole.

"I talked to the one making handbags, told them we were
thinking of launching our own line of PÖ bags, and asked
if they thought they could meet our quality requirements,"
Gillian said. "The marketing guy immediately began to talk
about the brands they're already making. It's quite a few
more than just VLG, but he really stressed their VLG production as an indicator of how good their quality is."

"It's good to know they're producing for more than one
customer. It means they should be able to stop making products for VLG and still maintain a solid business."

"And what a strange business it seems to be."

"What do you mean by that?"

"Well, when I mentioned the possibility of the factory's

manufacturing the PÖ line, his first question was whether I would want our bags to be identified as a product of China."

"What did you say?"

"I asked him what the other companies did," Gillian said. "He laughed and said they typically want them identified as products of Italy or France."

"How is that possible unless they're deliberately mislabelling the bags?"

"Maybe some of them are, but he said that as long as part of the production is done in, for example, Italy, the 'Made in Italy' label is legal."

"Part of the production?"

"He said the most common thing is for them to send the bags without the handles attached."

"The handles are made in Italy?"

"No, they're made in China and sent with the bags. They're simply attached in Italy."

"What a joke."

"It gets worse," Gillian said. "Some companies want the bags sent completely assembled except for the 'Made in' label. Evidently putting it on counts as part of the manufacturing process."

"How long has this been going on?"

"They've been making leather for years, but he said it's only over the past year that they've starting making finished goods for the brands."

"Does the luggage manufacturer operate the same way?"

"Identically. And that's not surprising, because the two companies are connected."

"What makes you think that?"

"Towards the end of our conversation, the marketing

guy said they have so much business that unless we move quickly there might not be any production capacity left in his factory. I then asked if there were any other options he could recommend. He said they have a sister company that's making luggage but is starting to diversify into handbags. It's the company making luggage for VLG. I asked him if they operate in the same way when it comes to labelling. He said they do and then warned me again about production capacity. He said that both factories are going to be facing that challenge."

"When we get them to stop manufacturing for VLG, that will free up some capacity," Ava said, and laughed. "Now I don't feel quite so bad about leaning on them."

"Do you think we can actually get them to stop?"

"We have friends who are going to persuade them that it's the best thing to do. And what you just told me should make it easier for them to say yes."

Gillian paused. "Amanda told me not to ask too many questions about how you intend to put pressure on VLG," she said hesitantly.

"Amanda was right."

There was another silence before Gillian said, "Do you want me to email you the information?"

"Please."

The younger woman sighed. "It's been a long day. Everyone here is very tired."

"It should be a satisfied tired — you did terrific work," Ava said. "Do you and the others want to join May and me for dinner tonight?"

"I don't know about Amanda, but I think the rest of us are ready to crash."

"Okay, go and get a good night's sleep. And tell Amanda that if she wants to join us we're leaving the hotel at seven forty-five."

"I will, right after I send you the information on Huadu."

Ava sprawled in the chair, a wave of relaxation washing over her. Twenty-four hours earlier they'd been a dispirited, almost depressed lot. Now they'd turned a corner and could be at least hopeful. They'd accomplished a lot in one day. Not enough to change the reality of their position, but maybe enough to start changing VLG's perception of theirs.

She walked over to the desk and checked the computer. Gillian's email had arrived. Ava opened it and copied the essential information into her notebook. When that was done, she forwarded the message to Xu with a note that read: 1. Here is the information that Lam needs for Huadu. Of interest is the fact that the factories are making products for multiple customers, so giving up VLG short-term shouldn't hurt their businesses that much. 2. Do you know if Lop and Sonny have talked? 3. Is Suen going to Chongqing? If so, when? 4. Did you talk to Lam about Huidong? 5. What did your perfumers have to say about the VLG brands I mentioned to you? Warmest, *mei mei.*

She looked at the bedside clock. It was already past seven. Maria would be up now, standing in her T-shirt and underwear at the kitchen counter as she made coffee. She had long, slim legs with a perpetual golden hue, and firm breasts. "Shit. What brought that into my head?" Ava murmured.

She stood, went back to the green chair, and thought instead about VLG's containers in the Port of Shanghai. What were they worth? Certainly millions, but how many? She ran some numbers, calculating how many cases of booze or perfume you could pack into a twenty-foot container, and then multiplied that number by an estimated cost and came up...confused. All she knew for certain was that if it was a number she couldn't figure, it was a number that would hurt VLG.

At seven-thirty she looked at her emails to see if Xu had replied. He hadn't. She had told Gillian that "friends" were going to persuade the factories in Huidong and Huadu to co-operate, but what if Lam wouldn't or couldn't help? She doubted that Xu would send his men into a territory controlled by the Guangzhou gang. Could she send Sonny with some of his friends? She felt a surge of impatience and reached for her phone to call Xu, but then stopped. He wouldn't leave her dangling. He was probably still working through her list of requests and she was certain he'd call when he had answers.

The hotel phone rang. *Xu?* Ava thought as she went to answer it.

"Hi, it's Amanda."

"Are you at the hotel?"

"I just arrived."

"Are you joining us for dinner?"

"No, I'm exhausted."

"I spoke to Gillian a little while ago and she filled me in on what you came up with. It's terrific stuff."

"It's crazy stuff. It's shaken my belief in brands. Who knew you couldn't trust the Italians?"

"Or the French, apparently."

"Any of them," Amanda said. "Will you be able to make good use of the information?"

"I sure hope so," Ava said, thoughts about Lam moderating her response.

"And how was your day? Did we make any progress?"

"We're rolling. Do you want details?"

"No, I believe you, and there's only so much my head can absorb in one day. I can't remember the last time I did an all-nighter."

"Then go to bed."

"I'm going to. Give May a hug for me and I'll see the two of you in the morning."

Ava went into the bathroom, put on some lipstick and mascara, and headed downstairs to meet May. The lobby was crowded and Ava didn't see her until she was almost at the door.

"Hey," she said.

May looked at her almost in surprise, then grinned and held her phone out towards Ava. "I've just spoken to Suki," she said. "Wait till you hear what her husband's cousin has in mind for VLG."

26

AVA WAS EXCITED TO HEAR ABOUT SUKI'S PLAN, BUT the combination of dinner's Pinot Grigio, jet lag, and emotional drain had done a number on her. She and May had eaten a quick meal at Mercato by Jean-Georges, one of the chef's three Michelin-starred restaurants at No. 3 The Bund.

"Are you okay?" May asked as they were walking back to the hotel. "We've had a terrific day and you don't seem particularly enthused."

"I'm tired and my mind is barely functioning," Ava said. "When I get like this, negative thoughts tend to push their way into my head. For example, I was just thinking that none of what we've done will matter if VLG is willing to absorb the losses until they find other factories."

"You do need to sleep," May said.

They were quiet as they strolled along the promenade. After a while, Ava began to sense tension coming from May. She wondered if it was about Xu.

"What's wrong?" she finally asked.

May hesitated, then took a deep breath. "I got a phone call from Pang Fai."

"She usually communicates through me," Ava said.

"I know. I wasn't sure how to handle it at first. I didn't want to put her off by telling her she should talk to you, so I thought I should at least listen to her."

"That was the right approach."

"She began by telling me that her agent was contacted by Raffi Pandolfo. He wanted to know if she was available to do some work for VLG. Raffi said they'd seen her in London and thought she deserved a much larger showcase than the one PÖ could provide. And when the agent didn't dispute that, Pandolfo told him that VLG has been looking for someone to be their face in Asia. He said it's a role that could eventually be expanded to other parts of the world."

"Fai is committed to us."

"And that hasn't changed," May said. "She told the agent that PÖ is the only design company she wants to work with and instructed him to say no to VLG."

"Does she or the agent know the kind of trouble VLG is causing us?"

"It wasn't mentioned."

Ava shook her head. "You had me worried there for a minute."

"It was upsetting to me as well, until Fai made her commitment clear," May said. "But that wasn't what was strange about the call. I think she contacted me for other reasons."

"Such as?"

"You."

"I don't understand."

"She asked me if you were safely back in Toronto. When I told her you're in Shanghai, her manner became less casual," May said. "She told me that when she first met you, it was in

Shanghai at a dinner with Xu and Tsai Men. She wondered if you and Xu have a relationship. I told her that you do, but it's strictly business."

"I told her that myself at the time."

"Well, she didn't remember, or more likely used Xu as an excuse, because then she asked if you have a boyfriend in Canada or in China," May said. "Ava, I didn't want to lie to her, so I told her that you don't."

"There's no harm in that."

"Yes, but then, after stumbling around a bit, she asked me if you're gay. She said some of the models at the London show were gossiping about you and she didn't know what to believe." May reached for Ava's hand. "I was caught off guard. All I could think to say was that I don't feel comfortable discussing your private life."

"Which probably led her to conclude that I am gay."

"Does that matter? I don't think it will bother her," May said. "In fact, I think the opposite may be true."

"What are you trying to say?"

"It's obvious she's attracted to you. When we were in London, she hardly left your side, and both Amanda and Chi-Tze caught her staring at you when you weren't looking."

"She likes men."

As they walked into the lobby of the hotel, May said, "Maybe that's what she wants everyone to think. But for the record, she stopped asking questions when I told her I was uncomfortable. And before she hung up, she reiterated her loyalty to PÖ." She reached down into her bag. "So, back to business. Here are the container numbers and copies of the air waybills for the goods that have gone missing."

"Thanks, and I'm sorry if I'm being overly sensitive," Ava said as she looked over the documents.

"*Momentai.*"

They were about to enter the elevator when Ava's phone rang. She glanced at the incoming number and didn't recognize it. "Ava Lee," she said, motioning for May to go ahead.

"This is Ban Lam in Guangzhou."

"How are you?" she said, feeling slightly unsettled that he'd called her directly.

"I'm okay, or as okay as you can be in this business," he said. "Xu called me a while ago to discuss that problem you have and to ask for a favour."

"Yes?" Ava said, her uneasiness growing.

"I told him it might be better if I was the one to give you the news."

Oh shit, Ava thought, her stomach knotting.

"I told him it's just too fucking funny for me not to tell you myself."

"I beg your pardon?" Ava said, raising her eyebrows at May, who was waiting for her.

"We own those factories in Huidong and Huadu — or at least we have enough shares to control them."

"Are you joking?"

"You know I'm not a man for jokes," he said. "Li helped finance the factories about five years ago. They've been making knockoffs for us ever since."

Ava was surprised at how casually Lam had dropped Li's name into the conversation. Li Kai had been the Mountain Master in Guangzhou until about a year ago, when he was running against Xu for the triad chairmanship. Things had soured between Xu and Li to the point where Li tried to have Xu killed. He obviously hadn't succeeded, and in the aftermath Xu — with Ava's active assistance — had struck a deal with Lam, Li's deputy. It was Lam who put the bullet into Li's head at their final meeting.

"So he had foresight in some things," Ava said.

"He wasn't always inflexible."

"Do you know that the factories are making real designer goods now?" Ava said.

"Yeah, but things haven't changed that much. In fact, it's probably improved our knockoff business."

"How?"

"Instead of copying originals, which involves some guess-work, we can work off the specifications that the designer brands provide."

"But Ban, how can you possibly be competitive in the knockoff market if you're using designer specs? I mean, it must cost you way more to manufacture to that level of quality."

"How much do you think it costs to make one of those designer bags or a pair of designer shoes?" he said.

"I have no idea."

"The factory is making two different bags for Plouffe. Do you know what they sell for?"

"Five to six hundred dollars."

"So take a guess what it costs to make one."

"One hundred dollars," she said.

"Between ten and fifty dollars, depending on the specifica-tions," he replied.

"C'mon. That can't be true."

"Shoes are different," he said. "A five-hundred-dollar pair of shoes costs about one hundred to make. That's why we don't sell our knockoff shoes in street markets."

"How about your profit margins?"

"They're about the same whether we're making a knockoff or filling a designer-brand order. In fact, the way it works now, when the factory gets an order for, say, five thousand designer bags, it makes the same number of knockoffs. It's improved our efficiency."

"What a business."

"It's all bullshit, isn't it. People are paying hundreds of dollars for a name. They think it improves their image when all it does is identify them as suckers."

Ava, like May, was very brand-conscious. Under normal circumstances she would have protested vehemently about being called a sucker, but part of her knew that Lam wasn't entirely wrong. "Thanks for all that information," she said.

"Anyway, the reason I called is that I want to tell you personally that VLG won't be getting anything from Huidong or Huadu unless you tell me otherwise. I've already phoned the plant managers and told them to stop any production we have underway, to put all the other orders on hold, and to recall three shipments that haven't left China yet."

"I don't know how to begin thanking you," Ava said.

"You just did, and don't make too much of it. The factories will just switch over to other brands. Business won't be declining."

"Still, I'm going to owe you."

"No, you're not. This makes us almost square."

"Hardly, but I'm not going to argue with you," she said. "Now, will someone from your factories call VLG to tell them the manufacturing of their products has been suspended, or will the factory wait until VLG calls them?"

"How do you want us to handle it, and what do you want us to say?"

Ava thought about it for a minute and then said, "Don't call them and don't take their calls. Let them guess why they've been cut off. When they do find out, I'd like it to come from us."

"Consider it done."

27

AVA STRIPPED AS SOON AS SHE WALKED INTO THE room, tossing her clothes onto the sofa. She put on a black Giordano T-shirt and went to the bathroom to wash her face and brush her teeth. Then she climbed into bed with her phone. No matter how tired she was, she owed Xu a call.

His mobile rang three times and she was about to hang up when he answered. "Ava, how was your evening?"

"I spoke to Lam, so I imagine you have some idea how it was."

"He was very happy to help."

"He did more than help. I'm going to owe him a favour now."

"He doesn't see it that way, and neither do I. What you did for him isn't so easy to repay."

"We can debate that some other time," Ava said.

"Suen left for Chongqing earlier tonight," Xu said. "He took three men with him. The local gang has arranged a number of meetings. They claim to have laid the groundwork, but that could just be them currying favour and getting ready to take the credit if Suen is successful."

"I can't imagine him not being successful," she said.

"The trick is to make sure the local gang follows up after Suen leaves. That's almost more important than getting the factories and exporters to agree to co-operate for a few weeks. We'll have to make sure the gangs keep leaning on the factories after Suen has left."

"Coercion works best when there are immediate consequences." Then Ava laughed. "I'm sorry, I don't know where that came from. I'm not thinking clearly."

"It sounds clear enough to me."

"Anyway, I'm sure Suen is more than capable of ensuring co-operation without my advice."

Xu went silent, and for a second Ava wondered if she'd lost the connection. Then he said, "I'm going over the list of things you want me to do. It seems the only one left is the perfume."

"Any luck with that?"

"Partially. Our people don't think there'll be any problem copying the scents you mentioned, but our glass man will need at least two weeks to perfect the bottles," Xu said. "And I imagine that you do want the bottles to be perfect."

"Of course."

"Then it's two weeks minimum."

"I understand. Can you ask them to start on the bottles tomorrow?"

"I will."

"You mentioned before that you're already making Rêves Blancs," Ava said. "Is it possible you could jack up the production?"

"I imagine it is, but why would you want us to do that?"

"If we flood the market and sell it at a big enough discount, we can downgrade the brand," Ava said. "We would find a way to cover any loss of profit you incur."

"There's no reason why we couldn't keep selling at the same price. But production can't be ramped up overnight."

"I know, and I'm not sure yet that I even want you to start," she said. "I'm thinking that Rêves Blancs and those other two VLG brands are weapons we can use down the road if the need arises."

"Okay," Xu said. "We'll keep it open as an option."

"That's more than fair, and much appreciated."

"Ava, how long do you think this will go on?"

"It will go on until one of us capitulates," Ava said. "But I know we can't expect you and Lam and all those factories to carry on indefinitely. I don't want to abuse friendships or over-extend favours. In the next week or two we'll get to a point where we'll know if VLG is going to bend. If it's not, then we'll have to revisit our strategy . . . and maybe even revisit our dreams of making PÖ an international brand."

"I certainly hope you don't have to do that," Xu said.

"It would be a worst-case scenario," Ava said, and then yawned so deeply that her upper body shook. "Xu, you need to excuse me. I have to sleep."

"I'll talk to you tomorrow. I'm sure there will be lots to discuss."

Ava put the cell on the bedside table, turned off the main light switch, and slid under the duvet. As a way of inducing sleep, she often imagined doing bak mei exercises. She drifted off at just the thought of it.

For many years her father had dominated her dreams. He would tease her with his presence at airports and hotels and office buildings — always neutral sites. But when she came too close, he would disappear, leaving her searching for him in vain. She never found him, though there were times when she thought she saw him in the distance or among a large crowd. But he was never there for long.

After his death, Uncle had replaced her father in her nighttime wanderings. Unlike her father, he eased her stress rather than being the cause of it. During times of emotional crisis and physical danger he would always appear in his black suit and white shirt buttoned to the collar, a cigarette dangling between his fingers. He would speak softly, the words measured and full of concern and love. He calmed her, and his presence had made dreams something she welcomed rather than feared.

Now she found herself in another dream with Uncle. He was sitting across from her in a crowded restaurant that looked familiar. He had a beer in front of him, Ava a glass of white wine. Several waiters were buzzing around a table on the other side of the restaurant. She was trying to get the attention of a server but was being ignored.

"We can't even get a menu," Ava said. "We should leave."

"Be patient. They will get to us eventually," Uncle said. "I am told this is the best Chinese restaurant in London."

"There are three servers at that table over there. What makes those people so special?"

"I believe the actress Pang Fai is sitting there," Uncle said. "Can you see her? She is the slim woman at the far end, with the sharply cut hair and the long, elegant neck."

"She is beautiful."

"And famous," he said. "But she is sad."

"How do you know that?"

Uncle shrugged. A slight smile tugged at the corners of

his mouth. "There are many things we never had a chance to talk about."

"Then tell me what you know about Pang Fai."

"She has a secret, one so dark that she has barely admitted it to herself."

"Why are you telling me this?"

"She is desperate to find someone she can trust," Uncle said. "She needs someone like you."

Ava looked across the restaurant and felt her heart skip a beat. Even in profile, Pang Fai was exquisite.

"I have her phone number if you want to call her," Uncle said, offering a pack of matches with a number written on the cover.

Ava took the matches, hesitated, and then picked up her phone. As she did, she saw that Fai was doing the same. Before she could enter the number Uncle had given her, her phone rang. She answered, certain it was Fai.

"I thought I would update you," a man's voice said.

Ava opened her eyes. She was in her bed at the Peninsula. Her cellphone was in her hand and Raffi Pandolfo was talking to her. She looked at the clock. It was just past midnight.

"Where are you? What time is it there?"

"I'm in Milan and it's five o'clock on a beautiful late winter evening."

"Why are you calling me?"

"I just finished a conference call with our marketing teams in London, New York, and Paris. I want you to know that the PÖ brand has now officially lost all prospects of doing any meaningful business in Europe and North America."

"You can't lose what you never had."

"You can lose hopes and dreams."

"That sounds almost romantic."

"I can be hopelessly romantic, I admit that," Pandolfo said. "But the real reason I'm calling is to ask you to reconsider your position. It may not be too late to salvage things. I don't really want to play a part in the destruction of Clark Po. He has talent. It needs to be nurtured."

"Is that you speaking or are you passing along a message from Dominic Ventola?"

"It's me, but I know that Dom shares the sentiment," he said. "Despite his bluster, he hasn't closed all the doors."

"Then call off your people and mend the damage you've done."

"I would like nothing more, but we have our terms."

"And we're not prepared to abandon ours."

"By clinging to them you're ensuring that PÖ won't ever be more than a pimple on the fashion world's ass."

"Don't be quite so sure of that."

Pandolfo paused. "You know, I had breakfast with Dom this morning and I said to him, 'That young woman Lee bears watching. There is an edge to her I really like, and I think when this PÖ business is resolved, we should consider doing other business with her.'"

Ava slid out of bed. She walked over to the couch where she had left her clothes and her bag. She took out the list that May had given her.

"Let me tell you a few other things that bear watching," Ava said. "Do you have a pen at hand?"

"Yes."

"I'm going to read some numbers to you. They're long, so I'll read slowly."

"I don't understand the point of this."

"Just write them down. Are you ready?"

"Go ahead," he said, sounding suspicious.

"OCE463987U96," she said. "Did you get it?"

"Yes."

"Good. And PPL948356YL23," she said.

"What are they?"

"The numbers of containers carrying VLG products," Ava said.

28

AVA SLEPT THE REST OF THE NIGHT UNINTERRUPTED and without dreaming. The room was bright when she woke. She felt energy coursing through her body and her head was clear. She glanced at the bedside clock. It was past ten. Next to the clock was the list of container numbers she'd given Pandolfo.

She checked her phone for messages and saw texts from Amanda and May, asking her to call when she was ready for breakfast. She texted them both. I just woke up. See you downstairs in half an hour?

She made coffee and turned on the computer. Sonny had emailed. Ava blinked. It was the first time she'd ever gotten an email from him. On my way to Shenzhen with Lop and some of his men. I'll phone you when we're finished, he wrote.

She scrolled down through the rest of the messages and quickly scanned a newsy one from her mother and another from her sister, Marian. Again there was nothing from Maria.

Ava finished the coffee and went to the bathroom. She brushed her hair and clipped it back while she brushed her teeth. Her mind drifted to thoughts of Maria, and then, almost inexplicably, to Pang Fai. It took a minute before she began to remember fragments of the dream, and another minute before she could see Uncle sitting at a table with her at a restaurant that looked like Hakkasan. May had planted that Pang Fai seed in her head, and Uncle had made it flower. "This is crazy," Ava murmured.

She dressed quickly in slacks and a button-down shirt, checked her phone, and saw that Amanda and May had responded that they would meet her downstairs. She put her phone, notebook, and the list of containers into her bag and left the room.

Amanda and May were already seated in the Lobby with a basket of pastries, a rack of toast, jams, and a large pot of coffee on their table. They both waved at her, and even from a distance she could see their broad smiles. May had obviously briefed Amanda on their success so far.

"So you told her?" Ava said when she reached the table.

"How could I not?" May said.

Amanda stepped around the table and threw both arms around Ava's neck. "I'm so lucky to be working with you and May."

"Everyone manufactures luck. This happens to be our turn," Ava said.

"You slept well?" May asked.

"I did, although Raffi Pandolfo did what he could to disrupt it," Ava said, taking the seat next to Amanda.

"He called again?" Amanda said.

"At midnight, to tell me they've shut us out of Europe and North America. But if we reconsider our position and accept their offer, they'll make everything right for PÖ."

"How did you respond?"

"I don't think I handled it as well as I could have," Ava said, looking at May. "I got irritated. I gave him the numbers of two of the containers we've misplaced."

"Oh, that explains it," May said.

"Explains what?"

"Suki phoned me first thing this morning to say she'd heard from two of the freight agents we persuaded to help us. They were contacted by VLG's import broker and asked about two containers. It must be the two you mentioned to Pandolfo."

"How did the agents respond?"

"As we agreed. They said they couldn't locate them and would have to get back to the broker."

"Hopefully there's more good news to come. Suen is in Chongqing already, and Lop and Sonny will be in Shenzhen this morning."

"Besides Chongqing and Shenzhen, what else is in the works?" Amanda asked.

"That's not enough?" Ava said.

"I was only —"

"I'm teasing," Ava said, smiling.

Just then May's phone rang. She listened for several minutes, nodding and smiling. "Thanks. Ava and Amanda are here. I'll let them know," she said. "That was Suki. The Customs Department has just told her that four television crews and at least six newspapers have confirmed for this afternoon."

29

AT TEN MINUTES TO THREE, TWO TAXIS CARRYING THE
PÖ team stopped at the entrance of the container terminal,
where Suki Chan was waiting in her SUV.

Years before, Ava had been inside Hong Kong's Kwai
Tsing Container Terminals and was astounded by the size
of the port. It was a like being inside a maze covering several
square kilometres, with walls that were thirty metres high.
Kwai Tsing handled about seventy thousand containers a
day, but as impressive as that was, the facility in Shanghai's
Waigaoqiao port area surpassed it by thirty percent. The
world's busiest container port was built on the coast facing
the East China Sea and extended south towards Hangzhou
Bay, where the Yangtze and Qiantang Rivers joined.

The taxis and Suki's SUV were dwarfed by long lines of
trucks, which in turn were dwarfed by rows of containers
above which quay cranes towered.

"It looks chaotic, but it isn't," May said. "The entire system
is supported by top-notch technology that can track every
container. That's why, when you use that technology to lose
a container, it's hard to find."

The taxis followed the SUV as it wove its way slowly past trucks and forklifts. Ava checked her phone. She hadn't heard from either Sonny or Xu, and she was getting anxious about what was happening in Shenzhen and Chongqing.

The SUV veered to the left and drove towards a square four-storey red-brick building with a sign reading CUSTOMS above double doors. To the right of the building was a row of warehouses. A cluster of television trucks and cars was parked in front of the one nearest the customs house. The SUV parked next to them and the taxis followed suit. Suki got out of her car and signalled for the others to wait where they were. She walked into the warehouse, and when she reappeared, a grey-haired man in a blue uniform was with her.

"This is my husband's cousin, Officer Ling," she said.

He nodded. "I told Suki she could bring some friends, but I didn't expect so many of you. I have to ask you to please stay in the background."

"We won't get in the way," Ava said. "But is it okay if we take pictures and video?"

"As long as you are unobtrusive."

"Officer Ling, we really appreciate your help," Ava said.

"The struggle against counterfeiters is endless. We're happy for the assistance that made this possible," he said and walked back towards the warehouse, where the television crews were gathered at the entrance.

"Does he seriously think these goods are counterfeit?" May said.

"Of course not," Suki said. "He's a good actor."

A group of customs officials appeared at the warehouse entrance. "Ladies and gentlemen," a voice boomed from a loudspeaker. The PÖ group edged closer, keeping to the right so they were out of the media sightline but still had a clear view of the proceedings.

"We invited you here today to witness the destruction of counterfeit goods that foreign manufacturers were attempting to smuggle into China. Putting a stop to this trade is one of the biggest challenges we face, but as these seizures prove, we are successfully combatting this illegal practice. Today we are going to destroy a shipment of counterfeit watches. It has a reputed value of more than six million renminbi but isn't worth a fiftieth of that. We also have a container load of alcohol labelled as one of the best Scotch whiskies. It is actually nothing more than cheap liquor," the official said. "Now I ask that you step just inside the warehouse."

The warehouse entrance was wide enough to accommodate the film crews and leave enough room for Ava and her group to stand to one side. Inside the brightly lit warehouse the watches had been dumped across the middle of the concrete floor, along with their boxes, which clearly displayed brand names. Off to the right, twelve cases marked "Dougal's Ten-Year-Old Single Malt Scotch Whisky" were stacked in three rows. Two large oil drums stood next to them. The customs officer who had spoken took a position near the watches. "Tell me when you have all the shots you need," he said to the media. Ava couldn't hear their comments, but a moment later the officer raised his right arm and then she heard a rumble.

Ava began recording the scene with her phone. A small steamroller appeared from the back of the warehouse and slowly drove over the watches. Ava heard glass popping and the crunch of metal being crushed. She made sure that she kept the brand names in clear focus. The steamroller finished its run, reversed back over the watches, and then did another length before reversing again.

The officer walked over to the cases of whisky. "There was too much liquor to dispose of all of it here," he said. "The rest has already been dumped into the sea. But for your cameras, we'll empty these bottles into the drums and do the same with the contents." Four officers stepped forward, opened the cases, and started pouring the whisky into the oil drums while the television cameras ran.

When they had finished, Ava saw the cousin smile at Suki. She gave him a wave and turned to Ava. "We should get going now."

As they walked back to their cars, Ava listened to Clark, Gillian, Chi-Tze, and Amanda talking excitedly about VLG's likely reaction to the destruction of their goods. In real dollar terms, Ava knew the product loss wouldn't affect the company, but the symbolism of the event would not be lost on them. Their power and influence in the East were not as secure as they had imagined. Then she caught herself. "Suki, when do you think VLG will know about their products being destroyed?" she asked.

"I'm sure their import brokers are already asking about the status of the shipments. If they haven't been told already about what's happened, they soon will be."

Ava looked at her watch. It was eight-thirty in the morning in Milan.

"You look preoccupied," May said.

"I'm trying to figure out when we should send the video to VLG."

"Me too. I thought maybe we should wait until their broker

tells them about the seizure and destruction. Then we follow up with the video in a one-two punch."

"I was thinking along the same lines, but I'm starting to feel that we're overthinking this and acting too passively. Why not send it now? Why not be the aggressor?" Ava said. "Let's see if we can put them on the defensive."

"You're right," May said abruptly. "Send it."

Ava stopped walking, took out her phone, and found Raffi Pandolfo's email address. She wrote, Greetings from Shanghai. I have two unfortunate pieces of news for you. The first is that an air shipment of VLG watches and an ocean container filled with Dougal Whisky were identified by Chinese Customs as counterfeits and were destroyed minutes ago. A video is attached. I can attest to the veracity of the video, since I took it. The second unfortunate piece of news is that this won't be the only such occurrence. Stay tuned for more. My warmest regards, Ava Lee.

Ava showed May the message. "What do you think?"

"It's perfect."

"Good," Ava said. She attached the video and hit SEND.

May looped her arm through Ava's as they recommenced their walk towards the taxis, where the others were waiting. "I can't tell you how good it feels to think about those men's reactions when they get that email," May said. "I understand about image. Having products bearing your name declared counterfeit and making purses and shoes in Chinese factories doesn't exactly mesh with the illusion VLG has conjured as one of the world's leading luxury-brand companies."

"Don't feel good for too long, because above all, they're going to be angry," Ava said. "We'd be naive to think they're not going to push back."

When they reached the taxis, Amanda approached them. "Did you hear from Sonny?"

"No. I sent the video to VLG with a note," Ava said.

"Already?"

"We decided it was time to go on the offensive. I know I said it might be better to let them find out things gradually, but we're at war."

"So now what?"

"I want to hear from Sonny and Xu before deciding on the next step."

"You don't need us around for that, do you?" Amanda asked.

"Why? What do you have in mind?" Ava said.

"We've been invited to a house party at a friend of Clark's and we'd like to go. It will give our collective heads a much needed rest," Amanda said. "You and May are welcome to join us."

"I can't," May said quickly. "I'll be spending most of the night on the phone with Wuhan. There are some business issues I have to deal with."

"And I'm going to stay available for Sonny and Xu," Ava said.

"But you don't mind if we go?"

"Not in the least. We can meet for breakfast again."

"Breakfast it is," Amanda said. "We'll just squeeze into one taxi and head out."

Ava walked over to Gillian, Clark, and Chi-Tze. "Enjoy yourselves tonight," she said. "I've sent the video to VLG, so they may ramp up tomorrow. I don't want you to lose contact with our customers, so be prepared to spend more time on the phone over the next few days. We need to keep our side of the story out there."

30

AVA AND MAY HAD A HURRIED DINNER AT YI LONG Court. May's first conference call was at six-thirty, and she thought she'd be busy until at least eleven. Ava kept checking her phone, becoming increasingly anxious as she waited to hear from Sonny or Xu.

"Why don't you call them?" May asked at one point.

"I don't want to seem desperate."

"It's Sonny and Xu."

"I still have a certain image to maintain."

"As if there's anything you could do or say that they wouldn't think was perfect."

Ava smiled. "That's only because I don't give them a reason to think otherwise."

"What else are you going to do tonight, besides wait?" May said. "I feel kind of guilty leaving you on your own."

"I have some other phone calls to make. You made a comment about brand integrity that hit home. I wonder how many VLG customers know that their bags and shoes may be labelled 'Made in Italy' but are actually made in part or entirely in China?"

"Are you going to muddy those waters?"

"I'll try. Elsa Ngan might be a useful resource."

"And Carrie Song?"

"No, she's done enough for us already. I wouldn't want to put her in an even more difficult position."

"Well, I'll leave you to it," May said. "I have to get upstairs and get organized for the first meeting. Call me if anything really urgent happens, and if you don't go to bed early, maybe we can have a nightcap."

After May left, Ava lingered in the restaurant. She finished a second glass of Pinot Grigio, thought about having a third, and then decided it would be better for her to take a walk. There was a chill in the night air, so she went to her room to get her Adidas jacket and cap. Before heading back downstairs, she checked her computer, hoping that an email or text had somehow evaded her phone, but none had.

The Bund was jammed when she exited the hotel. She stood at the entrance for a moment, weighing whether or not she was in the mood for being jostled and pushed by a slow-moving crowd. It didn't seem to matter what time of day it was or what the weather was like, the river and the promenade were magnets for both locals and tourists.

She gazed at the Huangpu River, the Oriental Pearl Tower, the World Financial Center, and the line of skyscrapers along the horizon. She started to walk towards the promenade but wasn't out of the Peninsula's driveway before her phone rang. She checked the number. It was Sonny.

"I've been waiting for your call," she said.

"We went to dinner to finalize the agreements," he said.

"And are they—" she began, and then stopped when she saw she had another incoming call. "Just a second, Sonny," she said before switching lines.

"Ava, I've just heard from Suen," Xu said.

"I'm talking to Sonny on the other line. Can I call you in a few minutes?"

"Sure."

"Sonny, I'm back," she said. "You were telling me that you finalized agreements."

"Yeah. It took all fucking day," he said.

Ava started moving back into the hotel. "Why so long?"

"We had to go to three factories. They're owned by different people, but they'd talked to each other and put up a common front."

"How did they know what we wanted them to do?"

"Lop told the guys in Fanling what the game was, and I guess they gave the factories a heads-up. In a way it wasn't a bad thing, because it saved explaining things and gave us more time to negotiate."

"How did the negotiations end?" Ava asked as she stepped inside the Peninsula.

"They won't take any more orders for now—" he said.

She lost the next few words as her phone sounded again. Ava saw it was an incoming Chinese number. *This is crazy*, she thought. "This is Ava Lee."

"Hello, Ava. This is Ban Lam in Guangzhou."

She hesitated, surprised by his call. Had something gone wrong in Huidong or Huadu? "Ban, I'll be right with you. I need to end another call. Don't hang up," she said, and then switched back to Sonny, "I have a call from Lam that I have to take. Stay by your phone."

"Okay, boss."

"Hi, Ban. I didn't expect to hear from you again quite so soon," she said.

"You sound worried," he said. "Don't be. I just thought you should know something. The VLG agent who supervises production and shipments from our factories in Huadu and Huidong was at the facilities today, to check on the progress of some orders. He didn't react very well when he was told there wasn't any progress, and that there wouldn't be until further notice."

"So he knows production has been halted?"

"He does."

"And how about the products in inventory and in transit?"

"He was told that they're not leaving China."

"That's great."

"The agent demanded to know who had made those decisions," Lam said. "He was told it was the people who owned the factories. He found that a bit confusing, since he had no idea the factories were connected in any way, let alone owned by the same group. He then asked who the owners were, and of course he wasn't given a direct answer."

"He must have asked why this was happening."

"He did. Our managers said they didn't know and didn't care. The order had come from upstairs and that was it."

"Did that end it?"

"No. He made some threats about lawyers and said they could expect to hear from Italy."

"I have to say that it sounds like it all went rather well."

"I thought so too."

"Thank you so much. Your support means a lot to me and my partners."

"You don't have to thank me again. Twice in two days is enough," Lam said. "If I hear anything else, I'll let you know."

Ava had been standing by the elevator while she spoke to Lam. Now she got in and rode to her floor. She hit Sonny's number as soon as she got off.

"Sorry, Sonny, I didn't mean to cut you off earlier, but it was Lam on the other line and I was worried that he might have some bad news for me."

"Did he?"

"No, it was all good. Now, how about you?"

"Pretty good, I think."

"What do you mean by 'you think,' and what does 'pretty good' mean?" she said as she entered her room.

"They won't take any more orders from that VLG outfit until we tell them they can," Sonny said, and then paused.

"What aren't you telling me?" Ava said.

"We had to buy the inventory they had on hand and commit to buying whatever they could recall."

"Who is 'we'?"

"Me and Lop."

"You mean Xu and I."

"The same thing, no?"

"Yes, the same thing," Ava said without hesitating. "And how much is it going to cost us?"

"About a million U.S."

"About?"

"Lop is sending one of his accountants to Shenzhen to finalize the amount."

"Sonny, if you don't mind my saying it, this doesn't sound like the kind of arrangement you and Lop would make on your own."

"We had problems with the Fanling gang," he said. "Shenzhen is their turf, and they weren't happy that we were messing around in it. It was only because it was me and Lop that they co-operated at all. Truthfully, if the factory owners had been left to us, there would have been a lot less talking and a lot more physical persuasion. But the Fanling guys wanted a peaceful solution, and we decided that the final outcome was more important than how we got there."

That might be the longest speech I've ever heard Sonny make, Ava thought. "You're absolutely correct about the outcome," she said.

"And don't worry about the inventory. One of the factories said they could help us peddle it."

"So they make a commission on top of their sales profit?"

"Lop thought it was the best way to go, since we have no idea how to sell the stuff."

"That's a good point," she said. "I think you did a great job. Please pass along my thanks to Lop as well."

"Is there anything else you need done right now?"

"No. Just stay on top of the accountant and make sure we don't get screwed on the inventory. When you know how much money is involved, call me," Ava said.

She'd been sitting on the bed as she spoke to Sonny. Now she moved to the desk to get her notebook and the names and addresses of the silk companies in Chongqing before she called Xu.

"What's going on? You sound harassed," he said.

"What hasn't been going on?" she said, taking a deep breath. "Two containers of VLG products were destroyed this afternoon by Customs. I sent the video to the guys in

Milan. Lam phoned to say his factories were contacted by the VLG agent and they told him they weren't shipping any more of their product. I'm sure Milan knows that by now. And Sonny just called to brief me on Shenzhen."

"I know about Shenzhen because I spoke to Lop a few minutes ago."

"Did he tell you that we're on the hook for a few dollars?"

"Yes, but don't worry about it."

"We'll pay."

"I said don't worry about it. By the time Lop is finished with the factories I'll be surprised if we owe anything."

"Pass along my thanks to him. He and Sonny did a great job," Ava said. "But right this instant, I'm more interested in how Suen did in Chongqing."

"He did quite well. We had to buy some silk, but nothing excessive. Our own factories will use it up over the next few months. He persuaded everyone who's been shipping to VLG not to take any new orders and to hold off on production. There are a couple of shipments in transit that they're trying to sidetrack. We won't know how successful that is for a day or two. So, overall, I think it's safe to say we've put a crimp in VLG's supply."

"Do I want to know how he persuaded them?"

"No, I don't think you do."

"Then I won't ask."

"And I told our perfumers and the glass manufacturer to speed things up. Maybe by tomorrow I'll have an improved deadline for those two scents you want them to make."

"Oh, that's fantastic," Ava said, and then she was alerted to yet another incoming call.

This time it wasn't from China and it wasn't from an

unfamiliar number. It was from Canada, and the number was all too familiar.

"Hey," Maria said softly. "Can you talk?"

31

AVA HAD NO IDEA WHEN SHE FINALLY FELL ASLEEP.

After her conversation with Maria, she had tried to work but found that her mind kept returning to Toronto. She turned on the television, but when that didn't prove a distraction, she pushed the green leather chair to the window overlooking the gardens and sat there staring out into the night. She wasn't sure how long it had been before she started to cry. The first tears sneaked out and she wasn't aware of them until she felt them trickling down her cheek. She wiped them away, but they were quickly replaced by others and. soon became a steady stream.

She went to the bathroom to get tissues. As she pulled a handful from the box she saw herself in the mirror. Her face was streaked with black mascara and her eyes were red and puffy. She hardly recognized herself, and the pain in the pit of her stomach was something equally strange. *What choice did I have?* she thought. Then she sobbed, her head lowered, her shoulders collapsing around her chest, her hands pressing down on the edge of the sink.

The intensity of her reaction caught her by surprise, but so had Maria. She had figured that Maria would state her case again and then back down when she saw that Ava wouldn't bend. Instead of backing down, Maria had issued an ultimatum. And Ava had responded the only way she could.

Ava walked into the sitting room with the box of tissues. She opened the bar, took out a bottle of white wine, and filled a glass. She went back to the window, where she reassumed her place in the chair. *Maybe I should have tried to meet her halfway*, she thought. *Except, what is halfway?* And the truth was, Maria hadn't seemed the least bit interested in having that kind of discussion. There was no compromise in her words or in her tone. Her mind was set — it was either live together or separate. *It's better to end this now rather than later, when it would be harder to untangle our lives and our emotions*, Ava told herself. Except she wasn't the one ending the relationship. It was being ended for her. She drank deeply from the glass. She looked out onto the gardens through a film of tears.

Ava finished the wine, went back to the bar, and took out a bottle of cognac. Her cellphone rang. She let it go to voicemail and then turned it off. The outside world was of no interest to her.

At one point she started to nod off, but the force of her head slumping forward startled her awake. She sipped more cognac and felt her head start to spin. *I should sleep*, she thought, struggling to rise from the chair. She collapsed onto the bed, still dressed in the clothes she'd worn all day and not bothering to wash her mascara-streaked face. She reached down and pulled up the duvet until it covered her like a cocoon.

She didn't dream and she didn't remember waking up

anytime during the night. When she finally opened her eyes, the sun was streaming through the window. Her mouth was dry; she felt dehydrated and her eyes burned. She groaned. *Why did I do this to myself?* she thought. It was a lament she'd made before, and nearly always after she'd tried to cleanse herself of emotional pain. She sat up and swung her legs over the side of the bed.

She rushed to the bathroom, drank three full glasses of water, washed her face, brushed her teeth, and stepped into the shower. Fifteen minutes later, she emerged wrapped in a thick terrycloth robe. She made a coffee and sat at the desk. She turned on her computer. *Maybe Maria sent me an email*, she thought. The idea filled her with as much dread as hope.

There was no email from Maria.

Ava reached for her phone. She had a dim memory of it ringing and her turning it off. Before she could activate it, the room phone rang.

"It's May. I've been trying to reach you on your cell since last night. I was getting worried."

"You could have tried the room."

"I did around midnight and there was no answer."

"I was sleeping," Ava said. "There's nothing to worry about."

"When I saw you make mention of a hard night in your email, I thought there might be more problems with VLG."

"No, it's the opposite. Sonny and Xu both called me last night to say things went well in Shenzhen and Chongqing."

"That's good to hear. So what was this hard night about?"

"Jet lag and a bit too much to drink."

"Still, it isn't like you. Are you sure you're okay?"

"I'm fine, May," Ava said, more sharply than she intended.

May hesitated. "I didn't mean to pry."

"I know you care about me, and I'm sorry if I was abrupt," Ava said.

"If you had a problem —"

"— I'd tell you," Ava said, reminded again how finely honed May's instincts were.

"Okay. So why don't you tell me about Sonny and Xu."

"VLG won't be getting any leather or silk from their suppliers in Shenzhen and Chongqing in the immediate future. It may cost us in terms of buying some inventory, but we should be able to turn most of it."

"Have you told Ventola or Pandolfo yet?"

"No, but I'm reasonably sure they know or are about to find out."

"Why do you think that?"

"Lam called me from Guangzhou last night. The VLG agent has been told they're cut off in Huidong and Huadu. He demanded to know who'd made that decision. Lam's people wouldn't tell him."

"But you're assuming that Ventola and Pandolfo will put two and two together."

"I am, and that they'll start calling around to their other Chinese suppliers to get status reports on the orders they have. And when they do, they'll get the same story. Even a thick-witted businessman would finger us as the prime candidate, and as we know, Ventola and Pandolfo are about the furthest thing from thick."

"That's not so bad, is it?"

"It's what we wanted. It's just happening a bit faster than we anticipated. I would have liked to have a few more jolts lined up and ready to go."

"How much more of their attention do we need?"

"Probably not much, if any."

"What do you expect to happen?"

"Like I said yesterday, after we destroyed the supposed counterfeits, they're going to be angry and they'll want to lash out," Ava said. "But the problems they're facing now are far bigger than just a couple of container loads of product. And what makes it harder is that they'll have no idea how extensive our reach is and how long we can carry on doing what we're doing. They must have factories waiting for raw material. They must have orders on hand for shoes and bags and luggage. How long before their customers get pissed off and cancel their orders and word gets out to the fashion insiders and media? So while I think they're going to be furious, I hope they're going to be even more practical and realize it's wiser to cut some kind of deal with us."

"And if they don't want to negotiate a deal?"

"We keep up the pressure. We lose more containers. We help customs offices in Hong Kong and Guangzhou find and destroy more 'counterfeits.' We unleash Xu's knockoff perfumes," Ava said. "We will cost them so much money and give them so much aggravation that they'll beg us to settle with them."

"I told Changxing a little about what's going on," May said. "He found some of it funny, especially destroying those real goods as counterfeit. He said Ventola has obviously underestimated how nasty and powerful we bitches are."

"And he meant that as a compliment?"

"He did. I know it's a back-handed compliment, but he was laughing when he said it."

"It's nice to know he has confidence in us. Maybe when

this is over and we've won, we can invite him to join us for a celebration in Shanghai."

"Let me mull that one over," May said.

"While you do, let me get dressed. See you downstairs at eleven. I'll leave it to you to find a place for lunch."

Ava put down the phone and went back to the desk. She turned on her cell and saw she had a message. She assumed it was May from the previous night, but found herself listening to the low, slow monotone of Raffaello Pandolfo.

"This is Raffi," he said. "I know you think you've been clever with Customs and your video, and now we hear we have problems with some of our suppliers that we believe you are most likely responsible for." His voice still a monotone but increasingly edged with menace. "I told you not to provoke us. You did, and then you went beyond that. Dominic is furious. He's been compelled to tell some of our partners about your interference in our business. I wanted to keep them out of it, but when he's that angry, he doesn't listen to anyone. So now the partners are involved and that is not a good thing for you. I don't owe you or anyone else associated with PÖ a warning, but you are in many ways lovely women and I don't want to see any unnecessary harm come to you. So I have to tell you — stop while you still have time and call Dominic and apologize. It's time you started listening to me."

Ava stared at her phone and then listened to the message again.

Is he talking about physical harm? Ava thought. *And partners. What kind of partners do they have that can deliver on that kind of threat?*

She thought about calling Pandolfo but immediately

discarded the idea. Reaching out to him would only make her look weak, and she knew that if Ventola and Pandolfo sensed any weakness, she'd never be able to get them to negotiate.

Should I tell May and Amanda about the call? she thought, and then quickly answered her own question. *No.*

32

AVA SAW AMANDA AND MAY STANDING NEAR THE
hotel entrance and was taken aback by how similar they
looked. If she hadn't known better, she would have mistaken
them for mother and daughter — a comparison May would
have found highly insulting. She had seen them together
many times, but May was usually wearing a designer suit
or dress, while Amanda was most comfortable in slacks
and a sweater or blouse. Today they both wore jeans with
a blouse and looked at the world through almost matching
large, round sunglasses.

"You look like sisters," Ava said as she joined them.

"I'll thank you for that comment, though Amanda may
not," May said. She lowered her sunglasses and looked at
Ava with concern. "Are you feeling okay? Your eyes are puffy
and a bit bloodshot."

"I've been sneezing and my eyes have been watering. I
must be allergic to something."

"Do you want to change rooms?"

"No, it could be something outside."

"I've reserved a table at the Dragon Phoenix restaurant

in the Peace Hotel. It's a short walk, but would you rather stay here?"

"Let's go," Ava said. "I'll survive."

"May briefed me on what happened last night," Amanda said cheerily as they left the Peninsula. "It sounds like we're making some progress."

"We're off to a decent start," Ava said, glad she'd decided to forego relaying Pandolfo's message. "How was the party last night, and how are Clark and Gillian?"

"Quite upbeat. Mind you, they were surrounded by people who adore them."

"That's not surprising when you consider how wonderful they are."

"And resilient," Amanda said. "I was talking to Chi-Tze this morning and we're both surprised at how well the Pos have handled this crisis — him especially. He could have fallen to pieces, but instead he's been working the phones like mad and is the most optimistic of all. He's been keeping Gillian's spirits up by saying that fighting to save their own business is better than working for anyone else. Plus, I have to say that Pang Fai's involvement in London got all their friends excited. Last night I must have heard ten times that there's no way PÖ can fail if she's supporting us."

They shuffled along the promenade for a few more minutes before the two buildings that made up the Fairmont Peace Hotel came into view. The hotel had what Ava thought was an odd combination of art deco and Renaissance architecture.

"The buildings were built decades apart," May said after Ava commented on it. "The south one dates back to the 1850s, when it was known as the Central Hotel. Then it became the

Palace Hotel and was converted into offices for the municipal government. It didn't revert to being a hotel until 1965, when it became part of the Peace Hotel."

"How do you know this stuff?"

"I read it online when I made the reservation."

"So the north building was the original Peace Hotel?"

"No, it opened in 1929 as the Cathay Hotel, and it was supposedly one of the most luxurious hotels in the world. Noel Coward finished writing *Private Lives* there. Like the south building it also functioned as municipal offices, but that ended in 1956, when it reopened and was renamed the Peace Hotel."

"They're gorgeous buildings."

"The entire Bund is gorgeous," Amanda said. "It's my favourite part of Shanghai."

"Not mine," Ava said. "I like it, but I prefer the French Concession. It's as if a small part of Europe was picked up and deposited there."

"Xu has a house there, doesn't he?"

"Yes. It's small, almost like a cottage, but it has a courtyard and a fishpond."

"It sounds charming."

"It is."

"It would be nice to see it one day," May said.

"I'm sure you will," Ava said, wishing she hadn't mentioned Xu.

They reached the hotel entrance and were just about to walk inside when Ava's phone rang. She saw the number she now recognized as Lam's. "I should take this," she said.

"We'll go to the restaurant," May said. "It's on the eighth floor."

"See you there," Ava said, moving away from the door. "Hi, Ban. Calls from you are becoming a habit."

"And weirder every time."

"What does that mean?"

"I just heard from some Italians," he said.

"You were contacted by someone from VLG?"

"No, I was contacted by someone who said they were affiliated with them."

"A shipping agent?"

"Hardly."

"Don't make me guess."

"The Camorra."

"God," Ava said, her stomach tightening. "Are you sure it was them?"

"We've done business with them in the past. The guy who was our contact then was the one who called me."

"But they're based in Naples, in southern Italy. Why would they be affiliated with VLG in Milan?"

"There are a lot of ways to interpret 'affiliated.' They could have been hired as muscle or maybe they do have a stake in VLG. Or it's possible that one of the other Mafia families the Camorra associates with owns part of it. I do know they have ties to the Mala del Brenta mob in the north," Lam said. "If any of those scenarios is true, it doesn't matter anyway. The guy who contacted me, Ricci, was quite clear that Camorra interests are involved."

"How do the two of you communicate?"

"Ricci and I both speak English just well enough that we can make ourselves understood."

"What does he want from you?"

"He said he needs help in China. He said that VLG has run

into some supply problems. He wants me to rectify them — for a fee, of course."

Ava shook her head. "He was actually specific about it being VLG?"

"He was."

"That's surprising."

"Ava, you know that in the past Li took contracts from all kinds of people to do all kinds of things."

"Of course I do, and one of them was a contract to kill me."

"Yes, and there were others — many others. Most of that work was done in China for Chinese customers, but once in a while there was a job outside that orbit. Two of those were contracts from the Camorra. Li arranged for an Italian government official to disappear while he was vacationing in Phuket. He also had a French drug dealer killed when he was in Laos, trying to bypass the Italian supply lines. What I'm saying is that there is history, a relationship, a level of trust between them and us."

"Ban, from your tone I'm starting to suspect that your Italian friends want you to do more than solve their supply problems."

"Ricci's exact words were 'Get the fucking plants to honour their obligations and we don't care how you do it,'" Lam said. "And then you and May Ling Wong were mentioned."

"In what way?" Ava said, the tightness in her stomach becoming a knot.

"He said they'd also appreciate it if we could inflict some pain and punishment on a couple of bitches named Ava Lee and May Ling Wong, who own a company called PÖ," Lam said. "He said you were the cause of the supply issues."

"Pain and punishment?"

"He wasn't precise."

"But the intent was clear enough."

"Very clear," Lam said. He took a deep breath. "My experience with them is that they have an extreme view of the world. When we worked with them in the past, there were never any limitations placed on us. To be absolutely frank — because I think you can handle it — it sounds to me like they want the two of you dead."

"Shit," Ava said. She fell silent while she fully absorbed the situation. "I got a message earlier from Raffi Pandolfo, one of the senior people in VLG. He said Dominic Ventola is very angry and contacted some friends to help him deal with us."

"I guess we know now who those friends are," Lam said.

"And now I know that Pandolfo wasn't just blowing smoke," she said. She paused, struggling to return the conversation to business. "Ban, during your conversation with Ricci, did he hint that they know you control the plants in Huidong and Huadu?"

"No, but their request for assistance wasn't limited to them. They've also asked us to help restart production in some factories in Shenzhen and Chongqing."

"Lop and my man Sonny closed Shenzhen for us, and Suen handled Chongqing."

"Do they have relationships there?"

"Only indirectly, through some local gangs. They paid the plants personal visits."

"No wonder they stopped shipping."

"We needed some diverse approaches," Ava said. "And speaking of which, do you think it's possible the Camorra has done the same?"

"What are you getting at?"

"Do you think this Ricci has contacted any other gangs in China, or in Asia, for that matter? Or do you think he's dealing only with you?"

"I seriously doubt they've gone anywhere else. As far as I know, Li was their go-to guy for just about everything in this part of the world. I seem to have inherited that role."

"How fortunate for us."

"Maybe for now, but I can tell you that these aren't people who let grass grow under their feet. If I don't deliver results, they'll find someone who can or may even try to do it themselves."

"How could they ever manage by themselves in China?"

"It would be difficult when it came to dealing with the factories. The language issue would be huge, and even if it wasn't, my plants would ignore them. And I can't imagine the other plants would want to anger people like Lop and Suen, people who are virtually on their doorstep," Lam said. "But you can't be so sure they wouldn't take a run at you and Ms. Wong. All they have to do is locate you, send a couple of their thugs, and hope they're smart enough not to get caught. And even if they do get caught, you know they won't talk."

"Did he mention a time frame for either of their requests?"

"I was asked to move as quickly as possible. He said that every day the plants aren't in production is costing them millions."

"How did you respond?"

"I thought it was best to play along."

"Of course."

"I told him I need a day or two to figure out the lay of the land with the factories, and that it will take my people at least an additional day to persuade them to resume production."

"How about dealing with me and May?"

"I said we'd do it when we could get around to it," Lam said. "That didn't make him very happy. He said taking care of you was as much of a priority."

"Do they know where we are?"

"Not specifically, though Ricci mentioned Shanghai as the most likely possibility. They sent me photos and some personal information about you and Ms. Wong to help us with our search."

"Did they mention Toronto?"

"It was identified as your home, but if they thought you were there they wouldn't go through me. They'd use locals or fly someone over from Italy."

"There are enough locals to go around," Ava said. "Toronto has its fair share of mafiosi."

"I wouldn't return to Toronto too quickly if I were you," Lam said. "You're safe as long as you're in China and the job is mine. It might be reckless to go back until these matters are resolved."

"How in the hell are we going to do that?"

"I've only just spoken to them. I haven't had a chance to really think about it yet," Lam said. "I thought you might have some ideas. I remember how imaginative you were when it came to dealing with the Li–Xu feud."

"That seems like a lifetime ago."

"I'm sure your imagination hasn't diminished in the interim."

"Let's hope not," Ava said.

"You'll talk to Xu?"

"Of course."

"He might have some thoughts about how we can manage this."

Ava sighed. "I didn't need this complication."

"We're in a business that doesn't run in a straight line."

"Except that it's not the business I'm in."

"If you say so." He laughed.

33

AVA'S KNOWLEDGE OF THE MAFIA AND ITS VARIOUS branches had come from books and films. During her years with Uncle they had run up against a Mafia group only once. That had been in Indonesia, where the Calabria-based 'Ndrangheta had established a money-laundering operation that had ensnared assets belonging to some of their clients. Ava had successfully recovered the funds, but it was a job that — at Uncle's insistence — she'd undertaken at arm's length.

Uncle had had dealings with the Mafia in the past and had a healthy respect for their willingness to do whatever was necessary to win whatever battle or war they were engaged in. He had preached maximum caution to Ava, and it was a lesson she absorbed and applied so well in Indonesia that — as far as she was aware — the 'Ndrangheta never knew of her involvement.

As she stood outside the Peace Hotel running through her conversation with Lam in her head, it was only too obvious that anonymity was a luxury she didn't have this time. The Camorra knew who she was. It knew who they all were. Her only hope was that Uncle's opinion about the efficiency and viciousness of the 'Ndrangheta didn't extend to the Camorra, but it was a hope she wasn't about to invest much faith in. Aside from knowing it was based in Naples, all Ava knew about the Camorra was drawn from an Italian film called *Gomorrah*, which portrayed the mob as greedy, vicious, and cruel.

She checked the time and knew she should be going inside to join May and Amanda, but Lam's call had killed her appetite and presented her with another dilemma. How much should she tell her partners?

Both Amanda and May were aware of — and had been party to — violent episodes in Ava's life. May had never been a target, but Amanda had been brutally attacked in Borneo and still carried a large scar over her eye as a result. Ava was reasonably sure that May could handle the news about the Camorra, but she had doubts about Amanda. The Borneo attack had shown Amanda, for the first time, how vulnerable she was. How would she handle it? Would it trigger horrible memories? That wasn't something Ava had any interest in finding out, but she knew she couldn't tell one partner and not the other about what had transpired.

I should wait until Lam and I have had a chance to think through our positions, she thought. *There's no point in alarming anyone until we have a much better idea of where we stand.* That was the decision she'd made as she walked into the black and gold marble lobby of the Peace Hotel, and it remained her decision when she left the elevator on the eighth floor and was led by a hostess to a table looking out over the promenade.

When she sat down, May said, "We ordered hot and sour

soup for you. It doesn't go that well with geoduck sashimi, but since they're both your favourites we figured you wouldn't mind the combination."

"Thanks," Ava said as Amanda poured her tea. "And the combination sounds wonderful."

"I also ordered lobster and scallops fried with ginger, chilis, and spring onions, and roasted crispy pork belly."

"The pork is my favourite," Amanda said.

"How can someone who eats as much as you do stay so thin?" Ava said.

"I worry a lot — but not as much as I used to when I was running my father's trading company. There's something special about being part of a team where the individuals care about each other. It takes whatever is negative and dilutes it."

"Even more important to me is that we all trust one another and have each other's back," May said. "It can make big problems, like the one we have now, seem surmountable."

"You're both correct," Ava said. She looked at both of her partners. Why wouldn't she trust them enough to handle Lam's news? In an instant she reversed the decision she'd made. "And speaking of problems, there's a new one."

"What is it this time?" May said.

Ava hesitated as she carefully gathered her words. "I need to preface this by saying that it will sound worse than it is. I believe, if we wrap our minds around it, we'll be able to manage it."

"I wish you didn't look and sound so ominous," May said.

"Well, we have been threatened, and I am taking it seriously," Ava said. "The phone call I took outside was from Lam, the triad Mountain Master in Guangzhou."

"Is there a problem with his factories?"

"Not yet, but he did receive a phone call from Italy. He was asked to take a contract to force resumption of production and shipping from the factories. They obviously don't know that Lam controls the plants in Huidong and Huadu."

"VLG called Lam? How would they know—"

"They don't know and they didn't call," Ava interrupted. "He was contacted by a man named Ricci, who's a member of the Camorra Mafia clan in Naples. They've done business together in the past. Ricci implied that the Camorra has an affiliation with VLG and that the plants' refusal to produce or ship VLG products is costing them money. I don't know if there's any truth in that. They could just have been hired to do a job, and given their lack of influence in this country, decided to subcontract it to Lam."

"They've hired Lam?" May said.

"They think they have," Ava said. She lowered her voice. "Ricci also made it clear that they want Lam to inflict some kind of personal retribution on us, me and May quite specifically."

"They actually asked Lam to do that?" Amanda said.

"Yes. And of course he agreed to it to buy some time, but he made it clear to me that the Camorra isn't patient. If he doesn't get results, he's sure they'll turn to someone else," Ava said. "That's the last thing we want, because as long as Lam has the contract and can keep stringing them along, we have a measure of control."

"What do you mean by 'personal retribution'?" May asked.

"They weren't definitive, but it's safe to assume they'd prefer an ugly outcome for us."

"They'd like to see us dead?"

"Maybe not, but I don't think they'd care if we did die."

"My god," May said.

"But we're not going to allow it to get to that point," Ava said. "We'll figure something out."

"Who are 'we'?" Amanda asked.

"Us and Lam. And I was going to ask Xu for his advice."

"How much time do we have to sort this out?" May said.

"I'm not sure, but I'd figure about a couple of days."

"And you're certain that if Lam doesn't help them, they'll go looking for someone else who will?"

"That's Lam's opinion, and he knows who he's dealing with."

"Ava, do you think that VLG — that Dominic Ventola knows about this?" Amanda asked.

"I sense there's a point you're trying to make," Ava said.

"Well, maybe they don't know what this Camorra group is really doing."

"Are you suggesting that if Ventola did know he might call them off?"

"I'd like to think he would."

"First of all, Raffi Pandolfo told me that it was Ventola, in a very angry state, who notified 'some friends' about VLG's difficulties in China. We have to assume that those friends are the Camorra, and that Ventola knows exactly who he's dealing with and what they're capable of," Ava said. "Even if he didn't, we'd have to contact him to find that out. And the second we did, he'd be talking to the Camorra and they'd know right away that Lam has spoken to us. I can't think of a result that would work to our benefit."

"I understand," Amanda said, her voice calm.

Ava looked at her and then at May, who also seemed unperturbed by the nature of the conversation. *I should never have considered not telling them*, she thought.

"So, how do we extricate ourselves from this situation?" May said as the hot and sour soup was served.

"I have a few thoughts."

"Are you going to share them?"

"Give me a few minutes to sort them into some kind of order," Ava said.

They all ate quickly, but their attention was obviously elsewhere. The soup lacked a spicy bite and was a bit bland for Ava's taste. She said no to a second helping and turned to the platter of geoduck sashimi that had been placed in the middle of the table. She mixed a large dollop of wasabi into some soy sauce until the sauce was a muddy brown. The clam had been cut into thin, translucent white slivers. She plucked one from the platter, dipped it into the sauce, and smiled as the clam almost melted on her tongue.

"The first thing I have to do is talk to Xu and Lam," she said as she reached for another piece. "We're going to need their support."

"Do you have any doubts you'll get it?" May asked.

"Lam has already indicated his general willingness to help us. Now I need to get specific with him. Xu doesn't know anything about this yet, but I don't think that matters. He'll help."

"Is there anything we can do?" Amanda said.

"If Lam and Xu agree to my idea, there are not only things you can do, there are things the two of you will have to do."

May's chopsticks were poised in midair, a sliver of geoduck suspended from them. She put the sticks back onto her plate. "I'm listening," she said.

"Can you lie low for a day or two? I mean stay off your phone and keep a very low profile. Have minimal contact with anyone, including Changxing."

"Could I tell him in advance?"

"Is he discreet?"

"When it's called for."

"Is he capable of telling staff, friends, and business partners that he has no idea where you are or what you're doing, and maybe expressing some concern about your well-being?"

"He'd ask me why I want him to do that."

"I don't want you to tell him anything specific. He'd have to do it on trust."

May nodded. "He would, I'm sure of it."

Ava reached for Amanda's hand. "And now you — how good an actress are you?"

"I've never done any real acting, outside of the time you got me to spin lies to those people in Macau, when I was trying to get those house plans for you."

"Well, we're going to need you in full drama-queen mode."

"Who will be the audience?"

"I'd prefer Dominic Ventola, but I suspect it will be Raffi Pandolfo."

34

AVA CALLED LAM FROM THE RESTAURANT AND EXPLAINED what she wanted him to do. May and Amanda listened intently to her side of the conversation as she laid out her plans. Ava, rather self-consciously, found herself avoiding their gaze. No matter how close they had become, she still felt rather strange spinning out her plans in front of them. Even when she had worked with Uncle, she kept her strategies to herself unless she needed his assistance.

As was his style, Lam listened without interruption. When she finished, he said, "It's certainly worth trying, and who knows, it may work. But Ava, I need to make something clear: if there's going to be a war with the Camorra, I don't want my gang involved."

"If it comes to that, I'm counting on Xu," she said.

"Have you spoken to him yet?"

"No."

"I expect he'll do what you want."

"He'll have to tell me that himself. For now I only need to know that you're firmly onside."

"I am as long as Xu is. But you'll have to let me know when I should contact the Italians."

"I won't know until I talk to Xu. I'll call you as soon as I have."

"Okay."

Ava put down her phone and looked at her partners. "Lam will co-operate. Now I have to talk to Xu, and that's something I need to do in person."

"And alone?" May said.

"I think that's preferable."

May shrugged. "I have a lot of work to do anyway, especially since it appears I'll be incommunicado for a while."

"And I promised our gang I'll meet them in Pudong this afternoon," Amanda said.

"I'll see if Xu's available," Ava said, hitting his number.

"Ava," he said.

"I'm glad I caught you."

"What's going on?"

"The problem we have with VLG just became more complicated. I need to talk to you about it."

"I'm listening."

"No, I'd rather do it person."

"It's that complicated?"

"Yes," Ava said abruptly.

"I'm at the house. Where are you?"

"At the Peace Hotel."

"I'll send a car to pick you up. When will you be ready?"

"Now."

"It will take about twenty minutes. Suen's not back yet, so Wen will come with the driver."

"Thanks," Ava said, ending the call and turning to May

and Amanda. "He's sending a car for me."

"Well, there's no reason for me to hang around until it gets here," May said. "I'll go and work at the hotel."

"I'll be in touch with both of you as soon as I get Xu's feedback," Ava said, and then looked at the platters of food they'd barely touched. "My mother would have a fit if she could see all this going to waste."

"I'll pack it up and take it to Pudong with me," Amanda said.

Ten minutes later they made their way to the lobby and hugged at the hotel entrance. Amanda got into a taxi and May began to walk back to the Peninsula. Ava watched them leave with a sense of relief. They'd handled the situation as well as she could have hoped.

A steady stream of luxury cars pulled up to the hotel. Ava thought she saw Wen more than once before she finally spotted him leaping out of the front passenger seat of the silver Mercedes. He waved at her and opened the back door.

"*Xiao lao ban*," he said.

She climbed in, settled back, and then closed her eyes as they made their way to the French Concession. She knew she had asked a lot of May and Amanda, and even more of Lam, and now she was about to ask Xu to commit to a course of action that had no predictable end. Under normal circumstances she wouldn't have any doubts about his reaction, but this involved the Camorra.

As the car wove through the Concession, she replayed in her mind the strategy she'd come up with. She didn't open her eyes until she heard Wen speak. The fruit vendor who guarded the entrance to the lane was leaning into the front window. "Everything's clear," he said.

When they reached the house, the gate swung open and the car turned slowly into the courtyard. She saw Xu sitting by the pond with a cigarette in his hand. When the car came to a stop, she reached for the door handle, only to hear Wen exclaim, "No, *xiao lao ban*, you must let me." She sat back until he opened the door.

Xu left his chair and crossed the courtyard to greet her.

"I'm sorry about this," Ava said.

"I'm not accustomed to seeing you look so worried," Xu said.

"Well, we've been blindsided."

"I know. I just got off the phone with Lam. I called him on other matters and he told me what's going on. I hope you don't mind that he did."

Ava shook her head. "He's been terrific."

"He does owe you some favours."

"I've cashed in several already."

"Some are weightier than others. He probably still feels he's in your debt."

"Even so, I don't like asking."

"Don't concern yourself about Lam. He's never been reluctant to say no," Xu said. "Now, do you want to go inside or sit by the pond?"

"Let's sit by the pond," Ava said. "Where's Auntie Grace? She usually meets me at the door."

"It's her naptime."

"I've never noticed that before."

"Whenever you're here, she stays up. She doesn't want you to think that she needs one."

"That's silly, I wouldn't care," Ava said, taking a seat by the pond.

"She does, though. She doesn't want to look too old in your eyes."

"As if I would think that."

"I don't pretend to understand how any woman thinks."

"Is that false modesty?"

"I wish it were."

Ava looked towards the house, still half expecting Auntie Grace to appear. "Xu, I'm genuinely sorry that I have to bother you with this latest problem. I thought we had things moving in the right direction until Lam called. His news was a bit of a shock."

"He was taken aback himself," Xu said. "But he mentioned that you have a plan to deal with it."

"Yes. I've asked him to convince the Italians to come to Hong Kong. I thought about Shanghai or Guangzhou, but Hong Kong is probably more neutral in their minds."

"It probably is," Xu said.

"Do you know the Camorra?"

"I don't know them specifically — Li's Guangzhou gang was their point of contact in China — but I certainly know of them, and over the years we've done business with them, again through Guangzhou," Xu said. "Like the triads, their organization goes back hundreds of years. As I remember, they have about a hundred gangs operating in a rather loose structure. I think there are about six thousand members in total. I'm sure VLG is involved with one specific gang rather than a group of them."

"Uncle was always wary when it came to dealing with the Italian Mafia, especially the 'Ndrangheta."

"From my experience, the Italian mobs aren't much different from one to another. Uncle would probably have been as cautious about the Camorra. They all think in the short term and nearly always opt for violence over negotiation."

"That's certainly part of their approach to resolving VLG's problems in China."

"You mean the fact that they want to hurt you and May Ling, or worse."

"Yes."

"As long as Lam has the contract there isn't much to worry about."

"I know, but he also says they're impatient. If he doesn't deliver, they'll find someone else who can."

"I understand," Xu said, taking out another Xiong Mao cigarette. "I wasn't suggesting that we ignore the threat. I'm simply saying that we have a little time."

"And I want to use that time to get them and the VLG executives to Hong Kong before impatience can set in."

Xu lit his cigarette, inhaled deeply, and blew the smoke away from Ava. "How will you go about ending the dispute? Lam says they want the factories to resume manufacturing and to ship what they have on hand. Are you prepared to do that before VLG gives you what you want?"

"No. It's the only leverage we have right now."

"You say that as if there's more pressure you can apply to them."

"There are a few more things we can do, but as long as the Camorra is part of the equation and May and I are targets, getting rid of that threat has to be the immediate focus."

"And you think that meeting them in Hong Kong will accomplish that?"

"This battle between us and VLG has been a series of shock tactics, of surprise attacks. They hit us first by trashing Clark and demeaning us in front of potential and existing customers. We retaliated with the containers and supposed counterfeits, and we probably raised the ante with the factories. They've hit back and increased the stakes one more time. Now it's our turn again, and we've got to match or surpass what they've done. And that most certainly includes some element of surprise."

"Lam said you want him to tell the Camorra that he's had you and May Ling badly beaten up."

"That's right."

"So your walking into a meeting in Hong Kong would constitute a surprise."

"Part of the surprise."

"What's the rest?"

"VLG has an affiliation of some sort with the Camorra. What neither of them knows is that the Shanghai triads don't just have an affiliation with PÖ, they are in fact major shareholders in the business, with many millions of dollars at stake."

"You and May would be comfortable making that public?"

"It would hardly be a public meeting, and I'm quite sure Dominic Ventola wouldn't want to broadcast that information once he knew he had to do a deal with us."

"And how would Dominic Ventola reach that conclusion?"

"I want you to tell them that you're prepared to go to war to protect your interests," Ava said. "And if it becomes a war, he'll be the first casualty."

35

XU DIDN'T SPEAK FOR A FEW MINUTES. HE FINISHED HIS cigarette, took another from the pack, and lit it with the dying embers of the first. His silence didn't concern Ava. He wasn't a man to react quickly or become emotional. She was sure he was processing everything she had told him, everything that Lam had said, and working through layers of relationships and agreements that she knew nothing about. Finally he reached down and put the second butt into the can of water by the chair.

"Do you want to go inside?" he asked. "Auntie Grace will be up now, and I feel like a drink."

Auntie Grace was emerging from her bedroom as they entered the house. She smiled at Ava and said, "I'll be with you in a minute. I need to freshen up."

"There's no rush, Auntie."

Xu sat in the living room on a bamboo chair with a padded seat. He placed his feet on the antique wooden tea chest that served as a coffee table. Ava sat across from him on a matching couch.

"You do know that if I tell the Camorra I'm prepared to

go to war, it can't be an idle threat?" he said.

"Yes, I know that."

"And you do know that while Lam is prepared to help in many ways, going to war with the Camorra isn't one of them?"

"He made that clear."

Auntie Grace joined them in the living room. "Welcome back," she said.

Before Ava could reply, Xu said, "Auntie, we really need a drink. Do I have any of the Macallan left?"

"Yes."

He looked at Ava. "Two glasses?"

"Sure," she said.

Auntie Grace walked to the sideboard, opened a door, and took out a bottle. She lifted two crystal tumblers from a shelf and carried the bottle and glasses to the table. She put them down rather deliberately. "It's a bit early in the day for a drink like this," she said.

"It is exactly the right time for a drink like this," Xu said.

"Just not too much," she said to both of them, and then turned and walked into the kitchen.

Xu sat up and poured each of them two fingers of the Scotch. "*Gan bei*," he said, lifting his glass.

"To our health," Ava said.

He took a sip and then leaned back again. "So, how do you see this playing out?"

"I want Lam to call the Camorra and tell them that he's taken care of May and me," Ava said. "We'll play it up a bit more from our side. Amanda is going to phone Raffaello Pandolfo and demand rather hysterically why they had to harm us. On top of that, May and I will make ourselves scarce until we meet them in Hong Kong."

"How would hurting you be a reason for them to come to Hong Kong?"

"It won't be. Lam will have to tell them that he's talked and met with the factories and then make the case that even pressure from him couldn't convince them to start producing or shipping again. He'll tell the Camorra he suspects the plants have been communicating among themselves and want to renegotiate their agreements. He'll recommend bringing them all to Hong Kong for a meeting with VLG, saying that if he can get them together in one room he's sure they can be made to honour their current contracts."

"Why does VLG have to be there?"

"Lam will say that the factories insist on dealing directly with the principals. Then he'll add that if the Camorra can't get VLG to come to Hong Kong, he doesn't want to waste any more time on the project and will withdraw from the contract."

"Will the Italians buy that?"

"Lam thinks so. It's his idea."

"He always was creative."

"So, what do you think?"

Xu sipped the Macallan, pursing his lips appreciatively. "It hinges on Lam's ability to talk them into coming to Hong Kong."

"It does, and we'll know whether he can soon enough."

"And if he's successful, then it falls on us to convince the Camorra that leaning on PÖ and the factories isn't going to get them what they want, and in fact it could be very messy and counterproductive."

"And I have complete confidence in your ability to do that," Ava said.

"Thank you," Xu said, suppressing a smile. "But that still leaves us the challenge of convincing VLG to abandon its anti-PÖ campaign."

"Not just abandon, but reverse," Ava said. "I'll handle that part of the meeting."

"There are a great many ifs attached to your plan."

"I've always found that if you take them one by one, it doesn't seem so daunting."

Xu shrugged. "I'll do whatever you want, but if Lam is successful and we go to Hong Kong, we'll be there in force. I'd involve Lop, Suen, and maybe a few more men from here."

"I'd ask Sonny to join us as well."

"That's a formidable crew," Xu said, topping up their drinks. "So now I guess we're waiting for Lam. When will he contact the Italians?"

"He won't do anything until you tell him that you're onside."

"I'll call him right now."

"Thank you."

"Then what?"

"May and I make ourselves scarce, a few hours later Lam tells the Italians that he's done a number on us, and then Amanda makes her call."

"And the invitation to Hong Kong?"

"I think Lam should wait at least twenty-four hours before contacting them again."

"And when he does, and if they agree to come, we're talking at least another two to three days before they get to Hong Kong?"

"Something like that."

"Where do you intend to stay during that time?" Xu asked.

"They don't know we're at the Peninsula. I see no harm in staying there until we leave for Hong Kong."

"Auntie Grace would be happy to have you here."

"May is involved as well. I can't leave her alone."

"I forgot about May," Xu said. "If you want to stay here in the interim, I'm sure we could find space for both of you."

"You know, I think it might be best if we stayed at the hotel until we know about Hong Kong," Ava said carefully. "To be safe, we'll keep out of sight and avoid using our electronic devices."

"Whatever suits you," he said. "I do have some phones that have never been used, if you and May want them."

"That would be perfect."

"Okay, now let me call Lam and get that resolved," Xu said, taking a phone from his jacket pocket.

"I'll go to the washroom while you do it," Ava said.

She didn't need to use the toilet. Her washroom visit was to give Xu the privacy to say whatever he wanted to Lam and the freedom to react to whatever Lam had to say. She ran a tap and splashed cold water on her face as she contemplated the situation. She thought it had improved markedly in the past few hours, and she had to credit VLG's clumsy attempt at second-party — no, make that third-party — intimidation. Instead of what was essentially guerrilla warfare, with a vague objective and no real timeline, everything had become tightly focused. The objective was now absolutely clear, and there would be a deadline measured in days rather than weeks or months, assuming that Lam and Xu were completely onside. And why wouldn't they be? She splashed more water on her face and looked at herself in the mirror.

Xu was still on the phone when she returned to the living room. She hesitated about taking a seat until he motioned to her. He covered the phone with his hand. "I'm talking to Feng. He's arranging to send the phones to your hotel."

"Say hello to him for me," Ava said. She knew Feng well. He was Xu's White Paper Fan, his administrator, and she had worked closely with him in the past.

Xu nodded as he continued speaking to Feng. When he finished, he slipped the phone back into his pocket.

"I thought you were going to call Lam," she said.

"I did."

"So quickly?"

"There wasn't that much to say. I told him I'm committed to doing whatever is necessary. He said he'd call the Italians tonight to tell them his men found you and May in Shanghai and that you've been dealt with, and that he's scheduled meetings with the plants close to Guangzhou for tomorrow."

"That's wonderful."

"It's too soon to say that, but at least we've made a start," Xu said.

"I should head back to the Peninsula to tell May."

"I'll have my car take you," Xu said, standing up.

Ava started to walk towards the door. Xu went with her, his hand lightly holding her elbow. As they stepped into the courtyard, Ava's phone rang. She looked at the incoming number and hesitated. It originated in China and looked familiar, but when she couldn't attach a name to it, she didn't answer.

"I'll let Lam know your new temporary phone number," Xu said as they approached the car. "He'll call as soon as he has some news."

"I'm anxious to get to Hong Kong. I'm anxious to resolve this," Ava said.

"If Lam is his usual efficient self, I imagine you'll be able to get there by tomorrow night," Xu said. "One way or another, we'll fix things for you and May."

Ava climbed into the back seat and waved at Xu as the car turned into the lane.

Wen was sitting in the front seat with the driver. He had become her regular escort and, it now occurred to her, her bodyguard. "The Peninsula Hotel," she said to him.

"Yes," he said.

As Ava took out her phone to let May Ling know she was on her way, she saw that the last caller had left a message. She checked it and heard an unmistakable voice.

"Ava, this is Fai. I don't know if you're still in Shanghai like May Ling said or somewhere else. I'm in Beijing and I'll be here for the next week; then I have to leave for a film shoot in Kunming. I just wanted you to know that I miss you and the others. Being with you in London was wonderful. It was like being part of a family where everyone looks after everyone else. It's never like that on a film set," she said, and then laughed. "There I go again, complaining about the hand that feeds me. My agent gets upset whenever he hears me talk like this, but I tell him that's just him protecting his interests."

There was a pause, and Ava thought the message was over. Then she heard a whisper: "Call me if you can."

36

PANG FAI'S VOICEMAIL HAD JOLTED AVA. IT IMMEDIATELY brought to mind her conversation with May and that odd dream with Uncle and Fai. The possibility that Fai could be gay hadn't occurred to her before then. As she was getting ready for dinner, Ava thought about their time in London. She remembered sitting next to Fai in a hotel bar. The actress was jet-lagged and tired, a condition not helped by several glasses of wine, and she had casually rested her head on Ava's shoulder. Then there were the intense hugs, and the way Fai touched her — gently, as if she were looking for reassurance, but affectionate at the same time.

It was also true, as May had said, that she stayed by Ava's side for most of the week. Ava had assumed that was because she was one of the few people Fai knew and she was in a foreign country whose language she didn't speak or understand very well. Then she thought about Fai's parting words, about feeling safe around Ava.

She pulled a final brushstroke through her hair and fastened it up with the ivory chignon pin. She was meeting May downstairs in the hotel restaurant. In the afternoon Feng had delivered the new phones to the hotel and Ava had given one to May. She knew she was being overly cautious about keeping their contact with the outside world to a minimum, but she also knew it was dangerous to take anything for granted.

She was the first to arrive at Yi Ling Court and was seated immediately. She ordered a glass of Pinot Grigio and had started to peruse the menu when her new phone rang.

"I'm in the restaurant already," she said, assuming it was May.

"And I wish I was with you," Lam said.

"I don't entirely believe that," Ava replied, laughing.

"Considering that you've been brutally attacked and your injuries are painful even to look at, I think you're right — I should steer clear of you."

"The Italians think that's happened?" Ava motioned to a waiter for the bill.

"I told Ricci a few minutes ago."

"How did he react?"

"I have to say they're not easy to deal with."

"How so?"

"He insisted on details."

"What do you mean?"

"He wanted to know where and when we found you and May Ling Wong, how many men we used, how badly you were hurt."

"Was it difficult to answer?"

"No. I was prepared, but I was still surprised he asked."

"Thank you for being careful."

"I've dealt with them often enough to have some idea of how they operate."

"How did you supposedly find us?"

"One of our associates knows a friend of May Ling Wong. That friend confirmed his hunch that she was in Shanghai. We phoned every five-star hotel in the city and were lucky enough to locate her in one near the Bund."

"And then?"

"We positioned men at and near every entrance to the hotel. One of our people spotted the two of you approaching. We waited until you were in the driveway before we attacked. My men used steel rods. It didn't take too many blows to inflict terrible damage. I told him that I wasn't sure you'd live."

"How did Ricci react to that?"

"It didn't affect him one way or another."

"So now what?"

"I told him I've scheduled meetings for tomorrow with the plants closest to Guangzhou and that I'll contact the others by phone. I promised to call him as soon as I have results."

"I'm concerned that he won't believe you couldn't convince the factories to co-operate," Ava said. "And what if their agents call the factories directly?"

"Ava, you aren't the only person who understands the need to construct and protect a backstory," Lam said. "We've already spoken to the factories. They know what to say."

"Sorry. I didn't mean to imply that you aren't on top of things."

"I know you're a demon when it comes to detail, but you should know it's a virtue many of us share."

"Sorry," Ava said again, now certain that she had offended him.

"Let it go."

"Okay."

"Assuming that my conversation with the Camorra goes as planned, when do you intend to get to Hong Kong?" Lam said.

"I'll leave tomorrow."

"Where will you stay?"

"Do you have a preference?"

"Hong Kong is your city, not mine."

"I like the Mandarin Oriental, so I'll probably stay there. It might be best to schedule the meetings at the Grand Hyatt or some other centrally located hotel."

"I'll tell the Italians the Hyatt is where they should stay and that's where we'll meet."

Ava thought about reminding Lam how important it was to have Dominic Ventola and Raffaello Pandolfo at the meeting, but she bit her tongue.

"I'll phone you the moment I know for certain what the schedule is," he said.

"We'll be waiting," Ava said.

She ended the conversation feeling annoyed with the way she'd acted. She was so accustomed to dealing with men who needed to be told what to do that it had become a habit. She wondered if she acted that way around Xu as well. It was something she needed to be more conscious of.

"Hi," May said.

"Lam just phoned to say he's contacted the Camorra to tell them you and I have been successfully assaulted," she said, as the waiter brought the bill. "We can fly to Hong Kong tomorrow. But right now I think we should have dinner in one of our rooms. It's best not to be seen in public."

"Why don't we go to my room. We should also alert the concierge that if anyone calls looking for us, they should say we've checked out."

"That's a good idea."

They walked down to the lobby and gave the concierge the instructions. When they got in the elevator, Ava drew a deep breath. "I hope Lam can convince Dominic Ventola to come to the meeting in Hong Kong."

"What if he can't?"

"Then he'll have to persuade the Camorra to take him a message. Either way, we'll bring this thing to a head."

"You always make it sound so easy," May said, as the door opened to her floor.

"How often do we fail?" Ava asked as they entered May's room.

"There's always a first time. And I have this awful feeling that when it happens, it won't be a minor event."

"What's happened to you? You weren't this negative when I left you earlier."

She sighed. "I spent too much time listening to Changxing."

"You didn't tell him what's going on, did you?"

"No, but the moment I told him I might be hard to reach for a little while, he launched into a lecture about how my working with you is adversely affecting the running of our own businesses."

"Is that true?"

"Not really — I have a terrific team in Wuhan. They make sure everything gets done whether I'm there or not."

"You need a drink," Ava said.

"You're right," May said, opening the mini-bar. She took out a bottle of white wine and gave it to Ava, along with a glass and the room service menu. "Do you know what you want to eat?" she asked.

"I think so."

"What do you have in mind?"

"I'll have steak frites."

"That sounds good to me. I'll have the same and I'll order another bottle of white wine."

After May got off the phone with room service, Ava raised her glass. "To friendship."

May sipped her wine. "Someone told me this makes a very good diet."

"Anyone who believes that is a drunk."

May looked at Ava with concern. "Ava, are you feeling okay?"

"Why do you ask?"

"I know my little joke wasn't that funny, but normally it would at least rate a smile."

"I've got too many things bouncing around in my head."

"In addition to the mess with the Italians?"

"Yes."

"Like what?"

Ava hesitated, then reached for her glass and drained it. "Some personal stuff."

"Tell me."

"I need more wine," Ava said.

"Don't use that as an excuse to stall."

"I'm not stalling. I just haven't decided what I want to tell you."

"You know you can tell me anything and everything."

"Not quite."

"What do you mean?"

"I've never discussed my love life in any detail with you."

"That's not because I've put up any barriers."

"I know," Ava said. "It's all me. I've just never been comfortable talking about it."

They heard a knock on the door. May got up to let in room service. The waiter rolled in their dinner on a cart and uncorked the bottle of white wine.

"I'm sorry," Ava said, when he had left. "I'm just a bit confused. Maria and I are at a crossroads. I like our relationship the way it is. She doesn't."

"Meaning?" May said, as she took a bite of steak.

"She wants us to live together, and in her mind that's a prelude to marriage and having children. I can't even get past the living together part of it."

"Surely you spend a lot of time with her when you're in Toronto."

"Of course, but we each have our own place," Ava said. She took a sip of wine. "I know this may sound terrible, but after two or three days together I'm always happy for her to go back to her own home. I like my solitude, May. I like being surrounded by my own things and having my own space. "

"Do you love her?"

"I do, but maybe not enough, or maybe not in the right way for her. She's quite desperate to settle down, to be part of a domestic duo. I don't feel the same."

"She's given you an ultimatum?"

"How did you know that?"

"Well, every conversation I've had with you about Maria left me with the impression that you're in control. That certainly isn't the impression you're giving me now."

They ate silently for a few moments. The steak was cooked to a perfect medium rare, the frites were crisp and salty, and the homemade mayonnaise had just a hint of lemon.

Ava was beginning to feel both stuffed and light-headed. "I should call Amanda," she said suddenly.

"Why?"

"She has to phone Raffaello Pandolfo to tell him we've been brutally attacked."

May shook her head. "I'll be so happy when this is over."

"You have lots of company," Ava said, reaching for her mobile.

"Yes," Amanda answered, almost immediately.

"Do you remember the conversation we had at lunch, just after Lam called? Well, it's time for you to become an actress."

"Who do you want me to call?"

"You can phone Pandolfo," Ava said. "When you reach him, you can say that May and I were attacked and there's some doubt that I'll live."

Amanda gasped, and Ava realized she might be forcing her to relive the nightmare in Borneo. "Are you okay?" she asked gently.

"Yes, I'm fine," Amanda said. "I'll call him soon."

"Things are starting to move in our favour," Ava said. "We need to keep pressing."

"I have no trouble pressing, but there's one thing I need to ask."

"What?"

"If you can get Ventola to come to Hong Kong, I want to be there with you and May when you meet with him."

"I'm pleased that you do, and we'll be delighted to have you with us," Ava said without hesitation.

Amanda paused as if she'd been expecting a different response. "Do you want me to call you after I talk to him?"

"Please." Ava gave Amanda their temporary phone numbers

"I'll speak to you later tonight then," she said.

Ava put down her phone. "You know, Amanda is a lot stronger than I've given her credit for."

"She wants to come to Hong Kong with us?"

"How did you know?"

"She called me about it earlier today. She was sure you'd say no and she wanted me to convince you."

"Why did she think I'd say no?"

"You'll have to ask her."

37

MAY MANAGED TO WALK AVA TO THE ELEVATOR WITHOUT tripping or stumbling. "I'm a bit drunk," she said.

"Me too."

"But happy."

"You mean 'happier.' Nothing is resolved yet."

"Whatever. We're a great team — me, you, Amanda, and Xu."

"Xu?"

"Don't start being defensive about him again. Every time I mention his name, you react like that."

"There's something that makes me nervous."

"What?"

"The idea of you and Xu getting into a relationship."

May was quiet. Finally she said, "Well, you can relax, because it will never happen."

"You don't want it to?"

"Of course I do, but I would never make the first move."

"And if he came on to you?"

"I've given him several chances and he's not shown the slightest interest," May said. "I am older than him."

"You don't look it."

"Thanks for that, but I like to think that even if I wasn't older, he wouldn't want to mix business and pleasure," May said. "That's how I normally think about things too, but I have these little moments of weakness."

Ava wrapped her arms around May. "I would never stand in the way of anything that made you happy," she whispered. "But I love you and Xu so much, I can't stand the thought of a relationship between you two causing tension among us."

"Don't worry," May said.

"I know," Ava said. She took a deep breath and noticed there were tears on her cheek. She wiped at them roughly with one hand.

"I've rarely seen you this emotional," May said.

"This Ventola business upsets me. I can handle whatever animosity is directed at me, but it bothers me to think about the pain Clark and Gillian have had to endure," Ava said. "And then there's Maria. I don't want to lose her, but I can't give in to what she wants. I'm starting to realize that she's going to disappear from my life."

"It will be her loss."

"Spoken like a true friend."

The elevator doors opened.

"Let's get a good night's sleep," May said. "Everything will look better in the morning, and with any luck we'll be in Hong Kong by this time tomorrow night."

When Ava got to her room, she sat down on the bed. She felt woozy from drinking too much or too fast. She quickly undressed, put on a T-shirt, and went to the bathroom to splash cold water on her face. She returned to the sitting area feeling more alert but knew she needed a distraction if she was going to stay awake for Amanda's call. She listened to Pang Fai's message again and for a moment thought about calling her, before deciding against it. She wanted to be sober if and when that happened.

She turned on the television and scanned the channels. A couple of films looked promising but she didn't want to jump in partway through. She settled for a mindless variety show that lasted nearly two hours. When it ended, she went back to the bathroom to brush her teeth and get ready for bed. She walked to the window and sat in the green leather chair with her new phone in her lap. Five minutes later it rang.

"It's done," Amanda said.

"How did it go?"

"Very well, I think. I did my very best impression of an overwrought woman. I even managed to force a few tears."

"Did he say anything?"

"He acted like he already knew about what I was telling him," Amanda said. "He was calm and didn't protest or deny anything."

"That's all?"

"He did say he'd tried to warn you, but that you'd been too stupid or stubborn to listen."

"That's true enough, I guess."

"The bottom line is that I think he bought the story."

"Now all he has to do is buy one more and we're on our way to Hong Kong."

38

AVA SLEPT FITFULLY, HER MIND ALREADY IN HONG Kong and frustrated that she wasn't physically there as well. She woke at just past seven feeling irritable and impatient. Two cups of coffee, an hour's walk back and forth along the Bund, and a long, hot shower didn't improve her mood.

She checked her emails and saw one from Raffaello Pandolfo. She smiled but didn't open it. What was in it was less important than the fact that he'd sent it. Sure that he was checking on her, she turned on her regular phone. The log showed two incoming calls from Pandolfo and another from a number with the Italian country code. She turned off that phone and reached for the one Xu had provided.

"I got calls from Italy on my regular phone. Did you?" she asked May when she answered.

"One call with a message. I didn't listen to it."

"Me neither."

"Someone also called my office in Wuhan early this morning and asked for me. Changxing has instructed the staff to say that I'm not available and they have no idea when I will be," May said. "The Italians are rather mistrustful, aren't they. They may not have entirely believed Lam."

"It's to be expected."

"Have you spoken to him yet?"

"It's too early. I figure he'll wait until about two, which is seven in the morning in Milan, before he calls Italy."

"Ava, have you thought about what we'll do if Lam can't convince them to come to Hong Kong?"

"He'll convince them."

"Are you saying that because you believe it or because it's the only option we have?"

"It isn't the only option, but it's the best one," Ava said.

"What else do you have in mind?"

"If it wasn't for the personal threats against us, I'd just keep tightening the screws in China and try to expand our activities elsewhere. The threats don't allow us that kind of time. I take them seriously and I can't pretend they'll disappear because of Lam's fabrication," Ava said. "So if the Italians won't come to us, we'll have to go to them."

"To Milan? You and me?"

"And Xu, Lam, Suen, Sonny, and however many more men we need."

"God, I hope it doesn't come to that."

"Me too, but if it does, we're not going into it without a full commitment."

"Can you get that from Xu and Lam?"

"We have it now."

"For Hong Kong."

"Geography is a detail."

May became quiet, and Ava knew she was thinking about the ramifications of what had just been said. She also knew that May had no idea about the ties that bound her to Xu and Lam, and she wasn't ready to start explaining them.

"Have you spoken to Amanda this morning?" Ava asked.

"Yes, about half an hour ago," May said, her voice lightening at the change of subject. "She's going to the factory in Pudong, but her bags are packed and she's ready to leave with us at short notice."

"And what are your plans for the morning?"

"I've scheduled a conference call with Suki to go over her plans for the next six months. You can join us if you want."

"I may just do that," Ava said. "When do you start?"

"Half an hour."

"Okay, I'll drop in, but first I'm going to book us seats on an early evening flight to Hong Kong."

Ava ended the call, feeling irritated again. What would happen if the Italians didn't come to Hong Kong? She had answered May's question quickly and, she hoped, convincingly, but the truth was she wasn't at all certain that Lam or even Xu would be willing to go to Milan. The hackneyed phrase about being a fish out of water came to her. Hackneyed or not, it was true, and one of the major reasons she wanted to get the Italians to Hong Kong, on triad turf. The situation would be reversed if they had to go to Milan.

Lam has got to get them to come to our territory, she thought. She went online, searching for flights to Hong Kong. She blinked in surprise; there were more than thirty-five direct daily flights and an abundance of airlines to choose from. She opted for the familiar, booking three business-class seats on a Cathay Pacific flight scheduled to leave at five-fifteen and arrive in Hong Kong around eight.

She checked the time. It was too early to call Lam, and she

didn't want to harass Xu. She sighed, picked up the phone and her bag, and left the room for the short walk to May's.

May had left her door ajar, and when Ava entered the room she saw her sitting at a small round table with a stack of paper in front of her. Suki Chan's distinctive voice tumbled out of the speaker. Suki spoke quickly and enthusiastically, her words falling over each other, leaving no room for interruption. Ava wondered sometimes if she ever drew a regular breath when she was on one of her verbal tears.

May motioned for her to sit. Ava opened her bag and took out a notebook and pen. Suki was talking about the possible expansion of their Beijing warehouse and logistics business, which they'd taken over only the year before. She was specifically urging them to buy and expand a cold-storage facility near the capital. They had recently done that in Shanghai and the business had been immediately profitable. As Suki reeled off numbers, Ava wrote them in her notebook. May had already covered spreadsheets with numbers and question marks.

Suki paused and May was quick to fill the silence. "Ava joined us a few minutes ago," she said.

"Do I need to repeat anything?" Suki asked.

"No, May can brief me on anything I missed," Ava said.

"Great. Now let me move on to the carbon-fibre container project."

May extracted another spreadsheet from her stack and placed it on top. Ava turned to a fresh page in her notebook. Of all the investments they had made — apart from PÖ — this was the one whose potential excited Ava the most. The world of ocean freight revolved around steel containers that were twenty or forty feet long, and there were close to twenty million of them in use. The company in which they'd invested had developed a container made of carbon fibre that weighed only ten percent of its steel counterpart. It was also collapsible, which made it much easier to store, non-corrosive, and well insulated, and it could float. The flotation aspect was proving to be a major selling point, Suki explained, because ten thousand steel containers fell off ships every year and were never seen again.

"I know you might find this funny after the way we've been losing VLG containers this week, but we've also made some recent sales because of the tracking system we can imbed in the skin of ours," Suki said.

"Explain that to me again," May said. "Changxing has a customer who's really concerned about the security of his shipments."

"It's simple enough. The composite in the panels of our containers is electronically transparent, so information from any built-in sensor can be transmitted wirelessly." Suki laughed. "It is virtually impossible to lose one of our containers."

"Then it's a good thing we haven't taken over the market-place yet," Ava said.

"We're a long, long way from doing that," Suki said. "As good as our product is, it still costs three times what a steel container does."

"But it pays for itself in less than two years, through savings in storage charges and fuel costs," May said.

"Not everyone is prepared to wait that long for a return on their investment."

"So what are the sales projections for the next six months?" Ava asked.

"I'll go major market by major market," Suki said. She began reading out a long list of numbers.

Despite her overriding concern about how Lam's morning was going, Ava found herself getting caught up in the minutiae of the carbon-fibre container business. As Suki moved past sales projections and into their longer-term marketing strategies, Ava was totally engrossed. So was May, who asked question after pointed question. May knew the transportation and warehouse business inside out and wasn't afraid to challenge Suki, sometimes in a manner that Ava thought bordered on rude. What pleased Ava was how professional Suki was in her replies. When the discussion ended, it wasn't because they had run out of things to say or because Ava had filled two pages of her notebook. It was because Ava's phone rang.

She stared at it blankly until the Guangzhou number registered. She hit the answer button and put the phone to her ear with a combination of eagerness and trepidation. "Ban, we've been anxious to hear from you."

"I've been on and off the phone with the Italians for the past hour."

"That sounds complicated," Ava said. She moved away from the table, leaving May to continue the discussion with Suki.

"It was, and we're still not finished."

"Oh," Ava said, now out of earshot.

"Don't be discouraged, at least not yet," Lam said. "One reason our talks dragged on was that Ricci isn't empowered to make the kind of decision we want. He had to speak to a man named Moretti, who in turn had to consult with a Franco Bianchi. I remember Bianchi. He dealt directly with

Li when he was Mountain Master. I think that when they initially contacted me, they didn't know that Li is dead and I'm the boss. I'm quite sure that Ricci and Morctti are under-bosses, and that they thought they were dealing with an equal when they talked to me. I should have picked up on that at the outset."

"They know you're the boss now?"

"They certainly do. I told them that until I spoke directly to Bianchi, nothing good was going to happen for VLG in China."

"Has that happened?"

"Five minutes ago. He apologized for their complex lines of communication and said he had misunderstood the leadership situation in Guangzhou. Otherwise he would have called me himself."

"What did you tell him?"

"Not exactly what you and I discussed."

"Pardon?"

"The more I thought about my original plan, the less plausible it seemed. In fact, I decided it was too weak to get you what you want, so I decided to up the ante," Lam said.

"How so?"

"I told him he has a far bigger problem with the factories and the shipments than he knows and that I originally thought," Lam said. "I said I had just discovered that the factories are at least partially owned by some triad gangs, specifically gangs in Shanghai and Wanchai that are controlled by Xu. Bianchi said he has heard of Xu but never had any dealings with him."

"Does Xu know you told him that?"

"I cleared it with him."

"Sorry," Ava said hurriedly, realizing that once again her question might have been inappropriate.

"*Momentai*," Lam said. "I said the triad ownership position has obviously changed the way I'm looking at my contract with the Camorra. I told Bianchi that we have to bring Wanchai and Shanghai onside if anything is to get done. He asked me if that's possible. I said yes. He asked me what it would take. I said I think I can broker a deal that both sides can live with, but that it will have to be done face-to-face. He asked me why. I said that Xu not only has part-ownership of the plants, he also has a connection with PÖ."

Ava wasn't quite sure what she'd just heard. "You said what?"

"I told him that PÖ has contracted all its clothing manufacturing to plants owned by Xu, and had been planning to develop lines of leather goods and shoes in Huidong and Huadu, in Xu's factories. I said VLG's public trashing of PÖ looks certain to cost Xu even more than their production was worth, and that's why he reacted the way he did with regard to the VLG products being made in his factories."

"How did Bianchi react?"

"He was stunned and then got quite angry — but not at me. He said it was Ventola who went after PÖ and that he did it on his own, without consulting them."

"Good god, that is a more intricate story."

"Maybe, but it lends itself to a simpler resolution," Lam said. "Bianchi now believes that Xu controls the plants and all he has to do is cut a deal with Xu to get their production and supply lines reopened."

"You say that as if you're certain that the Camorra has a financial interest in VLG and wasn't just hired to do a job."

"I am certain, because I asked Bianchi that specific question. He told me they've been partners in VLG for more than ten years. It's one of their most profitable and worry-free investments."

"That certainly gives them enough motivation to resolve the problem."

"And I made it very clear that the problem won't be resolved unless they meet with Xu."

"How can they say no?"

"I can't predict what they'll do," Lam said.

"No, you're right, I shouldn't be making assumptions. I mean, I never believed that Dominic Ventola would stoop to the level he did. Look how that's turned out."

"Ava, I also have to say that Bianchi was quite resistant to the notion of Ventola's being involved in any part of the negotiations."

"Ventola and Raffaello Pandolfo. I want them both there."

"I'll ask, but I can't promise," Lam said.

"What's the point in negotiating with the Camorra alone? I want to be certain that VLG understands its position. I want to be sure that Ventola commits to resurrecting PÖ and calls off his contract on May and me."

"Whether or not he's there, the Camorra will be made to understand that the contract is null and void."

"Ventola can go elsewhere. He has a vindictive streak and the money to indulge it. I don't want to spend weeks or months looking over my shoulder, and I'm not about to expose May and me to any kind of risk."

"Then I will insist they be there."

"Thank you."

"And if they refuse?"

"At the very minimum we'll continue our campaign to shut them out of China."

"Hopefully I won't have to issue that threat during my discussion with Bianchi," Lam said.

"I don't know many people who are more persuasive than you," Ava said.

"That's quite the compliment, coming from you," Lam said. "There is one more thing we should talk about and that's a meeting locale."

"Did you mention Hong Kong?"

"I saw no point in doing that until they had agreed to meet."

"Do you anticipate a problem?"

"If I were in their position, I'd most certainly have a problem with China."

"But Hong Kong isn't really China."

"To Hong Kongers it isn't, but I think most Europeans would think differently."

"Ventola and Pandolfo must know the city well. They'll understand it's a neutral site."

"The Camorra doesn't mix in the same circles."

"What are you suggesting?"

"Nothing in particular. I'll tell them Hong Kong is the best location, but if they don't agree then we need to have a backup proposal."

"Manila, Jakarta, Singapore...any major Asian city."

"Okay."

Ava drew a deep breath. "Ban, regardless of where we meet, you've done wonders. Changing the story was exactly the right thing to do. You've structured it in such a way that it's almost impossible for them to say no."

"That still may not get Ventola and Pandolfo along for the ride."

"Let's leave it to the Camorra to convince them."

"Strangely, I'm not sure who has the upper hand in that relationship," Lam said. "Bianchi was quite cautious and very polite when he spoke about Ventola. The man didn't build a fifteen-billion-dollar luxury-brand empire by being pushed around."

Ava leaned against the wall for a few minutes after ending her conversation with Lam. He had surprised her with his decision to tell the Camorra that the factories and triads were linked, and even more so by identifying Xu's organizations as principals. The surprise had morphed into something approaching shock when he said he'd told them that Xu had an interest in PÖ. Why did he have to mention it at all? If the intent was to coerce the Camorra and VLG to attend the meeting, surely the triad connection with the factories would have been enough. Ava didn't doubt his intentions — and the fact that Xu had agreed to the strategy mollified her reaction — but she still wished Lam had held back more in reserve. *I'm nitpicking*, she thought suddenly. *I told him to do whatever he had to do to get a meeting, and that's what he's done.*

"Ava, is anything wrong?" May asked, coming towards her.

"No. I was talking to Lam. He spoke to the Italians and thinks he's well on the way to getting them to meet."

"When will we know for certain?"

"He'll call back within an hour."

"Then why do you look so preoccupied?"

"He told them more than I wanted them to know."

"Like what?"

"He told them that Xu controls the factories they've been using and has a business relationship with PÖ."

"Not entirely untrue."

"No, but strategically it eliminates at least part of the element of surprise I was counting on."

"I'm not sure I agree with you that it was a wrong thing to do," May said. "It provides the Italians an immediate and compelling reason to have this meeting. It also gives them time to really think through the potential scope of the problem they have. That might soften their position."

"I see the sense in both those points," Ava said. "I just wish he'd discussed things with me first."

"I can't help feeling that's what's bothering you more than what he actually said," May suggested. "You do like to be in control."

39

THE CALL CAME TWO HOURS LATER. AVA AND MAY HAD
spent the time working on Suki's numbers, trying to calcu-
late how much money it would take to support the business's
growth. Or at least they tried to. Thoughts about the VLG
crisis kept intruding, and they took turns posing what-ifs.

"I'm hungry," May said at one point.

"Me too, but I'm not going anywhere until I hear from
Lam."

"Your phone will work in a restaurant."

"Yes, but I'm half expecting bad news and I want to be
able to really vent if I hear any."

"It isn't like you to be pessimistic."

"As you said before, I don't feel comfortable when I'm not
in control."

"That isn't exactly what I said."

"It's close enough."

"Ava!"

"Sorry, May," Ava said. "I'm not myself."

"Is it just this difficulty that's bothering you or is it what's
going on with Maria?"

"A bit of both, I think," Ava said, surprised by the emotion the question triggered in her.

"Both will pass."

"The sooner the better," she said, picking up another set of Suki's numbers.

Ten minutes later, Ava's phone rang. "This is Lam," he said. "I just spoke to Bianchi."

"You sound annoyed," Ava said, pushing her chair back from the table to create space between her and May Ling.

"He's not an easy man."

"But in the end?"

"They'll meet us in Macau."

"How did Macau enter the conversation?"

"They started off by asking us to meet them in Milan. When I said no to Milan, they suggested Rome, then Madrid, and finally Marseilles. I told them that none of those sites work for us, and they told me that Guangzhou, Shanghai, Manila, and even Hong Kong aren't satisfactory to them. Just when I thought we were at an impasse, Bianchi excused himself for a few minutes. When he came back on the line, he said Macau is acceptable."

"They must have contacts there."

"I would imagine that is the case."

"Do we?"

"I don't personally, but I'll be shocked if Lop or your old friend Sammy Wing don't have strong connections."

Ava felt a slight chill at the mention of Sammy Wing. He was the Mountain Master in Wanchai, a district of Hong Kong. In partnership with Li, he had arranged to have Xu and Ava killed. When that failed, Xu had decimated his gang, took over Wanchai, put Lop in place as the de facto boss, and let Wing continue on as a figurehead.

"Why would Sammy Wing do anything to help me?"

"Fear of what Lop might do to him if he doesn't."

"Even if Lop and Wing do help, I still find Macau an odd choice."

"It doesn't make me entirely comfortable, but it's better than Marseilles or Milan."

"True."

"That also wasn't the oddest part of the conversation."

"What else was said?"

Lam cleared his throat, and Ava's unease increased. "They want to have the meeting tomorrow."

"How is that possible? I mean, how could they get there that fast?"

"According to Bianchi, they have a private jet that can get them from Milan to Macau without a stop."

"It's probably VLG's jet."

"I don't know who it belongs to. All I know is that he said it was available and ready to leave within a few hours' notice."

"Why such a rush?"

"I asked the same question. I was told that every day the factories aren't producing goods is costing them millions of dollars."

"Did he mention the containers that have gone missing? Did he mention any of the other things we've done to create havoc with their business?"

"No, but he did raise your name," Lam said quietly.

"In what way?"

"He asked me if I'm one hundred percent sure that you and May Ling Wong have been taken care of. The question surprised me, and I have to say I was flustered for a second.

I'm not used to having my word doubted, especially when I was quite specific with Ricci," Lam said. "I asked him why we were still talking about it."

"He doesn't believe you, does he."

"No, I don't think he does. He said VLG arranged to send a buying agent not directly linked to them to the PÖ factory in Pudong first thing this morning. The agent pretended to be interested in acquiring the PÖ line for distribution in Switzerland. He probably went to see if you were there, or maybe just to get a sense of the mood of the place. He expected the atmosphere to be grim. Instead, everyone seemed quite cheerful. Bianchi said he can't understand how that could be the case if you and May Ling are as badly hurt as I made out. The agent even asked about the partners in PÖ, and your names were casually mentioned. Bianchi said he found that reaction odd. He said that at the very least there should have been some hesitation and apprehension."

"Shit," Ava said.

"Do your other partners know what our plans are and the stories we've been spinning?"

"Only Amanda Yee. I didn't share them with the others."

"Was Amanda at the factory this morning?"

"Yes, but I don't know when she arrived. She might not have seen the agent."

"Find out," Lam said. "We need to know who met with the agent and what was discussed. I have a feeling that Bianchi was holding some things back from me."

"I'll call as soon as we finish our conversation."

"The good thing is that I haven't lied to them directly. I keep saying that I've been told the deed was done, so if the shit hits the fan I'll pin the blame on some anonymous third party"

"They are a paranoid bunch, aren't they."

"They are indeed, and I think we need to take that into account when we go to Macau."

"How many of them are coming?"

"Bianchi didn't say."

"But you told him that Ventola and Pandolfo should be there?"

"I did, and he said that VLG will be well and properly represented."

"What does that mean?"

"I don't know, and I can only push so hard. Remember, they think they've hired me and that I'm working for them. I don't want them to raise any more questions. I'm certain I've already lost some credibility with them."

"I understand," Ava said. "So where does this leave us?"

"I told Bianchi I'll get back to him to confirm that Xu is available tomorrow. If he is, then we'll fix a time and location for the meeting."

"Have you spoken to Xu?"

"Not yet."

"Do you want me to do it, since the favour being requested is mine?"

"I think that's best."

"I'll do it now."

Ava ended the call. May was looking anxiously at her from across the table. "It looks like our Hong Kong flight schedule is well timed. We could be meeting with them in Macau as soon as tomorrow, but I need to confirm with Xu that he can be there then." Before May could ask any questions, Ava called him.

"*Mei mei*, what's going on?" he answered.

"Does something have to be going on for me to call you?"

"That's normally the case."

"And it is again." Ava laughed. "I just spoke to Lam. The Italians have agreed to meet with us, but in Macau, and they're proposing that it happen tomorrow. They have a private jet, so logistically they're flexible."

"And eager."

"I said the same thing to Lam. He doesn't find it unusual."

"So, Macau tomorrow," Xu murmured.

"Is that a problem?"

"I can clear my schedule, but I can't say I'm crazy about the idea of meeting them there. Macau still has too many local guns for hire who are easy to contact and will work for anyone."

"We're expecting a business meeting, not a pitched battle."

"You know I've never dealt directly with the Camorra, but I've had dealings with other Italian gangs and they were always volatile. They switch moods in a heartbeat. One minute they're your best friends, the next they're trying to cut your throat."

"Uncle felt the same way, but I don't think we have any choice about where the meeting will be held. Macau was the best compromise Lam could get."

"How many men does he expect will be there?"

"We don't know. We assume there will be several from the Camorra, and we've asked that Ventola and Pandolfo be there as well."

"Even if they don't enlist local support, we need to be cautious. The problem is we don't have any men on the ground in Macau."

"Can you send some from Hong Kong, from Wanchai?"

"I'll talk to Lop."

"I'm bringing Sonny with me."

"That's a good start. I'll have Suen with me, and I'll tell Lam to bring one or two of his people along," Xu said. "I'll ask Lop to provide anything else we need, once he figures out how many men we're dealing with and if they've hired any Macanese muscle."

"I can't imagine them doing that."

"Maybe not, but Lop will make sure we've got them covered no matter what happens."

"How will he do that?"

"I've learned that it's better to just give him an order and not worry about how it's carried out," Xu said. "Like you, he always finds a way to get things done."

"I'll call Lam and let him know that we're on for tomorrow," she said.

"When will you leave?"

"May, Amanda, and I are flying to Hong Kong tonight."

Xu paused. "Ava, are you thinking of bringing your partners to the meeting?"

"I was, before the meeting place changed to Macau."

"I don't think they should be there," he said. "We have no idea what's going to happen. It could get dangerous. No one doubts your ability to look after yourself, but May and Amanda are civilians. I'd be concerned about their safety and, on top of that, their well-being becoming a distraction for the rest of us. We don't want them to get hurt, and we don't want them to witness whatever happens if things go wrong."

"You're right."

"I'm glad you agree, because I was prepared to be insistent," Xu said. "Besides, I don't doubt for a second that they trust you to represent their interests. There is nothing they can add."

"I'll talk to them. I'm sure they'll understand," Ava said. "Now, when do you intend to leave Shanghai?"

"I'll fly into Hong Kong sometime tomorrow afternoon. I'll let you know the details when I have them. I'm assuming you'll take the jetfoil to Macau."

"It's my plan."

"I'm sure I'll land in time to travel to Macau with you."

"That would be ideal. You can reach me at the Mandarin Oriental or on the cellphone you gave me," Ava said. "Although I'm beginning to think that phone is irrelevant."

"Why do you say that?"

"Lam thinks the Camorra suspects he's been lying to them about May and me being assaulted."

"He said that?"

"He did."

"And the Camorra is still prepared to meet?"

"I guess whatever reservations they have are outweighed by the amount of money involved. May and I are small potatoes compared to that."

"Still, after a day of thinking about the possibility that Lam lied to them, they might decide on a change in priorities," Xu said. "Now I have even more reason to call Lop."

40

AT 7:45 P.M. THE CATHAY PACIFIC JET BEGAN ITS SLOW descent over the South China Sea into Chek Lap Kok airport. It had left Shanghai on time at 5:35 and Ava expected to be at the arrivals gate by 8:15. If the airport operated at its usual level of efficiency, they would clear Customs and Immigration, collect their bags, and be in Sonny's Mercedes half an hour later.

Ava and May had left the Peninsula Hotel in Shanghai at mid-afternoon, after Lam had confirmed arrangements with Franco Bianchi. The meeting was set for seven the following night in the Don Pietro restaurant, close to the Hotel Lisboa.

"They want to meet in a restaurant?" Ava said when Lam informed her.

"An Italian restaurant at that, but I don't think there's any intention to meet over dinner," Lam said. "Bianchi told me that one of his people knows the manager. Arrangements will be made to block off a large part of the restaurant, so we'll have privacy and still have the security of being in a public place."

"I guess there's no point in arguing about it," Ava said. "We're flying into Hong Kong tonight and will be staying at the Mandarin Oriental. Xu is arriving tomorrow. We'll jetfoil to Macau together."

"Are your partners coming with you?"

"Yes, but they won't be attending the meeting."

"Good. I'd be concerned if they were."

"Ban, when will you be arriving in Macau, and where do you want to meet?"

"I'll drive directly to Macau from Guangzhou tomorrow morning. I've booked rooms at the Grand Hyatt in the City of Dreams. Why don't you come there."

"We'll do that."

"Ava, has Xu mentioned how many men he's bringing?"

"Only Suen, but he's told Lop to provide as many more as are required."

"How will Lop know how many are needed?"

"I have no idea, but Xu seems certain that he'll figure it out."

"Lop is a piece of work," Lam said, "but I wish I had someone with even half his contacts."

"Are you coming alone?"

"No, I'm bringing two men."

"And did Bianchi tell you who's going to be with him?"

"I asked and he put me off. I reminded him that we expect senior people from VLG to attend the meeting. He repeated that the company will be well represented."

After her conversation with Lam, Ava called Sonny and gave him her flight schedule. She then quickly briefed May, and the two women went to their rooms to pack. May had been understanding when Ava told her she wouldn't be going to the meeting. She didn't have the stomach for violence and understood that there was potential for it. Ava didn't have to mention Xu's other reservations.

Ava phoned Amanda at the factory in Pudong to give her their departure details. Before she could, Amanda said, "Wait a moment, I want to go into a private office."

"Is this about the purchasing agent who was at the factory this morning?"

"I wish that's all it was," Amanda said tensely.

Now what? Ava thought.

"I'm in Chi-Tze's office," Amanda said a few minutes later. "She grabbed me the instant I arrived at the factory this morning. She told me that Dominic Ventola called Clark last night."

"How does she know that?"

"Gillian told her. Ventola said to Clark that he regrets the way things have been handled and promised him a place in the VLG organization regardless of what happens. Ventola also said that if Clark and Gillian can find a way to persuade Three Sisters to sell its rights and shares, there's still time to salvage PÖ."

"If Gillian knows all this, then she and Clark obviously discussed the conversation."

"They did. And thank god Gillian trusted us enough to talk to Chi-Tze."

"It's a bit late in the game for the Pos to change their minds," Ava said, biting back a feeling of frustration that was laced with anger.

"They haven't done that, at least, not according to what Gillian told Chi-Tze."

"But Ventola has planted the seed," Ava said. "I have to give him credit. He knew exactly what to say to entice Clark and to undermine us."

"Except nothing has resulted from it."

"Not yet anyway, but it's certainly one more reason why we need to resolve our issues with VLG tomorrow night in Macau," Ava said. "Speaking of which, I think you should tell Chi-Tze, Clark, and Gillian that we think we're getting close to a resolution. You can even tell them we're expecting something to happen within the next seventy-two hours. That might prevent Clark from considering doing something precipitous."

"Do you think we can reach an agreement that quickly?"

"If we can't, I don't like our chances of ever getting one," Ava said. She paused. "Is there anything else I need to know about Clark?"

"No, that's all, but I did tell Chi-Tze to stay close to Gillian and to let us know if she detects any reason for us to worry."

"Good. Now let's talk about that purchasing agent."

Amanda drew a deep breath. "He was here this morning and spent some time with Gillian and Chi-Tze. They thought he was a bit strange. It was like he was pretending to be interested in the PÖ line while he was really eyeballing the factory. He also asked Gillian about the ownership group."

"Did she mention May and me?"

"Only in the most general way. He just asked who the investors are and how many partners we have. She said the Po siblings and Three Sisters Investments are the owners. He asked who the partners are in Three Sisters. Gillian told him our names and nothing else."

"And he didn't press for more details?"

"No."

"Was he Chinese?"

"He was a Westerner. He said he was Swiss."

"Shit. Lam thinks he was sent by the Italians."

"Why?"

"To get a sense of our mood. And it seems everyone was so cheery that it stretched believability that two key owners of the business were supposedly badly beaten up less than forty-eight hours ago."

"How should they have acted? Gillian, Clark, and Chi-Tze think you and May are just fine and working towards a resolution to our problem."

"I'm not being critical."

"I know, but no one at the factory knows what to say or how to act right now, and putting on a happy face is the default position."

"Tomorrow we'll make sure they can be happy for a reason."

"I sure hope so," Amanda said. "When are we leaving for Hong Kong?"

Ava gave her the flight details and they agreed to meet at the Cathay check-in counter. Ava then explained to Amanda why she and May wouldn't be attending the actual meeting with VLG. Amanda was as understanding as May had been.

By the time they met at the airport late that afternoon, their thoughts about events at the Pudong factory were behind them and their focus was on the day ahead. The three women sat in the business-class lounge, and until it was time to board they talked about what they needed from VLG to repair the damage that had been done.

It was a two-and-a-half-hour flight to Hong Kong. Ava spent the time surfing the video channels, but her mind was so focused on VLG and the Camorra that she couldn't find anything to distract her. Things were moving quickly, even more quickly than she had hoped for. Part of her believed that was good, especially now that Ventola was trying to lure Clark, but she couldn't eliminate a nagging feeling that maybe it was too good. Except, why shouldn't it be? The Camorra believed that all they had to do was cut a deal with Xu. They probably weren't concerned about a few extra costs, given the profit margins they had. They had no idea that Xu's involvement with PÖ went far beyond a manufacturing arrangement. And as for May and Ava, why would the Camorra think that Xu, or anyone else for that matter, cared about an attack on them — assuming they still believed it had taken place. Either way, she wondered how they were going to react when she made her appearance.

Should she have asked Lam to lie to them about the assault? Doing anything else would have been careless, she thought, because there had been no indication that events were going to unfold the way they did. The important thing had been to buy time, to prevent the Camorra from hiring someone else to go after them in Canada, in Wuhan, or wherever. If the Italians had been unresponsive to Lam's request for a meeting, how long would they have waited before doing exactly that? No, the lie had been necessary. Even if they hadn't entirely bought into it, it created doubt.

And what was the connection between the Camorra and VLG? Were they really business partners or did VLG simply contract out jobs to them? And if they were partners, for how long, and which partner had control? It was inconceivable to think Ventola could be a Mafia don, but then Ava remembered Lam's remark about the way Franco Bianchi spoke of Ventola. What was the nature of their relationship that caused Bianchi to be so respectful?

As the plane began its descent, Ava looked out the window.

The sea below was sparkling like a star-filled sky on a cloud-less night. The flickering lights emanated from hundreds of ships coming and going from Hong Kong or anchored to wait their turn to enter the port. It was a familiar sight, and every time she saw it, she felt she was coming home. Until a dozen years before she hadn't considered Hong Kong a home at all, just the place where she'd been born and where her father and half-siblings lived. But after she began her business with Uncle, Hong Kong became a constant presence in her life, and the more time she spent there, the more she loved it. She thought of it as the world's bridge city: under British rule it was the entry point to most of Asia, and now it was the West's doorway to China. Having one foot in China and another in the West was sometimes a difficult balance, but whenever the territory tilted too far to one side, events tended to pull it back towards the centre. The most recent example had been Hong Kong's raucous democratic movement, which was dampened by the Communist government's willingness to wait it out. But just as the movement lost momentum, it had revived, the Chinese government made concessions, and balance was once again restored.

This duality — this tug-of-war between Chinese politics, culture, and customs and the British systems of law, governance, and education that had taken root more than one hundred years earlier — was one of the things that made Hong Kong fascinating to Ava. The city had all the raw energy and future focus of the mainland cities, but funnelled through the framework that the British had created and the population respected enough to maintain.

The plane touched down on the runway, and they disembarked and headed towards Customs and Immigration.

In less than the thirty minutes Ava had anticipated, the three women walked into the arrivals hall to find Sonny waiting for them in the same spot he always occupied, directly under the sign that read ARRIVALS. He waved when he saw them, a shy smile crossing his face. He wore a black suit, white shirt, and black tie. It was his normal style of dress. She had no doubt that Sonny had adopted it from Uncle, who always wore a black suit and white shirt buttoned to the collar, and that he'd never let it go.

The first time she had met Sonny, she was immediately intimidated. She'd never seen anyone whose combination of physical appearance and manner was so menacing. Over the years he had confirmed many times her initial impression, particularly when it came to protecting Uncle and, later, her. His devotion was absolute. Anyone who wanted to harm her would have to kill him first.

"Hey, boss," he said as Ava drew near.

"Hi, Sonny. Thanks for coming to meet us," she said.

He nodded and reached for her bag. She passed it to him and then stood on her tiptoes to kiss him on both cheeks.

"Hi, Sonny," Amanda said from behind Ava.

"Hey," he said. "I dropped Michael off at your apartment before I came here. He couldn't be happier that you're home."

"Where's the car?" Ava asked.

"The usual place."

She smiled. The airport police had always allowed Uncle to park at the curb in a no-parking zone. Out of respect for him, the privilege had been extended to Sonny.

They walked through the exit, turned right, and in twenty steps were at the car. Sonny opened the back door for them and loaded their bags into the trunk. The night was damp and chilly, made more so by a gusty wind.

May shivered as she climbed into the car. "I've never liked Hong Kong winters," she said. "The cold gets into your bones."

"The only thing worse is a Hong Kong summer," Ava said. "All that heat and humidity outdoors and arctic air conditioning indoors."

"The way you two are going on, I should apply for danger pay," Amanda said.

Ava laughed as she slid into the front passenger seat. "How's traffic tonight?" she asked Sonny as he started the car.

"Pretty good. I figure half an hour should get you to the Mandarin Oriental," he said.

The Mercedes joined the other outbound traffic. The airport was built on reclaimed land adjacent to Lantau Island. Their route would take them over the Tsing Ma Bridge, which spanned the Ma Wan Channel and linked Lantau to Tsing Yi Island. Ava knew they'd follow Route 8 over Tsing Yi into Kowloon, then journey south to Tsim Sha Tsui, where they'd connect with Route 3 and the Western Harbour Crossing that would take them to Hong Kong Island.

The Tsing Ma Bridge was more than two kilometres long and more than two hundred metres above the channel. It had been opened in April 1997 by Margaret Thatcher — one of the last official British events before Hong Kong was turned over to China on July 1 of the same year. Ava preferred taking the bridge during the day, when she could clearly see the profusion of freighters, tankers, pleasure craft, fishing vessels, and sampans below, but even at night it was a fascinating sight.

"That was a terrific job you did for us in Shenzhen," May said to Sonny.

"It wasn't so hard, and I had help from Lop and the guys in Fanling. In fact, Lop did most of the talking."

"But you were the one who was actually representing our interests," May said.

"That's true," Sonny said. He looked over at Ava. "On that subject, I was wondering, am I included in tomorrow's meeting?"

"Of course," Ava said quickly. "I should have made that clear. I'm sorry I didn't."

Sonny glanced at her again, and Ava expected him to tell her she never had to say sorry to him. Instead he said, "Who's going to be there?"

"Xu and Suen. Lam is coming from Guangzhou with two men. Then you and me."

"How about Lop?"

"He and Xu are working something out. Xu told him to make sure we're protected in any eventuality. I have no idea what Lop may think is necessary. We'll find out tomorrow, I guess."

"He's something else," Sonny said, a touch of admiration in his voice.

"So are you," Ava said.

He shook his head, but not too vigorously, and Ava knew he was pleased by her remark. Then he looked at her again. "I don't mean to intrude, but you haven't mentioned if May Ling and Amanda are going tomorrow."

"They aren't, but why do you ask?"

His face turned slightly red. Ava had rarely seen him look so uncomfortable.

"It's just out of concern for their safety if things go sideways."

"I would have hid behind you, Sonny," May said from the back seat.

"Me too," Amanda said.

"As pleased as I am that neither of you will have to do that, I still don't think we should joke about it," Ava said.

"Sorry to have raised the subject," Sonny said as they reached the Western Harbour Crossing. "I know it isn't my place."

The hotel was on Connaught Road in Central, Hong Kong's financial district. It faced Victoria Harbour and the Kowloon skyline, and behind it loomed Victoria Peak — the most expensive real estate in the city. Amanda and Michael had an apartment that was halfway up the Peak. Their goal was to one day be able to afford something closer to the top, something that would give them a better view of the harbour than the small slice they could see now.

"It makes the most sense to drop you and May Ling at the Oriental first," Sonny said as the car exited the tunnel to Hong Kong Island.

"Of course," Ava said.

"But I'll come back to the hotel after dropping off Amanda, in case you need me for anything," he said to Ava.

"No, don't bother doing that tonight. I'm going to stay in. I'm tired and we have a big day ahead of us."

Sonny nodded. "What are the plans for tomorrow?"

"Let me talk to Xu tonight. I want to know what time he's arriving and what his schedule looks like. We should travel to Macau together if possible. We'll coordinate our activities once I've spoken to him," Ava said. "Are you available if he needs a ride from the airport?"

"If he does, Lop will arrange it," Sonny said.

"Yes, of course," Ava said, reminded again how respectfully relationships were valued and guarded. She was sure that if Xu had suggested Lop arrange to pick her up, she would have reminded Xu that it was Sonny's job.

The hotel driveway was busy, forcing Sonny to double-park the Mercedes. He popped the trunk and got out. Ava and May stayed in the car until he opened their doors.

"Say hello to Michael. I'll call you in the morning," Ava said to Amanda.

"I know he'll want us all to meet for dim sum," Amanda said. "He might even ask your father to join us."

Ava shook her head. "It isn't the best time for socializing. Let me get this meeting behind me first."

"I understand," Amanda said.

A bellman came to get their bags. Sonny helped take them out of the trunk and then walked over to Ava. "My phone will be on at all times. I'm no more than half an hour away if you need anything."

"Thanks. I'm expecting that we'll leave here early tomorrow afternoon, but I'll confirm that as soon as I know."

"I'll be waiting," Sonny said. He looked at her, his expression betraying a hint of affection. "It's great to have you back in Hong Kong."

"And I'm happy to be here," Ava said.

Ava and May checked in and followed the bellman to the elevators. May had booked two rooms that had views of Victoria Harbour and Kowloon. Ava was on the twentieth floor, May one floor above.

"Do you want to eat or get a drink in the bar?" May asked as they ascended.

"No, I really am tired. I'll shower and then crash. I may

get up early to run in Victoria Park. If I do, I'll be back here by nine or so. We can have breakfast at the Mandarin Grill, or wait a bit and have dim sum at Man Wah."

"I thought you weren't in the mood for dim sum," May said.

"I'm not in the mood to have dim sum with Michael or my father," Ava said. "I don't need or want the distraction, and I certainly don't want to be answering questions about why I'm here and how long I'll be staying. We have enough to deal with."

41

IT WASN'T UNTIL SHE WAS INSIDE THE ROOM AND unpacking her bags that Ava realized she hadn't turned on either of her phones since she'd landed.

The new one had a message from Xu. He was arriving at one and would go directly to the Hong Kong–Macau Ferry Terminal. He said the TurboJet service left every thirty minutes and took fifty-five minutes to make the trip. He would call her as soon as he knew when he might get to the terminal. Where did she want to meet?

Ava did a quick calculation. If his flight was on time and traffic was okay, he'd reach the terminal by two-thirty. That would put them in Macau at around three-thirty or four and give them a chance to sit with Lam before the meeting with the Italians. She phoned him and was sent directly to voicemail. "We'll meet you at the TurboJet counter and will be there before two-thirty. We can travel together to Macau," she said. "Have you heard anything from Lop about what he expects when we get there?"

She picked up her usual phone and saw there had been three calls. She checked the log and saw the numbers for

Pandolfo and Maria, and a Chinese number that she thought was Pang Fai's. She guessed Pandolfo was still checking on her. She hesitated. There might not be any way for Pandolfo to know she'd accessed the message, but she wasn't going to risk it. She checked the time. It was almost nine-thirty. Maria had phoned an hour ago from her cell, and Ava was sure she'd be at her Consulate office by now. Had she had a change of heart? She felt a surge of optimism as she prepared to make the call on her new phone.

She sat at the desk, her hand trembling slightly as she tapped in Maria's number. The tremor surprised her. When the receptionist answered, Ava gave him her name and asked for Maria. There was a delay, one ring, and then Maria said, "Why are you calling me on the office line?"

"I have a temporary phone and I was afraid you wouldn't answer if you didn't recognize the number."

"That was sensible, because I might not have," Maria said.

"I saw you'd called but couldn't listen to your message. I thought I should call you back anyway."

"I'm glad you did, but you should know that I didn't phone to talk about us," Maria said quickly. "Or at least not about changing my mind."

"I didn't assume that was the case," Ava lied. "So that leaves me curious as to why you did phone."

"Well, I thought I should," Maria said. "I don't know what you're doing in Asia this time, but there are some strange things going on here, and I'm wondering if there might be a connection."

"What do you mean?" Ava said, her stomach turning.

Maria paused, and Ava could imagine her running her fingers through her hair, the way she did when she was gathering her thoughts. "I went to your condo earlier this morning," she finally said. "I wanted to pick up my things. I couldn't leave the key in the apartment so I went to talk to Bernard, the concierge on duty, about whether I should leave it with him or mail it to you. He said I should mail it and then asked me if you were out of town. I thought that was a strange question and I asked him why he wanted to know. He said that two men had been at the building about half an hour before looking for you."

"Two men? This morning?"

"I was there at about eight-fifteen, so it was before eight. And yes, two men. According to Bernard, they came into the lobby and buzzed your apartment, and when there was no answer they came to his desk and talked to him. He found them rather odd."

"In what way?"

"They said they were business acquaintances and had an appointment with you at eight, but Bernard said they didn't look or act like businesspeople. And I told him that I've never known you to have a business meeting at the condo."

"What did they look like?"

"He wasn't specific and I didn't press him," Maria said. "I also told him that it would be better if he talks directly to you and that I'd pass the message along."

"Which is what you've done, so thanks."

"Ava, these two men — they aren't a problem, are they?"

"No, of course not," she said quickly. "But I'll call Bernard just the same in case he has concerns."

"Yes, I think that's the best thing to do," Maria said. She paused, then added, "And I should tell you that I did mail your key back to you."

"That was considerate," Ava said, gathering her breath. Before she could say anything else, the phone went dead. *Well, I guess that's goodbye*, she thought, slumping back in the chair.

She reached for her regular phone, turned it on, and scrolled down until she found the number for the front desk of her condo. Then she used the phone Xu had given her to make the call.

"Bernard here. How may I help you?"

"This is Ava Lee. I understand from my friend Maria that I had some visitors this morning."

"Hello, Ms. Lee. Yes, you did. I hope you don't mind my mentioning it to Ms. Gonzalez."

"I'm glad you did," Ava said. "They claimed they had a business appointment with me at eight?"

"They did, and they said you weren't answering your buzzer or your phone. I told them that you probably weren't home. They asked if you were travelling, if you were out of the country. I said I didn't know and that it isn't my place to keep track of the whereabouts of our residents," he said. "Then they asked if you left any forwarding number or contact information. At that point I told them it wasn't information I had, and even if I did have it, I wouldn't have been allowed to share it with them."

"What were the men like?"

"Rather rude and rough-spoken."

"What did they look like?

"One was large and muscular and the other was short and sturdy. They were dressed casually, jeans and leather jackets."

"Were they white, Asian, black?"

"They were white, maybe Greek."

"Did they leave their names?"

"No."

"Well, Bernard, if they come back, I want you to be sure to get their names."

"I'll certainly ask. And if I get them?"

"Call me on my cell," Ava said, and recited the new number.

She stood and walked to the window. She looked out at Victoria Harbour and the splendour of its skyline, but none of it registered. Her mind was on Toronto and the two men at her condo. They had to be connected to the Camorra, who obviously hadn't believed Lam. One phone call from Italy to Toronto had sent them to her door. That concerned her less than the thought that they wouldn't stop there. Who else would they contact? She knew that, given enough time, they'd locate Maria and perhaps even her mother. And if they did, then what? Would they use them as leverage, as a means to get to her? *I need to buy some time*, Ava thought, and then shook her head. *I'm overthinking this, I'm overreacting. They were most likely just trying to find out if I was in Toronto, and we should have things resolved within the next twenty-four hours. Why stress out my mother or Maria?*

She unpacked her bags and went into the bathroom to get ready for bed. When she came back, she took a bottle of Chardonnay from the bar, poured a glass, and settled onto the bed to watch television. She wanted to find something funny, so she accessed the channel menu. There was a variety show on Pearl, but just as she was about to press the remote button she saw that Jade had scheduled a Pang Fai movie. Almost without thinking, Ava's hand reached for her phone and she went to Fai's message. *What the hell*, she thought, and then listened to Fai say, "Ava, this is Fai again. Call me when you can."

Ava picked up the new phone and entered the number. It went to voicemail. "Fai, this is Ava. I'm sorry I haven't called you sooner, but I've been involved in a rather complicated project. I'm not in Toronto; I'm in Hong Kong. Tomorrow is going to be a bit crazy for me, so if you try to reach me and can't, keep trying. I've also been using a new cell. Here's the number in case it doesn't appear on your phone."

She ended the call and looked at the television. The film listed in the guide was one of the dramatic, heart-wrenching films that Fai had made with Lau Lau. *Can I handle that tonight?* Ava thought. "No," she said out loud, and selected the variety show on Pearl.

42

THE MORNING FLEW BY. AN EARLY RUN IN VICTORIA
Park was followed by a long shower, half an hour on the computer, fifteen minutes getting dressed, and then a leisurely dim sum lunch with May and Amanda. All the while, Ava was checking her phones for texts and messages. Despite her decision the night before not to overreact, she found herself becoming increasingly concerned about the two men who had visited her condo. Had they returned? Had they gone to Jennie Lee's home in Richmond Hill? Were they following Maria? But there wasn't a word from either of them, or Bernard.

Xu had phoned from the Shanghai airport to say he was on schedule. If she didn't hear otherwise, she was to go as planned to the TurboJet gate at the Hong Kong–Macau Terminal.

"Have you heard anything from Lop?" she asked.

"Not yet, but he left for Macau last night. He had a couple of meetings scheduled. He'll meet us when we arrive, and I imagine he'll have information for us then."

Ava contacted Sonny and told him to meet her at the hotel at two.

Lam called as she was on the way downstairs to Man Wah for lunch. "We're about an hour away from Macau," he said. "I spoke to Xu. He said you'll come directly to my hotel when you arrive."

"Have you heard from the Italians?"

"Bianchi called about an hour ago to confirm the meeting place and time."

"So they're in Macau already?"

"Evidently."

"Did you ask if Ventola is with them?"

"No, and for the same reason that I didn't force the issue yesterday."

Ava started to argue that point and then stopped. Lam knew them better than she did and was astute when it came to managing his relationships. "How did he sound?"

"Businesslike."

"Did he mention me?"

"No. Why do you ask?"

"I think they sent some men to my condo in Toronto yesterday."

"Are you sure?"

"If they didn't, then the two rough-looking men who showed up are a coincidence that I can't explain."

"What were they told?"

"Nothing."

"Still, I can understand your concern."

"If they decide to bring my friends and family into the picture, I'm going to be more than concerned. I'm going to be furious."

"By the end of today there will be no reason to involve anyone else."

"I guess not."

"You sound less than convinced."

"I'm going to be demanding a lot of Ventola — assuming he's there. And if he's not, I'm not sure where that will leave .us."

"If nothing else, there will be a clear understanding of where each side stands."

"I need more than an understanding. I need them to reverse course."

"I'm doing all I can."

"I know, and I'm sorry if I seem ungrateful. I'm just worried," Ava said. "I have so many people relying on me. I don't want to disappoint them."

"Xu and I have just one person relying on us. That's you, and we're just as keen not to disappoint," Lam said, laughing.

Ava ended the conversation feeling only a bit better than when she'd started it. She walked into Man Wah and saw Amanda and May Ling sitting at a table next to the window.

"We're set," Ava said, taking a seat. "Unless I hear that Xu is going to be late, I'll leave here at two and meet him at the ferry terminal."

May and Amanda didn't speak and Ava sensed some tension. "What were you two talking about?" she asked.

May pursed her lips and looked across the table at Amanda.

"We were talking about Macau," Amanda said. "We were remembering the last time you were there, when you rescued Simon To."

"It's when we became friends," May said. "It was an important time in my life."

"And we started our friendship then," Amanda said. "I like

to think it's one we would have maintained even if I hadn't married your brother."

"It's a time I don't think of very often, and when I do, I don't remember it that fondly," Ava said.

"I don't blame you. You did get shot in the leg," May said.

Ava shook her head. "No, it isn't that. I shot a man in the head. I executed him. I can see his face, but now I can't even think of his name..."

"His name was Kao Lok," Amanda said. "And I'll never forget him. He was going to kill Simon."

May sighed and the table fell silent.

"We should order our food," Ava finally said.

The dim sum menu at Man Wah wasn't extensive, but it made up in quality what it lacked in choice. Ava had a particular fondness for the beef tenderloin puff with black pepper sauce and the dumpling stuffed with shrimp, crab, and coriander. She ordered double servings of both.

"Did you talk to Pudong this morning?" she asked Amanda as the server poured them jasmine tea.

"Chi-Tze phoned to make sure we'd arrived safely, but also to tell me that things are calm with Gillian and Clark, although they are wondering why we're in Hong Kong. She said they are convinced it has something to do with Lane Crawford," Amanda said. "I said that it does — indirectly. I guess it wasn't a complete lie."

The server came to the table with the puffs and an order of siu mai. Before Ava could reach for anything, her phone rang.

"It's Xu."

"Is there a problem with the flight?"

"No, I'm still on schedule, but I just spoke to Lop and there may be a problem with the Italians," Xu said. "He told me that a private plane from Milan landed in Macau around nine this morning, and then two hours later so did another. We were told there would be only one."

"Both flights originated in Milan?"

"Yes. Lop sent me the manifests and I went over them with Lam. Ventola, Pandolfo, Ricci, Moretti, and Bianchi were listed on the first flight. There were seven other names we didn't recognize, although at least two of them must be crew members. There were eight men listed on the second flight and we knew none of them," Xu said. "I've asked Lop to forward both manifests to you. Have a look and see if any names look familiar. Our hope is that they will include more people from VLG."

"And you and Lop are certain that the second flight is connected to us?"

"It's the most logical assumption."

"Shit."

"So either most of the executive team from VLG is in Macau or it's a small army of Camorra."

"I'll go through the manifests as soon as I get them," Ava said.

"Better news is that Lop has met with the heads of the two Macanese Chinese gangs that are still fully operating. They said they've had no contact with the Italians and won't have anything to do with them if they are contacted. They're also sending word to the freelance groups that they should keep out of any entanglements involving them."

"And the locals will listen?"

"Lop made it quite clear that he was issuing an order, not a request, and they all know who he is and what he's capable of doing," Xu said.

"That still leaves us enough to worry about with the Italians."

"Believe me, Lop isn't taking them lightly, and even more so after checking out the restaurant where they want to meet. He doesn't like it," Xu said. "It's surrounded by a spider's web of streets and alleys. It's an area that's hard to secure."

"What does he suggest?"

"He'd like to change the meeting venue. There's an executive boardroom at the Grand Hyatt, where Lam's staying, that he thinks would be perfect. It's off by itself, nowhere near the casino, and it's easy to monitor," Xu said.

"Why would the Italians agree to that?"

"Why would they object? It's neutral and it's private," Xu said.

"I'm not arguing with you. I just don't want to do anything that would put the meeting at risk."

"It's a suggestion. If the Italians aren't agreeable, we'll deal with it."

In the background Ava could hear a voice telling passengers to fasten their seat belts. "You should go," she said. "We'll see you at the ferry terminal."

"What was that about?" May said from across the table, a dumpling suspended in her chopsticks.

"Ventola and Pandolfo are in Macau," Ava said, and then looked at her phone as it sounded again. It was an email from Lop with the Milan manifests attached. She quickly scanned the names and didn't see any — other than those Xu had mentioned — that were familiar.

43

SONNY'S MERCEDES WAS PARKED AT THE FRONT DOOR of the Mandarin Oriental. He stood off to one side talking to a doorman, who was nodding enthusiastically.

"Sonny," Ava said. He glanced in her direction and then hurried to the car.

"Sorry. That guy was asking me about Uncle Fong." He opened the back door for her. "They used to go to Macau together to gamble. He said he hasn't seen Uncle Fong in months. I told him that he's given up gambling. He said that's a good thing, because Uncle had more bad luck than anyone he's ever known."

Ava waited until Sonny was behind the wheel before she said, "How did the doorman know you and Uncle Fong are acquainted?"

"He saw us together when we came here to pick you up for dinner."

"And what you said about Uncle Fong, is it really true?" Ava asked as the car eased onto Connaught Road.

"That's what he tells me, and I believe him, because he hasn't hit me up for money in a while."

Uncle Fong was an old colleague of Uncle's. He had no family and had squandered his entire life's earnings on the gaming tables in Macau. Uncle had left him some money, and Ava, out of loyalty and affection, augmented it with a monthly allowance.

"That's so nice to hear," she said.

Sonny drove west for a couple of minutes and then turned right into the Hong Kong–Macau Ferry Terminal. He stopped the car at the entrance and Ava climbed out. "I'll be about five minutes parking the car. I'll meet you at the gate," he said.

Ava took the escalator to the second floor, found the TurboJet counter, and bought first-class tickets for herself, Sonny, Xu, Suen, and the two other men. Xu had phoned before they left the hotel to say he had landed, and he immediately asked her about the manifests.

"I didn't recognize any names from VLG except for Pandolfo and Ventola," she said.

"That's unfortunate."

"Mind you, I didn't meet that many people when I was in Milan."

"We'll have to assume the worst," Xu said. "I should be at the terminal just after two o'clock. See you then."

Ava took a seat in the departures area to wait. Xu's tone had been calm, but his spare use of words told her he was concerned. She shuddered, and then told herself the Italians wouldn't be crazy enough to start something in a place that was virtually next door to Lam's territory and less than an hour away from Hong Kong.

Sonny's arrival provided a distraction. He smiled at her and then stood against a wall that gave him a clear view of the surroundings. Ava was going to tell him that wasn't necessary, but he had been a bodyguard for so many years that the habit was engrained.

About ten minutes later he stood at attention. She saw Xu approaching with two men in front of him, each carrying two bags. Suen trailed a few steps behind.

Sonny moved to Ava's side. The two men in front of Xu and Suen stopped to let them pass.

"Perfect timing," Ava said, as a voice came over the intercom to announce that the jetfoil was now boarding. "Here are everyone's tickets."

Xu and Ava hugged while Suen and Sonny shook hands. "These are Gui and Zhang," Suen said, nodding at the men who'd accompanied them. Sonny shook their hands as well, but Ava had already started down the jetfoil's ramp with Xu.

They settled into their first-class seats, Xu and Ava in the first row, the men sitting together several rows behind. They were a well-dressed, conservative-looking group. Xu discouraged tattoos and outlandish hairstyles; he wanted his men to be as nondescript as possible. Suen and his two companions were wearing slacks, plain shirts, and casual jackets with Polo or Tommy Hilfiger logos. Xu had on his standard black suit with white shirt and black tie. Ava matched his monochromatic look in black slacks and a white button-down shirt. Collectively, she thought, they looked like Hong Kong office managers on a day outing.

There were a few empty seats in first class, but economy was full. Ava knew it would be the same story on every boat, every half-hour, every day of the week. There was no legal casino gambling elsewhere in China, so over the past dozen years Macau had transformed into a giant money-making machine for the world's largest casino companies. Millions of gamblers found their way there each year, leaving more than US$45 billion behind in the city's thirty-three casinos. By comparison, Las Vegas's seventy casinos generated only $6 billion a year.

Macau hadn't always been dominated by gambling. In the 1500s the Portuguese had landed there and used the region as their trading base, paying an annual tribute to the Chinese government. This continued until 1864, when, after the first Opium War, they were granted permanent occupation rights, similar to what the British had in Hong Kong. Those rights eventually reverted and the territory was returned to the Chinese in 1999.

Ava had been there many times with Uncle to visit clients and collect debts. There were still vestiges of the Portuguese occupation in Macau's cuisine and architecture, but they were few and far between. The population of 600,000 was ninety-five percent Chinese, and almost no one spoke Portuguese. Unlike the British in Hong Kong, the Portuguese had no interest in creating legal, bureaucratic, or educational infrastructures. It was all about trade, all about extracting every dollar they could. Now they were gone and a foreign horde of even cleverer money-extractors had replaced them.

When Ava made her first trips to Macau with Uncle, the casinos weren't so omnipresent. In fact, compared to what she'd seen in Las Vegas, they were almost quaint. There were about a dozen, all operated by the same company, the Sociedade Turismo e Diversões de Macau. The company had been granted a monopoly in 1962, and over the next forty years, through a syndicate controlled by Stanley Ho, it was the sole operator in the territory. Ho's casinos, with the exception of the modestly sized Lisboa, were small, drab, and sometimes dingy, and they didn't offer much in the way of service, food, drink, or entertainment. Uncle hated them, even though they were sometimes a source of business. He didn't like the paper wrappings and cigarette butts that littered the carpets, which were sometimes damp from spilled drinks or, more often, spit. He didn't like the moneylenders who sat next to the gamblers with briefcases filled with cash. Uncle called them parasites and couldn't understand why the government would allow that practice, although the truth was the casinos encouraged them to be there and probably were getting paid by them. He also didn't speak kindly of Stanley Ho, whom he knew. This was unusual for Uncle, and Ava wondered if there was more behind his distaste than the way he felt about the casinos. There were rumours that Ho had triad ties, specifically to the Kung Lok gang in Hong Kong, but Ava never asked Uncle if that was the root cause of his feelings.

Quaint Macau had disappeared in 2002, when the Chinese government issued six new gambling concessions and the big boys from Las Vegas came rumbling in. The STDM's dozen modest casinos quickly found themselves with twenty new competitors — including the Venetian, Wynn, Sands, and MGM Macau — some of them exact replicas of their Vegas namesakes. And every year, it seemed to Ava, there was a new one being built or an addition being made to an existing casino.

The jetfoil pulled away from the dock and entered the channel that would take it out to the South China Sea. As the engines roared, it gained speed. Ava turned to Xu, raising her voice over the noise. "Have you heard from Lam about the meeting location?"

"We're still going to the restaurant," Xu said. "He pushed as hard as he could without upsetting them for a change of venue. Lop knows the decision. He'll add some extra men."

"But we're heading for the Grand Hyatt first?"

"Yes. Lop will be at the ferry terminal with enough cars for all of us."

"Where are you staying?" she asked.

"The same hotel. If all goes well, I'll stay for at least a night. Lam and I have some things to go over, and I've never really seen the place. Every time I've been here, it's been in and out," Xu said. Then he noted, "You didn't bring an overnight bag."

"I didn't think I'd need to stay in Macau overnight," Ava said. "My gut feeling is that this isn't going to be a long, drawn-out negotiating session. Besides, I have two partners waiting for me in Hong Kong who will be desperate to hear how things went, and I'd like to tell them in person."

"You could be right about the meeting being short," Xu said. "I've been thinking about the approach I'm going to take and have decided to be as direct and blunt as possible. It may not go down well, but from what I know about these guys and what Lam has told me, they aren't about subtleties."

"What are you going to say?"

He shrugged. "I'm still working on it, and I want to hear what Lam wants to say. Do you mind waiting until we're all together?"

"Of course not."

The jetfoil was bouncing over the sea. Ava turned around to see how Sonny was doing and saw that his eyes were closed. She was contemplating doing the same when her phone rang. The screen read PRIVATE CALLER. She hesitated and then realized it was the phone Xu had given her.

"Yes?" she said.

"Ava, this is Fai. I hope I'm not disturbing you," she said. "Where are you?"

"No, you're not disturbing me. I'm on a boat," Ava said over the engines, then quickly changed the subject before Fai could ask any questions. "Are you okay? You sound groggy."

"I just woke up. I couldn't get to sleep last night and had to take some pills."

"Are you still a bit jet-lagged from the London trip?"

"I don't know. I'm tired physically but my mind keeps turning. Sometimes I think I'm going crazy." Fai laughed.

"I know that feeling. Sometimes it takes a week after a trip like that for life to get back to normal," Ava said. "When do you leave Beijing to go to your film shoot?"

"It starts in Kunming and ends in Beijing. I leave in three or four days — I don't actually remember. That's how tired I am."

"You'll probably be better by then."

The line went silent, and Ava wondered if Fai had put down her phone. She waited for ten or fifteen seconds and was about to end the call when Fai said, "How long are you going to be in Hong Kong?"

"I'm not sure. I have a meeting tonight and if it goes well I could be out of here tomorrow," Ava said.

"Oh."

"But I might stay an extra day to see my father."

"I don't know Hong Kong very well," Fai said, sounding distracted.

"I read somewhere that you made a few movies here."

"Two films, and both times I was shuttled back and forth between the set and the hotel. I hardly saw anything else..."

I should let you go," she said suddenly.

"And actually I should go. I have to get myself organized for the meeting."

"All right," Fai said, again lapsing into silence.

"Call me whenever," Ava said. "I may be able to use my regular phone tomorrow, so try it first." She put the phone in her bag.

"Who was that?" Xu asked.

"It was Pang Fai."

"When you mentioned a film shoot, I thought that's who it would be."

"She's still fighting jet lag."

"I'm pleased she's working with you. She adds real glamour to the line," Xu said. "I didn't realize she'd become such a good friend."

"I think she really enjoyed being in London," Ava said. "You know, it wouldn't be a bad thing if we gave her some shares in PÖ."

"Assuming that after tonight the shares are worth having."

44

THE LAST TIME AVA HAD SEEN LAM, THEY WERE IN AN abandoned mah-jong parlour near the Happy Valley racetrack in Hong Kong. He had just put two bullets into Li, Guangzhou's Mountain Master and his boss. Xu had a direct hand in the killing, Ava an indirect one. Either way, if ever a death was warranted, Li's was. He had tried to kill both of them — Ava twice — and Xu was convinced that if Li lived he'd try again. Still, the execution had shocked her. Xu and Lam had been calm and composed and took turns assuring her that it had been an inevitable outcome. Inevitable or not, the death was convenient. It paved the way for Xu's election as chairman of the triad societies in Asia, and it vaulted Lam into the Mountain Master position in Guangzhou.

Ava hadn't thought much about Li's death since that day, but as the jetfoil neared Macau the memory flickered through her mind. "What kind of Mountain Master is Lam?" she asked Xu as Macau came into view through the water-spattered windows.

"Why do you ask?"

"I was thinking about the last time I saw him, in Happy

Valley, and then I remembered how he was when I met him in Huangpu and we began negotiating the settlement between the Shanghai and Guangzhou gangs. I found him to be low-key and thoughtful. I was wondering if becoming the boss has changed his operating style."

"You've been talking to him on the phone. What do you think?"

"I haven't detected any difference, but then I don't work for him or have to compete with him."

"He's still thoughtful and calm," Xu said. "But becoming the boss has affected him."

"In what sense?"

He turned to Ava. "When you're the deputy, your main concern is keeping your boss happy, and in Lam's case with Li, that meant worrying about the day-to-day business. The future wasn't his responsibility. Now it is, and he has thousands of men — and, by extension, their families — depending on him, and only him, to ensure their long-term economic security. Every decision he makes has to strike a balance between the immediate challenge and its long-term impact, and then when he makes the decision, he has to present it in a way that makes it seem the only possible decision that could have been made. There's no room for self-doubt. Your people can never see you confused or in a panic. I think that Lam understands and has mastered that part of the craft," Xu said. "If I was going to be critical of him, I'd say he is sometimes too careful, too risk-averse, and that's in both his opinions and actions. Li was the opposite, so maybe Lam's style is a reaction to that."

The jetfoil's engines cut back and the vessel slowed. Ava saw people stirring. Many in economy were already making their way towards the doors, anxious to be first off the boat and first to get through Customs. "They'll race each other to the casinos," she said.

"They just want to win their fair share of money before the casinos run out of it," Xu said.

The boat docked and now everyone except their group was at the doors or in line. They remained seated until the exit was completely clear and took their time walking to Customs and Immigration. There were only a few people waiting to be processed when they arrived. The booths were well staffed and the officers were trained to move people through as quickly as possible. A few minutes later they exited the terminal to find Lop and two cars waiting for them.

"Hey, boss," he said to Xu, and then nodded at Ava. "Nice to see you again."

"And you too, though we always seem to meet under difficult circumstances," she said.

"It's the nature of the work," Lop said.

"Speaking of work, I want to thank you for what you and Sonny did for us in Shenzhen."

"He's a good man and I like working with him. Any time he wants another job, he knows where to come," Lop said, smiling at Sonny.

"I don't mind lending him out from time to time," Ava said, "but I'm not giving him up." This time Sonny smiled.

"We should start moving," Xu interrupted. "Lam is expecting us."

"I thought that you, Ava, me, and Suen could take the first car," Lop said. "The other guys can go in the second."

"Who are the drivers?" Suen asked.

"All men I brought with me from Hong Kong. I've got five more at the Grand Hyatt and another group already positioned around the restaurant and near the Lisboa."

"Any sign of the Italians?" Xu said.

"One of my men went into the Lisboa for something to eat and thought he noticed some Westerners who looked tough enough to be part of their team."

"What were they doing?"

"Walking and watching, like us."

"How many did he see?"

"Six, but based on the manifests and the fact that Ava didn't recognize any names, I'm figuring there must be ten to fourteen of them in town."

"And there's no indication that they've hired local support?" Xu said.

"No."

"Good. Then let's go see what Lam is doing."

Macau was a peninsula attached to the Chinese mainland, across from the Pearl River delta. The vast majority of the population lived in an area of about six square miles, which made it the most densely populated territory on earth. Curiously, its inhabitants also had the world's longest life expectancy. The number of casino/hotel complexes on the peninsula had grown from twelve to twenty-three since Stanley Ho's monopoly ended in 2002, and had chewed up all the available land. The island of Taipa, directly south of Macau, took the overflow. Now there were about a dozen complexes there, including City of Dreams, the Wynn, and the Venetian.

The ferry terminal was in Macau, on the outer harbour — the Porto Exterior. Ava knew from her last trip that it was about seven kilometres from the terminal to City of Dreams. They would drive south from the terminal, cross the Governor Nobre de Carvalho Bridge, and enter Taipa. City of Dreams was near the northern tip of Taipa, on a stretch of land called the Cotai Strip.

The ride to City of Dreams was quiet. Everyone seemed taken with the surroundings, and Ava had to admit they were impressive. The closest counterpart was the Strip in Las Vegas, but it wasn't surrounded by sea and seemed almost suburban compared to the density of Macau and the Cotai Strip.

The Taipa skyline dominated the view almost as soon as they drove onto the Carvalho Bridge. A few minutes after reaching the island, the lead car began to wind its way into the maze of buildings that was City of Dreams. There were four towers, all about forty storeys high, surrounding a central pod. Two were dedicated to the Grand Hyatt Macau; the others were a Hard Rock Hotel and a Crown Towers Hotel.

As they entered the Grand Hyatt property, Ava felt a twinge of disappointment. She had anticipated something lavish or maybe even spectacular, but the hotel had a rather modest sign and its exterior was a wall of plain glass in an uninspired design.

The cars rolled to a stop at the hotel entrance.

"I have to check in," Xu said to Ava. "You can wait for me or go directly to Lam's suite."

"I'll wait," she said, and followed Xu and his men into the lobby.

The interior was everything the exterior wasn't. It was a huge, cavernous space with walls tiled in tan, beige, and white. The walls soared about sixty feet towards a brightly lit

ceiling made of coloured glass that resembled clouds. Strings
of crystals or glass hung from the ceiling like rainfall. The
floor was black marble and flickered under the light from
overhead. The lobby's size reminded Ava of a 1920s railway
station in a city like New York, except that its design was
lighter, airier, even verging on minimalist.

She and Sonny walked to the elevators. She was still
admiring the lobby when Xu approached with Suen and
Lop. "Lam is waiting for us," he said.

"Where are the other men?"

"Lop has given them their orders. If you don't see them
again, that's a good thing."

They bundled into the elevator and Lop pushed the button
for the thirty-seventh floor. "I was in Lam's suite earlier," Lop
said. "It has a separate living room, den, and dining room.
I think it's bigger than my apartment in Hong Kong, and
it has to cost twelve thousand Hong Kong dollars a night."

When the elevator stopped, Suen stepped out first, looked
both ways down the corridor, then waved them forward. Two
men were standing outside a set of double doors at the far
end of the corridor. One of the men opened the door before
they reached it. As Xu passed, he and his partner lowered
their heads in respect.

"Welcome," Lam said from the far end of the suite. He
stood in front of a window, the light framing him. He was
slightly taller than Xu, but thinner and wirier. As he walked
towards them, Ava noticed that his long, narrow face was
just starting to show his age. His white hair was tied back
in a ponytail. It was a youthful look, one he accentuated
with a pair of red-tinted round wire-framed glasses. He was
wearing a long-sleeved white silk shirt, black jeans, and tan

Ferragamo loafers. A year at the top of the Guangzhou gang didn't seem to have affected his appearance or manner.

Xu met him in the middle of the suite. They shook hands, Xu's left hand clasping Lam's elbow. "Good to see you," Xu said. "And thanks for all of this."

Lam took a small step to one side and peered past Xu. "I've only done what Ava wanted — which seems to be the case every time I get involved with her," he said with a grin. "Ava, come and give me a hug."

Ava crossed the floor. "All I've been hearing about for days is Three Sisters and PÖ," Lam said as he put his arms around her. "As lovely as you are, I'll be glad to put this business behind me."

"That's a view we share," Ava said.

"Well, hopefully we'll accomplish it. The Italians are here, including the two you were most anxious to meet."

"Lop said their names were on the flight manifest."

"So he told me, and Bianchi finally mentioned their names when I spoke to him about an hour ago."

"So he said they'll be at the meeting?"

"It was implied."

Xu looked at his watch. "That meeting is closing in on us. Perhaps we should take some time to talk about our strategy."

"My thinking exactly, but we also need to eat. I have a separate dining room in the suite, and the hotel restaurant, Beijing Kitchen, has a good reputation. Shall I get them to send up some food?"

"That sounds perfect," Xu said.

"Any preferences?" Lam asked.

"I eat everything," Ava said.

"Why doesn't that surprise me?" Lam said.

45

AT TWENTY MINUTES TO SEVEN XU, LAM, AND SUEN left the hotel to go to the Don Pietro restaurant, which was on a side street a few blocks from the Hotel Lisboa. Lop had made the trip from the Grand Hyatt several times and calculated it was ten minutes away, even in heavy traffic. One of his men who was familiar with the route was the designated driver. The plan was for him to drop off Xu and the others and then return to the Hyatt to pick up Ava. By the time Ava arrived at the restaurant, Xu and Lam would have had about thirty minutes to talk through various issues with the Italians.

"We need to lay the groundwork, to set the proper tone," Lam had said. "It will be all about business, but I don't see why it can't be collegial."

"But they need to understand that not only have we shut down part of their production, we can keep it shut," Xu said. "We want to negotiate from a position of strength."

"They might react badly if you're that blunt. They might see it as a threat," Lam said.

"The message can be subtle, but it has to be clear. They

need to know that we're not just posturing," Xu said. "My feeling, though, is that it will all boil down to money. They'll want to know what it will cost to stop the bleeding."

"And if they ask for a number before Ava gets there?"

"We stall."

"And then she walks in and —"

"We'll find out."

"I know we've talked about it, but I'm still not entirely sure it's the right approach," Lam said hesitantly. "It could be disruptive, and maybe worse than that."

"You might be correct, but I agree with Ava that if she walks into that meeting with us, we might not even have a meeting. They'll know we lied to them and they'll feel manipulated. They could explode, and then what chance do we have for a rational discussion? I want their attention for at least thirty minutes so they can understand who they're dealing with and what kind of power we can exercise. It might temper their ultimate reaction."

Lam turned to Ava. "I wasn't being critical of your idea," he said. "All I want is a resolution that benefits everyone in the long run, and every option has to be considered."

"I understand," she said.

"So we're agreed on her late arrival?" Xu said.

Lam nodded.

Ava reached over the table to touch his hand. "I can't tell you how much I appreciate your support."

"Let's hope you feel the same after the meeting."

At six-thirty Lam and Xu left the suite, leaving Ava and Sonny the sole occupants.

"I don't know why, but I have an uneasy feeling about this meeting," Sonny said.

"You're out of practice. This kind of thing used to be routine for you."

"Not meeting with Italians. That was always special. That always made Uncle nervous."

"I —" Ava began, and then stopped as her phone rang. She looked at the incoming number and had her own attack of nerves.

"Mummy, is everything okay?"

"Do you know what time it is here?"

"Six-forty in the morning."

"Exactly. So can you please tell me why two men came to my front door a few minutes ago asking for you?" Jennie said, her voice cracking.

"Did you let them in?"

"Of course not. I yelled at them through the door, but I could see them through the peephole."

"What did you tell them?"

"That I haven't seen or heard from you in weeks."

"Have they left?"

"Not yet. They hung around the door for a few minutes and I was afraid they were going to go around to the back. Now they're sitting in their car in front of the house."

"Do you want to call the police?"

"And tell them I'm scared because a car is parked in front of my house? They'd laugh at me."

Jennie's answer told Ava that her mother had already thought about calling the police and ruled it out. "Did the men say why they wanted to see me?" she asked.

"No."

"What did they look like?"

"Dark-haired *gweilos*. They looked Italian or Greek to me."

"Are you sure?"

"Ava, I've been living here long enough to be able to tell one *gweilo* from another."

"Okay, I believe you."

"I don't care if you do or don't. What I want to know is what the hell they're doing here."

"I'm in Hong Kong — actually, Macau — and we have a business problem I'm trying to resolve that does involve some Italians. There's a meeting in half an hour that should put it to bed. I can't imagine you'll see those men again," Ava said.

"And if you can't solve your problem?"

"I'll let you know."

"That doesn't sound particularly encouraging."

"Mummy, I'll solve it."

Jennie Lee breathed deeply into the phone. "I never interfere with your business, but I can't have it coming to my door or sitting in front of my house. That scares me."

"It won't happen again."

"You can't guarantee that. It will be enough for me if those two thugs leave."

"I promise you they will."

"I'll depend on you for that."

"Yes, Mummy," Ava said.

She closed her eyes, shook her head, and sighed.

"What's wrong?" Sonny asked.

"The Italians have paid a friendly visit to my mother."

"Fuck."

"This has to end tonight."

"Can you do that?"

"I don't have any choice."

"Whatever you need me to do…"

"Sonny, there isn't a person in the world I count on more than you," Ava said. "But it's important that we stay calm."

"I know. Uncle always said the same thing."

Ava was about to say something else when Sonny's phone rang.

"It's the driver. He's downstairs," he said.

"Then let's go."

46

THE BMW WAS AT THE ENTRANCE, THE DRIVER SITTING behind the wheel.

"He should be holding the door open," Sonny said.

"I don't think he drives for a living," Ava said.

Sonny grunted and opened the back door for her. He climbed into the front. "How were things at the restaurant?" he said to the driver.

"It was almost empty, and the boss has men surrounding it."

"By 'boss' you mean Lop?"

"Yeah."

"He's solid."

The driver looked shocked that Sonny would dare pass judgement on Lop.

"Did you go into the restaurant?" Ava asked.

"No."

"Then how did you know it was almost empty?"

"I could see through the windows, and there was a big sign on the door saying it was closed for a private function," he said, pulling out of the hotel driveway.

The car retraced the path through Taipa and over the Carvalho Bridge. They drove past neon signs advertising the Lisboa and the Grand Lisboa and into a part of Macau where the streets were lined with shops and restaurants.

"This is how I remember the place," Sonny said.

"In a few years they'll be gone as well, replaced by another casino," the driver said.

"Are you from Macau?" Ava asked.

"No, but I leave so much money here I might as well be."

Ava had a vague memory of the neighbourhood. She thought she had been there with Uncle, to meet a client who had taken them to a restaurant that specialized in snake. She remembered a glass cage in the window filled with serpents, from which the client had chosen several that were prepared in a variety of ways.

"Is there a restaurant near here that specializes in snakes?" she said.

"It's one street over. These three blocks have a lot of wild animal restaurants. They cook bats, raccoons, snakes, bears, and seals. I don't know how an Italian restaurant has managed to survive in this area," he said. "Speaking of which, there it is."

Ava looked to her left and saw a white neon sign flashing DON PIETRO above a green, white, and red canvas awning. The front window had modest painted depictions of the leaning tower of Pisa and the Colosseum.

"It does look quiet," Sonny said.

The car stopped directly in front of the restaurant. Ava was surprised that no one was guarding the door, but when she looked to either side she saw four Chinese men standing about twenty metres away. The driver got out of the car and waved at them. "I think it's safe to go inside," he said.

Sonny opened the door. Before Ava could climb out, her phone rang. Her first thought was that it was her mother and she felt the onset of panic, but when she glanced at the screen she saw 63 — the country code for the Philippines. *What the hell?* she thought, then jammed the phone back into her bag.

Sonny led her into the restaurant. The space was long and narrow, with a desk and bar on the left and a row of tables for two on the right. The back of the restaurant was only partially visible because a line of portable screens blocked the view. A large man stood in front of the screens, his feet planted, his arms folded across his chest, and his eyes fixed on Ava and Sonny. She guessed he was at least six foot two and weighed as much as Sonny. They walked slowly towards him. As they did, he turned his head and said something in Italian.

A second man appeared from behind the screens. He was as large as the first and dressed identically, in a black T-shirt and jeans.

"What do you want?" the first man said.

"We want to join the meeting," Ava said.

"This is a private function."

"Actually, I'm the reason there is a meeting," she said. "I don't think anyone will object to my joining it."

"There's no one else on the list."

Ava took a step forward. Before she could take another, the man to her right reached out and grabbed her arm. She flinched, and saw the second man step between her and Sonny. Her left hand searched for the man's elbow and she dug her nails into the nerve she was looking for. He screamed in pain and his arm fell helplessly to his side.

As the other man heard his partner yell, Sonny drove a fist into his ear. As the man staggered, Sonny grabbed him by the collar and drove his head into the bar. He collapsed onto the floor.

The man Ava had engaged with was now on his feet. He threw a punch in her direction. She sidestepped him, trying to find a good angle to deliver a phoenix-eye fist to his ear or nose. When she couldn't, she flicked a fingernail into his eye, drawing a spurt of blood. Before Ava could inflict further damage, Sonny was on him. He gripped the man's shirt, rammed his head into the bar, and threw him on top of his partner.

"Stay there," Sonny shouted at their prone bodies. "I have a gun. If you move, you die."

Ava heard raised voices from the other side of the panels. She pushed one back and saw seven men seated at a round table. Suen was standing behind Xu and an Italian who was even bigger and heavier than the two men out front was leaning against a brick wall.

"*La puttana principale!*" Dominic Ventola shouted.

Bianchi's man pushed away from the wall and took a couple of threatening steps towards them. Sonny caught him by the throat, lifted him off the ground, and propelled him back towards the brick wall. His head smashed against it and he slumped to the floor.

"Hi. My name is Ava Lee, and this is my colleague Sonny Kwok. We're here to talk about resurrecting the PÖ line."

47

LAM'S FACE WAS IMPASSIVE. XU HAD A SLIGHT SMILE on his. Raffi Pandolfo's mouth gaped and he looked to be in shock. Dominic Ventola turned away from her and Sonny and spoke rapidly in Italian to the three middle-aged men who were seated to his left.

"Your entrance was a bit dramatic but your timing is impeccable," Xu said. "We were just about to start discussing PÖ in some detail."

"What is this shit?" Ventola yelled.

"I think it would be polite to make some introductions first," Ava said. "Who are these gentlemen with you and Raffi?"

"My name is Franco Bianchi, and these are my associates Ricci and Moretti."

"Pleased to meet you," Ava said, noting how calmly Bianchi spoke and carried himself. He was about the same age as Ventola, equally stocky, freshly shaven, and with thick hair combed straight back. He was dressed in a long-sleeved black cotton shirt with red piping around the edges of the collar and down the front. He looked more like someone who worked at VLG than the man who ran the Camorra.

"I wish I could say the same," Bianchi said. "Was all that violence really necessary?"

"Sonny doesn't like being threatened at any time, and when I'm involved he tends to overreact."

Bianchi looked across the table at Lam. "You lied to us about her," he said matter-of-factly. "We thought you might have, but Ricci hoped the relationship between us and your organization was of such long standing that you would honour the association."

"Ava isn't just anyone," Lam said. "She has strong ties to Xu and I'm personally indebted to her."

Bianchi turned to Ventola. "I'm surprised you didn't do more research, Dom. It would have been useful for us to know that this woman is connected to these people. In fact, it would have been even more useful if you'd known that before she and her partners met with you in Milan."

Ventola shouted, "How could we have known?"

"He's right. We don't make a point of publicizing our relationship," Xu said.

"But now that we do know, I find myself confused," Bianchi said. "All this talk about getting our shipments moving and the plants going back into production, what was that? Window dressing?"

"No. We're prepared to do all that."

"At what cost?"

"Absolutely none, where money is concerned."

"Don't play games with me," Bianchi said, his tone sharpening. "I have no tolerance for bullshit."

Xu pushed his chair back from the table. "Let's make room for Ava," he said to Lam. "Sonny, will you bring another chair here, please."

Lam slid to one side. Sonny pushed a chair into the space and went to stand with Suen. Ava sat at the table, trying to catch Ventola's eye. He avoided her gaze. Pandolfo did the same.

"Where are your other men?" Ava said to Bianchi.

"What men?"

"The ones listed on your flight manifests."

Bianchi turned towards the man he'd identified as Moretti.

"Let them figure out who they are and where they are," Moretti said.

Ava looked at Xu. "Lop has the place surrounded. I'm not worried," he said.

"Well, I am worried," Ava said, leaning in towards Bianchi. "Two men showed up at my apartment in Toronto yesterday. Less than an hour ago, two more knocked on my mother's door and are now sitting outside her house in their car. Who sent them?"

"We did," Moretti said.

"Well, fuck you for doing that."

"Like Franco said, we thought Lam might have lied to us. We wanted to know for certain."

"And now that you do?"

"That's up to Franco."

"If you don't mind my saying it, I think we're getting side-tracked," Lam said.

"No, I need to finish what I want to say," Ava said sharply. "If anything happens to my mother or to any of my friends, I will come after you — Sonny and I will come after you."

"And regardless of how this meeting ends, I must tell you that nothing had better happen to Ava or her partners or her family," Xu said. "I promise you we will take revenge on anyone who harms them."

"You can safely assume that you'll never have to do that," Bianchi said.

"There are still those two men in Toronto," Ava said.

Bianchi looked at Moretti. "Call them," he said, and then added something in Italian.

Moretti took a phone from his pocket and turned his back to them.

"Can we now get back to discussing real business?" Bianchi said.

"I told you we shouldn't have come here," Ventola blurted. "We should have waited them out. We could have found other plants."

"You might have, but even if you did we would have eventually closed their doors to you," Xu said. "And all those minor inconveniences that Ava caused by arranging for goods to be seized and containers to go missing... Well, that would only have escalated. China would disappear for you as a market and as a source of supply."

Bianchi raised a hand. "Stop, that's enough. I may not believe you're capable of doing everything you say you can, but there's no doubt you can cause enough disruption that our business doesn't need."

"You're an owner in the business?" Ava asked. "We were never sure."

"Dominic and I have been friends since our childhood in Naples," Bianchi said. "I personally financed the very first Ventola suit collection, and I have supported him and Raffi ever since."

"Then you should understand our commitment to Clark Po," Ava said.

Ventola slapped an open palm on the table. "Forget Clark

Po," he said. "He's done, he's finished."

"Clark Po is the reason we're all here," Ava said to Bianchi.

"My understanding is that he's damaged goods."

"Only because Mr. Ventola criticized his collection and damaged his reputation," Ava said. "Luckily, we think the damage can be repaired if we move fast and convincingly enough."

"And what does that repair work have to do with us?" Bianchi asked.

"It has everything to do with Dominic Ventola," Ava said.

"How so?"

"We want him to make a public apology."

"That will never happen," Ventola said.

"Actually, we want him to do more than apologize. We want him to publicly admit that, when the PÖ brand declined his offer to join VLG, he lost control of his emotions and said what he did out of spite, and that in fact Clark is the most talented designer he's seen in years."

"Never!" Ventola shouted across the table.

Ava smiled at Bianchi. "Concurrently, we want Raffi Pandolfo to instruct his sales and marketing team to spend as much time calling customers to promote Clark as they spent denigrating him. We want them to insist that the PÖ brand be marketed alongside VLG."

"You're demented," Ventola said.

"Mr. Bianchi, you've just heard our demands," Ava said. "We don't want any money. There's no need for compensation of any sort. All we want is for Mr. Ventola to do the right thing. If he does, then it will be business as usual for you in China and in Asia."

"And if he doesn't?" Bianchi said.

"Then we'll be at war," Xu said.

48

TWO BOTTLES OF RED WINE AND TEN GLASSES STOOD in the middle of the table. Bianchi reached for a glass.

"Does anyone else care for wine?" he asked.

"Sure," Xu said. "We'll all have some."

Bianchi moved slowly, making a production out of filling the glasses. When he finished, he raised his. "*Salute,*" he said. He took a sip, looking over the rim at Xu. "'War' is a very big word."

"Beyond the economic repercussions, my understanding is that your organization has been known to respond to adversity with violence," Xu said. "I think it's only fair to warn you that we would be prepared to respond in kind."

"I'm not sure that taking us on would be clever," Bianchi said. "We're large — larger than our numbers in Naples might lead you to think."

Xu turned to Lam. "Ban, how many experienced, battle-tested men could we count on?"

"In China, counting Hong Kong, at least twenty thousand."

"And if we involved our brothers in the U.S., Canada, and Europe?"

"Another ten thousand."

"It is possible that you may be tougher than us," Xu said to Bianchi. "But we would be as determined, and we have the numbers on our side. Eventually we'd just overwhelm you...Not that we want it to come to that. I'd rather talk about Ava's proposal."

"Me too," Bianchi said.

"Am I correct in assuming that we've returned to discussing an agreement?" Lam said.

"I think so," Bianchi said.

"The only one on the table is Ava's," Xu said.

"Which I have no interest in discussing," Ventola said.

A sharp noise came from the direction of the restaurant entrance. At first Ava thought it was the sound of a car backfiring, but when she saw Suen and Sonny stiffen and walk towards the panels, she guessed it was a gunshot.

Bianchi looked at Moretti and spoke to him in Italian. Moretti's face was impassive when he answered, but Ava felt tension in his voice.

Suen pulled back a panel and he and Sonny headed towards the entrance. The two men whom Ava and Sonny had dispatched still lay on the floor near the bar and didn't budge when they passed. Before Suen and Sonny could reach the door, Lop walked briskly through it, carrying a gun in his right hand. He spoke to them but didn't stop moving. They followed him to the back of the restaurant.

"What's going on?" Xu asked.

"We have a problem outside," Lop said, eyeing the Italians at the table. "They have a dozen armed men out there. We have twice that number and we have them covered, but they're not backing down and things are close to getting out of control."

Xu turned towards Bianchi. "What are you trying to do? Start a war here and now?"

Bianchi shrugged and then twisted in his chair to look at Moretti and Ventola.

"This was always the plan," Ventola said.

"It was the plan only if we couldn't reach an agreement," Bianchi said.

"Once that fucking woman walked in here, I knew there wasn't going to be an agreement," Ventola said.

"That's your position but not mine," Bianchi said. "We haven't even discussed their terms yet."

"Fuck their terms."

Ava leaned towards Moretti. "Who did you call?"

"What?"

"When you used your phone, did you call Toronto or did you call the men who are outside?"

Moretti hesitated.

"Tell her," Bianchi said.

"The men outside," Moretti said.

Ava started to rise from her seat and Sonny took two quick steps towards the table.

"Ava, please be calm," Xu said, lightly touching her arm. He turned to Bianchi. "Before this goes any further, you must tell the men in Toronto to go away and to stay away from Ava's mother."

Bianchi looked at Moretti. "Do that. Do it now, and in English."

Moretti nodded and then dialled. "This is Moretti," he finally said. "Tell your men to leave the house. Nothing more is to be done. The contract is over."

"Does that satisfy you?" Bianchi said to Xu.

"Yes, but I find it regrettable that it wasn't done the first time."

"A misjudgement," Bianchi said. "I hope you understand that the woman's surprise appearance was disturbing. Not everyone is thinking clearly."

"Speaking of which, why do you have those armed men in the street?" Xu said.

"Why do you have even more?"

"Protection."

"For us it's the same," Bianchi said. "We're on unfamiliar ground. We wanted to be sure we could make a safe exit if negotiations failed."

"You should have no worries about your safety. You can ask your men to stand down."

"Not yet."

"Then that leaves about thirty armed men confronting each other. All it takes is for one hothead to lose control and we'll have a disaster on our hands."

"My men won't lose control," Bianchi said. "And they're not leaving without me and the others."

"*Puttana.*"

Ava looked at Ventola in surprise. She'd been so caught up in the exchange between Bianchi and Xu that she'd almost forgotten he was there. "That isn't helpful," she said.

"Fuck helpful," Ventola said. He stood up from the table.

Bianchi remained seated. Raffi Pandolfo, Moretti, and Ricci looked as if they couldn't decide what to do.

"Let's get out of here," Ventola said. "That's what we agreed to do if we couldn't reach a deal."

"Dom, sit down for a moment," Bianchi said. "The woman has made a proposal. I know you don't like it, but maybe there's room for compromise."

"My name is Ava Lee," she said. "I'd appreciate it if you would stop referring to me in the third person."

Bianchi nodded at her and then turned his attention to the still-standing Ventola. "Is it really impossible for you to mend some of the fences you've been tearing down?"

"Yes."

"We seem to be at an impasse," Bianchi said to Xu. "And you need to understand that I'm as loyal to Dominic as you appear to be to Ms. Lee. I can't go entirely against him."

"You'll have to pardon me for saying this, but that's terribly short-sighted," Xu said. "Not only do you risk losing China as a supply source and market, we've been looking at expanding into Europe and we need partners. From what I've observed and heard today, I think you would have been ideal. So there's a lot more at stake here than PÖ and VLG. I'd like you to take that into consideration."

"Franco, Xu is a man who can deliver," Lam said. "He's not only head of the triads in Shanghai and Wanchai, in Hong Kong, he's also chairman of the triad societies for all of Asia. The two of you working together would be formidable."

Bianchi pressed his fingertips together and put them in front of his mouth for a moment. "Raffi, would you find it impossible to ask your people to communicate with our customers in the way that Ms. Lee has requested?"

Both Ventola and Pandolfo seemed startled by the question. "Don't answer that," Ventola said.

"Humour me, Dom," Bianchi said. "Raffi, I'm waiting for an answer."

"We'd need a very precise message," Pandolfo said after some hesitation.

"And if you had that?"

"It would be difficult and certainly awkward, but not impossible."

"I won't agree to it," Ventola said.

"Would that satisfy you?" Bianchi asked Ava.

"You haven't mentioned the apology I requested."

"That was deliberate. Can you live without it?"

"No."

"No compromise?"

"No."

"Fuck you," Ventola said to Ava.

"Dom," Bianchi warned. He looked across the table at Ava. "You are asking Dom to humiliate himself in public."

"He humiliated Clark."

"I don't excuse his behaviour, but surely you can understand that he and your Clark are at different stages in their careers."

"That's all the more reason for Dom to apologize. He's like a shark that jumped on a minnow — Clark had no chance. And an apology from Mr. Ventola, no matter how humiliating it may seem to him, won't end his career. It's a bump in the road. In fact, if you spin it right, he can come out of this looking like a good guy."

"Ava makes a very good point," Xu said. "An apology framed in the right way could make Mr. Ventola look gracious instead of coming across as a bully."

"What if we depersonalized it?" Bianchi said.

"In what way?" Xu said.

"What if Dom says that the VLG team was hasty in its initial assessment of Clark Po's work, and that on second thought they see a lot about it that they admire."

"I still won't do it," Ventola said.

"Well, Ms. Lee, what do you think?" Bianchi asked, ignoring Ventola.

She paused and saw that Xu and Lam were both looking at her. "He would have to be a lot more complimentary. 'Admire' is a weak word."

"I'm sure we can find something stronger."

"I'm not going to agree to any of this," Ventola said.

Bianchi got to his feet, took Ventola by the arm, and led him away from the table. For several minutes they stood with their backs turned to the others as they talked — as Bianchi talked and Ventola listened.

When they returned to the table, Bianchi said to Xu, "Our group needs to have a private discussion."

"I'm not leaving the restaurant without a decision," Xu said.

"Why don't you wait at the bar," Bianchi said. "Give us a chance to review our position."

"We can do that," Xu said. "What about the men outside?"

"They stay until we decide what we're going to do."

Xu looked at Lop. "Tell our men to maintain the status quo, and make sure they stay calm."

"It might be wise if Moretti went with your man and delivered the same message to our people," Bianchi said.

"Yes, that's an excellent idea," Xu said.

49

AVA, XU, AND LAM WALKED TO THE BAR. SONNY AND Suen stood off to one side, their eyes flicking between the doorway, the room in the back, and the two men on the ground.

"Do you trust them?" Xu asked Lam. "Even if we reach an agreement, do you think they'll honour it after they leave here?"

"Bianchi isn't stupid and he's all business. He wouldn't have asked those questions of Pandolfo if he didn't think there's a deal to be done," Lam said.

"Maybe, but I need the apology, and Raffi Pandolfo and his team have to make a genuine effort to mend fences for us with the trade," Ava said.

"I agree. You've given ground. Now it's their turn," Xu said.

"What if they won't do it?" Lam said.

"Then I'll honour my word and we'll try to close all the doors to China."

"That wouldn't be good for any of us. Bianchi wants the deal," Lam said, as if trying to convince himself it would happen.

"I know, but Ventola doesn't and the two of them are very close."

Ava closed her eyes. She was tired. Conversation at the bar ebbed to a halt, and she wasn't sure how much time had passed before she heard a voice.

"Could you please join us," Ricci said.

The mood at the table had changed. Ventola's face was just as grim, but the others looked relaxed. Xu nudged Ava gently with his elbow as they sat down.

"This is a difficult situation for all of us," Bianchi said. "If we'd known each other's involvement with the various parties it would never have reached this stage. But here we are and we have to deal with it. We're prepared to co-operate."

"Along the lines we discussed?" Ava said.

"Yes."

"An apology, a glowing review of Clark's work, and Raffi Pandolfo's team hard at work promoting PÖ?"

"You never let up, do you," Bianchi said.

"I want things to be absolutely clear. Misunderstandings only lead to more problems."

"You have our agreement on all of those points," Bianchi said. "Naturally we'll be concerned about the specific wording."

"I'll be happy to let VLG draft the statements," Ava said. "We'll have to agree to them, but we'll be reasonable as long as the wording is fair."

"We can do that," Pandolfo said.

"I'd also like to see the marketing plan. We have a few contacts who will be interested," Ava said. "I also want to know how and when Raffi's people intend to contact the trade."

"I'll make all that information available to you," Pandolfo

said. "You and I can start on it right now if you want. If not, I'll email you the drafts tomorrow for your comments."

Ava smiled. "Thank you."

"I'm sorry we put you through this," he said.

Ava wondered if he was being sarcastic, but he looked sincere enough. She glanced at Ventola. His head was turned, his eyes fixed on some distant spot and his jaw clenched. She smiled at Pandolfo. "I assume I'll be dealing with you and not Mr. Ventola on these matters," she said.

"You will."

She looked again at Ventola and knew she couldn't leave it like this with him. "Mr. Ventola, I know you're still angry with us — with me — but you have to understand that we weren't trying to take anything away from you. All we want to do is support Clark Po and build our little company into something a bit bigger. That's how you started. That's how everyone starts. How would you have reacted if in the early days some giant corporation tried to put you out of business because you wanted to pursue your own dream?"

"He reacted the way you did," Bianchi said. "I reminded him of that when we talked."

"What?"

"His company was less than two years old when a French conglomerate tried to take him over. He resisted and they went after him. He fought them off for as long as he could, but when he felt desperate, he turned to me in the same way you turned to Lam and Xu. The most important thing in life is to have friends you can trust completely. I was pleased to be there for him."

"Is that true! I mean, about the French conglomerate?" she said.

"It is," Bianchi said.

Ava leaned towards Ventola. "Then you should understand how Clark feels."

"We'll make things as right as we can," Pandolfo said.

Ventola's shoulders slumped, and Ava thought she saw weariness replace the determination in his face. "I'll call the boy at some point in time," he said.

50

THE GROUP IN THE BACK ROOM BROKE UP. AVA AND
Raffi Pandolfo went into the front of the restaurant to start
drafting the announcement and reviewing the list of publications, blogs, and industry insiders it would be sent to. Pandolfo
was affable, acting as if there had never been a dispute.

While they worked, Dominic Ventola sat by himself at
the far end of the bar, drinking red wine.

"Dom's not naturally a nasty man," Pandolfo said at one
point. "He's just had to fight for everything. Nothing was
easy. There was a lot of rejection at the beginning. It started
with a father who couldn't accept his sexuality or his profes-
sion. He thinks he's closed that door, but every time he faces
rejection it comes back."

"He and Bianchi are extraordinarily close."

"We don't talk about that. They were young and stuff happened. That's all anyone knows."

"Okay, but Bianchi obviously has some influence over him
that — pardon me — even you don't appear to have. What
did he say to Dom that caused him to agree to this? Was it
really reminding him of his own early struggles?"

"It's a good story, but neither of them is that sentimental. Bianchi controls the purse strings. He told him that every single dollar we lost in China would come directly out of Dom's share of company proceeds."

"That would get anyone's attention," she said.

"At the end of the day it's always about money. Dom can talk all he wants about image and reputation, but what he wants more than anything is to be the most valuable fashion conglomerate in the world. That's the only score card that matters to him and Bianchi."

As Ava and Pandolfo worked, the tensions between the Camorra and the triad men shifted dramatically. In a show of goodwill, Sonny and Suen drove the Italians who had been injured in the bar to a private clinic. Lop and Moretti stood outside in the street with their men, and Xu and Lam were chatting with Bianchi and Ricci.

It took more than an hour for Ava and Pandolfo to create an announcement and a list of fashion media, bloggers, and customers to send it to that they were both happy with. "Before it goes out, I'd like to send this to my partners for their input," Ava said. "I can't imagine it will be substantive, but I'll contact you tomorrow with any changes they want to make."

"I'll run them past our team in Milan," Pandolfo said. "I'll try to show the announcement to Dom as well, but honestly I don't think he'll have much interest. We should aim to have it finalized by late tomorrow. When do you want to release it?"

"Right away."

"I can't say I blame you," Pandolfo said.

"And you have my number, so we're set."

Ava and Pandolfo walked to the back of restaurant, where Xu, Lam, Bianchi, and Ricci seemed to be involved in a lively conversation.

"We're finished," Ava said. "With any luck, we can make a public announcement by late tomorrow."

"And now what?" Xu said.

"I'd really like to catch the ten o'clock jetfoil back to Hong Kong."

Xu stood up. "I'll ride with you to the terminal."

It took ten minutes for handshakes, promises, thanks, and goodbyes. The Italians were reserved, but Lam grinned when Ava kissed him on both cheeks. "I can't thank you enough for all your help," she said.

"We're almost even now, but if this thing turns out as well as I think it might, I'll owe you again," he said.

Sonny and Suen had returned from the clinic and were waiting outside the restaurant. Lam's car was at the curb. "Sonny and Ava are going back to Hong Kong on the jetfoil," Xu said.

"I'll drive. Sonny can sit up front with me," Suen said.

"What were you talking about with the Italians?" Ava asked Xu when they were in the car.

"Business opportunities."

"And?"

"They're tricky. We'll see," Xu said. "They're staying here a few more days. Lam and I have agreed to have dinner with them tomorrow night and we'll explore things in more detail. Do you want to join us?"

"No, thanks. I've had enough of Macau."

"I imagine Ventola and Pandolfo will be staying as well."

"I know, but Pandolfo and I have agreed to communicate

by phone and email. I told him that if we need to meet, he can come to Hong Kong."

They reached the ferry terminal at five minutes to ten. "We're going to have to rush to catch the ten o'clock sailing," she said as the car stopped.

"Off you go," Xu said.

She leaned over and kissed him on both cheeks. "Thank you, *ge ge*," she whispered.

She and Sonny got to the jetfoil just before they disengaged the ramp. The first-class cabin was half empty. "Sonny, I'm going to sit up front by myself for a while," she said. "I have some phone calls to make."

"*Momentai.*"

She found a seat in the front row by a window, with no one within earshot. She phoned May first, then Amanda. She gave them a brief update on the outcome of the meeting and made arrangements to meet them later at the Mandarin, to provide more detail over celebratory drinks. She then called Chi-Tze, who quickly put her on speaker so she could also tell Gillian and Clark. She was still talking to them when the jetfoil docked in Hong Kong.

"We'll talk again first thing in the morning," she said as she walked down the gangway. "I'll send you the draft announcement as soon as I get to the hotel, but I think we should hold off saying anything ourselves until things are completely nailed down. When I spoke to Raffi, he was anxious that we coordinate our timing in terms of contacting customers. I think they want to do it first — it will be less embarrassing for them that way." She put her phone in her purse and waited for Sonny to get the car.

She thought about her work with Uncle, how most often

she was on her own, at arm's length from clients. When she was successful, it had generated a sense of accomplishment and sometimes relief, but rarely, if ever, the kind of joy she had felt when she picked up the phone to tell her partners they were back on track.

Sonny parked the car at the curb and opened the back door.

"Are you happy doing this?" she asked as he eased into traffic.

"What do you mean?"

"You are capable of doing so much more than driving my brother and my father around Hong Kong. I know you work for me, but we have geography working against us. It worries me that you might feel underused and underappreciated."

"Are you saying that because Lop said he'd hire me if he could?"

"Partly, but it isn't just Lop. Lam and Xu would be just as eager."

"Because of the way I handled those guys at the restaurant?"

"Everyone needs protection, Sonny, and who's better than you at providing it?"

"I would only disappoint them," he said.

"Why?"

"Because I can't do it on command," he said. "There was a time when I could and there was nothing I loved more, but Uncle helped me escape from that mentality. He rewired me to respond only to direct threats to him or me. And now it's you and me — that's all I care about. So you see, I'd disappoint them."

Ava felt her emotions swell again, but she had no idea how to respond to Sonny until they reached the Mandarin

Oriental. When she got out of the car, she put a hand on his cheek. "I'm so lucky to have you," she said.

"We're a good team, boss," he said, averting his eyes. "I'll be on standby tomorrow."

"If I need you, I'll call."

She walked into the hotel lobby and headed for the elevators. Amanda was coming down from the Peak to join her and May, but Ava wanted to have a quick shower and change first.

"Ms. Lee," the concierge said as she passed his desk.

"Yes?" she said.

"Welcome back to the hotel," he said.

"Thank you," she said, finding his behaviour a bit odd.

She phoned May as soon as she got to her room. "I'm here. Let Amanda know. I'll see you at M Bar in half an hour."

She was towelling herself off when she thought she heard the doorbell ring. She opened the bathroom door and listened but heard nothing. She put on a bathrobe and was starting to walk towards the closet when she heard the bell again. She went to the door and looked through the peephole.

Pang Fai stood in the corridor.

"Fai," Ava said, opening the door.

"I hope I'm not disturbing you."

"No, but this is unexpected."

"Can I come in?"

"Of course," Ava said. "How did you get here?"

"I remembered that you and May said this is where you stay when you're in Hong Kong," Fai said as she walked past her. "I checked myself in and then I persuaded the concierge to give me your room number. He was extremely reluctant but I managed to convince him. The perks of being a famous actress," she said wryly.

"You didn't have to go to all that trouble. You could have just phoned me."

"There are things you can't say on the phone."

Fai sat down on a loveseat that faced the television. She was wearing light blue jeans, a plain white T-shirt, and sneakers.

"What's going on?" Ava asked.

"Will you sit with me?"

"Sure," Ava said, feeling slightly uneasy.

Fai's hands were clenched and she held them between her knees. She didn't look directly at Ava.

"Were you really in Beijing when we talked?"

"Yeah. I flew in to see you."

"Fai, I don't quite understand —"

"Yes, you do. I'm sure you do," Fai said.

Ava's heart skipped a beat.

"I have less than a week before I go on a film shoot that will last a minimum of three months. Once I'm on the set, it's like being in jail. I can't get away. My time isn't my own," Fai said. She fell quiet, her eyes focused on her hands. Then she blurted, "I don't want to spend three months wondering if you're as attracted to me as much as I'm attracted to you."

Ava pulled back. Part of her had sensed Fai's purpose, but hearing it said was something different. "Fai, you've caught me completely off guard."

"I'm sorry," she said.

"You're also making an assumption about my being gay."

"Well, if you're not, this is going to be even more embarrassing than I imagined."

Ava drew a deep breath. "I am gay. But I'm confused about you."

"Because I've been married?"

"Yes, and the first time I saw you, you were with Tsai Men, and you made it clear that kind of arrangement with men wasn't uncommon."

"I've thought often about that night," Fai said. "I'm ashamed of the way I behaved."

"I admired your honesty."

"Except I wasn't being honest," Fai said. "I remember talking about men, sex, and money as if I'd invented them. There's a lot of competition between actresses and a lot of exploitation by directors and producers. I think being in the system for so long and being scrutinized by the media and the public had hardened me. But when I saw the way Xu respected you, I thought, *This woman is different.*"

"Why didn't you say something then?"

"How could I? You were with Xu and I knew nothing about you."

"You called me after that dinner, remember? You wanted to warn me about Tsai."

"That was my excuse. What I wanted was to hear your voice. Then I began to think about ways I could get closer to you, and I decided that representing PÖ was an opportunity."

"Was that the only reason you did it?"

"No. The money was also very good."

"And you seemed to enjoy London."

"I had a great time. It was wonderful being around so many strong, bright women," Fai said. "I flirted with you but you didn't seem to notice."

"I was preoccupied."

"I thought that. Still, it was discouraging and I began to think that I'd misread you. Then one of the girls told me that you definitely are gay. I asked her how she knew, and she said that just about everyone knows. She said you don't talk about it but you don't hide it either."

"I've never hidden it and I've always accepted it."

"All I've ever done is hide," Fai said, her eyes filled with tears. "I've never had a real relationship, because if it became known — or even hinted at — my career would be over."

"Given what I know about Chinese cultural attitudes, I can understand why."

"Understanding doesn't make it any easier or make me feel better about myself."

Ava looked at Fai. Her head was lowered and her face in profile. Even without makeup and wearing nothing more than a plain white T-shirt, she was one of the most beautiful women Ava had ever seen. "So what kind of relationship do you think we could have?" she asked gently.

"I want to find out. I'm tired of being afraid," Fai said.

"What does that mean?"

Fai hesitated and then said, "Are you attracted to me?"

"Yes, I am. But I have my own fears."

"Maybe we could support each other."

After a pause Ava said, "I've had a very exciting day. I'm going to M Bar to meet May Ling and Amanda for a drink to celebrate. Would you like to join us?"

"Yes."

"Don't answer quite so quickly. They're going to find it curious that you're here. You have to expect that they'll figure it out. They are discreet, but I don't know how secretive you want to be."

"I'd love to join you, and I'll tell them I'm here to see you."

"Are you sure about this?"

"I've never felt more certain about anything," she said. "Do you remember in London, when I said I feel safe around you?"

"I do."

"I can't remember the last time I felt safe around anyone. It might have been when I was a child."

Am I ready for this? Ava thought. *Do I really want to let this woman into my life?*

"Please, this has been hard enough already," Fai said. "Let's have a drink together with your friends."

"Okay, we'll go upstairs," Ava said. "They're probably there already and I still have to get changed."

"Am I okay dressed like this?"

"You look wonderful."

"And what will we do after the bar?" Fai said.

"What do you want to do?" Ava asked.

"I want to come back to the room with you."

Before Ava could react, her phone rang. She picked it up, thinking it might be Pandolfo or May Ling. But when she looked at the screen, she saw the country code she'd seen earlier that night. "Hello?"

"Ava, this is Chang Wang calling. I trust you remember me."

"Uncle Chang, of course I do."

"I'm glad I reached you," he said. "Tommy told me to give you his best regards as well."

Tommy Ordonez was the wealthiest man in the Philippines and a Chinoy — an ethnic Chinese who'd taken a Filipino name. Chang was his second-in-command. More important, Chang had been Uncle's boyhood friend and a lifelong colleague. She had met Chang and Ordonez when she and Uncle did a job for them a few years back; they had saved Ordonez about $50 million, along with his reputation.

"I think you tried to call me earlier, but I couldn't take it. And truthfully, Uncle, your timing isn't perfect now either."

"We have a problem over here, Ava."

"I don't do debt-collection work anymore," she said. "Since Uncle died, I've strictly focused on my investment business with May Ling Wong."

"This is an entirely different sort of problem."

"Then why would you come to me?"

"It's complicated, and it will take some time to explain."

Ava looked at Fai sitting on the couch and felt her heart skip a beat again. She put down the phone. "Fai, how many days did you say you have free before you start shooting?"

"Four."

Ava returned to the phone. "Uncle Chang, I'm meeting friends right now to celebrate a great moment for our company, and I can't keep them waiting. It's also possible that I'll be completely tied up until Sunday. Can your problem wait?"

"Do I have a choice?"

"Not if you want my full attention," Ava said. "And Uncle, that doesn't mean I'll be prepared to take it on."

He went silent and Ava could imagine him pondering his options. He was a careful man in both speech and action. "Then I'll wait," he said finally. "This problem won't have disappeared by then. And I do understand that your willingness to listen to me isn't a commitment to help."

"Shall I call you?"

"No. I'll reach out to you, since there's a chance I can get Tommy to sit in on the conversation."

"So, Sunday night?"

"Yes. Enjoy your celebration."

Ava saw that Fai's eyes were on her. "With any luck, it might last for days."

AVA LEE WAS IN BED, FLAT ON HER BACK, HER HEAD
propped up by three pillows. Her eyes were fixed on a long,
lean woman standing naked next to a window that looked out
onto Dianchi Lake. The woman stretched her arms above her
head and yawned.

"I don't want to leave," Pang Fai said. "But I have to get
moving."

"Stay."

"There will be more than a hundred people at the pre-
shoot party tonight. I have to be there. The director is angry
enough that I took the weekend off."

"Surely being one of the biggest movie stars in China gives
you some advantages," Ava said.

"I think the opposite is true," Fai said. "I'm expected to
set an example for the other cast members, and this director
hasn't been shy about making me feel responsible for the
success of the film."

"And how long will the shoot take?"

"We begin early tomorrow morning and then it's at
least ten weeks of work. We'll start here and work our way

northwest to Beijing — city by city, town by town — for about twenty-seven hundred kilometres."

"I think it's ridiculous to drag you and the whole crew from place to place like that."

"He's a fiend for authenticity," Fai said. "The whole idea is to have one lonely brave woman duplicating at least part of Mao's Long March. It's a challenging role. I play a farmer's wife who's brave — or foolish — enough to protest. I'm supposed to be a symbol representing the spirit of the march, but in reality show how Mao's Great Leap Forward betrayed his original ideals and brought unimaginable suffering to ordinary people. Mao may have wanted to accelerate agrarian reform, but his policies dispossessed farmers, brought on catastrophic food shortages, and caused the deaths of millions."

Ava smiled. The women were staying at the Intercontinental Hotel on the outskirts of Kunming, in Yunnan province, which was almost three thousand kilometres to the southwest of Beijing. They had arrived from Hong Kong, where they had spent the previous two days. During their time together in Kunming, they had left the room only three times — for lunch and dinner in the Shang Tao Restaurant and for late-night drinks in the Butterfly Bar.

They had known each other for months but had been lovers for only four days. The experience was proving to be momentous for both of them.

Over the years Ava had had a series of flings before meeting Maria Gonzalez, a Colombian woman living in Toronto, with whom she'd had a serious relationship. Maria had ended it just as Fai came into Ava's life. Ava had thought she loved Maria, but after these few days with Fai, she was beginning to wonder if she'd ever experienced real love before.

"I could meet up with you on the road here and there," Ava said.

"No, I don't want you to," Fai said. Being gay in China was still considered unacceptable, and public knowledge of Fai's sexuality would destroy her career. It was a burden that Ava, Hong Kong–born but Canadian-raised, could barely comprehend but knew to be true.

She feigned pain and pulled the duvet over her head.

Fai rushed to the bed, pulled back the duvet, and crawled in beside her. She nuzzled Ava's neck. "I'm going to miss you, more than I've ever missed anyone," she whispered. "No one but you and me will know that the misery I convey in this role is because you're not with me. When the film is done, I want to go away with you for weeks, or months, or for however long you can put up with me."

"Would you consider coming to Toronto? I have a condo in the centre of the city. There are lots of designer shops and every type of restaurant within walking distance. And we can be ourselves without you having to worry about how people will react," Ava said. "I also don't think you'd have to worry about being recognized — my neighbourhood is not that Chinese."

"I think my ego can handle not being recognized."

Ava reached down and gently lifted Fai's chin. She wasn't wearing any makeup and her hair was slightly dishevelled, but she was the most mesmerizing woman Ava had ever been with. The slightly square chin, strong cheekbones, modest lips, and proud nose were in almost perfect proportion. And then there were her eyes. They were large, almost Western, and had triggered gossip about who her parents really were. But it wasn't their size that Ava found remarkable; it was the way they pulled her in. In many ways her eyes reminded Ava of Uncle, her former partner, her mentor, and — in every way imaginable, except for bloodline — her grandfather. She had always thought that Uncle communicated with the world through his eyes rather than with words or physical mannerisms. Now she felt connected in the same way to Fai.

"When do you really have to leave?" Ava said.

"Now." Fai sighed.

Ava slid her hand down Fai's body until it rested between her legs. "I can't convince you to stay?"

"You probably could, but if we start again, how will we stop? I don't want to leave here feeling guilty."

Ava kissed her on the forehead. Fai rolled off the bed and reached for her underwear, which lay on a chair. As Ava watched her dress, her phone rang. She picked it up and saw that the incoming number had the Philippines country code.

"Shit, I forgot about this," she said.

"What is it?" Fai said.

"I think Uncle Chang Wang from Manila is calling. I don't know if you remember, but he phoned me in Hong Kong. I put him off then and told him to call me tonight." Ava pressed the answer button. "This is Ava."

"Good evening, this is Chang. I hope this time my call isn't inconvenient."

"No, I was expecting to hear from you. Is Mr. Ordonez there as well?"

"Tommy is in Singapore on business, so it's just me."

Tommy Ordonez was the richest man in the Philippines. Chang Wang was his second-in-command. Despite his name, Ordonez was Chinese. He had been born Chu Guang in Qingdao and moved to the Philippines as a young man. In an effort to blend into society — and to avoid periodic out-bursts of xenophobia — he had changed his name. It was such a common practice in the Philippines that there was even a word for it. Chinese immigrants who adopted Filipino names were called Chinoys, a play on Pinoy, Filipinos' informal term for themselves.

"I've always enjoyed our conversations, with or without Tommy," Ava said.

"That's a very diplomatic remark. It reminds me of something that Uncle would say."

He was referring to Chow Tung, Ava's former partner. He and Chang were both from Wuhan, in Hubei province, and had known each other since they were boys. After leaving China, they had stayed in touch for more than fifty years and helped each other innumerable times. The last occasion had been a few years before, when the Ordonez organization hired Ava and Uncle to recover stolen money. They had successfully returned close to fifty million dollars.

"I can't begin to list the things I learned from Uncle," she said.

"I miss him," Chang said quietly. "We used to chat most weekends. Some Sunday mornings I pick up the phone to call him and then realize he isn't there anymore."

"I feel that way nearly every day."

"I know how close you two were. He talked about you often. He adored you."

"And I loved him."

Out of the corner of her eye, Ava saw that Fai was now dressed and putting her makeup bag into the small suitcase she'd brought with her. Ava reached under the pillow and pulled out a black Giordano T-shirt that she slipped over her head. "Uncle, excuse me for just a moment. Don't go away. I'll be right back," she said, sliding out of bed and placing the phone on the bedside table.

She walked over to Fai and hugged her so tightly she could feel their hearts beating.

"I want you to call me every day," Fai said. "You can text and email me too, but I want to hear your voice. The best times are before eight in the morning and after six in the evening."

"I will," Ava said. "This is going to be a long ten weeks."

"But when it's over, I don't have any other immediate commitments, and I'm not going to let my agent make any."

"I'm determined to get you to Toronto. I know you'll love it."

"I'll love anywhere as long as I'm with you."

"And I feel the same way. But still, you'll enjoy the freedom we'll have there."

Fai nodded but Ava saw doubt in her eyes. *How can you explain freedom*, she wondered, *to someone who's never truly experienced it?*

"You'd better go back to your friend on the phone," Fai said.

"I'll call you in the morning."

"Please don't forget," Fai said.

Ava waited until the door closed before picking up the phone again. "Sorry, Uncle."

"That's not necessary. I realize this is rather an imposition on my part."

"Except I don't know what it is you're imposing."

"As I said to you the other night, we have a problem here in the Philippines that we need some help with."

"But I don't do debt collection work anymore. I'm partners in an investment company with May Ling Wong."

"Does she still live in Wuhan, and are she and Changxing still married?"

"Yes."

"I've known them for many years, although I haven't had any contact with them recently. She is very capable and I'm sure an ideal business partner."

"That's been my experience," Ava said. "She's also a good friend."

"As someone who doesn't have any family, I place enormous value on friendship. I was fortunate to have Uncle for so many years."

Ava didn't doubt Chang's sincerity, but she suspected he was stalling as he searched for a way to circumvent her less than enthusiastic reaction to his request for help. "And you still have Tommy."

"We're not friends in the way I was with Uncle," Chang said. "We have different tastes and personalities, and outside of the office we never socialize. Inside the business, though, we trust and support each other and think almost as one mind. For example, when I mentioned to Tommy that I wanted to involve you in our problem, he leapt at the suggestion."

"Perhaps I didn't make it clear enough. I'm not only not in the old business, I have absolutely no interest in or intention of returning to it."

"This has nothing to do with debt collection."

"Then I'm confused, because I can't think of any other way that I could be of use to you and Tommy."

"I could spend several minutes repeating what Tommy and I have said about your abilities, but my experience with you leads me to believe you wouldn't welcome that kind of flattery. Tommy also suggested that we offer you money, but I told him — aside from the fact that you're a wealthy young woman — this isn't the kind of problem you can put a price on," Chang said. "So I guess what it comes down to is I'm asking you to help us as a personal favour — the kind that Uncle and I did for each other over the years."

God, he's smooth, Ava thought. Despite her cynicism, her curiosity was aroused and she couldn't dismiss his request for a favour out of hand. "Uncle, you have my interest," she finally said. "What kind of problem can't you put a price on?"

"On the surface — and truthfully this is Tommy's main concern — we believe one of our most successful businesses could be at risk. And there are larger issues, Ava, that could have an impact not just on us but on many other people, in the Philippines and beyond."

"And what do you imagine I could possibly do to prevent whatever it is you're alluding to?"

"I allude, as you call it, because we lack hard information. We have suspicions but we need to confirm them. We need to determine whether we actually have a problem," Chang said. "And if we do have one, we need to develop a strategy to deal with it. But that all starts with having facts. We need someone we trust totally to confirm some things we've been told and to gather as much additional information as possible. As Tommy and I remember very well, you have an extraordinary talent for getting to the truth. The truth is what we're after, and we think you're the person who can find it for us."

"What is this potential problem?"

Chang hesitated. She thought she heard ice clinking in a glass and wondered if he was drinking. "Ava, I would like that explanation to take place in Manila," he said. "I know this will sound vague and maybe even conspiratorial, but I'm not comfortable explaining it to you over the phone. First, it's very complicated, and I'm not as well informed as some other people I'd like you to talk to. Second, this isn't something that can be explained in half an hour, or even several hours. I believe you should meet and take the measure of the people who've related at least part of their suspicions to us."

"And you have no one in the Philippines you can turn to?"

"Absolutely not. As I said, this is about trust, and the number of people who Tommy and I truly trust we can count on one hand. Of those, only one lives in Manila, and he's the first person we want you to talk to."

"Uncle, I really don't know what to say. I have other responsibilities now."

"Give us one day," he said quickly. "Get on a plane tomorrow and come to Manila for one meeting. If you decide to go back to Toronto or Hong Kong or wherever after that, the issue will never be mentioned again and we'll still be grateful for your time."

"I'm expected in Shanghai tomorrow for a business review that's scheduled to last several days."

"Postpone it," Chang said. "Please, Ava."

The word *please* startled her. It wasn't something she could remember Chang or Tommy Ordonez ever uttering. Not only was it out of character, in her mind it was an acknowledgement that she was their equal.

"I can't give you an answer this minute," she said. "I have to think about it, and I also want to talk to my partners and the people expecting me in Shanghai."

"Of course, do that," he said. "But there is urgency to this matter. Waiting four days to talk to you wasn't easy — more than once I reached for the phone. Can you possibly speak to them tonight?"

"Yes, I can, and I'll call you when I have."

"I'll stay up until I hear from you," he said.

"Uncle, you do understand this doesn't mean I'm leaning towards saying yes?"

"Please, give us that one day, Ava," Chang said. "My belief is that if you do, you'll commit to helping us get to the bottom of this problem."

He's dangling bait, she thought. She admired how skillfully he had handled his end of the conversation: He had started it by invoking their connection through Uncle. Then he'd complimented her while insisting that he thought she was above flattery. Finally, he had framed his request as a personal favour. She didn't know why he thought he had the right to ask for one, since he and Ava were hardly friends, but he had anyway and it had been exactly the right approach. Indeed, it was probably the only approach that had a chance of succeeding with her.

"Let me make some calls," she said.

ACKNOWLEDGEMENTS

Almost unbelievably, this is the tenth installment in the Ava Lee series, and as Ava's life expands and grows, so does our readership. The challenge for me with every new book is to meet (and hopefully exceed) those readers' expectations. I'm not the best judge of my own work and I always like to get feedback from the readers. So when you finish this book and if you've read these acknowledgements, please send me an email or go to our Facebook page and let me know what you think.

As always, writing this book was a journey, and one that I didn't take alone. I want to thank those who came along with me.

First, Carrie Kirkman and Mary Turner — style mavens and professionals in the fashion trade — made it possible for me to write intelligently (I trust) about an industry I didn't know that well. I have attempted to weave their inside knowledge and details into something coherent and plausible. If I've failed, it isn't because of them.

As always, I had the eagle eyes of friends and family scanning the original manuscript and page proofs for me. A huge thanks to my amazing daughter Jill and to great friends Catherine Roseburgh and Robin Spano.

My publisher, Sarah MacLachlan, and her team at House of Anansi Press were, as usual, unfailingly responsive and supportive. Laura Meyer, my publicist, is an absolute joy to work with, and I also have to mention the honest and completely professional support I get from Matt Williams and Barbara Howson: Barbara is the vice-president of sales and Matt is the vice-president of everything else.

But the truth is, these books wouldn't get published without the applied talents of my editor, the great Janie Yoon. Janie is very protective of Ava and doesn't let me stray in terms of her character and relationships. I value her input and expertise beyond measure.

My agents, Bruce Westwood and Carolyn Forde, continue to have my back. They are a remarkable duo and I can only thank the lucky circumstances that brought me into their orbit.

IAN HAMILTON is the author of ten novels in the Ava Lee series. The books have been shortlisted for numerous prizes, including the Arthur Ellis Award, the Barry Award, and the Lambda Literary Prize, and are national bestsellers. *The Water Rat of Wanchai* was the winner of the Arthur Ellis Award for Best First Novel and was named a best book of the year by Amazon.ca, the *Toronto Star*, and *Quill & Quire*. BBC Culture named Hamilton one of the ten mystery/crime writers from the past thirty years that should be on your bookshelf. The series is being adapted for television.